Roger Taylor was born in Heywood, Lancashire, and qualified as a civil and structural engineer. He lives with his wife and two daughters in Wirral, Merseyside, and is a pistol shooter and student of traditional aikido. He is the author of the four Chronicles of Hawklan – *The Call of the Sword*, *The Fall of Fyorlund*, *The Waking of Orthlund* and *Into Narsindal* – the epic fantasy *Dream Finder* and *Farnor*, the first adventure in this sequence.

Valderen

Part Two of NIGHTFALL

Roger Taylor

First published in 1993
by HEADLINE BOOK PUBLISHING PLC

First published in paperback in 1993
by HEADLINE BOOK PUBLISHING PLC

A HEADLINE FEATURE paperback

10 9 8 7 6 5 4 3 2 1

ISBN 0 7472 4149 X

Printed and bound in Great Britain by
HarperCollins Manufacturing, Glasgow

HEADLINE BOOK PUBLISHING PLC
Headline House
79 Great Titchfield Street
London W1P 7FN

Valderen

Prologue

Thus ended FARNOR . . .

There was turmoil. Fears that had hitherto hovered at the edges of awareness like uneasy dreams, rolled inexorably forward, proclaiming themselves beyond any denial. The rumbling doubts of years were focusing themselves into an indisputable and immediate certainty.

'*It is the spawn of the Great Evil.*'

'*And it hunts the strange mover.*'

Yet, as many doubts swirled about this enigmatic figure as fears swirled about the manifest evil.

'*His power is unknown.*'

'*He carries a darkness of his own that is beyond us.*'

But the speed of the events now unfolding demanded action.

Yet, what was to be done?

'*To stay one darkness will be to admit another, and who can say what consequences might flow from that?*'

'*And who can say what consequences will ensue should the mover fall? There has not been such a Hearer in countless generations. If the spawn of the Great Evil is abroad again, we may have need of such a one, tainted or no.*'

Silence.

The pain and the fear were faced.

'*If it is possible, stay the known evil, and admit the Hearer.*'

The conclusion was definitive.

But the prospect was fearful.

'Run, horse, run!'

Farnor's relentless, inaudible litany had become meaningless to him as his plunging journey carried him onward through the darkness, the creature drawing ever nearer.

1

He did not look behind – more for fear that he would lose his precarious hold on his terrified mount rather than fear of what he might see. For he knew how close the creature was. With almost every heartbeat he seemed for an instant to bond with it; to be possessed by its foul desires, to breathe in the heady odours of the terror of its fleeing prey, to feel his mouth slavering warm, his hair raised stark and stiff. But, worst of all, he would touch fleetingly on the ancient and malevolent will that was powering the still-green muscles and sinews.

Yet it was, perhaps, the stark horror of this that kept his mind focused on the reality of what was happening, rather than yielding to the urge to accept this crazed flight as some nightmarish figment from which he must soon awaken to safety and security.

For he knew that although he was fleeing, he was also fighting a battle of some kind. Whatever unholy kinship he had with this creature, he knew that he must resist to the end.

No.

He must resist. There would be no true end while he did. Only if he faltered would there be an ending.

Hatred and anger wove themselves into the twisted strands of his fear.

He would not fall to Rannick or his creature. He would choke it and slash it even as it seized him. And he would utter not a sound whatever happened.

'Run, horse, run!' he willed, silently.

Then, the fear that filled him was not his own. He had the feeling of another will steeling itself for a terrible ordeal. But it was gone before he could respond, and, once again, the pounding rhythm of the chase carried him, unwilling, but helpless, into the soul of his pursuer.

There was his prey, almost alongside now: high above, and dangerous hooves flailing, but only a few paces from the kill.

Muscles strained for the extra effort that would turn stride into leap . . .

And the prey was gone!

Ahead lay the looming darkness of a broad tree trunk!

Farnor started violently as he was jolted back into his own consciousness, the creature's surging reflexes alive in his limbs.

Through the din of his flight, he heard a crashing and stumbling behind him.

'Run, horse, run!'

The words rang in his head, but the voice was not his. Nor was the word simply, horse. It was rich in many meanings, but too, it was hung about with great fear.

And, he realized, his awful, pulsing bond with the creature was gone. He was wholly himself again. The presence of the creature was fading. For an instant, he hesitated, but even as he did so the voices filled his mind overwhelmingly.

'Flee, mover! It taxes us sorely to touch this thing so and we have no measure of our ability to help you. Your fate is in your own hands still. Flee!'

'It is done.'

'But the pain, the horror . . .'

'Is passed. And it is done. The spawn of the Evil has been deceived. It returns from whence it came. The mover is safe.'

But there was an awful doubt still. Doubt that robbed this achievement of any true solace for the pain and degradation of touching that which had come in pursuit.

'The mover carries a darkness. We may have committed a great folly.'

'We could have done no other.'

It did not lessen the doubt.

There was a silence; deep and profound. The truth could not be denied. They had allowed an alien darkness to come amongst them.

'It will be ever beyond us. We must call on those who Hear. The Valderen must judge where we cannot.'

And into the night Farnor, clinging to the neck of his exhausted horse, galloped ever northward into the land of the Great Forest. He was lost and alone, but he knew only one thing: he was no longer pursued. The creature was gone. He was free.

Now begins, VALDEREN . . .

Chapter 1

The castle gates swung open.

Nilsson turned to watch the swaying silhouette that was moving slowly through the shade of the archway. He had been assiduously resurrecting the old, long-forgotten habits that had, in the past, ensured both his survival and his advancement, though it took him some effort to keep his demeanour neutral as Rannick, astride his foul-tempered mount, emerged into the light. For while Rannick might not yet be the man that Nilsson's erstwhile master had been, his power was increasing almost daily and, as it grew, so his humanity inevitably diminished. Nilsson knew only too well that now he had chosen to stand by his new lord his life depended solely on the value that Rannick placed on him, and that this value depended in turn not only on his willingness to serve but on his ability to read and anticipate Rannick's moods accurately.

And it was especially important now, for he was certain that something had gone amiss during the fiery demonstration that Rannick had given the previous day. True, the roaring column of fire that had appeared out of nothingness had been both awe-inspiring and terrifying, and it had sent Gryss and the others away suitably cowed and humiliated. Yet, increasingly sensitive to his master's behaviour, Nilsson was sure that he had felt Rannick falter. Only slightly, admittedly, but the memory of it had lingered with him since. It was as if Rannick had been assailed in some way. And he had sensed, too, a grim, almost desperate, anger begin to mount in the man; an anger that had seemed to be building towards some appalling conclusion until it had suddenly evaporated into a surprised vagueness at the unexpected collapse of Gryss and the others on to their knees.

Rannick had stood for a long time apparently staring after the retreating figures as they stumbled away from the castle, supporting the beaten Farnor. But Nilsson, fearfully willing himself to absolute stillness lest he inadvertently attract Rannick's attention, saw that his eyes were abstracted and distant.

Then, as if in confirmation of Nilsson's conclusion, Rannick had silently beckoned for his horse and, without comment, ridden north.

Later, Nilsson had started violently from a troubled sleep to hear, he thought, the distant, shrieking howl of Rannick's creature. Though whether it had been reality or a lingering remnant of some fearful dream, he could not have said.

And now Rannick had returned.

Nilsson took a slow, silent, very deep breath as Rannick came to a halt in front of him. 'Lord,' he said, bowing slightly.

'We begin today,' Rannick replied tersely as he dismounted.

'Lord?'

But Rannick was walking away from him. Hastily Nilsson turned and strode after him across the courtyard. What had he missed? As they reached a doorway, Rannick turned and looked squarely at him. 'We begin our conquest of this land, Captain,' he said. 'I am fully ready now. All opposition has been ended.'

Opposition? There was more in Rannick's tone than a reference to the mere quelling of Gryss and the others. So something *had* happened yesterday. Yet too, there was a strange exhilaration about Rannick that Nilsson had not known before. Something else must have happened during the night; something profound. He asked no questions, however. Time, and silent, watchful awareness, would eventually give him such answers as he needed. Petty curiosity now, might well kill him. 'As you command, Lord,' he replied, as Rannick turned and disappeared into the building.

Thus Rannick's early cautious steps along what he knew as the golden road of his destiny became a purposeful and determined march. Having finally had his own way in the matter of the treatment of the villagers, Rannick seemed content now to leave the day-to-day pursuit of his schemes in Nilsson's hands and, beyond a general overseeing of matters, he interfered scarcely at all with detailed plans. Nilsson however, took few chances, and submitted almost his every intention and the reasons for it to Rannick for his approval. Increasingly he was finding Rannick difficult to anticipate.

Rannick, though, was learning. Learning more and more about

the nature of the men that he now commanded, not least about their peculiar, savage expertise and how it could best be used to further his ends. He knew that to speak openly on such matters would be merely to display his ignorance and, in so doing, diminish his authority.

Fascinating though this learning was however, it was secondary to his avid study of his growing power and the mastering of the subtleties of its use. For hour upon hour he secluded himself in a room at the top of the castle's highest tower, a room which overlooked the woods and peaks to the north as well as the sweep of the valley southwards. No one knew what arts he practised there but, although nothing had been said, it was acknowledged that the room was forbidden to all others, on pain of immediate death. And the light that flickered fitfully from its windows at night, was like a baleful, eye, surveying not only the castle yards but the entire valley. More than a few of Nilsson's men complained that they could feel it watching them even when they were indoors. 'Well, be careful what you say and do, then,' he offered them, by way of reassurance. 'And what you think.'

And too, unannounced, Rannick would take his evil-tempered horse and ride off to the north. Sometimes he would return the same day. Sometimes he would be gone for several days. These mysterious absences unsettled Nilsson badly, particularly the longer ones. They brought to his mind the spectre of his new lord not returning, either through some unforeseen hazard or, worse, through choice. But he could say nothing. As he had many years before, he could only have faith in the path that he had chosen, accepting the arbitrary behaviour of his lord and continuing with the task that had been placed in his hands: the conquest of the land.

Only a few weeks ago such a notion would have seemed absurd to him. Indeed, but weeks ago, it *would* have been absurd. Then, he and his men had been a haunted and broken force. But, no longer. Now they had been renewed. Now their every ambition could be fulfilled, with time, patience and careful planning. Despite the dark uncertainty of Rannick's leadership, the prospect exhilarated Nilsson, though he allowed no outward sign of this to show.

Such knowledge as he had gained while journeying through the land beyond the valley had told him that it was large, sparsely populated and possessed of no great military might. That his own troop was small for such a grandiose scheme as conquest was of little consequence. With the correct tactics, any society could be brought low by a small, determined group. Had not he and his men been part of such a group once before? And held in thrall a far more vigorous people than inhabited this land. And too, he knew that his group would grow. There were always malcontents who could find no place in any ordered society, however benign. People within whose darker natures lay deep, stagnant pools of anger and hatred that needed only the right impetus to stir them into corrosive, consuming whirlpools of desire and resolve. Such people would emerge from the shadows and flock to the new banner that would be raised, like flies to a carcass.

However, tactics, recruits, and motivation notwithstanding, Nilsson knew all too well that Rannick's power was essential to the success of the venture. Only with this could they be assured of a victory sufficiently complete to ensure that they would *retain* their grip on the land. And Rannick's power would be with them only insofar as these early ventures were successful.

Thus, as Nilsson began to play his part in Rannick's great scheme, the villagers grew increasingly used to the sight of groups of armed men passing down the valley, to return days later, triumphant and noisy, with pack animals and wagons loaded with produce, furniture, and many other items of plunder, and, not infrequently, pale and fearful captives. They grew used also to the small but steady stream of ill-favoured individuals let through by the guards who sealed the valley to the south; individuals who sought directions to the castle with conspiratorial leers, taking it for granted that the villagers were party to the ravaging activities of Nilsson's men.

Given almost a free rein by Rannick, Nilsson implemented his original intention with regard to the villagers, namely that they be left alone while they caused no trouble. He did it quietly, off-handedly, almost, so as to avoid attracting Rannick's attention but he was explicit with his men. 'Leave them alone. Just let them know it's in their interests to stay quiet and co-operative. We'll need them to grow most of our food eventually. If any of you make trouble here, you'll answer to me personally.' He was not unreasonable, however; he knew his men's needs. He smiled knowingly. 'Besides, we'll get plenty of everything else we need from the other villages we . . . visit.'

Without openly declaring it, he affected that this was now

Rannick's will, and while his men knew that this was not so, they also knew enough not to dispute the point. At least, not while they could indeed get everything they wanted elsewhere.

The villagers themselves watched the unfolding events both fearfully and sullenly. The fate of Katrin and Garren Yarrance had made a stark and chilling impression on them, as had the account from Gryss, Harlen and Yakob of the strange power that Rannick now possessed. And fretting round the edges of these horrors was the mysterious disappearance of Farnor. Where had he gone that night after he had left Gryss's cottage? Had he gone to the castle and been quietly slain? Or had he fled over the hill to seek help from the capital? Or, the wilder notions went, had he fled north to the Great Forest? Some said that food and supplies had been taken from the Yarrance farm, and others were convinced that they had heard something howling beyond the castle on that fateful night. Speculation however, added only confusion to the dark ignorance that was slowly swamping the village.

Yet, inevitably, there was a certain amount of businesslike, if surly, contact between Nilsson's men and the villagers. Food was required. Repairs had to be made to parts of the castle. Horses had to be tended. Servants were needed. Occasionally there were overt threats made to reluctant workers, but the worst threat was the unspoken one which cried out every time a marauding band returned with booty and captives. 'Women for pleasure. Men and children as hostages. Think yourselves lucky this isn't happening to you.'

It was a matter discussed only in subdued whispers and with the closest of friends, for already there were those who were turning away from Gryss and the Council and the traditional, if informal, hierarchy that had overseen village life for generations. They were turning instead towards the power that could enforce its will with muscle and steel.

Gryss sat alone in his cottage, resting his head on his hand. His face was drawn and his eyes were red. He had been weeping. He had not wanted to, even though the wiser part of him knew that he needed to but the enormity of what was happening, and his part in it, had eventually swept aside his unhappy resistance and, for a while, he had sobbed like a beaten child into the silence of his old cottage.

Despite himself, he was tormented by the knowledge that he should have challenged Nilsson and his men when they first arrived, down-at-heel and exhausted. He was certain now that they could have been turned away while they were weak and had no measure of the village's vulnerability. Perhaps there would still have been some problem with Rannick and the strange creature with which he had made his unholy alliance, but that too might have been dealt with had Nilsson and his men not been there. And now, though he knew all too well that he should stand against Nilsson and Rannick, and tell the villagers to do the same; knew that he should use what remained of his authority to unite them into a powerful opposition; because of his earlier weakness and indecision, he could not.

Now he could only say, feebly, 'No, we mustn't do this, we mustn't do that, look what might happen to us.' And, again, by way of demonstrating the taunting rightness of this advice, came the steady stream of other poor souls, less privileged in their proximity to the seat of the power that was spreading like nightfall across the land.

How did I come to this? he thought bitterly, wiping his eyes awkwardly on his sleeve. Step by wretched step, came the equally bitter reply from somewhere within himself. And, in truth, he could not see how it could have been otherwise when he looked back over what had happened. But this gave him no consolation, and his mind was constantly filled with the words, 'if only', swirling round and round like autumn leaves caught in the coming winter wind. If only Farnor had not planted the idea of tithe gatherers in his head when Nilsson's men had first appeared in the distance. And yet again, if only he had stepped out and spoken to them as their ragged column had moved past the waiting villagers . . .

Gradually however, his mood became grimmer, until, angrily, he dashed the endless, tangled chain of tiny linked events aside and forced himself to look to the future. It was filled with the frightened faces of more and more captives, torn from their peaceful lives and brought in thrall to Rannick's terrible castle through no fault of their own; playthings and pawns in whatever dire game he was playing. Yet, while to Gryss these people were strangers, their very ordinariness marked them as his friends and neighbours. After a while, as he sat there, head bowed, he began to realize that the burden of their silent reproach would

9

eventually become more than he could bear; would become more awful to him than any consequence that might ensue from his facing and denouncing Rannick and Nilsson.

He stood up and went into the kitchen. Wiping his face with a damp cloth, he gazed at his reflection in a mirror on the wall. Like the ring that hung at his threshold, this too was a relic of his youthful travelling days, though he could not now remember exactly how he had come by it. Unlike the ornately carved ring, however, the mirror was of a very simple design. Its plain frame was black, though he could not imagine what paint or stain had been used to make it thus, as it had neither sheen nor texture. Indeed, when examined closely it seemed to have the quality of the blackness of a starless night, an infinite, aching depth. It disturbed him when he chose to think about it. And the glass was as bright and vivid as the frame was dark, almost as if the one had drawn all the light and radiance from the other. Further, throughout the years its brillant clarity had shown no signs of ageing or tarnishing – unlike himself, he mused. It gave, as it had always given, a cruelly accurate reflection of what it saw.

Gryss stared at the old man who was gazing pathetically out at him. Then the watching face became scornful. With an effort, Gryss straightened up. His inner battle was not yet finished; fear and self-doubt could never truly be vanquished but somewhere within him a tide was turning. Still there was a great chorus shouting for safety and security, for acquiescence to what was happening so that he could spend the remainder of his life in peace. But, increasingly, its voice was becoming strident and hollow and, though unwelcome, colder but wiser counsels were beginning to prevail. Safety he might possibly attain, though he had doubts about even that, knowing Rannick's disposition, but he could never truly know peace if others suffered when some effort on his part might help them.

The terrible, slaughtered images of Garren and Katrin Yarrance hovered perpetually at the edges of his mind, and, all too frequently, his stomach churned with his impotent distress at not knowing the fate of Farnor. But while he could not mend his earlier mistakes, perhaps he had learned enough to avoid making any more.

Yet what could he do? The inexorable question. Direct opposition to Rannick would mean death, or worse. And what retribution would such opposition unleash on the village?

10

The expression of the old man in the black-edged mirror became baleful. For an instant it seemed to Gryss that he was the shallow, ephemeral image and that the face in the mirror was the real person. He turned away sharply, his breathing suddenly painful, so powerful and frightening was this impression, and so severe the judgement in the eyes that had looked into his.

The shock cleared his mind. What he could do, first of all, was use his head: he could *think*.

Somewhere there was a solution. The energy that was draining out of him in whining self-pity must be redirected towards finding that solution, however elusive and difficult it might prove to be. And he did not have the luxury of time at his disposal. With each day, he reasoned, Nilsson's men would travel further and further abroad on their plundering raids; and too, in addition to those strangers who were wandering into the valley, like lesser predators following the scent of another's kill, not all those who returned with the raiders were captives; some were, beyond a doubt, recruits. Rannick's power would draw the worst out of men, and the worst of men. Gryss needed no military training to know that the armed strength of the garrison was growing relentlessly.

But what was Rannick up to? What could be the purpose of such a force? He obviously did not need it just to hold sway over the village. Gryss dismissed the questions before they began to lead him astray. They were irrelevant, at the moment. Whatever Rannick's intentions were, all that mattered now was that they be frustrated.

He returned to his favourite chair. It creaked welcomingly as he sat down and settled himself comfortably.

A dark measure of his position came to him first. He could do little or nothing alone. Further, whatever opposition he decided upon, he would have to persuade an increasingly large number of the villagers to accept and follow it as time passed. But who was to be trusted? There was no reason to suppose that the doubts and fears which were assailing him were not assailing everyone else, and, in all conscience he could not reproach anyone for throwing in their lot with the new masters of the valley. Yet this was only an intellectual conclusion; despite the truth of it, deep within himself he felt his benevolence fighting a stern battle with a powerful, emotional, reaction of anger and revulsion at such behaviour.

11

Still, he flattered himself that at least he could identify those most likely to succumb to this, and keep them away from any plans that he might instigate. He reverted to his original question, and amplified it. Who was to be trusted? And who was going to be any use?

The first names that came to him were Garren and Farnor, and the shock of the emptiness that followed in their wake made him grimace. Tears started to his eyes again and he brushed them away roughly. The dead were dead, and should be buried, he shouted inside his head, so that he could pass this momentary crisis under cover of the noise. He forced himself to think of the living. Yakob he could trust, certainly. Harlen too, though he found it hard to imagine him as any great tower of strength. That would be the role of Jeorg, of course. His heart was full of a black and awful rage at Rannick and Nilsson and his various injuries were healing well, though it would be some time before he had the full use of his arm again. The only real problem with Jeorg would be keeping his tongue under control. Also, Gryss knew to his cost, it would be politic to keep Jeorg's wife well away from any plotting and scheming. She was unequivocally of the opinion that what was happening was 'none of their business' and that it should be left to those 'better suited to such matters' or 'no good would come of it'. To her mind, the logic of her husband's cruelly beaten body was more than sufficient to sustain her argument, and she never elaborated on who such others 'better suited' might be. It would be a brave man who attempted to take her to task on such details.

It was not an uncommon view in the village, and, in her case, Gryss could sympathize completely.

There were others who could be relied on: Gofhern the blacksmith, Kestered the valley's finest leatherworker, Bellan the school teacher. Gryss weighed them all carefully. None of them was a fighter, of course, but they were men who could hold their peace, and who were not afraid to ponder intractable problems. And, as with himself in his capacity as a healer, their skills brought them into contact with more people than most. This alone would keep him better informed of the attitude of the villagers than if he were alone.

Then Marna's name came to him. He frowned. Much as he would have preferred to, he could not exclude her from any plans, as she would inevitably scent them out. And despite

Farnor's beating and subsequent mysterious disappearance, she was still quite capable of undertaking some wild venture of her own if she thought that nothing was being done. Whatever he decided to do, he would somehow have to find a way of involving her that offered her no danger.

He settled on the group that he should approach initially: Yakob, Harlen, Jeorg and, reluctantly, Marna. Perhaps Gofhern, Kestered, Bellan and others later but, he realized, that would not be solely his responsibility by then.

He stood up, stretched, and went to stand for a while at the front door of the cottage. It was a fine summer's day and everything about him was as it should be: birds singing, bright flowers everywhere, the air alive with rich scents, and all manner of small creatures bustling through the hedges and long grasses. Subtly marring it, though, was the darkness of the unexpected that now lay over everything like a clinging miasma. Throughout the years since his return, he had walked down into the village, knowing that while no two days were ever the same, he would meet nothing and no one that he would not have wished to meet. That had been such a truth in his life that it had never actually occurred to him before. But now, who could say what might lie around the familiar bends in the road? One of Nilsson's men? Oddly restrained but arrogant and unpleasant for all that, and not infrequently drunk on ale 'freely given' at the inn. Or some sharp-eyed stranger seeking the way to the castle? Guards returning from duty downland? Or perhaps even another column of armed men returning from a raid over the hill and bringing with them more captives.

He picked the carved iron ring up and examined it thoughtfully. The soldiers etched into its surface seemed to reproach him. They were waiting too, but they were armed and ready; at some time in the past they had seen their destiny and prepared themselves for it. He found himself making an ironical inventory of all the weapons that he knew lay in the valley: a handful of rusty swords that had accumulated over the generations from who knew what sources; an equally small handful of bows which, like the swords, were a greater danger to the users and their immediate neighbours than to any enemy they might be levelled at; and, incongruously, he seemed to remember having seen two old pikes lying in a barn somewhere, though he could not recall now whether or not they hadn't been made into pitchforks.

The fate of the pikes, however, was of little consequence. Not in his wildest imaginings could he envisage disciplined, serried ranks of villagers marching resolutely up to the castle to face Nilsson's men; that, indeed, was a task for others 'better suited'.

Which still left Gryss with his original problem. What could he, and his potential co-conspirators, do?

He put the ring down gently but the bell tinkled faintly, invoking a cursory rumble from the dog somewhere in the cottage. Closing the door behind him, he set off towards the village. The darkness of everything that Rannick and Nilsson had brought to the valley was still with him, but for the first time in many weeks he felt almost at ease with himself. It was a feeling that grew as he visited first Yakob, then Jeorg – 'Just to see how he's getting on,' he said, smiling excessively at Jeorg's wife – and finally Harlen. He gave no indication of his intentions, simply asking them to come round to his cottage that evening, 'Just to talk about a few things.'

The only threat to his unexpected euphoria was the absence of Marna. It took him some time to turn the conversation so that he could ask, casually, where she was. Harlen smiled and shrugged. Gryss had a brief vision of the young woman crawling along ditches and hedgerows in order to avoid the guards who were now permanently on duty down the valley. He dismissed it as calmly as he could. 'Bring her with you, Harlen,' he said as they parted. 'There're things I want to talk about that she'll be interested in.' Then he turned on his heel and left quickly before Harlen could summon up any questions.

Thus, in the early evening, all his would-be allies were gathered in his cottage.

He made no preamble, but set out his ideas immediately. There was a silence when he had finished. Yakob eventually broke it. His initial reaction was the same as had been Gryss's own. 'All very fine, Gryss,' he said. 'We'd all like to do something. But what can we do? We can't throw them out of the castle. We can't get out of the valley.' He threw up his hands. 'We don't even know what it is that Rannick and these people are up to.'

'And they *are* leaving us alone,' Harlen added, reluctantly reciting the growing response of the villagers. 'Who knows what they'll do if we start to make trouble?'

Gryss nodded. He suspected that this careful treatment of the villagers was Nilsson's tactic, and that it had been adopted quite specifically to disarm troublesome local opposition. Rannick, he was sure, would not have hesitated to wreak havoc on the village had the whim so taken him.

He submitted this to his friends. 'Just discussing it like this, now, makes me think that perhaps Rannick's fully occupied on some greater design of his own,' he concluded. 'I can't see that he's leaving us alone because he regrets . . .' He hesitated. 'What he did to Katrin and Garren.'

Yakob scowled and shrugged. 'Maybe,' he said. 'But whoever's idea it is, it's a good one, and it'll work. Everyone's seen those other poor souls being hauled in, and everyone knows it could be them next if they make trouble.' Anger and regret filled his face. 'It's horrible to talk like that, I know,' he went on. 'But it's true. Those people are suffering on our behalf.' He brought his hand down on the table. 'If only we'd seen them off when they first arrived.'

Gryss was no more indulgent with Yakob than he had been with himself a few hours ago. 'Well, we didn't,' he answered curtly. 'And we can't be wasting our time breast-beating and howling over what we should have done. We did what we did because it seemed right at the time. Now the harm's been done and what we have to do is make sure we don't perpetuate that mistake by letting Rannick and Nilsson get away with whatever it is they're doing, without any hindrance.'

Yakob made to speak again but Gryss lifted a hand to stop him. 'Do you agree or don't you?' he demanded. 'It's that simple.' He paused briefly. 'If you don't, then fair enough. I'll involve you no further. All I'll ask of you is that you keep quiet about this meeting.'

There was a brief, injured silence, then Yakob said heatedly, 'You've no call to speak like that. Of course we want to do something.' Harlen and Jeorg both nodded in agreement. 'But I presume we'll be allowed the odd moment to speak about our regrets, won't we? It's not as if anything springs immediately to mind that we *can* do, does it?'

Gryss bridled a little at this rebuff but he fought back a scowl and managed to look appropriately contrite. 'You're right, Yakob. I'm sorry,' he said, insincerely. 'I've no doubt I can rely on you to guard against my impetuosity.' This time it was Yakob who bridled, at the sarcasm that Gryss had failed to keep out of

15

his voice, but Gryss continued quickly, 'As for what to do, I'm afraid we must succeed in what we failed to do before. We must get news of what's happening to the capital.'

For the first time since she had sat down at the long wooden table, Marna looked up. She did not speak, but she leaned forward a little. Gryss noted the movement. 'There'll be plenty for you to do here, Marna,' he said, partly to reassure Harlen, but mainly in an attempt to forestall any folly that she might be contemplating.

Unexpectedly she nodded understandingly and said, 'Of course, Gryss.'

Gryss looked at her narrowly and made an immediate resolution to watch her very carefully. When they were alone, he would speak to her a little more bluntly.

Yakob reverted to practicalities. 'I suppose it's all we can do,' he said. 'But how? There are far more guards downland than there were when Jeorg tried to leave, and if anyone's lucky enough to get past them, there's no saying how far over the hill these raiding parties of theirs are reaching now.'

'I'll go again,' Jeorg said resolutely. 'If Rannick's in the castle, I'll take my chance on dodging his men.' He tapped his head. 'I go through the route continually in my mind, and I've still got the maps and notes we prepared, wrapped up safe and sound at the bottom of my pack.'

Yakob and Harlen looked unhappy, but Gryss nodded. 'You're still the best choice for the job,' he said. 'But we've got to be far more careful this time. They'll kill you without a doubt if they catch you again, and who knows what reprisals they might take against the rest of the village?'

'I know,' Jeorg replied, his voice untypically soft. He tapped his head again. 'I go through *that* continually as well. And don't think I relish the prospect of trying again. The whole idea frightens the breeches off me'. He paused, and then almost spat out, 'But doing nothing's rotting me. And it's no guarantee of safety for the village. Rannick'll turn on us sooner or later, I'm sure. You all know what he's like.' He looked around the table. His pain was reflected in the faces of his listeners, but no one disagreed.

Despite the grimness of this assessment, Gryss was strangely heartened by the fact that they had all apparently reached the same conclusion as himself about Rannick's probable conduct.

Jeorg continued, 'And talk around the matter as much as you like, it comes to the same in the end. We can't fight them. That's a job for soldiers. So someone has to tell the king what's happened so that the army can be sent to get rid of them.'

A long silence followed this pronouncement. 'We must work out when and how, then,' Gryss said eventually, his voice a little hoarse.

'I can watch the guards downland,' Marna said.

'No!' Both Gryss and Harlen spoke together sharply. Gryss deferred to her father. 'You keep away from them,' Harlen said. 'You don't need to be told why they're bringing women back from their raids, do you?'

Marna's face coloured in a mixture of anger and embarrassment. Such directness from her father was unusual. 'Just keep away from them,' he said again, quietly but authoritatively. The other men around the table nodded. Marna's face became stony, but she did not speak.

'*I'll* keep an eye on the guards,' Harlen went on, turning back to Gryss. 'They're used to me wandering about down there. It shouldn't be too difficult to find out how many there are and how they come and go.'

Gryss nodded. 'I suppose we'll have to think like soldiers ourselves,' he mused. 'We must watch all of them all the time. Find out exactly how many there are, what they do, who's in charge, and so on.' He grimaced. 'I suppose we'll have to get to know them. Find out their names. Find out who likes to drink, who likes to gamble, who likes to gossip. As we learn about them, perhaps other ways of quietly causing them problems will come to light.'

Marna's restraint broke. 'And what am I supposed to do,' she demanded, 'if I'm to keep away from them?'

With unexpected inspiration Gryss said, 'You can do as you've already been doing. Find out what the young people are thinking.' Marna's eyes became menacing. 'And the women,' Gryss added hastily and with some earnestness. 'It's important, Marna. Only Jeorg here's married now, and his wife's views are all too well known. But sooner or later, there's going to have to be a lot more than us involved in this, and we can't do anything if the women are against us.'

Slightly mollified, Marna sat back in her chair and surveyed her fellow conspirators. Gryss added to his resolve to watch her carefully: he would have to give her plenty to do as well. He had seen the look of resolute determination that flickered briefly in her eyes, and it alarmed him.

Chapter 2

'This must be the cause of all the fuss.'

A booted foot prodded cautiously.

'Careful, it might be dangerous.'

'No, surely not, it's only . . .'

'No.' A respectful but definite interruption. 'Be careful. Something's disturbed them profoundly. I told you, I Heard it clearer than I've ever Heard anything. And this *must* be the cause of it all. Just look at it. It might be more than it seems. We must be careful.'

Insistent. 'But it might be injured. Its face is badly bruised.'

Female, newly arrived, and impatient. 'For pity's sake, the two of you. If *it* doesn't die of its hurts, *it* will die of old age while you stand around debating matters.' She laid a heavy and scornful emphasis on the word it.

The young woman pushed the two men aside and knelt down by the object of their attention. 'Go and tend that horse, Marken, if you're bothered about this one. I'll let you know if it suddenly turns into a tree goblin and tries to drag me to its lair.'

The older of the two men looked briefly at his companion for support, but found only an anxious preoccupation with their discovery. Scowling, he set off across the clearing towards the quietly grazing horse that the girl had indicated.

The other man abandoned his momentary reverie. 'Edrien, that's no way to talk to Marken,' he said to the girl. 'He's our Hearer, child. You should show more respect.'

The girl frowned impatiently. 'I know, Father,' she said, a little repentantly. 'But he fusses so, at times.'

'He fusses because he Hears and we don't, Edrien,' her father persisted. 'And I've never seen him so agitated about a Hearing before.' A note of annoyance came into his voice. 'And what he Hears he notes, which is more than you've ever done. You just apologize to him when he comes back.'

Edrien's frown deepened and her mouth formed a reply which she noticeably pondered and then rejected before saying, 'Oh, very well,' with a great lack of conviction. 'But is it all right if I see if this thing is alive or not?'

The man allowed his daughter this last sarcastic barb, then he crouched down beside her and nodded. 'Take care though,' he said, softly but firmly. 'There's something odd about him, to say the least. Look at his clothes. And his hair, for pity's sake – it's black! And so's his horse. Wherever he's from, it's beyond the Forest, for sure.' Surreptitiously, and keeping his hand well out of the sight of his daughter, he drew a knife.

Edrien reached out and gently held her fingers against the throat of the motionless figure lying on the sunlit grass. 'He's not dead, anyway,' she said after a moment.

'That may not necessarily be good news.' It was Marken, returned, leading the horse uncertainly.

Edrien looked up, her face angry, but catching her father's eye she swallowed her intended reply. 'I'm sorry I was – a little short – Marken,' she said flatly, her jawline taut.

Marken gave a slight, sharp nod by way of acknowledgement, then turned to her father. 'His horse is exhausted, Derwyn,' he said. 'He must have been riding like someone demented.'

Derwyn shook his head. 'I'm surprised he got this far. There must be *some* reason for it.' He turned to Marken. 'Can you Hear anything?' he asked.

Marken closed his eyes, and raised his hand slightly for silence. It was an unnecessary gesture. Both Derwyn and Edrien stood motionless, watching him intently. The gentle rustle of the surrounding trees filled the small clearing. 'No,' he said, after a moment. 'Less than usual, if anything. Whatever was causing the disturbance has ended.' There was doubt in his voice, however. 'But there's a – tension, here – an expectancy – even a bewilderment. It's very strange. It's as if they're waiting for us to do something.'

'What?' Derwyn asked.

Marken shrugged apologetically. 'I don't know,' he replied.

Edrien looked at the two men. 'Shall I see if it's safe to move him?' she asked.

'I suppose so,' Derwyn replied, though he still kept his knife discreetly ready. He'd seen more than one 'unconscious' animal, suddenly spring to life, all teeth and slashing claws. And he'd never come across any animal remotely as devious and savage as a man bent on treachery.

Gently, Edrien lifted up the eyelids of the unconscious figure, then, carefully, she tested his limbs. 'I can't feel anything serious. I think he's probably just fallen off his horse and cracked his head.'

Derwyn stood up. His lined face creased further as he frowned. 'Well, that's as may be, but if he's a faller we can't risk throwing him over a saddle while he's unconscious; there's no saying what hurt we'd do him. And wherever he's come from, or for whatever reason, we can't leave him here. We'll have to tie him to a stretcher and take him back to the lodge. See what Bildar makes of him.' He turned to Marken. 'Find some suitable branches and ask if we may take them,' he said.

Marken nodded and disappeared into the trees. Derwyn turned to his daughter. 'Go and help him, Edrien,' he said, adding as she stood up, 'And be pleasant, please. Like me, he's older than you, and unfortunately no longer has the advantage of knowing everything.'

His slight smile silenced Edrien's reply before it formed.

Within a short while the three were walking their horses slowly through the forest. Derwyn's horse was hauling a crude but well-rigged stretcher, to which the body of the still-unconscious new arrival was tightly and skilfully lashed. The springiness of the two main supporting branches absorbed much of the impact of the small jolts that occurred as the trailing ends were dragged over the forest floor. Derwyn kept a careful watch for anything that might seriously jar the passenger. Behind him came Edrien and Marken, leading the other horses. There was little conversation as they walked along, and the tread of the horses was so soft that the sounds of their passing were lost in the gentle rustling of the trees and the birdsong that filled the sunlit air.

As Derwyn halted and he and Edrien moved to ease the trailing ends of the stretcher over a large root protruding above the grassy forest floor, the figure on the stretcher muttered something. Edrien looked up. 'I think he's waking,' she said.

Derwyn looked at him thoughtfully for a moment. 'Well, we've not far to go now, we'll get him back to the lodge and let Bildar look at him anyway. Keep an eye on him. See if you can make sense of anything he says.'

21

The small procession set off again.

Darkness swirled around Farnor. At his heels, the fearful menace came ever closer.

'Run, horse, run!' The phrase wove incessantly in and out of his head through the pounding progress of the exhausted and panic-stricken horse. Then there was no horse and no sound and he was moving alone through the darkness. All around were menace and fear. Voices called to him: his mother and father, Gryss, Marna, and poor, beaten Jeorg. But he could not understand what they said. And there were other voices too, alien and strange.

Yet these were but flitting dreams. In truth, he knew that there was nothing but the flight and the fear and the terrible rasping of his breath and the pounding of his heart. There had never been anything but the flight and fear, in all its gasping horror, nor would there ever be.

Then the darkness began to cling about him, tangible and awful. A myriad cloying fingers catching at his legs, his arms, his whole body. But he must not stop. Even to falter would be to bring the creature down upon him, with its fearsome, rending jaws, and its terrible will, lusting to feast upon the fear that so filled him.

Yet the darkness would not be gainsaid. It tugged and snatched at him, relentlessly draining the strength from him, wrapping itself about him tighter and tighter like some great spider's web.

Until finally he was powerless to move.

Utterly spent, he was held fast, swaying helplessly in the black emptiness.

Faint sounds drifted to him.

It was still there! Pursuing him!

He began to struggle. He would not die to this creature – Rannick's creature – like some bleating sheep.

No!

'No!'

'Father!'

The voice burst upon him, urgent and nearby. With it came shifting shadows within shadows. Something touched his face. He shied away from it violently and struggled to free himself.

'It's all right. It's all right.' An anxious female voice, speaking with a strange accent, washed over him, and the darkness broke

22

silently into countless shimmering lights. 'It's all right. It's all right,' the voice said again.

Farnor took in the gentleness of the voice even as the lights about him became bright, welcoming beams of warm sunlight, scattered by a wind-shaken canopy of branches and leaves.

The menace had gone!

Relief flooded through him.

But still he was bound!

With a panic-stricken cry, he began struggling again.

'No, no!' the woman's voice protested. 'You're safe. No one's going to hurt you.' Then, apparently to someone else, 'I don't think he can understand me.'

Hands touched Farnor's face, and the silhouette of a head intruded itself against the leafy background. 'I said, you are safe,' the head said loudly and with painstaking slowness. 'Do not struggle. You have had a fall. You might be badly hurt.'

'I doubt that, Edrien,' came a man's amused voice. 'Not the way he's wriggling. And I don't think he's deaf either, judging from the look on his face when you shouted at him.'

Though the nightmare horror of the creature and the chase had slipped away from him, much of Farnor's fear returned. He was a captive, held by some strange-speaking people. Had he fallen into the hands of Nilsson's men? Was he being carried back to the castle? He redoubled his struggling.

The head disappeared and another one replaced it. Farnor stopped briefly and screwed up his eyes to examine his captor, but the sunlight flickering through the leaves was too bright for him to distinguish any features.

'Do you understand me, boy?' the new head said quietly, but also with a strange accent.

'I'm not a boy, *sir*,' Farnor said, viciously polite as an unexpected surge of anger ran through him, at this form of address.

Somewhere there was a soft chuckle. 'I gather you do understand me, young man,' the head said again.

'Who are you?' Farnor demanded. 'Are you Nilsson's men? Where are we? Where are you taking me . . .?'

The head shook and a waving hand appeared, seeking silence. 'Calm yourself. No one means you any harm and we've all got a great many questions to ask. But for now, my name's Derwyn, I'm Koyden-dae. I'm afraid I know of no peoples called Nilssons – a very peculiar name, I must say – but if the Nilssons are your

23

kin then I'm sure we'll help you to get back to them in due course, if we can.'

Farnor gaped.

'Although I must admit, I wouldn't know where to start looking,' Derwyn continued. 'Indeed, I've no idea how you came to be here. It's all very strange.' He became explanatory. 'We were drawn out to look for something when our Hearer felt a great disturbance. And we found you. And your horse. That's safe too, but you've been riding hard by the look of it. We—'

'I can't understand half of what you're saying,' Farnor interrupted heatedly. He struggled against his bonds again. 'But if you mean me no harm, then why am I trussed up like a Dalmas Day fowl?'

Derwyn's brow furrowed. 'I can't say that I understand *you* particularly well, young man,' he replied. 'Your speech is a little strange. But we thought you were a faller, albeit only off your horse, and you might have been badly hurt. We bound you to this stretcher so that we could take you back to our Mender at the lodge without injuring you further.'

Despite his anxiety, Farnor felt the reassurance in Derwyn's voice and, almost in spite of himself, he relaxed a little. 'I'm not hurt,' he said more quietly. But as if they had been waiting for the opportunity, the pains from his beating by Nilsson and his subsequent headlong flight through the forest returned to give him the lie. He stiffened and grimaced.

Derwyn nodded knowingly. 'So I see,' he said, with some irony. 'Just lie still. We've not far to go to our lodge, now. Then our Mender can look at you properly and we'll find out just how badly you're not hurt.'

Farnor was inclined to dispute the matter further, but all the spirit seemed to leave him. His entire body was beginning to throb, and his mind whirled with innumerable, half-formed questions.

'Relax. Lie still,' Derwyn said again, and his head disappeared from Farnor's view. The soft command coincided exactly with the demands of Farnor's body and it did as it was bidden. Almost immediately sleep began to creep over him, helped in no small degree by the gentle swaying of the stretcher and the sunlight above him, broken into countless dancing shards by the shaking leaves.

'He's asleep, Father,' he heard the female voice say softly in the distance, but he could not muster the strength to deny it.

A dreamlike, twilight interval followed, as he drifted in and out of the sleep that he so desperately needed. He was aware of shimmering lights, then a dark coolness. Then warmth and sunlight again, with an open sky overhead. And many voices, speaking with that same strange accent. And hands, lifting him gently and laying him down, and searching about him, expertly, purposefully, for injury. He woke briefly to a deep silence and a momentary vision of an odd, cave-like room. Then there was darkness again, folding over him to take him away from his aching body.

And into this darkness came the other voices that he had heard before. The voices that were inside his head. The great family of voices. But whereas, in the past, they had been distant and faint, now they were clear and distinct, and he knew that they were speaking softly, as if for fear of disturbing him.

Some part of him told him that he should be frightened; that he was hearing voices where there were no people; that he had indeed fallen and injured his head – or worse, that he might even be going mad. But he *had* heard them before, and he could feel no real alarm, for the voices brought with them subtler meanings than those contained in the words alone. Many questions were being asked, and there was bewilderment, doubt, and even fear, but there was nothing that offered him any threat. Indeed, when he became the focus of debate, a sense of surprise and wonder dominated all responses.

'He can Hear us even now.'

Again, wonder. And a realization that this was the truth.

'It is strange. There's never been such a one before.'

Denial.

Farnor felt a sudden, almost giddying, sensation, of great spans of ages arching back into times long past, when many things were very different. It was as if in a single instant, he heard every one of Yonas's tales being told, plus ten score more, and each more enthralling than the last. A fleeting glimpse of innumerable great histories, of peoples growing and moving across the world. Of the coming of great darkness and terror, of terrible conflicts, and courage and heroism, cowardice and treachery, sacrifice and victory. Of the return of light and wonder and knowledge. And finally, trailing into the here and now, of guilt, of lapsing vigilance, of a recent, frightening – return?

And, within the blink of an eye, it was all gone.

'He will Hear our every word.'

'No. He's but a solitary Mover. And a sapling.'

'And what have we to hide?'

Silence.

'He may be our salvation.'

Doubt. Fear.

'He may presage our downfall.'

Denial again.

'He may presage strange and troubled times, but our true downfall cannot lie in the power of the Movers any more than it did before. We are First Comers after the Great Heat and our hold on the world goes even beyond that – into the times unknowable.'

This opinion was given unequivocally, though strands of doubt ran through it.

'Who are you?' Farnor found himself asking into the silence that ensued, though no sound came to his lips.

The silence deepened.

'There. He Hears us almost as we Hear ourself. Say what you will, there's not been one such in generations beyond counting.'

'Who are you?' Farnor asked again.

'Rest, Mover,' came the reply. 'You know us well enough. We have turned away the abomination for the nonce, though it cost us great pain and fear runs through us as it has not done in many ages. Rest your limbs, we feel their pain. And make your peace with your own kind. You have frightened them also.'

'I don't understand anything you say,' Farnor replied.

Amusement filled him. 'Rest,' came the gentle instruction. 'We'll disturb you no more with our chatter.'

And in the word, rest, came so many images of peace and stillness that it was beyond Farnor to resist them, and he drifted back into sleep again.

Bildar, the Mender to Derwyn's lodge, scratched his chin unhappily. 'He's not seriously hurt,' he said. 'But he's got severe bruising and muscle damage, and, like his horse, he's absolutely exhausted.'

Derwyn shrugged a little. 'Well, I suppose only he can tell us why he was riding so hard,' he said. 'And I presume it's the riding that's caused the bruising.'

'Not all of it, I'm afraid,' Bildar said, shaking his head. 'At least, as far as I can tell. Some of it's a little older than the rest and it looks as if he's had a nasty accident to his arm. But, for the most part' – he looked unhappily at Derwyn – 'it looks to me as if he's been beaten – badly beaten.'

'Beaten?' Derwyn queried, a puzzled frown forming on his lined face.

Bildar nodded, and lifted his clenched fist to amplify his meaning. 'Badly,' he repeated. 'I'd say he was lucky not to have suffered some internal injury. As it is, he's going to be very sore for quite a time.'

Derwyn turned to Marken, who shrugged. He looked around at the trees surrounding the wide, circular green where they were sitting. 'I've no idea,' he said, in answer to the unspoken question. 'I don't even know what's brought him here, let alone how he came to be injured. And I can Hear nothing. It's almost as if they were deliberately keeping quiet. I've never felt anything quite like it.'

Derwyn leaned on the wooden table in front of him and rested his head on his hand. 'But who'd want to beat a young lad like that? Who'd beat him so hard that he'd flee his homeland and ride both himself and his horse to a standstill?'

'That's not completely beyond understanding,' Marken replied a little sourly, casting a glance at Edrien. 'But more to the point, why did they let him through? Why wasn't he gently turned about? We don't suffer from outsiders and fringe dwellers here, but the Koyden-ushav and the Koyden-d'ryne do and that's what normally happens there to anyone who wanders in without an invitation.'

'Perhaps it's *because* they're not used to outsiders here,' Edrien offered. 'Perhaps he caught them by surprise.'

Marken shook his head. 'No,' he replied, gently but definitely. 'They weren't taken by surprise. I've been Hearing vague whispers about – someone beyond – someone unusual – for some time now. And there's been an odd feeling of – expectancy . . . in the air.' He looked at his listeners and shrugged. 'I'm sorry I can't be clearer.'

'You mean, they *knew* he was coming?' Derwyn asked, his eyes widening. 'And *you* knew?'

'No,' Marken replied, a touch irritably. 'I told you, it's not that clear. But they certainly weren't taken by surprise. When I Heard

27

them, it was like nothing I'd ever Heard before. Vivid, intense. There was some great upheaval, a bewildering debate of some kind, then suddenly something was coming into the Forest and we were to find it.' He shivered slightly. 'And there were great washes of all sorts of emotions, not least outright fear.'

Derwyn straightened up and then leaned back in his chair. He looked around him. Warm sunlight filled the clearing, while a soft breeze, full of woodland sounds and scents, prevented it from becoming too hot and gently stirred the surrounding treetops. Quite near to the table, several birds were hopping to and fro in search of insects and worms. Occasionally a noisy squabble would break out and one or two of them would fly off into the trees, seemingly to sulk for a little while before returning.

'Such a beautiful day,' Derwyn said, putting his hands behind his head then letting them fall on to his knees. 'I don't know what to make of all this. It's so strange. And it all feels so – bad. I almost regret not strapping that lad over his saddle, pointing him south and sending him back on his way.'

'I think that might have been to his death,' Marken said, after a long pause. 'Whatever was causing the upheaval amongst them was no small thing.'

Derwyn turned and looked at him. 'This has disturbed you far more than you're admitting, hasn't it?' he said.

'I'm afraid so,' Marken replied. 'I've no clear reason for it, but I don't feel any happier about the arrival of this young man than you do. Valderen are Valderen, outsiders are outsiders—'

'We're all people, Marken,' Edrien interrupted, with some petulance.

Marken assumed a look of scarcely controlled exasperation and Derwyn shot his daughter an angry glance. 'Valderen are Valderen, and outsiders are outsiders,' Marken repeated deliberately. Then despite himself his irritation surfaced. 'And no one's talking about them not being people, you silly girl.' Edrien bridled, but another look from her father made her keep silent. Marken continued, 'We're Forest dwellers and they're not. They live in the plains and the mountains and presumably know the lore of such places, just as we know the lore of the Forest. But throughout our known history and our legends, contact between us has been infrequent and usually associated with evil happenings.' He looked at Derwyn. 'We must tend this boy, of course. See that he's fed and rested. And listen to his tale, if he's willing to tell it. But we must be' – he searched for a word – 'circumspect in any judgements we make about him. Or anything he says.'

Derwyn's eyes narrowed as he looked at the Hearer. 'Have you Heard things that you don't want to tell us about?' he asked.

Marken shook his head slowly. 'No,' he replied doubtfully. 'But something's wrong. Unsettled, turbulent.' He hesitated and his face became agitated. 'You'll have to forgive me, Derwyn, I suddenly seem to find myself not where I thought I was. As if I'd been walking uphill without realizing it, and suddenly turned to find myself looking out over a totally unfamiliar treescape.'

Derwyn looked concerned, and even Edrien forebore to make any caustic observation, so disturbed did Marken seem. 'I don't understand,' Derwyn said.

'Nor do I,' Marken replied after a long pause. 'That's the problem. Everything is at once so clear and so vague. It's clear that something portentous is about to happen – or perhaps has happened – but vague about what it could be, or might have been. Or when, or how it will affect us.'

'How long have you had these feelings?' Derwyn asked gently.

'I don't know,' Marken replied. 'That's what I was trying to say. It's as if I've had them almost for years, but for some reason have only just noticed them.' He looked at Derwyn. 'I'm sorry,' he said, standing up and putting his hand to his head. 'Even talking like this is – changing things.'

There was a long, uneasy silence, in which Marken stood motionless, staring into the trees, while his companions watched him, uncertain what to say or do. Then, abruptly, he seemed to reach a decision. 'I'm afraid I'll have to go away for a little while. I'll have to find – a quiet place – calm myself, order my thoughts.'

Edrien frowned, puzzled by this remark, but Bildar and Derwyn exchanged shocked glances. Derwyn stood and took Marken's arm and looked at him intently. After a moment however, he nodded slowly, and, with reluctant resignation, said, 'You must do as your judgement tells you, Marken.' He sat down again, but it was almost as if he could not trust his legs to support him. Then, clearing his throat awkwardly, he became practical. 'Do you want a companion to tend to your needs?' he asked.

'No, thank you, Derwyn,' Marken replied. 'I'll have to be truly alone.' He affected a slight heartiness. 'And I've not lost all my Forest skills yet. I'll survive for as long as I have to.'

Derwyn was too well acquainted with the old Hearer to dispute the matter with him. 'As you wish,' he said helplessly. There was another uncomfortable silence. 'When will you go?' he asked eventually.

Marken looked pained. 'Now,' he said. 'I'll get some things from my lodge and go immediately. There's nothing needing a Hearer for a little while, and' – he looked from side to side, restlessly – 'matters aren't going to resolve themselves by us sitting talking about them.'

'Whatever you wish,' Derwyn said again softly.

Marken gave a curt nod and made a small, awkward gesture of farewell to Bildar and Edrien, then turned and walked off into the trees.

Edrien stood up hesitantly, her mouth hanging open in bewilderment. 'What's the matter?' she asked her father uncertainly. 'What's happened? What's he doing? Where's he going?'

Derwyn motioned his daughter to sit down, and, leaning back in his chair, put his head in his hands.

'Father?' Edrien insisted.

Bildar laid a hand on her arm. 'A minute,' he whispered. 'Give him a minute.'

Edrien turned to him, the same questions on her face, but Bildar waved a finger for silence.

'Damnation,' Derwyn said suddenly, his face grim. He slapped the table with his hand, and the birds feasting nearby rose as one and scattered noisily into the trees.

'What's the matter?' Edrien tried again, her voice both anxious and impatient. 'What was Marken talking about? Why's he gone off like that all of a sudden?' Guilt tinged her expression. 'Was it something I did?'

Derwyn looked at her sharply, as if surprised to find that he was not alone. His dark expression faded almost immediately into regret as she flinched away from it. He took her hand. 'No, no,' he said reassuringly. 'I'm afraid it's something far more serious than your acid tongue.'

'What, then?' Unsettled by her father's sudden change of mood, Edrien let a petulant note waver into her question.

Derwyn scowled irritably. 'I don't know, Edrien,' he said, echoing her tone. 'And neither does Marken. Nor Bildar. Nor any of us. Something's troubling him deeply; very deeply. And he needs to go to what the Hearers call a quiet place.'

Edrien frowned. 'But—'

Bildar cut through the angry family tension that was beginning to develop between father and daughter. 'Marken's a Hearer, Edrien,' he said, risking the obvious. 'No one knows what they Hear, or how, or why. But they're our only contact with *them* and we need them if we're to live here in any semblance of harmony. We have to weigh what they say, and we have to trust their judgement.'

Edrien's lip began to curl slightly.

'No!' Bildar said softly, but with great force. 'You're young, and you take things for granted. Just listen for once. That's the way it is, even though we don't truly understand it.' He became quite stern. 'And we don't denounce because we don't understand. We think and we listen and we watch and we stay silent until perhaps, one day, the light dawns.' He tapped his temple with his finger.

United to her by blood, Bildar had an authority over Edrien that was in many ways greater than her father's. She nodded, but did not speak. Bildar cast an anxious glance at Derwyn and hesitated before continuing. 'Your father's concerned because we don't know when, or even if, Marken's going to come back.'

The remainder of Edrien's antagonism drained away into shocked disbelief. 'What do you mean, you don't know *if* he's coming back?' She looked at her father and then back at Bildar, a frightened girl suddenly trying not to peer out of the young woman's eyes.

Seeing his daughter thus downed, Derwyn's own darkness faded a little. 'We've no answers to any of your questions, Edrien,' he said gently. 'Hearers are Hearers. If Marken could've told us the how and why of everything then he would have done. All we can do now is accept whatever problems his leaving presents us with. His own troubles are far greater. If he needs anything at all, it's to know that his friends, his people, will be carrying on as he's always shown them, trusting in the knowledge that this is *their* will and that they'll not leave us without guidance for long.'

Edrien looked in the direction that Marken had taken. Her face was pale and she seemed suddenly near to tears, but her father's appeal to friendship and trust had forbidden any response other than concern for Marken now.

'You mean he's just – going to wander off somewhere and sit under a tree and think?' she said, her voice unsteady.

Derwyn shrugged, but did not reply.

Shaking her head rapidly, as if to clear it, Edrien took refuge in practicalities. 'You men are so illogical,' she announced. 'How can he wander off without knowing what he's doing, or where he's going? What in the Forest's name does—'

Bildar interrupted, a little impatiently. 'I told you,' he said. 'He trusts himself, and what he Hears. And we must do the same. It's a rare thing for a Hearer to leave like this but it's happened to others before now.'

Edrien let out an exasperated breath. 'If you say so,' she conceded reluctantly. 'But I don't understand what's happening at all. Marken's probably not been away from the lodge, alone, in years. How's he going to manage?'

'He'll manage well enough,' Derwyn said, though his voice lacked conviction. He looked up at the sunny sky. 'It's summer, after all. And he's well rooted. Try not to fret.'

Questions still tumbled around Edrien's mind, but she gave voice to none of them. After a moment she said conspiratorially, 'Should I go after him quietly? Keep an eye on him?'

Derwyn smiled and shook his head. 'No,' he said. 'Leave him be.' He stood up briskly, slapping his knees loudly with both hands as he did so, to signal an end to the debate. 'What you can do though, is go and see if that young man's awake yet, and if he is, bring him to my room. He's at the heart of this business, and I think it's time we called him to account.'

Chapter 3

Farnor started awake at the sudden light. As he made to sit up, however, pains throughout his body forced him down on to the bed again immediately. He let out a noisy breath.

'I'm sorry, did I startle you?'

Carefully Farnor turned his head in the direction of the voice. Gradually his eyes focused on a young woman. She was holding a small lantern which seemed to be the only source of light in the room.

If room it was, he thought, as his eyes adjusted further. For there were no familiar beams over his head, no windows, nor even, for that matter, flat walls and straight corners. With a cautious effort, he levered himself up on to his elbows and gazed around, his companion momentarily forgotten.

The chamber proved to be roughly circular, and the walls rose up and curved inwards to become a crudely domed ceiling. What held Farnor's attention, however, was not the unusual shape of the room but the fact that both walls and ceiling were decorated with dark, shadowy lines that twisted and curved and wound about one another in what seemed to be a completely random pattern. He recalled from the haze of the immediate past that at one point he had imagined himself to be in a cave. But this was no cave. At least, not one such as he had ever known. It was warm and dry and fresh smelling, and, despite the peculiar walls and ceiling, it had almost a homely air about it. And the bed was wonderfully comfortable.

He stared at the walls intently, following the twisting lines up and over and down again until he found that he was looking at the wall immediately by his bed. The light grew brighter and the lines began to cast shadows. Tentatively he reached out and touched one of them. 'They're like roots,' he said, softly, in amazement. 'Tree roots.'

A laugh made him recall his visitor. Just in time, he remembered to move slowly as he turned around. The woman had moved closer to his bed, and was holding the lantern high in order to help him with his inspection of the wall. Her thin face was full of laughter. 'Of course they're tree roots,' she said. 'What else did you expect to see down here? Rooks' nests?' She laughed again.

For an instant Farnor felt indignant at this response, but his indignation crumbled before the confusion and bewilderment that suddenly rushed in upon him. He covered his eyes with his hands and slowly lay back on the bed.

'Are you all right?' the young woman asked, anxious now.

Farnor nodded. 'I was just hoping that I was dreaming,' he replied.

'No, you're not dreaming,' came the response, with flat simplicity. 'Why should you be?'

Farnor scowled and, removing his hands from his eyes, turned towards his questioner. 'Who are you?' he asked, none too politely.

'Edrien,' came the answer, brusquely echoing his tone. 'Can you get up? My father wants to see you.'

'And who's he?' Farnor demanded.

Edrien's eyebrows rose. 'His name is Derwyn,' she replied, with studied calmness. 'He's the Second of this lodge. And it was he who said you had to be looked after. If I were you, I'd be prepared to answer questions rather than ask them. Are you well enough to get up, or not?'

Farnor nodded, then grimaced as the general throbbing of his body concentrated itself suddenly in his head. 'Yes, I can get up,' he said. 'But only slowly, I think.' Gingerly he eased himself upright and prepared to swing his legs out of the bed. Then he stopped abruptly and peered under the blankets. When he looked up, he was wide-eyed. 'Where are my clothes?' he asked, urgently.

Edrien flicked a glance towards a nearby chair where Farnor saw his clothes, neatly stacked.

'Could you pass them, please?' he asked with awkward politeness.

Edrien scowled. 'I'm not your servant, boy,' she said, heatedly. But she gathered up the clothes and tossed them to him.

34

'Thank you,' he said weakly. Then he looked at her expectantly.

'What now?' she demanded.

'I want to get dressed,' he replied, making a vague gesture to the effect that perhaps she might leave him, or at least turn around.

Edrien cast an impatient glance towards the ceiling, and turned round. 'I don't know who you imagine helped to get you into that bed last night,' she said stiffly. 'Or helped Bildar with his examination.'

Farnor made no reply, but he coloured violently as he hastily struggled into his clothes.

'I'm ready now,' he said eventually.

'Splendid,' Edrien replied caustically. 'Are you sure you don't want a satchel over your head when you speak to my father, in case he looks at you?'

'Now, listen—'

'This way,' Edrien continued, cutting short his attempted rejoinder. It was fortunate that she led the way, as Farnor doubted that he could even have found the door, which lay amid the tangle of roots and was as irregular in shape as the rest of the room. Following Edrien through it, he found himself in a narrow corridor, the walls and ceiling of which were also lined with roots. He had little time to look around however, as Edrien was motioning him forward busily. After a short but rather steep upwards journey they reached another door. Edrien threw it open, and Farnor raised his arm to protect his eyes from the bright sunlight that flooded in.

Edrien doused the lantern and placed it on a shelf by the door. Then she took Farnor's arm firmly and pushed him towards the door. 'Come on,' she said.

Eyes screwed tight, Farnor found himself in a wide, grassy clearing, surrounded by trees. Closing the door, Edrien marched off again, with another, 'Come on.'

'Where am I?' Farnor asked, as he caught up with her.

'I told you. My father's lodge,' came the unhelpful reply. Before he could enquire further however, they had reached the edge of the clearing. Edrien stopped by a huge oak. 'Boys first,' she said, holding out her hand. Farnor did not notice the taunt in her voice, but turned to see a ladder fastened to the trunk of the tree. As his eyes followed it upwards, it tapered giddily until it was eventually lost in the foliage.

He returned his gaze to the waiting Edrien, and pointed a questioning finger up the ladder. The impatience on Edrien's face faded, to be replaced momentarily by concern. 'What's the matter?' she asked.

'Nothing,' Farnor replied hastily then, clearing his throat, he asked awkwardly, 'Does your father live up a tree?

The impatience returned. 'Of course he does,' Edrien replied, crossly. 'Where else would he live, for pity's sake?' She stepped past him. 'Here, follow me.'

Farnor watched in amazement as she clambered effortlessly up the long ladder, for the most part taking two rungs with each step. Hesitantly he started after her. Having, in the past, helped to build ricks and barns and repair wind-damaged roofs, Farnor was not unduly disturbed by either heights or ladders, but this was the first vertical ladder he had climbed and he soon began to feel alarmingly exposed. Despite being aware that his progress was becoming painfully slow, he made no effort to emulate Edrien's light-footed ascent but concentrated instead on ensuring that he had a good hand grip and had both feet on each rung before taking the next step.

'You're very slow,' Edrien informed him unnecessarily when he eventually reached the top and, with some relief, carefully stepped on to a wide timber platform. 'Anyone would think you'd never climbed a ladder before.'

'I'm stiff,' Farnor replied defensively.

Edrien grunted. 'This way,' she said.

The platform curled around the wide trunk of the tree, rose up through a small flight of steps, and then floated out into space to reach what Farnor presumed must be a neighbouring tree. As he stepped on to it, it moved a little. He desperately wanted to ask if it was safe but Edrien was almost at the other side. The thought came to him that she was a lot lighter than he was, but he set off after her in resolute silence, holding very tightly on to the ropes that apparently supported the structure.

Edrien turned and watched him walking across, her head inclined to one side a little. 'You *are* stiff,' she said when he arrived, her voice puzzled and almost sympathetic. 'Never mind, not far now.'

Nor was it. Another platform carried them round to the far side of the tree and Farnor found himself looking open-mouthed at a door set in its trunk. But was it the trunk? He looked from side to side, and then upwards along the . . . wall? . . . that housed the door. Where it was visible, it was covered seamlessly in bark, yet surely it couldn't be a tree trunk. It was far too wide. Then he noticed what appeared to be window set in it. As if to confirm that he was indeed high in the woodland canopy, he peered over the handrail behind him, but he could not see the ground below; only dense summer foliage.

Then he looked around. There were other 'walls' of bark. And there were more windows – and doors! Doors served by platforms such as he was standing on. And there were other platforms too, winding to and fro between the leafy branches; some wide, some narrow, some slung on ropes, others carried on beams and intricate frames, some, alarmingly, with no apparent means of support whatsoever.

He had little inclination to stand and study this strange scene, however, as its dominant feature was becoming the number of faces that were appearing at the many windows and staring at him with a blatant curiosity that was both embarrassing and disconcerting. For a frightening instant he felt completely disorientated. His mind seemed suddenly to run out of control as if it were searching for something ordinary and familiar on to which it could latch and from which it could measure everything else. Images of his mother and father, and Marna and Gryss, and Rannick and the creature crashed in upon him, cacophonous and confusing. His stomach lurched violently and he felt himself swaying.

'Steady, boy!' A hand seized him and shook him vigorously. He looked round to see Edrien, her face shocked. 'What in the Forest's name is the matter with you?' she said. 'Haven't you had enough falling for one day?'

Farnor did not answer, nor did he make any effort to free himself from her unexpectedly powerful grip.

Edrien shook her head in bewilderment. 'You look awful,' she said, again almost sympathetic. 'Do you want to go back to the root room and rest some more?'

The vision of the return journey, across the platform and down the ladder, took away most of what was left of Farnor's speech. 'No,' he whispered hoarsely, shaking his head violently. 'I'm fine, really. I just felt a little dizzy.'

'In you go then, if you're sure.' Edrien opened the door by which they were standing and ushered him through.

The inside of Derwyn's lodge proved initially to be even more disorientating than the outside. Not because its shape followed the eccentric contours of the exterior, but rather because it did not. In many ways, Farnor felt that he could have been stepping into nothing more unusual than the entrance porch of an ordinary cottage. A large and exceptionally well-appointed cottage, he had to concede, but an ordinary cottage nonetheless.

He had no time to debate however, as Edrien's guiding hand shepherded him along a short passageway and thrust him through an open doorway. Two men were sitting by an open window. They both stood up as Farnor entered. He noticed immediately that the one who stepped forward to greet him was obviously Edrien's kin. There was a look about the eyes and the jawline that was quite distinctive. The similarity ended there, however, as the man's face was lined and weatherbeaten, and, though oddly light on his feet, he was heavily built, in marked contrast to Edrien's slight frame. Farnor looked at him uncertainly, his mind too full of questions to formulate any one of them clearly.

The man smiled. 'My name's Derwyn, young man,' he said pleasantly, pulling round a chair and gently easing Farnor into it. He indicated his companion. 'And this is Bildar, our Mender. He's been looking after you since we brought you back.'

Farnor half rose to greet the other man, but a quiet gesture returned him to his seat. 'Are you feeling a little better now you've had a chance to rest?' Bildar asked.

'He's very wobbly,' Edrien said, before Farnor could reply. 'He seems to have quite lost his tree legs.'

Farnor scowled at this intervention, but Derwyn's smile broadened. 'I've a suspicion that perhaps he's never had tree legs, Edrien,' he said. 'Strange though that might sound.' He sat down again and turned his attention back to Farnor. 'But first things first. Are you hungry, young man? And do you have a name?'

Farnor hesitated, almost expecting Edrien to answer for him again. 'I'm a little thirsty, sir,' he said eventually. 'And my name is Farnor, Farnor Yarrance.'

'Farnor Farnor Yarrance,' Derwyn echoed. 'Two names the same, that's unusual. Is that always the way with your people?'

Farnor looked flustered. 'No sir,' he said, hastily. 'It's just Farnor Yarrance. Farnor is my given name, Yarrance is my family name.'

Derwyn nodded slowly and thoughtfully, as if he were having a little difficulty taking in this information. 'Ah, a sirename,' he decided. 'And do you have a stock and branch name, or a tree dubbing?' he went on, expectantly.

Farnor gaped.

'Apparently not,' Derwyn concluded, after an brief but awkward silence. He glanced up at his daughter. 'Ask your mother to join us, would you, Edrien? And bring us something to drink.' He glanced at his companions.

'Just water for me – and for Farnor, I think,' Bildar answered.

Derwyn nodded, and Edrien left the room, a hint of indignation in her posture.

Derwyn and Bildar smiled at one another knowingly.

Farnor glanced about the room. There was nothing about it to indicate that it was built in a tree, high above the ground. Except for the occasional mysterious bump here and there, the walls were quite straight and plain. Strangely, to Farnor's eyes, the ceiling was not lined with beams but was flat. It was also decorated with a complicated pattern of leaves and branches. In places, Farnor thought that he could see birds and tiny animals worked into the ornate pattern.

He recollected himself with a start. 'I'm sorry,' he said, flustered. 'I've never seen a room with a painted ceiling before.'

Derwyn nodded. 'Where've you come from, Farnor?' he asked abruptly.

Farnor lifted a hand as if to point, then after gazing round futilely for a moment, lowered it again. 'From the village,' he said, vaguely. 'But I don't know where it is from here. I'm afraid I don't know where I am.'

'How did you come here, then?' Derwyn went on.

'I – I – rode north,' Farnor replied, stammering unexpectedly. As he spoke, he felt waves of alarm passing through him. He leaned forward and wrapped his arms about himself.

'Are you all right?' he heard Bildar asking.

He nodded. Then he shook his head. 'No. Yes. I don't know,' he said, uncertainly.

Bildar was by his side, a cool hand feeling his forehead. Gradually the surge of panic receded into the depths from whence it had come. 'Yes, I'm all right, now – I think,' Farnor said, after a moment. 'I'm sorry, I don't know what . . .' His voice tailed off.

'You've had some kind of a shock, I'd say,' Bildar said, sitting down beside him. 'But whatever's—'

Some pent-up wildness within Farnor was released. 'Shock!' he heard himself crying out, his voice cracking with an almost childish incredulity. 'My parents murdered, my home burned, me beaten like a dog – and then pursued by . . .' He wrapped his arms about himself again and began to shiver violently as some other, darker compulsion welled up inside and silenced him. Gritting his teeth, and driving his fingers painfully into his arms, he forced himself to stop trembling.

Derwyn and Bildar, both standing by his side now, were looking at him in horror. Derwyn's arm was extended to warn Edrien, who was standing with another woman in the doorway, not to enter.

'He has no fever. Nor any contagion that I can find,' Bildar said, in answer to the unspoken question on Derwyn's face. He touched his own temple discreetly. 'But he seems to be appallingly troubled. We must be patient with him. I think perhaps we can do nothing but tend him until he can find the strength to speak of what's happened.'

'Don't talk about me as though I weren't here,' Farnor said angrily.

A flash of reciprocal anger lit Derwyn's face, but Bildar laid a restraining hand on his arm. 'I apologize,' he said to Farnor, before Derwyn could speak. 'It was ill-mannered and thoughtless of me. A Mender's way, I'm afraid. But you'll understand, I'm sure, that you've come to us as mysteriously as if you'd dropped out of the sky. Almost like something out of an ancient tale. Your appearance and your speech tell us that you're not Valderen, or even of the Forest, and suddenly you talk of the most fearful happenings. We're concerned for your pain, as we would be for one of our own, and we're concerned for what your pain might mean for us, if evil things have driven you from your home and land, Farnor Yarrance.'

Farnor put his head in his hands but did not reply.

Derwyn frowned thoughtfully, then crouched down in front of Farnor. 'Tell us what you can, when you can, Farnor,' he said. 'You may stay in our lodge until your body's truly rested, and your spirit's more at peace.'

Farnor looked up sharply, his face riven with conflicting emotions, greatest amongst which was anger. Gradually however, he seemed to gain control of himself again. 'Thank you,

Derwyn,' he said, his voice subdued. 'I seem to be full of dreadful thoughts and feelings that I've never known before. I'm sorry. I can't stay, I have nothing . . .'

Derwyn rested a hand on his arm. 'For such time as you need to recover yourself, you'll be our guest, Farnor,' he said. Then he straightened up and affected a heartiness which, in truth, he did not feel. 'I've no doubt that as you get better we'll find some chores to keep you occupied.'

Farnor nodded dully.

Derwyn indicated his daughter. 'I'll not ask you any more questions now, Farnor. I should've let you rest more, you're obviously still too distressed. I'll leave you in Edrien's charge.' He looked thoughtful. 'You're not used to lodges – homes – like ours, are you?' he asked.

Farnor shook his head.

'Incredible,' Derwyn said softly to himself, then, 'Well, ask Edrien if there's anything you want to know, but don't wander off without her. And do as she tells you. That way, you should come to no harm.'

He beckoned Edrien into the room and, taking her to one side, spoke to her softly. 'Watch him carefully, listen to him, and learn what you can about him – without actually questioning him. He's probably more likely to confide in you than in old hollow trunks like me and Bildar.' He glanced back at Farnor, who was sitting motionless with his head bowed. 'For all he looks a bit odd, he seems to be a well-set-up lad. I'd say he's been a hard worker in his time, judging by his hands. But even I can tell he's broken inside in some way. I fancy he'll need a lot of help and a lot of patient tending, so keep a rein on that acid tongue of yours, my girl. Do you understand?'

Edrien nodded. 'I think so, Father,' she replied, tartly. Then she went over to Farnor. 'Is it true you've never seen a lodge in a tree before?' she asked bluntly.

Farnor looked at her suspiciously, but saw that the question was sincere. 'Yes,' he replied.

Genuine amazement filled Edrien's face. 'I'll help you with the ladders and the ways, then,' she said. 'I never realized . . .'

Derwyn laid a hand on her shoulder. 'Go with Edrien now,' he said to Farnor. 'It's growing dark. She'll find somewhere for you to sleep tonight, and tomorrow she'll find you a room of your own and show you around. Then perhaps we can have another talk.'

No sooner had Farnor and Edrien left, than Derwyn's concern showed on his face, and he started to pace up and down. The woman who had accompanied Edrien came into the room. Her movements were soft and fluid and seemingly quite without effort. She sat in the chair that he had been using. 'You can stop that before you start,' she announced, with a purposefulness markedly at odds with her gentle demeanour. 'There won't be a leaf left on the tree if you carry on pounding up and down like that.'

Jaw set, but making no reply, Derwyn sat down by the window and leaned on the sill, his head on his hand. The setting sun threw the shadows of the branches outside on to his face, deepening its already well-defined furrows. 'What do you make of it all, Angwen?' he asked. 'Have we taken a cuckoo into our nest?'

The woman laughed softly. 'It'd be a rare bird that could throw Edrien out of anywhere,' she replied. 'That black hair makes him look strange, but from what I've just seen and from what little she's told me, he seems a fragile kind of a soul.'

Derwyn nodded. 'My impression, too,' he said. 'But' – he stood up and walked over to his wife – 'somehow he's cost us our Hearer, and impressions or no, I want to find out a great deal more about him, and as quickly as possible.' He sat down opposite his wife and turned to Bildar. 'How long?' he asked simply.

Bildar shrugged. 'I've no idea,' he replied. 'What he's said should give you some clue to the state he's in. What was it? His parents *murdered!* His home burned. Burned, Derwyn.' He gave a slight shudder. 'And then something about being beaten and pursued, just as we'd worked out for ourselves. He's been through some fearful ordeal, and I doubt he's Edrien's age. All I can suggest is that we wait, and in the meantime keep an eye on him. I'll have another look at him tomorrow, but as far as I can tell there's nothing wrong with him physically that time won't put right. I think we'll have to be very careful about how we question him, though.'

Derwyn looked unhappy. 'You may well be right,' he said, after a long pause. 'But, apart from the disturbance that Marken was talking about, it worries me that something might be happening – beyond, that could affect us. Suppose whoever was pursuing him returns to the search. And the people who

42

murdered his parents and burned his home. What if they come looking for him?'

Bildar made no reply.

Derwyn went on, his expression becoming increasingly troubled. 'Or suppose he's a criminal of some kind, fleeing from . . . some . . . lawful pursuit?'

'That's not what you feel, is it though?' his wife asked, her eyes fixed on his face.

'No,' Derwyn replied. 'All I feel is that an injured sparrow has fallen into our care, but . . .'

Angwen smiled and her manner became mocking. 'First a cuckoo, now a sparrow,' she said. 'What next, Derwyn? An eagle messenger from one of the cloud lands? A white swan from the snow mountains? Or perhaps the raven from the great castle of light?'

'Stop that,' Derwyn demanded, impotently, with a jabbing finger. 'This is serious.' But his scowl had become a reluctant smile.

'Of course, my dear,' Angwen replied, agreeing completely and conceding nothing, as was her usual way. 'But of the many things he might be, I can't see him being a criminal, can you?'

'He *might* be,' Derwyn insisted. 'How can we tell? Just because he's hurt and fragile looking?' His eyes widened. 'He's got a temper, and he's shown it already.'

'And you haven't, I suppose?' Angwen retorted.

'That's different,' Derwyn replied defensively.

Angwen raised her eyebrows, mocking again.

'You're not helping, Gwen,' Derwyn spluttered in exasperation.

'Yes, I am,' his wife replied simply. 'You've been fretting about this boy ever since you found him, instead of thinking. You're trying to do too much, too quickly, and you're not stopping to look at the obvious.'

Derwyn's eyes widened in feigned surprise. 'And what obvious is that, my dear?' he inquired, sitting back and affecting an expression of rapt expectation.

Angwen leaned forward a little. '*They'd* never have let him in if there'd been any great evil in him, or if any such evil would have been drawn after him,' she said, quietly and seriously.

Derwyn sighed noisily and nodded. 'Marken said more or less the same thing,' he conceded. 'I suppose you're right.' His face relaxed somewhat. 'Perhaps I have been a little too – agitated about this business so far.' He paused, and his eyes became distant. 'But, seeing the lad lying there, with his strange clothes and his black hair,' he grimaced slightly. 'He really did look like something out of an old tale. And now this business with Marken.' He shook his head. 'Gone to find a quiet place, for mercy's sake. Where does that leave us? I've heard of that kind of thing happening to Hearers but I scarcely gave it credence. I certainly never thought it'd happen to us, to Marken. This is his root lodge.'

This time it was Angwen who sighed. She rested her chin on her hand pensively. 'Well, we'll have to see what he has to say when he comes back,' she said after a moment.

'*If* he comes back,' Derwyn said significantly. 'That's the problem, isn't it?'

'He'll be back,' Angwen said.

'You seem quite confident about that,' Derwyn said, looking at her earnestly. 'Most of the stories I've ever heard about Hearers wandering off to find a quiet place have involved them *never* coming back.'

Angwen did not reply. Instead she began twisting and turning her hands slowly, bending and straightening her long fingers, and apparently studying them in great detail. Derwyn watched her in silence. Angwen moved now as she had when they had first fallen in love, and through the years he had never tired of watching her subtle, elusive grace. He had never seen the like in any other woman. Still it touched the young man housed inside him. And too, he knew, that there was no pointless vanity in her present examination; she was not looking at her hands, she was ordering her thoughts. Angwen had many kinds of grace.

'Marken's well rooted,' she said eventually. 'But that's not what will bring him back. He'll come back because they want him to. They protected the boy in some way, they drew Marken and thus you to him in a quite unprecedented manner. And there are other lodges round here that could have served the same end, aren't there?'

Derwyn pursed his lips. That thought had not occurred to him.

'But when the boy's safe, Marken suddenly senses confusion all around him. *Their* confusion, as much as his own. Confusion that he thinks might have been rumbling on perhaps even for years. And he's got an inquiring mind, Derwyn. His every fibre would have wanted to stay here and learn about that boy. I don't think he simply walked away. I think he was drawn away.'

'They want to tell him something.' Derwyn said, on an impulse.

Angwen nodded. 'Yes,' she said, simply. 'I think so. Marken, the boy, us, we're all at the centre of this. They wouldn't have let the boy in on some whim, would they? Nor chosen Marken to search him out, nor had him brought here. And, from what both Marken and the boy said, I think they may well have turned away his pursuers.'

She paused and continued looking at her hands. When she spoke again she was almost whispering. 'Think, Derwyn. We live in harmony with them, but it's they who are the stronger and the older, and we who are really the outsiders. They've little or no need of us. They respect us, perhaps, or they fulfil some ancient obligation, who can say? But they aren't as we are, and generally they leave us to our own destinies.'

Derwyn's brow furrowed a little.

'You know it's so,' Angwen replied. 'Many's a child wandered off to perish, and many's an injured hunter bled to death, where a whisper from them would have found them.'

Derwyn grimaced. Angwen's clarity of vision was sometimes difficult to deal with. 'A cold respect,' he could not help saying.

Angwen looked at him sadly. 'But it is so,' she said. 'And how could it be otherwise? Either they interfere with our lives or they don't. And if they did, what would we be then? Clinging parasites, useless and draining? Noisy pets? Either way, as captive as if we were bound in cages. Yet this time they did interfere. More than we've ever known.' She nodded her head conclusively. 'They have some need of this boy. This boy who isn't even Valderen. And he in his turn needs us if he's to survive here.'

'And you think Marken will be told what's to be done with him?' Derwyn asked.

'It's logical, if nothing else,' Angwen declared.

'But if that were the case, they could've told him what he needed to know in the first place,' Derwyn said, although he was reluctant to challenge the optimism in his wife's words.

Angwen nodded again. 'I doubt it's that simple,' she said, reflectively. 'They aren't as we are. Marken spoke of great confusion. Perhaps they don't know what they want. Perhaps what they want is beyond our understanding.' She shrugged her shoulders. 'Perhaps it's difficult for them to make themselves Heard, or perhaps Marken, or any Hearer for that matter, simply can't understand fully what he's Hearing—' She stopped abruptly. 'But that's all conjecture and vagueness,' she concluded, smiling and holding her hands out, palms upwards, with a small shrug of defeat. She raised an eyebrow. 'What does the bold hunter's intuition tell him?'

Derwyn smiled and raised his head in mock imitation of an animal testing the air. 'My hunter's instinct tells me that I *have* been dithering where I should've been thinking, and that, as usual, you're probably right,' he said. 'There's obviously something special about the boy. And, without a doubt, he'll need us while he's here. And who else but Marken could be the link to tell us what's happening? I'll be patient and await events.' Then his smile faded abruptly and his expression became almost fearful. It was as if a black cloud had suddenly appeared in a bright summer sky, to obscure the sun and throw the land below into cold shadow.

'What's the matter?' Angwen asked, leaning forward, her eyes abruptly anxious.

Derwyn forced a smile, but it merely served to accentuate his look of distress. 'There's a bad feeling in the air, Angwen. All around. Change coming. Change for us. Change for them. Darkness . . .' Slowly, like Farnor before him, he wrapped his arms about himself protectively.

Chapter 4

Farnor slept restlessly, though it seemed to him that he scarcely slept at all, so many times did he start awake violently. Yet sleep he did, he knew, for when he slept, he dreamed, or, more correctly, he slipped from the torment of his waking thoughts into the torment of nightmare.

Awake, he played fitfully with all that had happened, seeking to arrange the events of the past weeks into some form of order, seeking some kind of pattern within which he could find his place, and thence decide what he must do next. But no such pattern emerged. Everything that had happened had seemingly been wild and arbitrary: the silent arrival of the creature, heralded only by a few slaughtered sheep; the unexpected arrival of Nilsson and his men, and the confusion with the tithe gathering that had enabled them to become established at the castle and to take control of the valley before their true character was known; and the mysterious transformation of Rannick from village misfit to . . .

To what?

To some kind of manic . . . chieftain? . . . possessed of powers that previously Farnor had heard of only as wild fancies in Yonas's fireside tales where they were invariably possessed only by those beings who had walked out of the great burning from which all things had come, and who had moved about the world, shaping it through the ages until it had become as it now was. Beings who were now all long vanished.

For all the fever of his anguish, however, Farnor was too close to the soil, to the reality of the mysterious cycle of the growth and death of things, to squander his energies wildly denying what he knew to be true. The how and the why of Rannick's transformation were questions which capered for the most part at the edge of his thoughts, dancing to the centre only rarely and being almost immediately dismissed from the whirling circle there, where

47

lodged his overpowering desire to destroy Rannick. His dominant concerns were profoundly practical. What was the extent of Rannick's power? How readily could it be used? How often? And at what cost? For surely nothing was ever truly without cost? There was a balance in all things.

And, most intriguing of all, for what, and how much, did Rannick rely on the creature? For it was the creature he had sent in pursuit when he had felt Farnor's angry presence, not some battering wind or scorching fire.

And yet, mysteriously, the creature had failed.

Memories of the times when he had found himself at one with the creature returned, welling up inside him like vomit. They were not memories that he relished, but he sensed that they were important. He had seen the terror in men's faces, indeed he had *felt* – and lusted for – the terror in their hearts, as they looked on it . . . him. And they had been fighting men at that; men used to wielding swords and axes to defend themselves against savage enemies. Yet they had fallen without resistance, like corn before the scythe.

But still, he, Farnor, fleeing in panic, had escaped the creature, though he was sure it had been only a few paces behind him at the end. When he solved that mystery he would have the makings of a weapon which he could wield against both Rannick and the creature, he was sure. For even though he had no measure of his own strange abilities, nor any conscious control over them, he knew that Rannick understood – and feared – them.

Not that this conclusion was reached so straightforwardly. It emerged and retreated repeatedly, like a wild animal preparing to cross open ground. Looking, listening, testing the air, waiting for those silent inner voices that would urge it forward, then vanishing again into the tangled undergrowth of childish terror and frenzied blood-red hatred, of despair and grim determination, that seemed to have possession of Farnor's soul.

And in between this waking confusion, he slept, sometimes tossing and turning, muttering and crying out incoherently, at other times lying motionless while his mind soared off into eerie dreamworlds where the terrors and the furies of his waking thoughts ran hideous riot.

Yet, unvarying throughout, there ran the simple thought that he must return to the valley. He must finish what he had set out to do. He must find Rannick and somehow kill him. No sense of ordered law coloured this thought, neither the far distant king's, nor even the village council's. His parents had been cut down at Rannick's foul whim, and he was tied to that event inexorably. That the bonds were of his own making, he could not know. All he knew was that his every endeavour must be dedicated to the destruction of the murderer of his mother and father. What might lie beyond that end was one torment that never came to him.

He was thus little rested when finally he awoke to see leaf-greened sunlight percolating through a carved grille covering the window and dimly lighting the room that Edrien had found for him. He jerked upright, gazing about him, alarmed. 'Who's there?' he demanded of the silence about him.

There was no reply. And the room was quite empty. Yet for some time he could not shake off the feeling that he was being watched, or perhaps listened to.

Eventually, however, his aching body made itself felt, and the impression faded. Then a lifetime of early rising forced him out of bed. He looked about him as he dressed. The room was simply furnished, containing only the bed, a couple of chairs, and an odd circular table set with tiers of drawers, the like of which he had never seen before. And everything, he realized gradually, seemed to be made of wood – even a bowl on the table, which at home would have been earthenware, was wood. He picked it up gently and examined it closely. At first he thought that it had been elaborately painted, but as he looked at it he saw that it was made out of many different-coloured pieces of wood, tightly jointed together in some manner that he could not discern. For the first time since his parents' death he felt a distant stirring of wonder; pleasure even.

It shrivelled however, as soon as it touched the baleful thoughts that blew through Farnor's mind like biting winter winds. Its last residue faded as he ran his fingers lingeringly along the smooth rim of the bowl when he laid it down. The bowl became merely functional and unnecessarily ingenious. As did the wooden handles to the drawers in the circular table, and the peculiar hinges to the door.

His inspection was ended by a sharp knock on the door. As he moved to open it he noticed for the first time that a sword was hanging behind it. He was about to examine this unexpected find when a second, more impatient knock made him snatch open the door irritably.

49

Edrien bustled in. 'Hello,' she said cheerfully. 'You're up at last, then? I gather the dawn horns didn't wake you. Bildar said I should leave you until you woke up on your own.'

Without waiting for a response, she walked across the room to the window, where she fiddled with something that Farnor could not quite see. Silently, the grille covering the window divided and the two halves swung apart to form decorative panels on either side of the window. Bright sunlight flooded the room.

Blinking, Farnor moved to the window. He ran a hand over one of the panels. There was a quality about the delicate carving that, for some reason, reminded him of the ring that hung outside Gryss's cottage, but he was in no mood to pursue the idea. Then, very tentatively he tapped the glass. 'Well, at least something around here's not made of wood,' he said.

Edrien looked at him, puzzled, but did not comment. In the light, Farnor noticed for the first time that she had pale brown eyes. It came to him that he had never seen such a colour before. And her hair was light brown as well. Like an autumn leaf, he thought, unwittingly poetical. But the eyes drew his attention again. They looked squarely at him and there was a look in them which seemed to challenge him. He turned away, uncertain how to deal with this strange young woman.

'I suppose you're hungry by now, aren't you?' she said, unexpectedly.

Farnor nodded cautiously, wary of some taunt.

'Come on, I've arranged breakfast for you.' With a flick of her head Edrien turned and walked briskly towards the door. Farnor glanced again at the sword hanging there as he followed her out. He was about to ask about it when he realized that he was standing on a narrow platform below which was nothing for some considerable distance except dense foliage and a few large and unwelcoming branches. Involuntarily he froze, his hands tight around the rail in front of him.

'Sorry,' Edrien said, turning back to him. 'I forgot you don't know anything about trees, do you? I'll walk more slowly.'

'I know quite a lot about trees, thank you,' Farnor managed, straightening up and releasing the handrail as casually as he could. 'I've just never lived in one, that's all.'

'What kind of lodge did you live in, then?'

The question made Farnor wince, as visions of his home and his parents rushed into his mind. Edrien however, was looking away

50

and did not notice. With an effort, he set the memories aside, and did his best to give a brief description of a typical village house as they walked along. From time to time his telling faltered as the platform swayed a little, or worse, creaked. He noticed that Edrien made a conscious effort not to smile whenever, instinctively, he reached out and clutched at the handrail.

'How strange it must be, living on the ground all the time,' she mused when he had finished.

'Not as strange as living in a tree,' he retorted, more defensively than he had intended.

Edrien scowled a little and looked around. Walkways were all about them, above and below and on every side, sweeping hither and thither through the enormous leafy bower. Bark-covered walls appeared here and there, punctured by doors and windows. The whole perspective of the place bewildered Farnor.

'There's nothing strange about living in the trees,' she said, a little indignantly, after this inspection of her domain. 'How else are you supposed to live? It's what all normal people do. We've always . . .'

'I've never seen such splendid trees,' Farnor interrupted hastily, suddenly anxious not to antagonize his guide. 'There are some fine trees in the valley, but nothing to compare with these. They're so big. So alive and vigorous looking.'

A proprietorial smile replaced Edrien's scowl and she looked around again. 'Thank you,' she said, as if she had just been paid a particularly pleasant compliment, then, 'Are you going to be all right on this ladder?' she asked, her tone concerned. She suddenly slipped through a gap in the handrail and dropped down so that only her head and shoulders were visible above the platform.

'Yes,' Farnor said quickly, in preference to giving a more considered answer.

Edrien nodded and then disappeared. Gingerly, Farnor peered cautiously over the edge to locate the ladder. Edrien was just bouncing down on to the platform below as he did so and her face turned up to look at him. He turned around and, tightly gripping two well-worn uprights, he cautiously swung a leg from side to side until it made contact with the ladder.

I suppose I'll get used to this eventually, he thought, unconvincingly, as he began the descent.

It was not a particularly long ladder, but by the time he reached the bottom, his hands were sore and his arms were aching.

'I see you're still very stiff,' Edrien said. 'But I watched you that time. I think you're holding the ladder too tightly. Can't you relax a little? I'm sure it would help.' She seemed pleased at having arrived at this diagnosis.

'I'll try,' Farnor mumbled then, hastily changing the subject, 'Where are we going?'

'To Bildar's,' Edrien replied. 'He wants to have another look at you, to make sure you're all right.'

'I thought we were going to eat somewhere,' Farnor said, an old reluctance to place himself in the hands of a healer rising within him.

'Bildar will feed us,' Edrien said, setting off again. She grinned expectantly. 'He's an excellent cook.'

As they walked, Farnor became aware for the first time of people on the other walkways. Some of them called out to Edrien, who shouted back or just waved in acknowledgement. Farnor felt extremely self-conscious, all too aware of the contrast between his lumbering, awkward gait and Edrien's light and easy movements. It did little to help him that almost everyone they encountered stared at him quite openly and with considerable curiosity. Once or twice he saw individuals swinging under the handrails of the platforms to pursue whatever errand it was they were on by climbing rapidly from branch to branch. Occasionally he saw Edrien move as if to do the same, only to recollect herself at the last moment. 'Doesn't anyone ever fall?' he asked tentatively.

'Oh yes,' Edrien replied, simply. 'But not often. It's not nice.'

Farnor nodded in pained understanding, uncertain how to continue this particular line of conversation.

He was spared any further difficulty, however, by a group of people coming along the platform towards them. For the most part they were young men and women of around his own age, and their chatter and laughter rose up to complement the sunshine streaming through the leafy surroundings. Farnor was unpleasantly surprised by a twist of sneering anger that suddenly sprang to life within him at the sight and sound of them. He found himself reminded of the darkness that had come to his own homeland unbidden and undeserved and, without realizing it, he held his breath, as if to suffocate this unwelcome response.

There was a brief, confusing flurry as the group reached them and, amid noisy and simultaneous greetings, Farnor found himself introduced very quickly to several people. Vaguely he tried to cling to one or two of the names, but further references to families and relations passed him by completely. He was a little unsettled by the fact that each of the newcomers peered at him intently, especially at his hair. This was not as unsettling however, as the form of greeting which they adopted, which was not, as he was used to, to shake hands, but to grip both his arms firmly just above the elbow. After three or four such welcomings Edrien saw his discomfiture and intervened. 'Gently,' she said, prizing someone away from him. 'He's had . . .' She hesitated for a moment '. . . a nasty fall recently,' she decided. 'He's badly bruised. And we have to get down to Bildar's now.'

There were some noisy apologies and much understanding nodding, but the group seemed content to stand and stare until Edrien vigorously shooed them on their way.

As the group retreated noisily, Farnor remained where he was, holding on to the handrail as the swaying of the platform, which had been another concern during the encounter, subsided.

His head was trying to tell him that having withstood so many people standing in one place, the platform, and whatever supported it, must undeniably be extremely strong, but his heart and his stomach were not listening. Somewhat to his distress, he still felt a lingering anger at the happiness of the people he had just met.

'Are you all right?' he heard Edrien asking, yet again.

He relinquished his hold on the handrail and hugged his arms. 'Yes,' he said. Then, rather than discuss his inner confusion, he added, 'But does everyone have such powerful hands?'

Edrien's forehead furrowed and she looked down at her own hands. They were long and delicate. 'I've never thought about it,' she said, with a shrug. 'Come on.'

A few minutes and two more ladders later, they reached a door which Edrien announced as being the entrance to Bildar's lodge. She was beginning to enjoy the authority of her role as guide to this strange young man. Looking over the handrail, Farnor saw that they were about the height of the Yarrance farmhouse above the forest floor. For some reason, the mere sight of the ground made him feel much safer, even though he knew that a fall from such a height was just as likely to seriously injure or kill him as a fall from much higher.

Edrien knocked vigorously on the door and pushed it open without waiting for permission. She ushered Farnor in.

Any reservations he might have had about visiting the healer disappeared as he stepped inside and was greeted by the savoury smell of cooking. Somewhat to his embarrassment, his stomach rumbled noisily. Edrien laughed and Farnor looked a little guilty. 'I didn't realize I was quite so hungry,' he said uncomfortably.

Bildar emerged from a steamy doorway and gestured the two arrivals forward. He gripped Farnor's arms very gently. 'You must be extremely hungry by now,' he said, without any preamble. 'That's if I'm any judge of the average young man's stomach. And you, Edrien, I know, will eat anything, any time.'

'We were once a starving people,' Edrien said immediately.

'Not within our known history,' Bildar replied.

'But—' Edrien began.

'—we must preserve the trait against harsher times in the future.' Bildar concluded the exchange as if by rote.

'Something like that,' Edrien conceded.

Bildar cuffed her gently. 'That tongue of yours was always too glib, young Edrien,' he said, motioning both of them towards a table. 'I don't suppose it's ever occurred to you that you might be just plain greedy, has it?' he went on, as they sat down.

Edrien shook her head wisely. 'Not for a moment,' she said, pursing her lips earnestly.

Bildar grunted.

Farnor watched this apparently regular ritual in silence. Again, he felt unfamiliar whirls of anger rising in response to the love and friendship permeating it. There was a bitter taste in his mouth. He shuffled on his chair unhappily.

Then, almost as if he had read Farnor's mind, Bildar said, 'Last night, you told us that your parents had been murdered, Farnor.'

Farnor looked up at him, uncertain what was about to happen following this unexpected bluntness. Bildar's dark brown eyes held him fast.

'There's nothing I've ever found that can ease the pain you must be suffering, except time. But I've known others thus hurt, and you can speak to me about anything, at any time, as the mood takes you. Do you understand what I mean?'

Edrien looked pained and disconcerted by the abrupt mention of this dark topic which she had been assiduously trying to avoid since she collected Farnor, and she glanced nervously from Bildar to Farnor several times as the old man was speaking.

Farnor returned Bildar's gaze. There was neither offensive intrusion nor simpering pity in it and, under the impact of Bildar's directness, he felt the small knots of anger within him dissolving into confusion and regret and many other lesser feelings that he could not name. 'Thank you,' he said inadequately, after a moment.

Bildar held his gaze for a little longer, then, rubbing his hands together slowly, he said, 'I'll get your food.'

As Bildar fussed out of the room, Farnor caught Edrien's eye. She gave an embarrassed smile and looked awkwardly away from him without speaking. Bildar's gentle but stark reference to Farnor's tragedy seemed to have left her exposed and vulnerable in some way. She was uncertain how to behave.

Equally uncertain himself, Farnor gazed around the room. It was obviously much lived in, and was full of splendid disorder. Shelves, stacked untidily with all manner of books, lined much of the walls, and where spaces were available they were filled with boxes, jars, ragged heaps of papers, various ornaments and many small wooden carvings. Farnor noticed several carved wooden inkstands, and it occurred to him that they were very similar to the one that Gryss owned and used so meticulously. He did not dwell on this strange coincidence, however, for his attention was drawn by the cutlery with which he was absently toying. Even *they* were made out of wood. Spoons, forks, knives. He picked up one of the knives and examined the delicate patterns carved into both blade and handle. Then he tested its fine, toothed edge gently against his thumb. It was surprisingly sharp. How did they make such articles? he wondered. And how could they sharpen them?

Bildar ended any further speculation however, by returning with a large tray on which stood two steaming dishes. 'Here we are,' he said. 'This'll get you started.'

Edrien bowed slightly as the dish was placed in front of her. 'Thank you, Woodfar,' she said. But hunger had swept away Farnor's usual politeness and he began eating the thick soup ravenously and without comment. Edrien gave Bildar a slightly shamefaced look as Farnor plunged on with his meal, oblivious to all around him. The old man raised his finger a little for silence. 'Eat,' he mouthed to her.

Only as he demolished the last of the soup did Farnor's awareness of his surroundings begin to return. He looked at his host and his guide guiltily. 'I didn't realize I was so hungry,' he said again.

Bildar smiled, and Edrien laughed outright. 'No,' they both said, simultaneously.

'You can't ignore the needs of the body for long, whatever's happened to you,' Bildar said, chuckling understandingly. 'You fill your trunk, young man. Your need is honest. And it's not as if we're short of anything here.' Then his eyes widened, and he lifted his head up and sniffed. 'Oops,' he said, suddenly flustered, and scuttled quickly out of the room, knocking a brightly coloured figurine on one of the shelves as he swung the tray around wildly in the process.

Involuntarily Farnor reached out to catch the tottering statuette even though it was on the other side of the room, but it lolled gently from one side to the other a few times, then finally settled back on its base. 'I thought it was going to fall and break,' he said, self-consciously dropping his hands into his lap.

'Break?' Edrien queried.

Farnor leaned forward and stared across at the statuette with narrowed eyes. 'Is it made of wood as well?' he asked hesitantly.

'Of course,' Edrien replied. 'What else could it be?'

'Well, pot, perhaps,' Farnor offered, feeling himself moving towards a strange conversation.

'What's pot?' Edrien's question confirmed his concern.

He waved his hands vaguely. 'Earthenware,' he said, adding quickly as he saw her begin to frown, 'Clay, baked hard. And painted.'

'I've heard of that.' It was Bildar, returning with his tray, laden this time with plates filled with meats and a variety of vegetables. 'The Koyden-ushav do it, I've heard. They say they can make the clay as hard as a good heartwood, and shape it into all manner of things.'

'You means axes and knives and things?' Edrien asked, eyes widening.

Bildar smiled and shook his head. 'No, only plates and jugs and ornaments,' he said. 'It's hard, but it's brittle. Like glass, in a way, but not clear.'

Edrien nodded knowingly. 'And you thought that was made out of . . . pot?' she said to Farnor, indicating the figurine.

'Yes,' Farnor replied, reaching out to take the plate that Bildar was offering him. 'It reminded me of an ornament we had at home. I remember my mother was very upset when—' He stopped abruptly, as a rush of memories took possession of him. He felt a tightening in his chest and throat. Bildar watched him carefully and Edrien's eyes flicked unhappily between the two of them again, searching for guidance. Breathing deeply, Farnor ruthlessly crushed the memories. That time had gone now. It had no place here, or anywhere, ever again. All that mattered now was to survive so that he could pursue his intention to destroy Rannick. 'She was very upset when my father broke it,' he said, coldly and dismissively.

Edrien looked relieved, but Bildar frowned slightly. 'Eat, the pair of you,' he said tersely, after a slight pause.

They ate their meal in comparative silence, while Bildar sat nearby and surreptitiously watched Farnor closely. 'How do you feel now?' he asked, when they had both finished.

Edrien belched loudly, making Farnor jump and calling a reproachful look from Bildar. She apologized insincerely, with a laugh.

'I feel much better,' Farnor said, more restrainedly, and patting his stomach. He moved cautiously in his chair. 'But I'm still full of aches and pains from—' He stopped.

'From the beating you told us about?' Bildar said.

Farnor nodded.

'I'd like to look you over again, Farnor, if you don't mind,' Bildar went on. 'Just to make sure nothing serious has been done to you.'

Farnor did mind. Even Gryss was someone he used to avoid if he was unwell. He preferred to do as the animals did, namely, retreat to a quiet place and lie still until he was well again. Now however, as in the past, he was trapped by circumstances. Previously subject to the will and cunning of his parents in such matters, he was now subject to the concern and hospitality of his new hosts; not to mention that hint of taunting that seemed to be flicker occasionally into Edrien's eyes. 'Whatever you say,' he conceded, with as good a grace as he could manage.

Bildar shepherded him into another room, after asking Edrien if she would clear the table and wash the dishes. She hesitated for a moment, and gave him a dark, narrow-eyed look before she finally stood up and began gathering the dishes together.

It was against a distant background of irritably clunking dishes, rattling cutlery and splashing water, that Farnor submitted to

Bildar's examination. His eyes were peered into. Muscles were poked and prodded and massaged. Limbs were moved up and down, then from side to side, and pushed and pulled, and twisted this way and that, all while Bildar whistled softly and tunelessly to himself. Occasionally he gave a click or a noncommittal but knowing grunt, or he asked a question: Did this hurt? Did that? Can you feel this? How many fingers am I holding up? Have you passed any blood?

This latter reminded Farnor of something else.

'No,' he announced when he returned a few minutes later from yet another room, having learned something else intriguing about these tree dwelling people.

Throughout, Bildar made notes on various papers that were scattered about a small writing desk, which he wheeled around the room as he moved to and fro. Seeing Farnor's curiosity he showed them to him. They were simple pictures of a human body, viewed from the front and the back and various other angles. Each view was peppered with dots, all of which seemed to be joined to one another by finely drawn lines, each of which bore a legend of some kind in a neat but very tiny script. The whole effect was more than a little bewildering. Bildar made a half-hearted attempt at explaining the pictures, but abandoned it very quickly when Farnor's mouth started to drop open. Finally he sat down at a small desk and began slowly leafing through the papers, whistling tunelessly again.

Farnor, sitting on the edge of the couch where most of the prodding had been done, fastened his shirt and gazed around the room. Unlike the room in which he had eaten, this one was quite orderly. Such books as were to be seen, were neatly arranged, and there were many pictures on the wall, though pictures was not the most appropriate word, he decided, as they seemed to be simply larger versions of the diagrams on which Bildar had made his notes. There were also one or two devices consisting of poles and pulleys and ropes that he chose not to examine too closely.

'Tell me what happened,' Bildar said abruptly, laying down the papers.

Farnor looked at him suspiciously.

'What happened,' Bildar repeated more insistently, 'when you were beaten?'

Anger suddenly welled up inside Farnor. This was none of this man's business. He would find some way to repay him for his hospitality. But this prying was not acceptable.

Bildar was looking at him narrowly, then quite abruptly, his authoritative manner vanished, and he began to flick through his papers again. 'It's not that important, if you don't want to talk about it, Farnor,' he said with a smile. 'But you've been lucky. There's nothing seriously wrong with you. I thought so last night, but I wanted to make sure.' He stood up and walked to a cupboard. 'I've got some liniments and salves that will help to ease your stiffness and help mend some of the bruises and muscle damage.' He retrieved a small bottle and a jar and handed them to Farnor.

Part of Farnor wanted to refuse them angrily, but he could not respond thus to such simple kindness. 'Thank you,' he muttered, taking the two items.

'That's for the bruising and that's for the stiffness,' Bildar said, indicating which was which. He sat down again and leaned back, pivoting his chair on to two legs in a manner that, to Farnor's eyes, seemed quite perilous. Looking at Farnor shrewdly, he said, 'It occurs to me too, that being a – ground dweller, you might find all the climbing you'll have to do round here quite a strain. You'll find the salve helps with that quite a lot.' He nodded to himself, pleased with this small piece of cultural perceptiveness. Then he cocked his head to one side, and said conspiratorially, 'Judging by the lack of noise, I think Edrien's finished the washing up. It should be safe to go out now.' But he kept discreetly behind Farnor as they returned to the first room, as if anticipating some form of assault.

Edrien was standing looking out of the window, her shoulders hunched a little. Bildar smiled. 'Ah, you've finished, I see,' he said heartily. 'I'm sorry. I didn't think I was going to be so long.' He shrugged apologetically. 'But we had more to talk about than I'd thought.' He turned to Farnor as if for support.

Finding himself in the middle of what was obviously a small private feud, Farnor gave an inconclusive movement of his head.

Bildar ploughed on. 'Come back and see me if you have any problems with your injuries,' he said to Farnor, adding with quiet significance, 'Or anything else.' He turned to Edrien. 'You're going to show him round a little more, are you?' he asked.

'Yes,' she replied. 'Then Father wants to see him.'

Bildar nodded. 'Yes, of course,' he said. 'You've caused quite a stir, young man. I haven't heard the branches in such a twitter in many a year. Not since . . .'

His reminiscence was interrupted by an angry hammering on the door.

Chapter 5

The door was pushed open roughly before Bildar could reach it. Silhouetted against the sunlit green background was a tall, hulking figure.

With a loud cry, Farnor leapt to his feet, knocking his chair over with a noisy clatter. 'Nilsson!' he shouted, half fearful, half challenging. His face was white and his eyes wide and staring, but in his right hand, glittering in the leaf-filtered sunlight, was the long-bladed knife that had killed his mother.

Edrien screamed and backed away hastily.

The figure in the doorway faltered, and immediately Bildar stepped forward to stand in front of him. Hesitantly, Edrien moved across to join him, though her eyes were fixed on Farnor, who was crouching, watching the intruder tensely, with the knife held unsteadily, but dangerously in front of him.

'EmRan, what the devil do you think you're playing at, crashing into my lodge like that?' Bildar shouted angrily.

The new arrival ignored the complaint. 'Where's this outsider, Bildar?' he demanded, moving into the room, and forcing Bildar to step to one side.

Farnor looked at him balefully, and extended the knife further towards him menacingly. The man was tall and heavily built, not unlike Nilsson, and he was probably of a similar age, but though his face was angry and determined, his eyes lacked the chilling coldness that Nilsson's possessed. Farnor met his gaze unflinchingly.

'Nasty-looking piece of work,' EmRan said after a moment, though without attempting to come any closer.

'You're no silver birch yourself,' Bildar retorted acidly, taking hold of his arm. 'Now perhaps you'd explain your disgraceful conduct.'

The big man seemed to swell with rage, but Bildar did not move except to straighten up in response. 'You can explain to me now, or you can explain to the lodge Congress later,' he added, as quietly resolute as EmRan was noisy. 'But explain yourself you will.'

EmRan faltered, then snorted. 'I needed to see – him!' he said, levelling a finger at Farnor. 'I needed to see what it was that had managed to sneak in and drive our Hearer away.'

'What you needed to do, EmRan, was rein in your temper and think,' Bildar replied angrily. His tone became caustic. 'Or should I perhaps stay silent in the light of your deep and profound wisdom; your ability to know *their* will in this matter; your apparent ability to see the future and know that Marken's gone for good?' He began to shout. 'I'd lay a fair wager that Marken's really gone off in search of a quiet place because he can't face listening to your ranting any more . . .' Edrien laid a hand on his arm, but he shook it off and continued his tirade. 'Now, if you want to sit and talk like a civilized person, then you're welcome to my lodge. I'll introduce you to our guest and you may sit and debate. Failing that, get out, or take the consequences!'

For a moment Farnor thought that EmRan was going to strike the old man but, as abruptly as he had entered, he spun on his heel and left, slamming the door behind him. The sword hanging behind the door swung from side to side, further deepening long-established scratches in the wood, as the sound of EmRan's heavy footsteps faded into the distance.

Farnor remained where he was, with the knife held out in front of him. Bildar looked at him intently. 'Put that away,' he said, eventually. 'You're quite safe. Even EmRan's not that wild. And we don't point weapons at one another here unless we intend to use them.'

Farnor seemed unable to take his eyes away from the door. 'I did,' he said, after a moment. His voice was soft and unsteady, and not without some surprise. 'I did,' he repeated, as if to confirm his intention.

Bildar nodded. 'I feared so, from the look of you,' he said, quietly. 'You looked terrified. But he's gone now. Put it away. Unless you're going to use it on me or Edrien.'

Farnor's face twitched nervously at this rebuke, and he made to put the knife back in his belt. It was no easy task, as his hands were trembling violently. 'Who was that?' he asked, stammering a little as he forced his hands to be still.

Bildar made a dismissive noise, but Farnor noticed that he too was trembling and that Edrien was visibly shaken. 'EmRan's a blustering loud-mouth who thinks he should be the lodge's Second,' he replied, picking up the chair that Farnor had knocked over and returning it to him.

With an effort, Farnor forced his gaze away from the door. 'I'm sorry, I don't understand,' he said. 'What's a Second? Why did he look at me like that? What was he talking about? What—?'

Bildar held up his hand to end the questions, and then turned to Edrien. 'Are you all right?' he asked.

Edrien nodded. 'Yes,' she said, 'I think so. EmRan startled me, that's all, bursting in like that. I actually thought he was going to hit you when you shouted at him. Should I tell my father, do you think?'

'Oh yes,' Bildar said, without hesitation. 'Tell him everything. After all, he's not EmRan, is he? He won't go charging about in a wild rage threatening anyone. But he'll want to know the full tale so that he can use it to some effect if need arises.' He guided Edrien gently to a chair, then he sat down himself and looked at Farnor again. 'Don't you worry about EmRan,' he said. 'He always shouts before he thinks. I'm sure you've got someone like him in your own lodge. And, unfortunately, your arrival *has* caused a bit of a stir. Derwyn will explain it to you.'

Farnor made to speak, but Bildar, seemingly anxious not to be questioned further, continued hurriedly. 'Derwyn's our Second, to answer one of your questions, a sort of – leader – a chief, I suppose.' He made a vague gesture. 'But not like a king, or a great war leader. Not someone that everyone follows blindly.'

'Like a senior elder in our village council?' Farnor offered, still trembling inside, and a little relieved to be returning to more mundane matters. 'Someone that people turn to when they have disagreements or problems they can't sort out themselves?'

Bildar smiled. 'An elder,' he mused. 'A nice word that. A little more dignified than Second, too. Yes, I think that's as near as we'll get to answering your question without giving you a very long history lesson,' he decided. 'But you can see why EmRan's quite unsuitable for the job.'

Farnor nodded and then lowered his head. 'I'm sorry about the knife,' he said. 'I thought he was someone else. He gave me a bad fright.'

'You gave both of *us* a fright, pulling out that knife like that,'

Edrien said. 'My father said we should leave it with you, so that you'd feel safer. But . . .' Her voice faded.

Bildar laid his hand over hers. 'I gather that you thought it was this person, Nilsson; the one who beat you,' he said to Farnor. 'Presumably he too is a large and noisy man.'

Farnor sat up and took a deep breath. His inner trembling fluttered into life again at the mention of Nilsson's name. 'Large,' he managed to say, 'but not noisy. He – menaces – simply by looking, just by – being there.' He wrapped his arms about himself briefly, then he shook his head as if to dispel unwanted memories, and his hand drifted absently to his knife again.

Bildar let the subject go. There was an awkward silence until Farnor said, 'I seem to be causing you a lot of problems.' He looked from Bildar to Edrien. 'If you'll let me know how I can repay you for your kindness, I'll be on my way as soon as I can.'

Bildar took his hand from Edrien's and laid it on Farnor's arm. 'You owe us nothing, Farnor. A little food and the use of an empty bed hardly burdens us. We'd have done no more and no less for one of our own.'

Farnor nodded, uncertain what to say. 'Even so,' he replied eventually. 'I must go back home – to my valley. But first I must do some service for you, to thank you for your help.' He paused, and then spoke as the thoughts were occurring to him. 'If you hadn't found me, I'd probably have died. I had some supplies with me, but—' He stopped and turned abruptly to Edrien. 'Where's my horse?' he asked, wide eyed. 'I'd completely forgotten about it.'

Edrien laughed at this sudden change, dispelling the last remnants of EmRan's disturbing visit. 'Your horse is fine,' she said. 'As are all the bits and pieces in your saddlebags.' Her laughter died away and she looked at him seriously. 'Judging by what you had with you, I gather that you were intending to live outdoors for some time when you left.'

'You had a good look, then?' Farnor said, with some indignation.

'Oh yes,' Edrien replied easily. 'All of us. We thought there might be something in your bags to tell us where you came from, or what had happened to you.' She tried unsuccessfully to avoid smiling as she spoke, then she gave up. 'But mainly we were just curious,' she admitted finally, grinning broadly and leaving

Farnor even more indignant, yet incapable of offering her any reproach.

'Why must you go back?' Bildar asked casually.

Farnor opened his mouth to say something, then seemed to change his mind. 'The valley's where I belong,' he said instead. 'It's my home.'

Bildar nodded. 'I thought that your home had been destroyed,' he said. 'And that you'd been driven out by this . . . Nilsson.'

Farnor's jaw tautened. 'I have to go back,' he repeated. 'I have matters to attend to. Family matters.'

'Matters involving the use of that knife in your belt?' Bildar said.

Farnor turned away from him. 'I have to go back,' he said again, coldly. He stood up. 'I'm grateful for the meal and all the kindness that you've shown me, Bildar. But I suspect the problems I've brought you will only be solved by my leaving. If my horse and my supplies are all safe, then I'll go as soon as possible.' He turned to Edrien. 'Will you take me back to your father's . . . lodge? I'd like to thank him, and at least offer to repay him for what he's done for me. Then you can show me where my horse is and how I can get on my way.'

Edrien looked at Bildar for guidance. Bildar raised both hands and motioned Farnor to sit down again. Farnor however, remained standing where he was.

'Farnor, you're free to go any time that you wish,' the old man said. 'I don't know what your people are like, but we place great value on each individual's personal freedom. There's no question of keeping you here any longer than you wish. You must see Derwyn, of course, but I imagine that he'll answer you as I have, with regard to any form of payment.'

There was such a weight of qualification in his voice however, that Farnor sat down again.

'But there are some problems about your leaving,' Bildar went on. 'Not the least of which is that we don't know where you came from.'

Farnor frowned. 'What do mean, you don't know where I came from?' he asked.

'Just what I said,' Bildar replied. 'We know where we found you, but how you came there . . .' He shrugged.

Farnor looked flustered. 'I rode north. Through the valley. You must know, surely . . .'

Bildar shook his head. 'South of here lie the mountains. That's all we know. Doubtless there are many valleys there, but we never go near them. None of the Valderen go near the edges of the Forest, except in some extremity.'

'But—'

'We're the most southerly of the Koyden-dae, Farnor, and our hunting ranges are northwards. South is an unknown country to us.'

Farnor grimaced irritably. 'Well, take me back to where you found me then,' he said. 'The way I was riding, I must have left tracks that a blind man could follow. I'll find my own way back.'

'Quite possibly,' Bildar agreed. 'But' – he looked down briefly – 'there are other matters to be considered.'

Farnor's eyes narrowed. 'What other matters?' he demanded suspiciously.

Bildar rubbed his chin with his hand, a perplexed expression on his face. 'You're an outsider, Farnor, but they let you in,' he said after a long pause. 'They must have had their reasons for it, and I suspect they won't let you out.'

Farnor looked at him in bewilderment. 'You said something about "they" to EmRan,' he said. 'Who are you talking about? Who are "they"?'

Bildar looked at him uncertainly. 'They,' he said, as if stating the obvious, and waving his hand towards the window.

'I don't understand,' Farnor said, looking at the window, his brow furrowing. 'Who do you mean?' He searched for something familiar. 'Are there – soldiers – armed men keeping you here, as well?'

Bildar smiled and shook his head. 'No, of course not,' he replied. 'I told you. We're a free people. No one constrains us.'

Farnor put his hands to his temples. 'If no one constrains you, who are *they*, and why would they stop me leaving?' he asked, trying to keep the impatience from his voice.

'They,' Bildar replied, pointing to the window again.

Farnor took a slow breath and then looked at the window again. There was nothing to be seen beyond it however, except bright, gently waving foliage. He closed his eyes for a moment and his frown deepened. He was about to ask, 'Who are they?' once more when he changed his mind and turned to Edrien for assistance. Her light-brown eyes searched his for the source of the confusion that was leading him into this futile circular debate with Bildar.

An impulse led her to it. 'The trees, Farnor,' she said. 'The trees. They let you in. And if they did that then they want you here for some reason. Father thinks that's why they've taken Marken away. To find out what it's all about.'

Farnor looked at her dubiously, a faint smile hovering uncertainly at the edges of his mouth. 'The trees,' he said, raising his eyebrows. '*They* let me in?'

Edrien nodded, her eyes fixed on his face.

'Nothing to do with the fact that my horse was running fit to plough through a mountainside? The *trees* let me in?'

Edrien nodded again and gestured at Bildar. 'We think so,' she said.

Farnor's smile broadened, though it was not without some nervousness. 'I'm sorry. If this is some kind of Valderen joke, I'm afraid it's beyond me.' He stood up again. 'I think I'd like to go now, unless you've got a *real* reason for wanting me to stay.'

Edrien looked at Bildar, concerned. Bildar turned to Farnor. 'It's so difficult,' he said. 'We really need Marken here. We need to know what they want.'

Farnor's smile faded and he looked at the two of them uneasily. He opted for a further apology. 'I'm sorry if I'm being slow,' he said, 'but I really don't know what you're talking about.' Increasingly unsettled at this bizarre turn in events however, he endeavoured to be stern. 'I'd like to leave now. I want to be on my way as soon as I've fulfilled whatever obligations I've incurred here.'

He moved towards the door. Without comment, Edrien stood up and joined him, though she seemed a little puzzled at his manner.

'We're not joking, Farnor,' Bildar said as Edrien reached out to open the door. 'It's as Edrien said. It never occurred to me – to any of us – that you wouldn't know.' He gave a little, self-reproving smile. 'You'd think I'd be aware of the obvious at my age, wouldn't you?' he said, half to himself. Then he looked at Farnor, his expression open and his manner straightforward. 'This is the Forest. The Great Forest. The place of the trees. The *ancient* place of the trees. *Theirs* is the power here, should they choose to use it. They allow us to live here. No one knows why, but they do, and we're thankful for it and we live in harmony with their needs, as best we can.'

Farnor remained motionless while Bildar spoke. Then he looked from the old man to Edrien and back again. He could find no hint of mockery in either of them. Nor, for that matter, any hint of madness. 'You really believe this, don't you?' he said cautiously, after an awkward pause.

Bildar smiled. 'An odd word, believe,' he said. 'You might as well say that I believe in this table, or the sky, or Edrien here. But yes, I believe it. I believe it because it happens to be so. And it will remain so whether I, or you, *believe* in it or not.'

Farnor glanced out of the window at the swaying branches. 'How do you know all this?' he asked, self-consciously. 'Do they – talk to you?' He cleared his throat, still fearful that he was being made the butt of some joke. 'Do they – walk about?' He wiggled his first two fingers in demonstration.

For a moment Bildar's face clouded angrily, but his voice was level and calm when he spoke. 'No, of course not,' he said, with wilful slowness. 'At least, not in the way that we do.'

'Then how can they prevent me from leaving?' Farnor asked, a faint note of triumph in the question.

Bildar, still making a deliberate effort to remain calm, touched his forehead. 'They can reach into our minds if they wish,' he said. 'Make their thoughts yours. What you thought was left, will be right; what north, south; what up, down. And you'll wander back here. Or wherever they want you to go.'

Farnor, just coming to terms with the idea of a people that lived in the trees, felt unreality closing about him. Desperately he wanted to laugh and pour scorn on this foolishness, but the old man's manner forbade it. As did Edrien's now sober presence. And, unbidden, came the memory of his last joining with the creature. How it was preparing to make its final leap when suddenly, he, the fleeing prey, was no longer there. 'How can you know all this?' he asked again, though speaking to reassure himself that he was not in some eerie dream, rather than to elicit an answer.

Bildar relaxed a little. He shrugged. 'It's the way we are, Farnor. We all know it. It's in our blood, in our history, in everything. It's – obvious.' He held up a hand to forestall Farnor's inevitable further questions. 'But there are some among us who – Hear what the trees say. They can tell us when a tree may be felled, or branches taken, bark stripped. When a tree may be used as a lodge; when not. Many, many things that we need to know if we're to stay here in peace with them.'

Farnor looked at him uncertainly, his mood still teetering between scorn and fear. He remembered the word that EmRan had used. 'Are you a Hearer?' he asked.

Bildar shook his head. 'It's said that all the Valderen are Hearers to some extent, but no, I'm not. Not as we mean it.' He looked at his hands. 'I'm just an old journeyman Mender. More at home with flesh and bones and protesting people than bark and sap and the whispering leaves.' His voice became low and pensive. 'And the voices that sing in the mind between sleeping and waking.'

Farnor clung to practicalities. 'Is there someone here who is a Hearer, then?' he asked. 'Someone who can' – he was about to say, 'ask the trees', but the words refused to form – 'find out whether I can go or not?' he managed.

Bildar shook his head. 'I'm afraid not,' he said. 'Marken was – is – our Hearer, but he's gone off in search of a quiet place.'

'When will he be back?' Farnor persisted.

Bildar shrugged and looked at him sadly. 'Today, next week, never. We don't know,' he replied. 'That's the trouble. That's what's caused all the stir. It's not good for a lodge to be without a Hearer.'

Farnor put his hand to his head. He was about to ask why the Hearer had gone, but as it obviously involved him in some way he decided against it. 'How can I find out what I'm supposed to do, then?' he asked instead.

Bildar looked at him squarely. 'I don't know,' he replied. 'Perhaps you're right. Perhaps you should just saddle your horse and ride south. See what happens.'

Farnor looked out of the window again. He was shaking inside. How could he believe all this nonsense? Yet there was no doubt that Bildar and Edrien believed it, and presumably everyone else around here did so as well. As he looked at the sunlit leaves and branches beyond the window, they seemed to take on a menacing, purposeful motion of their own, and he seemed to sense countless eyes peering at him, watching his every movement. And ears listening to him. Listening to the hidden discourses of his mind. Worse, the sensation was not unfamiliar.

He looked away sharply. He must not allow Bildar and Edrien's strange beliefs, however sincere, to infect him. It would be at best discourteous and at worst perhaps downright dangerous to mock their ideas, but equally it would be madness to allow himself to be drawn into believing them himself. What he needed now was plain, simple common sense.

But even as he reasoned thus, he remembered the distant voices that he himself had heard in the recent past: voices that were full of many emotions, and that seemed to belong to a great family; voices that he knew were from somewhere beyond him, just as surely as was his contact with the creature.

Then he recalled the voices that had urged him to flee from the woods. And that had directed him away from the valley! Had directed him to the north! And in the wake of these exploded the memory of those he had heard as he lay half awake, half asleep, in the root room. Voices that had given him a fearful, giddying, perspective of countless ages gone and yet still present, as they judged him in some way.

'He can Hear us even now.' Such depths of meaning resonated in that word, Hear.

'. . . never been such a one before.' Deeply puzzled, awe-stricken, almost.

Dismissive. '. . . but a solitary Mover. And a sapling.'

A sapling!

'What's a Mover?' he asked Bildar sharply.

Bildar started at the unexpectedness of the question, and Farnor heard Edrien catch her breath.

'Why?' Bildar asked.

'What's a Mover?' Farnor repeated.

'Where did you hear the word?'

'What does it mean?' Farnor insisted.

There was a short silence in which Farnor and Bildar stared at one another.

'It's what they call us.' The answer came from Edrien. 'Where did you hear it?' She echoed Bildar's question.

Farnor could feel the blood mounting to his face. He blustered. 'I – I heard it from one – one of the people we met when we were coming here.'

Edrien and Bildar exchanged glances, then Edrien shook her head. 'It's not a word we normally have cause to use,' she said. 'Apart from in children's games, the only people who might call us Movers are Hearers, when they're telling of some particularly significant Hearing.' She stepped towards Farnor and looked him squarely in the eye. 'Where did you hear it?' she demanded.

Farnor was reminded of Marna's inexorable curiosity. This, he could contend with . . . for some time, at least.

He set his jaw. 'I don't remember,' he said defiantly. Edrien's jaw stiffened in imitation of his own.

'Leave him, Edrien,' Bildar's voice came between them like a protective shield. 'It's probably nothing.'

Reluctantly, Edrien stepped away from him, though her eyes did not leave his face. As surreptitiously as he could, Farnor took a few deep breaths in an attempt to calm himself. He shut out of his mind the clamouring implications of what he had just been told. He must get away from this place. There was too much strangeness beneath the seeming normality here. He must get back to the valley. The thought brought an acrid taste to his mouth, and his original resolve flooded through him, oddly warm and reassuring. There was nothing for him anywhere until he had won vengeance for his parents: until he had killed Rannick.

'I think I'll do as you suggest, Bildar,' he said, as soon as he could trust himself to speak without his voice trembling. 'If someone can take me back to where I was found, I'll head south and see what happens.'

Bildar nodded an acknowledgement, but did not speak.

As Farnor opened the door, he noted again the sword hanging behind it. Edrien remained standing where she was, looking at Bildar intently. After a moment he motioned her on her way with a flick of his head.

'Thank you, Bildar,' Farnor said, emptily, as he stepped through the doorway.

As he followed Edrien along the platform, Farnor tried to make casual conversation, but she looked preoccupied and, apart from occasional warnings about various hazards on the way, she said nothing.

Finally they reached Derwyn's lodge, Farnor flushed and puffing heavily.

'Your bags are all here,' Edrien said coldly, as they entered. 'But I'll have to speak to my father before you go. You'll need someone to take you to where you were found.' She pointed to a chair. 'Just wait here. I'll go and find him.'

Farnor sat down, his outward stillness belying his mounting inner agitation. Resolutely, he refused to think about the voices that he had heard, about trees, about Movers, about anything to do with this place, except that he must leave, and leave quickly.

He had come to this strange place, and fallen among these strange people, by the purest chance, and while he was grateful for the rest and shelter he had received, he belonged back in the valley; where his enemies were; where his vengeance lay. The image of his slaughtered parents returned to him horribly; his father limp and broken, his mother bloodied and startled.

He drove his fingernails into the palms of his hands as, in a flickering instant, he found himself reliving all that had happened since that day, concluding with his panic-stricken flight from the valley. But that would not happen again. Whatever else might happen, he would not flee again. He would not betray his parents twice. Next time he would stand and take whatever he had to take until Rannick was dead at his feet.

The image of the dead Rannick displaced that of his dead parents. He nodded to himself. Yes. That image he would keep before him constantly, until it eventually became a reality. And nothing, *nothing*, would be allowed to interfere with his pursuit of that ambition.

As if to challenge this resolution, memories returned to him of sitting safe and warm amid an excited group by a crackling fire, listening to Yonas, his ringing tones bringing to life vivid tales of great warriors who had made similar vows. Warriors who had valiantly stood their ground against all odds, despite cruel, perhaps fatal wounds, and who had yielded to nothing until they had slain all their enemies.

You're living in the spurious glory of a child's tale, the memories sneered. And with this taunt came, quite unexpectedly, the cold realization that, stripped of Yonas's dramatic telling the reality could be only pain and horror. Had he ever seen two dogs fight and the winner walk away unscathed? No. Had he ever seen any conflict in which both participants did not suffer? No. And, more profoundly, had he ever learned or achieved anything worthwhile without toil and effort and, sometimes, much inner distress?

No.

So then, it would probably be with Rannick.

No.

So it *would* be with Rannick. He wasn't living in some child's tale. His intention was the intention of a clear-eyed adult. He could see through the magical facade of Yonas's telling and he

72

could see what was truly required. And he would do it.

As he sat waiting for Edrien to return, his aching body felt like a testament to this renewed resolve, and he twisted his clenched fist into a large and painful bruise on his leg.

And if Rannick is too strong? persisted a lingering doubt.

He felt a darkness gathering in him as the pain from his leg spread through him.

I will do what I have to do, he vowed.

The darkness overwhelmed him.

I shall kill Rannick for what he has done, no matter what the cost.

And if that cost is your death . . .?

Silence.

It will be of no great importance. There is nothing left for me now, anyway.

In the stillness that followed this stark conclusion, he stood up and, limping a little, walked slowly over to the open window on the far side of the room. He stared out for some time at the brilliant, shimmering greenery. 'Wave away, branches, leaves,' he said. 'Whatever you are. Whatever you think I am. I have duties elsewhere.'

Then he added menacingly, 'And don't seek to defy me.'

Chapter 6

'Who are you talking to, Farnor?'

Farnor spun round with a start. The speaker was Derwyn. 'No one,' he answered, then, with a shrug, 'Well, myself, I suppose.' He looked at Derwyn's face, but he could read nothing there.

'You sounded quite grim,' Derwyn said.

Farnor shrugged again, but did not reply.

'Edrien told me about your problems at Bildar's,' Derwyn went on. 'I'm sorry about EmRan. He's always apt to act before he thinks, but that was inexcusable. I'll speak to him about it.'

Farnor made to dismiss the incident – he was anxious to sever all ties with this place, but Derwyn continued: 'And I'm sorry for not telling you about – them,' he said, nodding towards the treescape beyond the window. He smiled awkwardly. 'It never even occurred to me that you wouldn't know about them. I suppose we must seem very strange to you.' Yet, to Farnor, the very ordinariness of the remark gave the lie to it. Almost in spite of himself, he smiled.

Derwyn leaned on the windowsill beside him. 'Most important of all, however, is that Edrien tells me that you're anxious to leave,' he said.

Farnor straightened up. 'Yes,' he replied. 'There are things that I've got to do and I'd like to set off as soon as possible.'

Derwyn nodded.

'But not until I've repaid you for your kindness and hospitality,' Farnor added hastily. 'I'm afraid I've very little in the way of things that might be of value to you, but if there's anything you'd like me to do – any work – I can sharpen a good edge if you need any doing.' Out of the corner of his eye he saw Edrien and Angwen come into the room. He glanced at them briefly. Edrien was stony faced, but Angwen smiled at him warmly as she introduced herself. Farnor shuffled his feet awkwardly.

'Sit down, Farnor,' Derwyn said, motioning him back towards the chair that he had just left. 'Don't concern yourself about any kind of repayment, you owe us nothing. But I'll be honest. I hoped that you'd stay a little longer with us. Few of us – few of the Koyden-dae, certainly – have had the chance to meet someone from outside, and it seems a shame to let such an opportunity slip away, without a word. Unless it's some truly pressing matter that draws you back, can't I persuade you to stay for a little while? Just so that we can talk. Learn a little about one another. I know Bildar's said that you're not seriously hurt, but I'm sure a little more rest wouldn't go amiss after what you've been through. And your horse would certainly benefit from it. It was in an even worse state than you when we found you.'

Farnor looked round the room anxiously. Edrien was sitting with her arm resting on the windowsill, staring out into the greenery. Farnor noticed a squirrel on a nearby branch gazing into the room curiously. Angwen too, sitting nearby, was gently scrutinizing him.

The reference to his horse had pinioned his immediate hopes however. After its unrestrained headlong chase through the forest it would almost certainly be in need of considerable rest. Indeed, he reflected, it was a matter for some wonder that it had not fallen and injured them both badly. And he could scarcely ask to borrow one of Derwyn's for his homeward journey. He had, after all, no intention of returning.

But despite Derwyn's plea, he wanted to be away from here. Some instinct told him that each day he spent here would make it harder for him to leave; would soften his grim resolve. 'I really do have matters that I must attend to,' he said apologetically. 'I'll have a look at my horse. Perhaps I'll be able to walk it most of the way.'

Derwyn nodded again, but did not speak.

Farnor's eyes drifted around the room once more. He was unwilling to meet Derwyn's gaze directly. Edrien was still staring out of the window, and Angwen was still looking at him, as if she were expecting him to continue. 'Perhaps your Hearer will come back when I've gone,' Farnor offered, for want of something to say.

'Perhaps,' Derwyn agreed, adding casually, 'But who's to say? Who knows what he's Heard? Or what they want of him? Who knows anything about Hearers, really?'

There was another difficult silence.

'And perhaps EmRan won't be so much trouble, if I leave,' Farnor said.

Derwyn chuckled, as did Angwen. 'EmRan will always be trouble,' he replied. 'It's in his nature. But don't you fret yourself about that. I don't think there's any problem there that can't be handled, one way or another.'

Despite his anxiety to be away, Farnor pursued the matter. 'But losing your Hearer's a bad thing for you, isn't it?'

Derwyn's face became more serious. '*If* we've lost him, it's not good, to be sure,' he replied. 'But he only went yesterday and I for one am not going to start fretting about him yet.'

'But if he doesn't return?' Farnor insisted.

'If the lodge is struck by lightning, if this, if that,' Derwyn answered, with an expansive shrug. 'We'll carry on somehow. It won't be the first time a lodge has lost its Hearer unexpectedly. I'll concede I never expected to lose ours, but they'll provide.'

Farnor let the last remark pass. 'I still feel I'm responsible in some way,' he said. 'And that everything will get back to normal when I've gone.'

Derwyn looked at him curiously, as if searching for something unusual about him. 'You probably are the cause of Marken leaving, Farnor,' he said. 'But that's not to say it's your fault. Or that you could've done anything other than you did.'

'I don't understand,' Farnor replied.

'Nor I,' Derwyn said bluntly. 'That's another reason why I'd like to persuade you to stay for a day or so.' He leaned forward, his face concerned. 'Something very strange is happening, Farnor,' he went on. 'Something that involves us all. I'll not press you about staying, or talking about anything you don't wish to talk about, but we know that you have deep and terrible troubles. Troubles which, I suspect, came suddenly, without warning. And *we* in our turn find ourselves suddenly called out to go in search of you, an outsider, when you were injured. I can scarcely believe that, even now. Then our Hearer suddenly decides he must find a quiet place.' He shook his head. 'I appreciate our ways are not your ways, but you must understand that these are matters of great strangeness and import to us and that your affairs and ours are linked in some way.'

'I don't know what to say, or what I can do,' Farnor said unhappily. 'I know nothing of trees and Hearers.' He let out a noisy sigh. 'Didn't Marken say *anything* about why he had to leave?'

Derwyn pursed his lips. 'Nothing helpful,' he said. He frowned a little. 'He said that something portentous was going to happen – or had happened. He couldn't even tell which. And that he had felt a sense of expectation amongst them for some time. Something to do with – someone unusual – someone from beyond. But all very vague.'

Farnor turned away from him.

Derwyn finished his tale. 'I asked him how long he had sensed these strange feelings and he said that he didn't know, but it was suddenly as if he had known of them for many years, and for some reason hadn't noticed them.'

Farnor shook his head. 'I can't help you with any of this,' he said, looking restlessly about the room again. Abruptly he blurted out, 'My village was attacked by – bandits – and I ran away, in a panic. That's all that happened. I'm certainly nothing special. I don't know anything about Hearers and Movers and talking trees. I'm just a farmer's son – a farmer. I must get back to my land. And my people.'

At the word Movers, Angwen raised her head slightly and caught her husband's eye significantly. Derwyn opened his mouth to say something then appeared to change his mind. 'Don't upset yourself, Farnor,' he said. 'I didn't mean to pry into your grief. It seems that we've all got questions that can't be answered.' He turned to his daughter. 'Edrien, take him down to the stables, would you, and show him where his horse is.' He smiled at Farnor. 'Let's confine ourselves to practical matters, farmer's son. When you've examined your horse, let me know what you want to do. If you still want to leave, we'll take you to where we found you and go south with you as far as we can.'

When Farnor and Edrien had left, Derwyn turned to his wife. 'He Hears,' she said. She held out her hand and snapped her fingers. The squirrel, which had been silently watching the proceedings, scuttled a little way along the branch and then with two swift jumps, landed on the window sill. Angwen picked it up and held it in front of her face. Its nose twitched and Angwen wrinkled hers in imitation. 'He Hears, doesn't he, little one?' she said. 'That's why you wouldn't come in, isn't it? *You* could tell. A strange, black-haired Hearer is someone to be long watched before you come too close, isn't he?' The squirrel ran up her arm and sat on her shoulder. Angwen offered it a piece of fruit from a bowl on the table. The squirrel examined it shrewdly, then, turning it over a few times with its front paws, began nibbling it. Angwen lifted the animal down and put it back on the window sill.

Derwyn looked unsure. 'You're certain?' he asked.

'You're the one with the instinct, hunter,' Angwen said mockingly. 'I'm supposed to be the logical one, but even I can feel that he's tormented, driven. There's a great deal that he's not told us about. Perhaps he can't face it himself yet.'

Derwyn nodded. 'He couldn't have heard anyone talking about Movers, could he?' he said. Angwen did not reply.

'What shall we do?' he went on.

There was a tiny flurry as the squirrel scratched itself vigorously. Then it leapt out into space and, with a series of bounding jumps was soon far away from them.

'As you said, let him go,' Angwen replied simply, watching the retreating squirrel.

'But—'

'Let him go,' she repeated. 'The alternative is to hold him here in some way. And the mood he's in that'll probably mean locking him up somewhere. He's got problems enough without that.'

'I wish I knew what they wanted,' Derwyn said fretfully. 'I wish Marken was here.'

'So do I,' Angwen said. 'But he isn't, so all we have is our own judgement.'

'We can't lock him up, for pity's sake.' Derwyn mused. 'I suppose we'll *have* to let him go.'

'Don't sound so reluctant about it,' Angwen said, half laughing. 'After all, they let him in, and if he wanders off then they'll decide where he goes. Perhaps for some reason they're just using us to give him shelter while he recovers. Perhaps they need him to leave to be able to use him.'

Derwyn shook his head. 'There's more to it than that, I'm sure. Only yesterday you were reminding me that they don't normally interfere with our affairs. How much less likely are they to interfere with the affairs of an outsider?'

'Unless, as Marken said, he's special,' Angwen replied, significantly. 'And he *is* a Hearer, I'm sure.'

Derwyn sat down and rested his head on his hand. 'Someone special,' he muttered. 'Forest protect me. The ordinary's difficult enough to deal with.' He gave a theatrical sigh. 'I wonder if I can persuade EmRan to take over as Second.'

Angwen laughed, then wound an arm around his neck and kissed him on the cheek. Derwyn rested his head on her arm. 'I'll see what the lad wants to do,' he decided. 'Then when that's been cleared up I suppose we'll have to have a lodge Congress about it.' He unwound his wife from about him. 'Though I don't think that's going to do much more than add more unanswerable questions. And EmRan's going to be a real pain.'

Angwen patted his head, patronizingly. 'There, there. You'll live, I'm sure,' she said, insincerely.

On the Forest floor, far below, Edrien and Farnor were nearing the stables. Farnor was walking quite slowly.

'What's the matter?' Edrien asked.

'Just my legs,' Farnor admitted reluctantly. 'I've never done so much climbing in all my life.' He bent forward and rubbed his throbbing thighs and calves.

Edrien watched him patiently, though, like all Valderen, a climber since she was a child, she was at a loss even to begin to understand his discomfort. Echoing her mother's conclusion, she blurted out abruptly, 'It's very strange. You're a faller if ever there was one, Farnor. I don't think you've got two drops of Valderen blood in your veins. But I think you're a Hearer. I think you Hear the trees and that they've brought you here because of that.'

Farnor remained stooping, head lowered, apparently concentrating on his weary legs. 'Is it far to the stables?' he asked, affecting not to have heard her remark.

'No,' Edrien replied, simply. 'Why don't you answer my question?'

'You didn't ask one.'

The reply came so quickly that Edrien momentarily reverted to her childhood and stamped her foot angrily. 'Are you a Hearer?' she demanded.

'I'm not Valderen. You said so yourself,' Farnor replied, wilfully evasive. He looked around. 'Where are the stables? I want to see how my horse is.'

With an effort, Edrien tried a softer approach. 'Farnor, having the gift of Hearing is a great honour – a very special privilege. One that enables a man or a woman to help and guide the people of their lodge . . .' Her voice faded as she met Farnor's unreadable gaze. She made to say something else, then changed her mind and turned away sharply.

The trees under which they were standing were widely spaced and very tall. High above, Farnor could see walkways and platforms winding in and out of the canopy, and, here and there, there were dense shadows in the foliage that he presumed were lodges. For a moment he had a vision of having to lower his horse from some towering eyrie. Edrien's voice dispelled it. 'Come on, we're nearly there,' she said flatly, setting off again.

As they walked, Farnor finally identified something that had been troubling him: the sound that mingled with the wind-stirred branches and birdsong was the sound of human voices; many voices.

He looked upward. 'How many people are there up there?' he asked.

Edrien followed his gaze and frowned. 'I haven't the faintest idea,' she said irritably. 'You ask the strangest questions. You'll be wanting to know how many birds are up there next.'

Farnor let the matter lie. Perhaps it had not been the most sensible of questions. Nevertheless, he was drawn to look up again. His eyes narrowed as he listened intently. Although individual voices came and went, shouting, laughing, there was a steady continuous hubbub. And too, there were other sounds; footfalls along the wooden platforms, a door slamming, a dog barking? And other sounds that he could not identify. It might have been a silly question, he mused, but he would have liked an answer to it even so. There were a great many people up in that dense green canopy.

'Come on.' Edrien's shout brought him out of his reverie. He began running towards her, until his legs reminded him that they had had more than enough vigorous exercise recently, and reduced him rapidly to a leisurely walk.

A little further on, they came to an area where the trunks of the trees were seamlessly joined together with bark-covered walls such as Farnor had seen on the lodges, except that here they reached down to ground level. A faint smell of stables reached him, suddenly bringing back an unexpectedly vivid and not particularly welcome memory of the farmyard at home.

Edrien however, walked on past these walls and towards a large, rounded hillock that welled up out of the Forest floor. It was covered with dense shrubbery, through which rose a widely spaced cluster of particularly tall trees.

Farnor gazed up at them giddily. 'No one lives up these, then?' he asked.

Edrien was regretting her brusque dismissal of his previous question a little and, remembering her father's injunction to watch her tongue, she answered as pleasantly as she could, 'No one lives up most of the trees. I don't suppose your lodges at home cover absolutely everywhere.'

Farnor conceded the point with a nod.

'Most of the lodges are where they are because they're where they are,' she went on unhelpfully, with a disclaiming shrug. 'They've always been there. I don't suppose anyone knows exactly why.' She paused and nodded to herself reflectively. 'I'd never thought about it before, to be honest,' she announced, after a moment, giving Farnor a puzzled, slightly surprised, look.

'I expect some trees are more suitable than others,' Farnor offered vaguely.

'Oh yes,' Edrien replied. 'I don't know much about it myself, but choosing a tree for a lodge is quite a performance.' She leaned forward confidentially. 'There's an awful lot of talk goes on amongst the gnarls before any decisions are made,' she said, slightly disdainfully.

'The gnarls?' Farnor echoed.

Edrien pondered the question for a moment. 'The Congresim,' she answered, pursing her lips severely and screwing up her face by way of explanation. 'The old folks. Father, EmRan, you know, all our wise and revered parents and—'

She stopped suddenly, and her hand leapt to her mouth. 'I'm sorry, Farnor,' she said desperately, her eyes widening. 'I forgot. I didn't think – I –' She bit her bottom lip and looked up into the trees as if for forgiveness.

'It's all right,' Farnor said. 'No amount of words, thoughtless or otherwise, is going to have any effect on me now. Finish telling me how the trees are chosen for the lodges.'

'Well,' she stammered awkwardly, 'it seems to be mainly talk, as I said.' She looked at him hesitantly. 'Marken has a big say in what happens, of course, because a tree can't be built in without their goodwill. But after that, it's all: How big should this be? How big should that be? Should this branch be trimmed? Should that? I don't understand much about it really. And the Climbers make most of those decisions anyway, as far as I can gather.' Recalling something, she clapped her hands. 'If you were staying, you'd be able to see a first climb,' she said excitedly, her confusion evaporated. 'I'd forgotten in all this upheaval.'

Farnor looked bewildered.

'One of my cousins is starting his own lodge,' Edrien went on. 'All the talking's finished and the first climb will be in a few days. As soon as all the local Climbers are here.'

Farnor raised his hands to stop this sudden flow. 'What are you talking about?' he asked.

'The first climb,' Edrien said again. 'It's . . . it's . . . a celebration to start the building of a new lodge.' She waved her hands up and down rapidly. 'There's the drums – and the race. You must stay and see it—'

'I can't stay,' Farnor said, cutting across her enthusiasm none too gently. 'I have to go.'

Edrien looked at him expectantly for a moment and then sagged a little. 'If you must, I suppose you must,' she said. 'I'm sorry I got excited, it's just that . . .'

'It's all right,' Farnor said. 'I shouldn't ask so many silly questions.'

'Not very silly, I suppose,' Edrien said. 'I'm sure I'd ask a lot of strange questions if I suddenly found myself in the open lands with lodges all piled up on top of one another.'

Farnor looked at her uncertainly, and then gave a little laugh. 'They're not piled up on top of one another,' he said. 'They're next to each other, side by side, with spaces in between – big spaces.'

'Oh,' Edrien replied, flatly, her eyes flicking from one moving hand to the other. 'Are you *sure* that everywhere isn't covered with lodges?'

'I'm certain,' Farnor replied.

Edrien looked at him. 'You look a lot less grim when you smile,' she said. 'And I don't think I've heard you laugh since we found you.'

But the laugh was already echoing reproachfully through Farnor. It mingled with the residue of the excitement that Edrien's enthusiasm for the first climb had created, to fill him with a bitter sense of betrayal. Laughter and celebration were not his to enjoy now. They were for other people; people whose slaughtered parents were not crying for revenge. Guilt welled up, foul, inside him.

His face darkened. 'I thought we were nearly there,' he said starkly.

A slight spasm of pain passed over Edrien's thin face, but it was gone on the instant. 'Yes,' she said, pointing. 'They're just here.'

Farnor found himself following her down a wide pathway that had been cut into the hillock. Neatly trimmed embankments rose up steeply on each side of the path, and an almost vertical face sealed the end of the artificial chasm. Set well into this face was a large double doorway. Edrien swung expertly on one of the doors and dragged it open, then stepped inside. Farnor glanced dubiously at the embankment lowering ominously above him before following her.

He did not know what he had expected to find in this underground chamber, but images of cold and damp and darkness had predominated. He was thus considerably surprised to find himself in a huge chamber, which, despite the pervasive smell of horses, contrived to be light, airy and dry. It was also very high and, at seemingly random intervals, great irregular pillars swelled up from the floor and shouldered themselves purposefully under the unevenly curved roof. Farnor gave a soft ejaculation of surprise. 'This is amazing,' he said, staring around.

Edrien glanced at him. 'It's only another root room,' she said, though had Farnor been listening carefully enough, he would have heard no small amount of proprietorial pride in the casualness she affected.

Inquisitively, Farnor walked over to one of the large pillars and examined it closely. It had a rough-hewn appearance, giving the impression that it was simply a column of earth or rock that had been left by the excavators of the chamber, but as he looked at the surface carefully he saw that it was an irregular and complicated weave of what he took to be tiny roots. His eyes drawn inexorably upwards, he saw that the roof was similar to that in the room in which he had first awakened, though here the twisting timbers were both bigger and more numerous. And the place was filled with light, he realized. Further, it seemed to be daylight. He looked around for lanterns and lamps, but though there were one or two illuminating odd corners there were none that could account for the general brightness. 'Is there a hole in the roof?' he asked in bewilderment.

With a concerned frown, Edrien looked upwards urgently. 'Of course not, no,' she said, with some indignation, after a brief inspection.

'Where's the daylight coming from, then?' Farnor retorted.

'Mirror stones, of course,' Edrien replied. 'How else could we get the daylight into here?'

Farnor was tempted to pursue this intriguing answer, but part of him foresaw an endless tangled skein of enquiries ensuing about these strange people, and little profit to be gained from it in the end if he was going to be leaving shortly.

He nodded, as if the answer had been adequate, and then turned his attention to the lower reaches of the chamber. Around the edge were stalls in which the horses were kept. Some were small rooms cut into the sides of the main chamber, others were just fenced areas. In the distance, there was a large corral in which several horses were grazing quietly, bathed in a brilliant sunlight. Looking up, Farnor saw that the brightness came from a great swathe of tiny lights, sprinkled almost like stars across the broad, uneven dome of the roof. The mirror stones, he deduced, in some awe, though the sight told him nothing about them, and again he deliberately chose not to pursue the matter.

Edrien was talking to him. 'I said, your horse is over here,' she repeated, pointing to one of the stalls. 'It's been groomed and tended and, unlike you, doesn't seem to be much the worse for wear after its journey, apart from being hungry and tired. What's it called?'

'Called?' Farnor echoed vaguely. 'I've no idea. It's just one of the inn horses. It doesn't have a name.'

Edrien's forehead furrowed. 'I've never heard of an inhorse,' she said. 'Do you have outhorses as well?'

Farnor paused as his mind teetered abruptly sideways in search of a meaning to this remark. 'No, no,' he said, hastily, as he discovered it. 'It's not an inhorse, it's an inn horse.'

Edrien looked at him blankly.

'The horse belongs to the inn,' Farnor explained. 'It's the innkeeper's in a manner of speaking. Everyone provides food for it and the others that are kept there, and the innkeeper tends them. Although actually, he usually gets some of the children to do all the hard work.'

Edrien nodded sagely at this last remark; perhaps after all there was not a great deal of difference between the Valderen and these outsiders, but, 'What's an inn?' she asked, as they reached the stall which held Farnor's horse.

'Just a place where people sit and drink, and talk, after they've finished their work,' Farnor answered.

'What, everyone?' Edrien exclaimed. 'All together? Like a great communal hall?'

Farnor felt the bounds of normality slipping away from him again. 'No,' he said, with a hint of desperation. 'It's just a . . . house . . . a lodge . . . where people can go and . . . drink and talk,' he repeated, adding weakly, 'If they feel like it.'

'A meeting house,' Edrien decided. 'Where community matters are decided.'

Farnor shrugged. 'I suppose so,' he said, rather than risk becoming entangled in any further discussion.

'It sounds like one of our ale-lodges,' Edrien said.

The distinct note of disapproval in her voice however, encouraged Farnor not to pursue the topic further.

They entered the stall, and Farnor began to examine his horse. There were some cuts on its legs and flanks, obviously caused by the undergrowth through which it had careened, but he could find no serious injuries. 'You've looked after it very well,' he said. 'Thank you.'

'You're welcome,' Edrien said, patting the horse's nose gently. 'It's a nice animal, even if its colour does make it look grim.' She looked at Farnor's hair. 'Does *everything* have black hair, out there?' she asked, frowning.

Farnor reached tentatively to run his hand through his hair but stopped halfway and gesticulated vaguely. 'No,' he said awkwardly. 'Horses – and heads – come in all sorts of different colours.'

Edrien looked relieved. 'I thought everyone couldn't be quite so fierce-looking,' she said. 'It'd be awfully depressing.'

Farnor looked at her helplessly. 'The horse is fine,' he said, after a moment. 'I'll pack my things and be on my way, then. Unless your father's found anything he wants me to do.'

Edrien looked at him enigmatically. 'Your horse isn't fine yet, Farnor. You can see that. It's still tired. A day or two more will make a big difference to it. And to you. And—' She stopped.

'And?' Farnor prompted.

Edrien turned away from him as if gathering up courage. Then she looked squarely at him. 'You don't know what a disturbance your coming here has caused,' she said, calmly, though Farnor could see that her whole body was tense. 'You really don't. Outsiders just don't come here. Not to the lodges of the Koyden-dae. It's something that hardly ever happens even in our great tales. And if they come to the Forest at all they come from the north and the east, to the Koyden-ushav and Koyden-d'ryne. But we're the deepest dwellers of the Valderen, the oldest of the old. No one ever comes here.'

Farnor looked at her, held by her quietness far more than he could have been by any amount of impassioned urging.

'We have Marken bursting in, half fearing for his sanity, so vivid was the Hearing he had. Telling us we had to find something – something that was disturbing them – in the south, of all directions, when our ranges are all to the north. And then we find you, lying there. Black-headed and black-horsed, like something out of a dark dream. There's something very special about all of this; about you, and your being here. You're here for a reason. You must stay.'

Farnor began to look about him, as if for escape. 'I just rode here by accident, that's all,' he said, with a helpless gesture. 'Or rather, the horse carried me here. The last thing I remember is . . .' he faltered as the horror of the pursuing creature returned to him '. . . is hanging on to the horse and then – blackness.' Taking a deep and shaking breath, he reached up and began patting the horse's neck nervously. 'There's nothing special about me. Nothing at all. I'm just an ordinary person. Just as you never leave your forest, so no one from my village ever went over the hill – out of our valley – until—'

Edrien snatched at a passing thought. 'Until someone from the outside came to you, and drove *you* out,' she said, eyes wide with realization. 'And now you've come from the outside to us.'

'No,' Farnor said defensively, moving round to the other side of the horse to hide his face.

'Yes,' Edrien insisted, following him. She seized his arm and swung him round. Again, despite his confusion, he was surprised at the strength of her grip. 'They came from the outside to destroy your life, and now you've come from the outside to us. What for? You've got to stay and help us find out what it all means.' She was almost shouting. '*They* have never let an outsider in before. Not ever. They want you here. You must—'

Farnor yanked his arm free. 'Must! Must! Must!' he shouted,

full in her face. 'I don't *have* to do anything, girl. And I certainly don't have to listen to this foolishness about *them* any more.' He waved his arms about wildly. 'They're trees out there. Just trees. Plants, like flowers and grasses, just bigger and older that's all. Things you climb in and lie under and chop down. They're not gods, thinking creatures, they're . . . they're just lumps of wood, for pity's sake.' He snatched out the knife from his belt and drove it several times into the side of the stall, prizing out great splinters of wood. 'Look. That's all they are. Plain old wood. For making planks and beams, or bowls and knives and forks, and whatever else you people make of the damned stuff.'

Edrien backed away from him, her face a mixture of alarm and anger.

Suddenly Farnor felt as if he were being borne away on the echo of his own ranting voice. He seemed to be looking at the great root chamber from some other place, a pounding mixture of fear and rage swirling through him, possessing him. To the heart of his being he knew that he must destroy the cause of all this pain and horror. He must return to the valley and destroy Rannick utterly, and if needs be, any who stood before him or espoused his cause, no matter what the cost to himself. As his fury consumed him, he felt his will rise up like a screaming wind. Then it was moving across the Forest, towards the mountains that lay to the south, time and distance set at naught. Angry, malevolent. Seeking, searching. Hideously intent.

Abruptly, he was overwhelmed. Some greater power rose up and engulfed him; returned him brutally to his body in the great root room.

For an instant, he found himself staring again into the pale, fearful face of Edrien, then he plunged into darkness.

As he fell, a deep, powerful voice rang through his entire being. 'No, Mover. Not until more is understood of your true purpose.'

Chapter 7

Farnor opened his eyes abruptly; suddenly wide awake. He was greeted by the sight and sound of Bildar, starting away from him violently with an agitated cry. 'You frightened me to death,' the old man gasped, patting his chest vigorously. 'I thought you were unconscious.'

Farnor found that he was sitting on the ground, leaning against the uneven wall of the stables. He looked around. Derwyn, Angwen, Edrien, and several other people had formed a loose semi-circle about him. Like Bildar, they all looked startled. 'What's the matter?' he asked. 'What's happened? What are you all doing here?'

Edrien stepped forward and knelt down by him. 'You fainted,' she said. 'You were shouting at me, then all of a sudden your eyes rolled up and you fell over.'

'Fainted,' Farnor blustered, as he leaned ungallantly on her to struggle to his feet. 'Nonsense. I've never fainted in my life. I must have slipped on something.'

Derwyn and Bildar exchanged hesitant glances, but Edrien stormed in. 'You fainted, you donkey,' she shouted. She shuffled her feet vehemently in the dusty straw. 'You're as natural-born a faller as ever I've seen, but even you couldn't trip over straw.' Her tirade rose to a climax. 'Especially as you were standing still at the time.'

'I'm afraid you gave Edrien rather a bad fright,' Bildar intervened hastily, with an air of conciliatory concern.

'No, he didn't,' Edrien lied angrily. Derwyn put a hand on her arm.

Farnor clung to the easiest release from this strange predicament. 'Well, whatever happened, I'm fine now, and I'm leaving,' he said to Derwyn. 'Too many odd things are happening to me here. And I'm causing nothing but difficulties for everyone. I belong in my own village, with my own people. There are things that I have to do.'

Derwyn stepped forward and gripped both of Farnor's arms supportively. 'We'll pack your things, Farnor,' he said. 'We'll happily give you supplies. And we'll take you to where we found you and accompany you as far south as we dare, back along your own tracks.' There was reservation in his tone. Farnor stared at him, expectantly. 'But I doubt you'll get far. My every instinct tells me that you'll be back here before nightfall.' He paused, significantly. 'And I think yours does too.'

Farnor shook himself free from the grip, impatiently. He was going to sneer, '*They* don't want me to leave, I suppose?' but the venom was gone. He might perhaps choose to deny to the Valderen that he heard the voices of . . . someone . . . talking to him, but he could not deny it to himself. Just as Nilsson had effortlessly destroyed any pretentions he might have had towards being a fighter, and as Rannick and the creature in full cry had left him with nothing except headlong and desperate flight, so the power that had just drawn back his hurtling will, and the voice that had spoken to him, had told him that he was no longer wholly master of his own destiny.

He looked round at the watching group. There was more in their faces than concern for a fallen boy.

'What happened?' he asked again. 'Why are you all here?'

There was an awkward silence. Angwen stepped forward and took his arm. 'Something moved us,' she said, her voice, like the way she moved, at once gentle and irresistibly strong. 'Derwyn and I were already down when we met Edrien running for us.' There were various nods and mutters of agreement from the others.

Uncharacteristically, Farnor probed Angwen's reticence. 'What moved you?' he asked coldly.

There was no hesitation however, and again Angwen's straight-forward gentleness swept his antagonism aside. 'Edrien said that it was talk of the trees that agitated you, but it was they that we Heard. Not well, not clearly – we're none of us true Hearers – but it was unmistakable.'

Farnor lowered his eyes from hers, and slowly she released his arm. 'And it was unlike anything any of us have ever known,' she concluded, the softness of her voice tinged with awe.

Farnor listened to the silence that filled the great chamber.

Even the horses seemed to be waiting for something. Then his own horse shook itself noisily and broke the spell. He turned to Derwyn. 'I don't know what to think,' he said. 'You've been very kind and generous. Indeed I probably owe you my life. But everything about – this place – your people is so – disconcerting. I need to be back with my own kind. People who concern themselves with sheep and cattle' – he gave a dismissive shrug, then concluded incongruously – 'and turnips.' He put his hand to his head. 'I feel that my sanity will go if I stay here,' he went on. 'For all your kindness, I don't belong here. And while I don't know what's happening, I *do* know that I have matters to attend to at home which can't be set aside for any reason. I *must* leave.'

'This matter is a family matter? A matter of honour?' Derwyn asked.

Farnor nodded reluctantly, sensing what was to follow.

Derwyn stepped very close to him. 'You're going to seek vengeance for your parents,' he said softly, but with great intensity. It was a statement, not a question. 'Listen, younger to elder, for a moment. Vengeance is no way for a young man. It's no way for anyone. And you'll die, or worse, destroy yourself and perhaps others who care for you, if you pursue it. There will be law somewhere in your land. Seek that. And if there's no law, then seek to bring it there.'

Farnor heard tones in the voice that could have been his father's. Something stirred deep inside him; struggled to reach into the cold emptiness inside him, where the only warmth came from the image of the death of Rannick.

But the power of the image was too strong and he clung to it fearfully. It was all that he had left.

He met Derwyn's gaze. For all his kindness and, doubtless, wisdom, the man did not understand. Indeed, could not understand, unless *his* parents had been arbitrarily, brutally murdered. Straightening up, he said, 'I thank you for everything that you and your people have done for me, Derwyn.' His manner was formal and respectful. 'I would impose on you for just one more thing, if I may, and that's to accept your offer to take me back to where you found me. I want to leave today. Now.'

Derwyn's eyes were pained as he held Farnor's gaze, then defeat and regret came into them, and he nodded. 'As you wish, Farnor,' he said, sadly. 'I'd have liked you to have stayed, for many reasons. To have talked about your people. And our people. And other things. But' – he lifted his hands in a gesture of resignation – 'you know your own mind. I'll do as you ask.'

An unhappy silence pervaded the members of the group as they made their way out of the chamber. However, as they stepped outside, they were met by a large and noisy crowd, filling the wide defile that led down to the stables.

Derwyn nodded, as if this was what he had anticipated. He raised his hands as people moved forward expectantly. 'My friends,' he shouted above the hubbub. 'I know what strange call brought you here. We all Heard it too. And I know that the lodges have been alive with gossip and rumour about this young man ever since he came amongst us so unexpectedly, yesterday—'

Questions came from all sides before he could continue. He waved his arms a few times in an attempt to beat down the rising clamour, then he gave up and, putting his fingers into his mouth, gave a piercing whistle. 'I myself have far more questions than answers, I'm afraid,' he said into the ensuing silence. 'But' – he seemed to reach a decision – 'we'll hold a Congress meeting tonight, and I'll tell you what I know for certain, and also what I think. And then we can talk and conjecture and see if we can muster a little wisdom to help us make some sense of what has happened.'

This declaration ended much of the questioning, but, as the centre of the attention of the crowd, the focus of the pointing fingers and craning necks, Farnor felt as he had when he climbed his first vertical ladder the previous day: exposed and extremely vulnerable. As he walked along, flanked by Derwyn and Angwen, the trailing crowd did nothing to lessen his discomfort. The children especially, were particularly forthright in their curiosity, coming close and staring up at him, wide eyed and unblinking. One or two of the older ones, on the pretext of satisfying the curiosity of their younger relatives, carried them up to Farnor and encouraged them to reach out and touch his black hair, showing them, by the way, how it should be done.

It was thus some time before they reached the tree which led to Derwyn's lodge, and Farnor was, by then, more than a little ruffled. Derwyn went first up the ladder, closely followed by Angwen. Farnor watched her and wondered how she could possibly be so graceful when climbing a ladder.

He knew that his own marked lack of grace, or even agility,

would be highlighted by the contrast, and that such confidence as he had acquired so far would not withstand the scrutiny of the crowd now watching him keenly. For a moment he considered asking Edrien to go ahead and bring his packs down, but some residual pride prevented him. That and the fact that such an action would leave him alone and feeling even more foolish in the middle of this curious crowd.

As he set off up the ladder he thought that he heard Edrien whispering some kind of injunction to silence, in the midst of which, he caught the word, 'Faller.'

It was however, a useful reminder to him that what he was doing was dangerous, and he forced himself to concentrate as he began to pull himself slowly upwards. Only occasionally now did he need to put both feet on one rung before he continued, but each time he did so he seemed to sense the silence of the crowd below deepening under Edrien's gaze.

Determinedly he refused to look down. Indeed, he did not need to look to feel the eyes of the crowd fixed on him unremittingly. He was glad however, that they were silent, though there was the occasional giggle, or worse, anxious gasp, both of which were followed by a rush of 'Ssh . . . Ssh . . .', embedded in which, like a barbed arrow, came again the dread word 'Fallep'.

When he reached the first platform he stepped off the ladder and, looking down at the crowd, risked a wave. The upturned faces were, for the most part, smiling, and there was some tentative waving in reply, together with a little, possibly ironic, applause. There were also quite a few shaking heads to be seen however, as the crowd started to disperse, noisy again now, freed from Edrien's stern restraint.

Then, swiftly, Edrien was trotting up the ladder. As she swung off it next to him, she silently motioned him along the platform. More relaxed now, at the prospect of leaving, an old walking habit reasserted itself and Farnor glanced around to see if there were any landmarks that he could identify in the mass of branches and leaves, but there was nothing. How could these people find their way about up here, where everything looked the same? The sooner he got away from this place, the better.

Yet even as he thought this, it occurred to him that at some other time perhaps, to come here would have been a wonderful thing, with so much to be seen, and so much to be learned. He had a fleeting vision of himself as an old man, like Gryss, sitting in his cottage surrounded by mementoes of the strange places he had visited in his foolish youth, but it was gone before he could dwell on it. That was a future that now could never be.

As he walked along the platform after Edrien he became increasingly aware that there were far more platforms, walkways and lodges up here than he had noticed before. And too, he became acutely conscious of the fact that he was still the object of a great deal of scrutiny: every person they encountered, and any that he saw nearby, all stared at him intently.

A short walk, and a few ladders later, however, he was once again entering Derwyn's lodge. It was no small relief to be away from all that increasing curiosity.

Edrien led him along a wide passage and opened a door to reveal a small cupboard. 'Here's everything that we found on your horse,' she said brusquely. 'Bring it through. You'd better check what's there, in case anything fell off during your journey. I'll get you some fresh food and water before you go.'

Farnor ignored the reproach in her voice and dragged the saddlebags into the room that she had indicated. As he checked the contents, Derwyn entered and sat down. He watched Farnor silently, but Farnor avoided his gaze until, satisfied that nothing had been lost from the bags, he had painstakingly refastened them and had no alternative but to look at him.

'Everything is there that you need?' Derwyn asked.

'Yes, thank you,' Farnor replied, adding self-consciously, for want of something to say, 'I think I was lucky not to lose them, the way I was riding.'

Derwyn nodded, understandingly, and then glanced out of the window. 'I don't want you to think I'm obstructing you in any way, Farnor. You've made your wishes quite clear. But it *is* late in the day, and it'll be dark before we even reach the place where we found you. I don't know how good a tracker you are, but frankly I think you're going to find it very hard to find your original tracks in the dark, and there seems to be little point in you camping out there.' Farnor looked at him in silence. Derwyn continued. 'Also, that region is not one that any of us are familiar with and, to be honest, I'm not too anxious to be travelling over it at night. We'll take you right away, if you insist, but would it really disturb your plans to postpone your journey for a few hours and leave say, at dawn?'

Farnor looked out of the window. The light suffusing the trees was now that of a bright sun, low in the sky, leeching the colour from everything that it touched and etching long, dark, wavering shadows through the mote-filled air. Derwyn's request was too reasonable, and too reasonably put, to be denied. Besides, memories of the creature reaching out to him through the night were beginning to hover about him. 'I didn't realize I'd slept so late,' he replied weakly. 'And I *would* prefer to travel in the daylight – if you don't mind me staying here another night.'

Derwyn smiled in a fatherly way and stood up. 'No, we don't mind, Farnor,' he said.

Farnor patted his saddlebags comfortingly, uncertain what he should do next. 'And anyway, you have your Council meeting tonight, haven't you?' he said, to fill the silence.

Derwyn took a sudden deep breath, and muttered something under his breath that Farnor did not quite catch, but which he took to be an oath. Then, with a hasty 'excuse me', Derwyn left hurriedly. Farnor heard his footsteps resounding through the lodge accompanied by a great deal of agitated shouting, until finally it ended in a ripple of female laughter and the slam of a door.

Angwen was still laughing when she came into the room. 'It's a good thing you reminded him, Farnor,' she said. 'There'd have been *real* uproar after what he said at the stables if he hadn't summoned the meeting after all.' Then she rubbed her arms and moved over to the open window. As Edrien had in his room that morning, Angwen casually touched something by the window. This time, two glazed panels swung silently into the opening. What struck Farnor most forcefully however, was not the silence and seeming efficiency of whatever mechanism worked the windows, but the fact that the room seemed to become brighter, as if the windows were gathering more sunlight than had come through the open window and were scattering it into the room. There were so many fascinating things about these people . . .

'I think you're wise to leave your journey until the morning,' Angwen said, breaking into his thoughts. 'Night tracking's so difficult, even when you're used to it. Do your people do much hunting?'

'No, no,' Farnor stammered. Somehow, this strangely beautiful woman disconcerted him profoundly. 'We're farmers. We catch the odd rabbit for the pot now and then, and perhaps a fox or a wild dog if they've been worrying the sheep.' Unbidden, the memory of the motley gathering in the farmyard came to him, with Gryss sternly forbidding the carrying of bows, and Marna slipping through Gryss's guard so that she could accompany them. Then, other memories threatened to come in the wake of these: the now childish-seeming excitement at passing for the first time beyond the bounds of the valley as he had always known it; of looking up giddily at the clouds moving over the swaying castle walls; his strange contact with the creature . . .

Suddenly agitated, he turned away from Angwen's gaze and twitched his hand nervously over his mouth as if wiping it.

'I'm sorry,' Angwen said. 'Does it bring back too many painful memories to talk about your people?'

Farnor's hands fretted a little more before they settled on his knees. 'No,' he lied, then, smiling uncertainly, 'A goose walked over my grave, that's all.'

Angwen clapped her hands. 'We say just the same,' she said, laughing. 'How strange.'

Her laughter seemed to fill Farnor just as it filled the room, and he felt a great easing. 'What's going to happen at this Council meeting tonight?' he heard himself asking.

'The Congress meeting?' Angwen corrected. She gave another rich laugh. 'If Derwyn manages to notify everyone, it'll be full of talk about you, Farnor. Talk, talk and more talk. All about the grim, black-haired outsider on his grim, black horse; the strange intruder who's cost us our Hearer.'

Farnor grimaced and self-consciously ran his hand through his hair. 'Does no one round here have black hair?' he asked.

Angwen shook her head. 'No one,' she confirmed. 'And, unfortunately, it's a colour that's always given to the invaders and the evil mages in our legends.' She smiled broadly.

'You don't seem to be very concerned about it,' Farnor said.

Angwen laughed again. 'We're a civilized, rational people, Farnor,' she said. 'We love our legends and our stories – and our history, as far as we know it – but we don't confuse myth and reality any more than you do, I should imagine. You were just an injured man, a faller, plain and simple. You needed help, and we gave it to you.'

'But I've caused you problems, nevertheless,' Farnor said. 'You've lost your Hearer because of me.'

Angwen wrinkled her nose a little as she pondered this remark.

'We haven't lost him, Farnor,' she said, looking at him seriously. 'He's gone to find a quiet place for himself. It'll all resolve itself. They'll provide.' She leaned forward, her expression uncertain now. 'Edrien's told me how talking about the trees upset you so much,' she said, watching him carefully. 'I've tried to imagine what it's been like for you, finding yourself here in this strange place all of a sudden. But I can't really. I know we're only people like your own, but so many of our ways, our ideas, our thoughts, must be so different that I can't begin to put myself truly in your place.' She reached out and took his hand. 'All I can do is perhaps put you in *our* place a little,' she went on. Brown eyes held Farnor. 'Remember this above all: that nothing is to be feared. It is only to be understood.'

Farnor started. Hadn't Gryss said something like that? But memories of the creature close behind him bubbled into his mind to dismiss the recollection, and he could do nothing but challenge the assertion. '*Nothing* is to be feared?' he echoed disbelievingly.

Angwen released his hand and smiled. 'That's the ideal to be striven for,' she said. 'But none of us is perfect.' She laughed, and then quite abruptly became serious again. 'But think about it, Farnor. Fear is important to us. It galvanizes us at times of danger, and helps us to survive. But constant fear is not to be borne. It's an oppression and it has to be opposed. And to understand what causes the fear is to learn its strengths and weaknesses. And to learn how to avoid it, or perhaps even overthrow it.'

Farnor tilted his head on one side. 'You talk like a soldier out of one of Yonas's tales,' he said.

'Yonas?' Angwen queried.

'He's a Teller,' Farnor replied, his face brightening. 'He's one of the few people who come from over the – from outside the valley. He travels all over, telling his stories in return for food and shelter.'

Angwen smiled appreciatively and her face became pensive. 'I remember an old woman who used to teach here once . . .' She paused, as if trying to recollect something. 'Uldaneth, she was called. And *she* used to tell splendid tales.' She chuckled to herself. 'She could be so fierce. Even the men used to scuttle when she told them to do something. She'd poke them with her stick and order them about.' She thrust an imaginary stick forward and laughed. 'But everyone loved her.'

Farnor waited.

Angwen looked at him strangely. 'And she was an outsider too. And her hair was black as well!' She ran her hand absently over her own hair and her eyes became distant. 'Fancy forgetting about Uldaneth,' she said softly.

Farnor was loath to disturb the silence which hung about Angwen after this revelation, but his curiosity was too strong. 'Where did she come from?' he asked

Angwen shrugged and smiled again. 'I don't think anyone knew,' she said. 'And I don't think anyone felt inclined to ask. She just seemed to belong here naturally.' She shook her head slowly. 'I can't even remember when she left now.' There was another long, thoughtful pause. 'How strange. I haven't thought about her in years,' she concluded a little sadly, Farnor thought.

Then she shook off her pensive mood and reverted to the question that Farnor's earlier comment had implied. 'The Valderen were a fighting people once,' she said. 'And it's still reflected in many of our traditions.'

'The swords by the doors!' Farnor exclaimed.

Angwen nodded. 'The Threshold Swords,' she said. 'Yes, that's one thing. From a long time ago.' She became thoughtful again. 'The strength of a people depends on the willingness – *and the ability* – of each to defend both himself and his neighbour against those who would unjustly impose upon them.' She was talking half to herself. 'Yes,' she reflected, softly. 'That spirit is still with us even though we've known no conflict in generations.'

Despite himself, Farnor found his curiosity engaged again. 'Who did you fight against before?' he asked.

Angwen started slightly, as if her thoughts were elsewhere. 'Bildar's a better person to answer that than me,' she said. 'It's a long, complicated tale.'

Farnor risked a gentle taunt. 'Are you afraid that if you tell me I'll understand you better and thus be less afraid?'

Angwen's head went back and she laughed delightedly. 'I think you have me there, Farnor,' she said, as she recovered. Then she looked at him strangely again. Farnor saw a mother's eyes looking at him. 'Forest forbid that you should ever feel afraid here, of all places, Farnor,' she said softly.

He turned away from her.

'I'll risk telling you a little,' Angwen said, mockingly, after a moment. 'It'll perhaps help you to understand us.'

She leaned back in her chair. 'Back in the times you were asking about, our ancestors came here to hide from a foe so awful that He seemed set to destroy all living things. For generations we helped to hold the bounds of His conquest, until eventually He was destroyed.' She paused, momentarily, her face troubled, but the doubt in it passed, like a small cloud from in front of the sun, and she continued. 'During those times, war was waged in many ways, Farnor. On terrible battlefields, on the oceans, even in the air above us. And in the hearts and the minds of whole peoples as He sought to lead them astray, disguising His evil with sweet words.'

Farnor found himself spellbound as Angwen's voice began to rise and fall to some subtle rhythm, just as Yonas's would when his tale gathered momentum.

'And as people searched for means to oppose Him, old skills, old knowledge was rediscovered. For some of us here, in the Forest, came the ability to know the . . . minds . . . of the trees, to Hear them, as we say now. And with that, came the knowledge that the very trees amongst which we sheltered had a will, a sentience, of their own. A will that had silently supported us in our struggle and that had worked to deceive the enemy when His armies had tried to drive us out.'

Farnor began to frown a little.

'Listen, and then you *will* understand a little better, and be a little less afraid,' Angwen said, her face counselling patience. 'That's how it began. And we've lived in harmony with one another ever since.' She raised a cautionary finger. 'It's not that we fully understand one another, even now. Not by any means. In fact I doubt that such a thing is possible, we're so different. But we understand enough to respect one another's right to be and, through our Hearers, to talk, as best we can, when we must impinge on one another.'

Farnor's frown was deepening. 'But people keep saying, *they* let me in, for some special reason of their own, and *they* might well not let me out,' he said, half angry, half afraid. 'And—' He was about to mention the overwhelming will that had possessed him before he fainted in the stables, but some inner voice prompted him not to. 'Bildar said that theirs is the power here. That they can reach into minds, make people do what *they* want. That we – people – are merely tolerated.'

Angwen put her hand to her head as she searched for words

that would ease Farnor's distress. 'What Bildar said is both true and not true,' she said, after a moment. She looked at him earnestly. 'But I told you, *they're not like we are*, Farnor. Almost everything about them is beyond our true understanding. They may have needs, ambitions, desires, affections, but I doubt we'd understand them, even if they could tell us about them easily. And I doubt they understand ours. Their power to control us is undeniable, but power is only power when it's used, and they don't use it, except to keep outsiders away. And that's why your coming here has caused such a stir.' She smiled ruefully. 'I'm afraid that in our lack of understanding of what's happened, we've become frightened.'

Angwen's sincerity and concern was beyond any doubting and Farnor looked at her unhappily. 'And you've no Hearer to advise you now, because of me,' he said.

'I told you before, don't concern yourself about it,' Angwen said. 'That will resolve itself.'

Farnor looked at her helplessly. 'And what am *I* to do, in the meantime?' he asked.

Angwen met his gaze. 'Whatever you want,' she said, simply. 'Now you've made me think about it. Do as your heart moves you. But as much as you can, stay . . . calm . . . and quiet . . . within yourself. And, above all, listen to the quieter voices within you. Whatever it is they want from you, if anything, I'm sure you'll learn in due course.' She became practical. 'And I'm sure they mean you no harm. The Forest is vast and there are many dark and dire places in it to which you could have been led to die, had that been their will. And don't forget, they've roused us to come to your aid twice now. Nothing like that has ever happened before, ever.' Still watching him, she nodded, as if confirming to herself that her conclusion was correct. 'Do as your heart moves you,' she said again. 'If tomorrow, you still want to leave, then leave. All will be well.'

Farnor nodded slowly. Angwen's logic chimed with his determination. He would leave tomorrow.

Set back on his original intention, however, the gentle magic of Angwen's telling faded, and darkness bubbled up inside him again. He would return to seek out Rannick – and, if necessary, the creature – and destroy them both. That was his duty. That was all he truly had now. And if the trees didn't like it, then they could tell him directly, and take whatever consequences ensued.

Come into my mind at your cost, he felt something say, deep within him.

He sat with Angwen in silence for some time, then she looked about her suddenly. 'I hadn't realized how dark it was getting,' she said.

She stood up and touched what Farnor had taken to be a round woven basket hanging from the patterned ceiling; an ornament, he had presumed. Immediately a tiny light glowed at the centre of the basket, and then abruptly flared up to light the whole room. Standing up and screwing his eyes against the brightness, Farnor looked at it intently. The basket proved to be of delicately carved wood and it contained a glass globe. He turned away, blinking.

'What a marvellous sunstone,' he said to Angwen, who was watching him with some amusement. She raised her eyebrows in surprise. 'Sunstone,' she said. 'What a nice name. I'm afraid we call them lightrocks, even though we use them as much for heating as lighting. I gather you use them too.'

Farnor nodded. 'Yes, but all ours are very old now, and it's difficult to find new ones. We have to look after them very carefully. And we've none as good as that. It's so bright. Where do you get them from?'

Angwen smiled. 'From the mountains up north. Anyone who's travelling up there for any reason usually brings some back. And there's always plenty at the Solstice Mart. I'll give you some when you leave tomorrow,' she said. 'And a striker.'

Guiltily, Farnor raised his hands to refuse the offer, but Angwen shook her head. 'It'll be a gift to your people from my people, Farnor. You can't refuse a gift of light, can you?'

Taken aback by this impulsive gesture, Farnor did not know what to say. Sunstones were precious in the valley and much cherished by their owners. He was just composing a suitable sentence of thanks when Derwyn returned. He looked harassed.

'What's the matter?' Angwen asked quietly, wrapping her arm around him.

Derwyn cast a glance at Farnor but spoke to his wife. 'EmRan's being particularly troublesome,' he said. 'More than I thought he would be.' He pulled a rueful face. 'And I'm afraid it didn't help that Farnor threatened him with a knife.'

Angwen grimaced slightly and nodded.

Farnor felt suddenly trapped. Though no explanation was asked for, he blustered one out. 'He barged into Bildar's like a mad bull. I thought he was someone else. Bildar and Edrien saw what happened. They'll tell you. He frightened them, too.'

'Don't upset yourself, Farnor,' Derwyn said, kissing Angwen and unwinding her arm from about him. 'It's just an unfortunate thing to have happened. And EmRan's thrashing about and clouding the issues that we really need to be discussing.'

'I can leave now, on my own, if you wish,' Farnor offered.

Derwyn shook his head hastily. 'No, no,' he said. 'That will make things far worse. With all the confusion there is at the moment, that might even bring the hunt down on your head, and Forest knows what the consequences of that would be.' He sat down and looked up at Farnor, his face unhappy. 'I didn't want to get you involved in this, but drawing a weapon against another is a serious matter amongst us, Farnor. From what I've heard from Bildar and Edrien I'm satisfied that your behaviour was reasonable, and that it was EmRan who was in the wrong. But now it's been raised publicly . . .' He paused uncomfortably for a moment. 'I can't force you, but I think it would be better for all of us if you could come with me to the Congress tonight and say why you did what you did. And tell them whatever else you feel you can.'

Farnor looked at Angwen, alarmed at this unexpected turn of events. She nodded slightly, and laid her hand on her heart significantly. 'Everyone speaks freely and without fear of reproach in the Congress, Farnor. Go and listen to them. Understand their fear. And then speak to them so that they'll understand yours.'

'And if they don't understand?' he asked.

Neither Derwyn nor Angwen replied.

Chapter 8

As Farnor followed Derwyn along the ways that led to the Congress Hall, sunstones hung along the walkways and through the branches were bursting silently into life. Gradually, the great tree canopy was turned into a flickering, many-greened cavern by the myriad lights sweeping and twisting through it in long, glittering skeins. It was a sight that might have held Farnor spellbound had he noticed it, but he was too preoccupied with safely negotiating the walkways and ladders along which Derwyn was leading him: that, and the leaden, almost desperate, feeling inside him about what was going to happen.

Although Derwyn had tried to hide his concern about the Congress, he had been unable to keep it from his eyes and, unsettling Farnor even further had been the reference to him bringing the hunt down on himself if he decided to leave immediately. He tried not to dwell on the images that this presented but it was all far from reassuring. Conflicting thoughts harried him. He had been well treated – very well treated, in fact, and the worst that he had had to suffer was some blatant curiosity. But EmRan's violent intrusion at Bildar's lurked in his mind like a menacing shadow. For a terrifying moment he had truly thought that it was Nilsson hulking there in the doorway, pursuing him even into the depths of the Forest. But how would all these people see it?

Surely Bildar and Edrien would speak for him; explain what had happened? They too had been badly frightened. If he had somehow broken one of their laws, then it had been through ignorance, and no harm had been done. Then regrets began to mingle angrily with his circling justifications; he should have left as soon as he was able, he shouldn't have stayed to eat, he should have asked for his horse and pack as soon as he had wakened this morning.

'Not far now.' Derwyn's voice brought him sharply back to the present. For the first time he became aware of the noise. All around him was the clatter of feet on the swaying walkways and the clamour of voices. And as the voices impinged on him, so too did the sight. As he looked around, he saw walkways everywhere, all crowded with people moving purposefully in one direction. And there were more than he could see, he knew, for the leaves about him were alive with shadows.

Several people pushed past him as he paused, forcing him against the handrail. 'Careful,' he heard Derwyn saying crossly to the culprits. 'Faller.' This last word brought about some rapid head-turning and hasty apologies. Those who really saw him, however, paused and gaped openly, until Derwyn nudged them on their way. 'Quite a stir,' he said to Farnor, swinging on to yet another ladder. 'I haven't seen this much interest in a Congress meeting for a long time. It's going to be quite an entertaining evening.' Farnor sensed that he was smiling, though it was difficult to tell in the shifting shadows. Even so, he felt little reassurance in the words.

'Last one,' Derwyn said, as Farnor dropped down on to the walkway. It was wider than any Farnor had seen before, and it felt more solid under his feet. The sense of stability this gave him made him feel a little easier. As they walked along, the walkway was joined by others, and after a while it began to spiral slowly downwards, becoming wider as it dropped and as yet more walkways joined it. Progress, however, became slower as these tributaries brought with them increasing numbers of people.

Eventually they reached the ground, though Farnor deduced this from the feeling underfoot rather than from anything he could see amidst the noisy press of bodies. Being borne along by a crowd was a new experience for him, and it was not one he enjoyed. Indeed, once or twice he felt panic welling up inside him. There must be more people here, in this one place, than in the entire valley at home, he thought. Derwyn, sensing his unease, kept very close to him. 'It's not normally this bad,' he shouted above the din. 'And we're nearly there now.'

Looking ahead, Farnor saw the area they were moving towards was ablaze with lights. Despite the strange structures that he had seen thus far in his stay, he was expecting to see some kind of building similar to the Council Hall at home. Instead however, he found himself walking along a curving avenue of trees. It was wide enough to allow the crowd to spread out, to Farnor's relief, but the trees had an ominous quality about them as they loomed high into the darkness above him; darkness which was made yet darker by the bright lighting below.

Like great sentries, he thought.

Then the avenue widened out suddenly, like a river reaching the sea, and the crowd disgorged itself into a large circular clearing lit by brilliant sunstones that were both mounted on the trees and slung overhead by some means that Farnor could not make out. 'This is your Congress Hall?' he asked Derwyn.

Derwyn nodded and pointed ahead. It took Farnor some time to realize what he was looking at, so strange did it seem. And even as he drew closer he could not see exactly how it had been built or how it was supported. For, rising from the ground was what appeared to be an enormous tangle of branches. It reminded him, in its intricate random pattern, of the strange, fine weave of rootlets that had lined the walls and columns of the stables, but here the branches were both much thicker and more varied, ranging from those with a girth of perhaps a man's height and more, to twigs scarcely the diameter of a little finger.

Gazing at the confusion, Farnor saw that the branches curved around the sides of the clearing until they merged subtly with the surrounding trees, while above him they rose up and curved forward like a great arched roof, though their final destiny was hidden from his view by the bright lights. The whole conspired however to make him feel that he was once again standing in a huge root room rather than on the Forest floor.

As they drew nearer, Farnor began to feel both awed and intrigued by the eerie splendour of the place. Eventually his curiosity overcame his immediate preoccupations. 'How did you build all this?' he asked, lowering his voice.

Derwyn patted his shoulder and gave a rueful chuckle. 'If you're leaving tomorrow, I haven't remotely the time to tell you,' he said. 'Something this size is the work of generations. Growing, nurturing, shaping.' He tapped his head. 'Not to mention thinking, if it's going to work properly.' He stopped suddenly and looked around, as if it was something that he had not done for a long time. Then he nodded. 'I almost saw it with your eyes, Farnor,' he said, with a mixture of pride and surprise. 'New and different. And I have to admit, it's as fine a Synehal as you'll find for many a day's ride.'

'Synehal,' Farnor muttered to himself.

'I don't know what it means exactly,' Derwyn said, taking the utterance as a question. 'I think it means, place of sound, or place of hearing, or some such. It's not a Valderen word. I think it's from one of the ancient languages, from before the time we came to the Forest.'

Farnor nodded casually in response, his gaze still travelling to and fro across the wild, yet ordered, tangle of trunks and branches that seemed now to him to be embracing much of the clearing.

'Come on,' Derwyn said briskly, taking his arm.

As they walked on, passing underneath the branch-woven roof of the Synehal, Farnor noticed that the hubbub of the crowd was being replaced by a resonant silence. He looked about him. Such people as were talking were doing so softly, heads bent forward.

Then he saw that Derwyn was leading him towards a large raking platform set at the end of the clearing. Several people were already sitting on it, though Farnor noted that it was no ordinary platform such as might have been built for some village festival; rough planks set on uncertain trestles. Rather it was a continuation of the roof and wall of the Synehal. The great branches that dominated the structure threaded their way through the labyrinth to come together at this point, and thence sweep forward in a broad fan across the floor of the clearing. And, whether natural or manmade, Farnor could not decide, the upper part of the fan was shaped into curved and stepped tiers which were being used as seats. The lower, broader part flattened out and then sloped gently down to the ground.

As Derwyn led him up this slope, Farnor felt himself to be increasingly the focus not only of the curious attention of everyone present; but even of the Synehal itself. Every part of the structure seemed to emanate from this region. He felt very small and not a little afraid. It was all he could do not to take hold of Derwyn's hand.

And worse, Derwyn was leading him towards a podium that stood on, or, more correctly, seemed to grow from, the centre of the platform. The intensity of the focus upon him seemed to increase with each step he took, until he thought that it would become unbearable. When they reached the podium, however, the sensation faded suddenly and was replaced by a feeling of calm and stillness. Derwyn sat down on a high-backed, ornately carved seat at the very centre of the podium and motioned Farnor to a broad bench which stood slightly lower and to one side. Both men had their backs to the gathering crowd, and were facing those who were already seated on the benched tiers.

Derwyn leaned across and laid a hand on Farnor's shoulder. 'I don't know how your affairs are dealt with at home, Farnor, but here every man may speak freely, and may not be reproached outside the Synehal for so speaking. If you're asked anything, answer if you wish, you're under no compulsion. But, if you'll take my advice, if you do choose to answer, be as truthful as you can.' He gave Farnor's shoulder a final reassuring slap. 'And don't be afraid to speak your mind,' he said determinedly.

Though Derwyn had spoken softly, Farnor sensed that the sounds were being caught and thrown out high and wide over the clearing, like the wind itself blowing through the branches. And there was a tone in Derwyn's voice that told him that the words were not for him alone, but also a reminder to others present. He nodded, and then looked round nervously at the crowd. 'Is this everyone in your – village?' he asked.

Derwyn glanced round and smiled. 'It could well be,' he said, and the gently hectoring tone returned to his voice. 'It's a refreshing change to see so many people taking an active interest in the Congress's affairs. Most of them usually prefer to sit at home in their lodges whenever there are decisions to be made.'

Farnor saw a ripple pass through the crowd as faces were casually turned away to examine some feature above or below, or on their neighbour's face. The ripple was accompanied by a sudden bout of awkward coughing. 'They can hear what you say,' Farnor said, on impulse.

Derwyn nodded. 'And what you say, too,' he replied. 'And you'll be able to hear what's said just as well, when things get started.' He remembered something. 'And if you speak, just speak as you do normally. Don't shout.'

'But how—' Farnor began.

Derwyn raised a pleading hand. 'You'll need to stay a *very* long time if you want to learn about that,' he said.

Gradually the tiered seats in front of them began to fill up. Farnor watched each new arrival warily, searching for some clue as to what was about to happen. He noticed that though Derwyn appeared to be much more relaxed and reassured seated in what must be his official place, there was still a tension about him. He felt profoundly uneasy.

Then Derwyn spoke. There was a strong note of humorous irony in his voice. 'I think we have enough here to begin. I must say that I find this sudden interest in the Congress's affairs most heartening. I do hope that this level of attendance will continue throughout our more routine meetings.'

'Your humour's misplaced, Derwyn Oakstock.'

Farnor started at the sound of the voice. It was as if someone was sitting next to him. Derwyn touched him lightly on the shoulder, then pointed. Farnor saw that one of the figures on the tiered seats in front of him had stood up. It was EmRan.

'No formality, EmRan,' Derwyn replied easily. 'We're only here to welcome a guest.'

'We're here to decide what to do with an intruder. An intruder who drew a knife on me,' EmRan retorted angrily.

There was a murmur from the crowd in the background. Derwyn raised his hand calmly and the murmur faded.

'Menacing someone with a weapon is a serious matter,' Derwyn acknowledged, earnestly. 'One that we must discuss in the fullest detail before we disperse.'

'What's to discuss, man?' EmRan's voice burst around Farnor, making him scowl and shake his head. 'Just look at him. Black-haired, lowering, abomination. No good will come of him being here.' He pointed a wagging finger at Derwyn. 'They've taken our Hearer because you've sheltered him. We've got to get rid of him before more harm's done. If you can't do it, then you must stand down and make way for someone who can.'

'Your willingness to serve the lodge as its Second is well known, EmRan,' Derwyn said, with a sincerity in his voice that was more cutting by far than any sarcasm could have been. 'I'm sure it's a constant solace to us all to know that such selflessness is still to be found.'

Farnor caught the sound of subdued laughter coming from somewhere. EmRan looked about him indignantly and the laughter faded.

'However, I'm not altogether certain what your concern is,' Derwyn went on. 'Apart from the specific complaint of your being threatened with a weapon, which, I agree, must be dealt with, all you've given us is abuse of our new arrival, an accusation against *them*, coupled with one against me, an appeal for a dire sentence where no trial has been held, and an election speech.'

This time the laughter was quite open.

EmRan leapt to his feet. 'You may choose to mock me—' he began. But he was shouting, and his voice welled up to fill the entire Synehal like a roll of thunder. There was a universal lifting of hands to ears and an immediate hiss of disapproval rose up like a biting wind. EmRan dropped his hands to his sides and then sat down with an air of angry resignation.

'I wouldn't presume to mock you, EmRan,' Derwyn said softly, as the sound died away. 'This is an arena for reasoned debate and I merely listed the items you yourself had raised, in an attempt to gain some clarity.' He held out his hands to encompass all those seated on the tiers. 'For it's clarity we need, my friends, if we're to make sense of the unusual circumstances we find ourselves in. I'm sure I don't need to remind you that we have a long tradition of hospitality to all travellers—' There was a mumbled interruption from EmRan in which Farnor caught the word 'outsider'. Derwyn turned towards him, his face darkening. 'Just as we have a tradition of respecting the speech of others, EmRan,' he said acidly. Turning back to the body of his listeners, he continued. 'Marken came to me before dawn yesterday in a state of high excitement. Gave me quite a shock, I can assure you; clamouring on the door at that time – as you know, he's not exactly noted for his excitable nature. Summarizing his tale however: he had been woken by a Hearing; one the like of which he had never known before, so clear was it. There had been some great commotion to the south. The feeling that was given to him, very vividly, as he kept on telling me, was that our help or perhaps our judgement was called for, as a Mover lay at or near the heart of the disturbance.'

Briefly he outlined the search that they had made, ending with the discovery of Farnor and the return to the lodge. 'In these last two days I've learned a little of this young man's recent past, and I think you too should hear it. Whether or not he wishes to relate these events to you is, of course, his choice entirely, and I have advised him so, as many of you will have heard. I should add, in all honesty however, that in any event, his story will leave you with more questions than answers. I must also tell you that, despite my exhortations that he should stay so that we might perhaps learn more about why he was allowed to come so far into the Forest, his dominant wish is to leave us as soon as possible. It was only the nearness of night that kept him here so long. He attends on us here purely at my request.'

EmRan stood up and pointed at Farnor. 'If you were called to exercise your judgement on their behalf, what possessed you to pick up something like that?' he said.

'The same judgement that would make me help any faller,' Derwyn replied, a cold anger suddenly permeating his whole manner. He dispelled it almost immediately, however, with a soft laugh, before it could provoke an equally angry response. 'And this one is a faller, my friends, believe me. He'll have your hearts in your mouths every two paces.'

Farnor heard murmurs of confirmation from the crowd and there was much smiling and many nodding heads amongst the listeners seated along the tiers.

'But, answering your question further, EmRan, raven-headed he may be' – Derwyn became mockingly dramatic – 'like some demon from an ancient tale.' Then, serious again. 'But Forest forbid that we judge one another by our looks. Suffice it that I felt no harm in him when I found him. Nor have I since, nor has Bildar. And Marken, too, heard nothing.'

'But Marken's gone now,' EmRan said. 'And why else should he have been taken from us except as a punishment for your faulty judgement?'

Farnor caught a dangerous glint in Derwyn's eyes. 'We're all of us capable of faulty judgement, EmRan,' he said. 'That's why we have this forum. But I wouldn't presume to dispute the judgement of a Hearer who feels the need to find a quiet place.' In spite of himself, his anger spilled out into his voice, though he actually spoke more softly. 'Or have you developed hidden traits in your middle years? Do you wish to become our Hearer now, as well as our Second, in your anxiety to be of service to the lodge?'

EmRan's mouth worked angrily. 'They have taken Marken from us because we haven't done as they wished with this' – he jabbed his finger towards Farnor – 'person,' he managed eventually.

Derwyn shook his head. 'You weary me, EmRan,' he said. 'You accuse me of faulty judgement when you'd judge a man by the *colour of his hair and his horse!* And you'd argue the judgement of a Hearer about a Hearing! And do you seriously think that *they* would have been disturbed by a solitary rider? That they could not have turned him about? Led him into a mire?

Over a cliff? Destroyed him in countless ways, had they wished?'
He leaned forward. 'And consider for a moment why they should
make themselves Heard to so many of *us* when he collapsed in the
stables?' He patted his chest. The hollow sound echoed around
the Synehal like a drumbeat. '*Us!* The ungifted ones. Why should
they send perhaps two score or more of us running from our
lodges to tend someone you call an unwanted intruder?'

EmRan waved his arms as if to dash away such protestations.
'He drew a knife on me,' he blustered.

Derwyn put his hand to his head in despair, and a general sigh
of irritation washed over the platform. It was, however, larded
with no small number of angry voices supporting EmRan's
protestations.

'We're all concerned about what's happened,' Derwyn said.
'Indeed, I think it's fair to say that we're all a little frightened.
But we're also civilized people, and we're here to discuss these
events rationally. You're lashing out blindly in your fear,
EmRan, and you're serving no good end by so doing.' His voice
rose a little and boomed through the Synehal. 'Consider the logic
of what you've been saying. What would you have done if you'd
come upon this man? Slain him where he lay, like an exhausted
animal? *Murdered him?*'

Before EmRan could reply, Farnor, increasingly unnerved by
his accuser's ranting, jumped to his feet. 'My name is Farnor
Yarrance,' he said hurriedly, but remembering just in time not to
shout. 'I didn't come here through any choice of my own. I was
pursued by . . .' He hesitated. If he told the truth, he could not
begin to answer the questions that would follow. Moreover, his
own ability to Hear the trees might slip out, and who could say
what would happen as a result of that?

He must lie.

'I was pursued by the people who killed my parents and burned
down my home. I have had only kindness and help from Derwyn
and his family. And Bildar. And I thank them.' He pointed at
Emran. 'But it's true, I drew my knife against that man there.' He
pulled the knife from his belt and held it high. It glittered in the
light of the bright sunstones. He was aware of a shocked response
about him, not least from Derwyn, but he ignored it. 'I drew it
because he crashed into Bildar's lodge unannounced and unin-
vited, like the very bandits who'd pursued me.' His anger
suddenly vanished, and his voice fell. 'I thought you were one of

110

them, come to kill me. I'm sorry. I meant no harm, but I couldn't have done anything else. All I want to do now is return home.' There was a deep silence all around him as he sat down again, his head bowed.

He heard Derwyn's voice, very gentle. 'Sheathe your knife, Farnor. This is not a place of weapons, and you've made your case far more eloquently than I or anyone else could have done.' He patted him on the shoulder, then leaned back in his chair of office and looked at EmRan, who was sitting, grim-faced and motionless. 'This was as Bildar told it to me also,' he said. 'And my daughter. Your conduct needs more explanation than does this young man's. I think that in a quieter moment, EmRan, you might consider apologizing to our guest, and to our Mender, and to my daughter, for your reckless intrusion this morning.' Then, despite an obvious effort, his anger showed again. 'What possessed you to do such a thing? And then to blame someone for defending their hearth – indeed, defending someone else's hearth?' He shook his head in disbelief. 'For what you did you could have been cut down on the spot, and no reproach to anyone. We must forgive Farnor for drawing a weapon in this place, he can't be expected to know our ways, but perhaps it's fortunate, EmRan, that his people don't maintain the tradition of the Threshold Sword, or this might have been your wake tonight instead of a Congress meeting.'

Silence descended on the gathering.

'Who else wishes to speak?' Derwyn said quietly, after what seemed to Farnor to have been an interminable interval.

'I do.'

Derwyn started violently and turned in his seat to look for the speaker. Farnor followed his gaze. A pathway was opening through the crowd and a frail-looking figure was walking along it. A murmur rose from the crowd to fill the Synehal like a great wind howling through the trees. Gradually Farnor began to hear a coherent pattern in the sound. 'Marken!' Derwyn's voice crystallized it. He stood up. Farnor joined him and the two stood side by side to watch the Hearer's progress. Hands came out to support the old man, but he waved them aside. Derwyn left the podium and moved down the sloping platform to greet him, his face full of both relief and enquiry, although, 'You look tired,' was all he could think of to say as he reached him.

Marken nodded. 'Nothing that a little sleep won't mend,' he

said. He did not alter his pace, however, and Derwyn found himself being almost dragged along by the old man whose eyes were fixed on Farnor, now standing alone at the top of the slope, silhouetted against the bright lights.

Still contending with his own tumbling emotions at this unexpected return, Derwyn said, inadequately, 'Have you anything to say to the Congress?'

Marken cast a quick glance over his shoulder at the crowd, and his intense expression gave way to a brief, wry smile. 'Quite an outbreak of public-spiritedness,' he said with heavy irony as they reached Farnor. 'But no. I've nothing to say at the moment. However, I do have a lot to say to this young man.' He seemed anxious to begin.

Derwyn, easier now, pulled a wry face. 'You'd better say something, or we'll be here all night,' he said, knowingly.

Marken looked again at the crowd and then nodded. He went straight to the chair that Derwyn had been sitting in and spoke immediately. 'You don't need a Hearer to tell you that strange things are happening,' he began. 'Stranger than any of us have ever known. I left yesterday because I felt within me a need – a great lack – a profound confusion. I thought that somewhere there would be a place where I could perhaps still my mind and find some . . . clarity. However, as you may suppose by my early return, I found no such place. And I found no answers. But I did find some of the questions that I need to ask.' He held his hand out towards Farnor. 'I must speak with this young man alone, in friendship and mutual enquiry, for he has been overwhelmed by events far stranger than any that we have experienced, and he's in need of our help. Go back to your lodges knowing that, and also that at the worst he is not our enemy.' He paused and bowed his head for a moment. Then he nodded. 'As I learn, so shall I speak.' He waved his hand dismissively. 'Go back to your lodges. Pursue your ordinary lives, for in them is the wisdom that will sustain us.'

Questions came from all sides. Marken stepped away from the chair and Derwyn took his place. He held up his hands. 'We came here to talk about the angry drawing of a weapon and to discuss the unexpected loss of our Hearer. The first one has been dealt with, in my view, and the other has been resolved by our Hearer's equally unexpected return. There might well be plenty to talk about, but there's nothing here that now requires any communal debate.' As he spoke, the Synehal carried his voice over the hubbub, but when he had finished and was turning to leave, the questions returned with as much force as before. He allowed himself a little anger. 'Having been away for a whole day, Marken returns to find the lodge like a chicken house with a fox in it. Much we've learned from him over the years, it seems.' Pausing, he looked around at his audience, and gradually the noise faded. 'Then he tells us that he has no answers. So why do we ask him questions? We look to our Hearer for advice. He's given it to us – go back to our lodges, pursue our ordinary lives. What he learns he'll tell us about.' He smiled. 'Having been so anxious for him to return, let's be glad he's back and let's follow his advice.' Taking advantage of the ensuing, if somewhat stunned, silence, he formally closed the Congress and moved away from the podium.

His authority prevailed and the crowd started to break up, immediately, though the Synehal filled with the muffled rumble of the still-repeated questions as neighbour turned to neighbour. Derwyn watched them, his smile gone. The relief at the return of the Hearer was almost palpable, but so too was the uncertainty that the arrival of Farnor and the departure of Marken had provoked. He had tried to seize on the first and dismiss the second lightheartedly, but he knew that he had not been totally successful.

As he looked round for Marken, several of the people who had been sitting on the tiered seats began to head towards him.

Marken in the meantime had been standing by Farnor, having taken his elbow in the powerful grip that Farnor was beginning to recognize as normal amongst these people. He looked at the old Hearer, though even as he did so, he realized that he could not have guessed how old he actually was. For although Marken had the demeanour of an old man, and greying brown hair, there was, nonetheless, an oddly youthful cast about his features, and, particularly his eyes, which managed to shine through even his manifest tiredness.

Marken guided him down the slope of the platform. 'The Synehal isn't the place for the conversation that we must have,' he said very softly. 'We'll go to Derwyn's.'

'Shouldn't we wait for him?' Farnor asked, somewhat bewildered by Marken's urgency. Marken glanced back. Derwyn was engaged in what appeared to be a heated conversation with several men and women. Marken chuckled softly. 'Derwyn's a good Second,' he said. 'But he never could finish a meeting properly. A brisk manner and swift legs is what you need, and Derwyn's always been too polite.'

Before Farnor could offer any protest, he was being propelled through the dispersing crowd. Unlike their behaviour at his entrance however, the crowd did not open before Marken, but tended rather to close around him as greetings were shouted to him, and hands came out to grasp his arms and pat him on the back. Somewhat to his surprise, Farnor, too, now found himself subjected to similar treatment, though he noticed that most of the people who took his arms tended to be looking at his hair. It was thus some time before they were able to walk on unhindered.

'Can we slow down a little?' Farnor asked. 'My legs have done more walking and climbing these last two days than in a month at home.'

Distressingly, he felt a frisson of bitter anger following in the wake of his casual reference to home, but Marken dispelled it with an immediate, if rather absent-minded, reply. 'Oh, yes, of course. Forgive me, I wasn't thinking. There's such a lot I need to talk about with you.'

Farnor stopped abruptly. Marken continued for a few paces before he realized that he was alone. He turned round, his face questioning.

'I don't mind talking with you,' Farnor said defensively. 'But I'm leaving tomorrow morning at dawn, come what may. Now you're back, there's even less reason for me to stay.'

Marken looked at him thoughtfully for a moment, and then nodded. 'Of course,' he said. 'Whatever you want, Farnor. Whatever you want.'

Farnor looked at him suspiciously. The old man's acquiescence had been a little too easy for comfort. But also, it left him nothing to argue about.

'Just so that you understand,' he said, awkwardly.

Marken pursed his lips and nodded sagely. 'Of course,' he said again. 'Of course.'

Derwyn caught up with them eventually. He had been running and was panting a little. Marken chuckled. 'Trouble getting away again?' he said, maliciously.

'Shut up,' Derwyn replied testily. Marken's chuckle became a laugh.

They walked along in silence for a while, Marken continuing to acknowledge the hails of passers-by but resolutely declining to slow down, Derwyn and Farnor following like sheep.

For the first time that night Farnor looked round at the trees festooned with glittering sunstone lights, their great leafy canopies magically lit from within. The long dust-carried shadows of people moving about the walkways flitted through the branches like silent night birds. As he gazed upwards he began to walk more and more slowly until finally he stopped. 'This is beautiful,' he said simply.

Marken and Derwyn stopped abruptly and turned to stare at him. Then his gaze drew theirs inexorably upwards to peer into their familiar domain. They stood in silence for a long time, then both of them said simultaneously, 'Yes, it is.'

'We should look at it more often,' Derwyn added, setting off again. 'Much more often.'

They completed their journey at a much slower pace.

When they reached Derwyn's lodge, Farnor slumped heavily into a chair and blew out a rueful breath as he massaged his legs.

'I need to speak to Farnor alone,' Marken said to Derwyn just as he too was about to sit down. Derwyn cast a longing look at his chair and then a reproachful one at Marken.

'And *I* need to talk to *you* alone before you leave,' he said, purposefully. He glanced upwards. 'I'll be skyside with Angwen if you want me.'

As Derwyn closed the door, Marken drew up a chair and sat down opposite Farnor. He leaned towards him earnestly. 'I heard your tale to the Congress, Farnor,' he said. 'And I heard the lies in it.' His eyes widened determinedly before Farnor could begin to mouth any denial. 'I can understand why, but tell me none.' He brought his face close to Farnor's. 'Tell me nothing but the truth as you know it. It may be that your life hangs by the finest of threads.'

Chapter 9

Farnor tried to tear himself away from Marken's brown-eyed gaze, but found that he could not. For a moment he felt as though the walls of the room were closing in to bind him to this place forever. He took a deep breath to still the panic he could begin to feel rising within him.

Marken leaned back in his chair and watched him carefully, as though trying to gauge the effect of his words. After a moment, he seemed satisfied. He held up his hand to forbid any speech. 'I'm sorry to be so brutal, Farnor,' he said. 'But my problem is that I sit here looking at you and I see an ordinary young man. A little unusual looking by our lights, but an ordinary young man nevertheless. And, to be honest, someone who's not a little lost and alone, at that. Yet I know that, in some way, you're the centre of an upheaval the like of which I've never known. I can hardly describe to you the turmoil I was in when we found you.' He put his hands to his temples. 'So much going on. So many Hearings. Such vividness. Such intensity. I felt battered and numbed.' He looked intently into Farnor's eyes. 'You must realize, Farnor, that a Hearer's a poor vessel for the tasks he has to undertake. Most ordinary people imagine that we literally hear voices in our head saying, "Do this. Don't do that. This will be all right, that won't," and so on. But it isn't so. We Hear voices true enough, but they're vague and distant and garbled. And also they're much more than voices. Such words as can be made out are laden with countless layers of subtle meaning. You understand what I mean, don't you?'

Despite himself, Farnor nodded.

Marken continued. 'And we often find ourselves on the fringes of what appears to be some . . . debate . . . argument . . . what you will, so that it's difficult to know what we're supposed to be Hearing, and for whose benefit. And even when we receive the answer to a question we've asked, it frequently has almost a casual, offhand quality about it, and its interpretation is invariably debatable.' His manner became more resolute. 'But the call to seek you out had no such vagueness. It was as clear as a frosty winter sky. It actually came into my dreams and woke me. Never, never, in all my years, have I known such a thing.' He drove his fist into his open palm. 'And the shock of it seems to have given me – a new insight, a clarity of vision. It's made me see clearly for the first time things that have been under my nose for years.' He leaned forward, resting his elbows on his knees.

'I see now, Farnor, that there's been an unease in the Hearings for a long time,' he went on. 'Several years, in fact. As if something had happened somewhere that had unsettled the entire Forest. It was slight, and subtle, but it was there nevertheless, except that I didn't have the wit to see it until yesterday. And even then I couldn't truly believe it at first. That's what drove me out to try to find somewhere where I could perhaps order my thoughts, see some kind of a pattern in events. But I wasn't allowed to. As I walked, there was a hubbub all about me, washing to and fro. Then, for the second time, I was spoken to directly.' He looked away from Farnor and shook his head, as if in disbelief. 'It was more unnerving awake than when I was asleep. This voice – or perhaps several voices, I couldn't really tell – coming to me from a great distance. As though someone was shouting from the far end of some great echoing cave, or through a blustering wind . . .'

He paused, and Farnor intruded anxiously, making to stand up. 'I don't know what all this is about,' he said. 'All this nonsense about—'

Marken's hand seized his and prevented him from rising. 'Stop that,' the old man said powerfully. 'I'm not Derwyn and the others to be fobbed off with your foolish protests. And I told you to tell me no lies.'

Farnor tried to speak again, but Marken's look forbade him. 'Listen to me, young man,' he said. 'I'm not so old that I don't see a long, interesting and useful life ahead of me still. But I'm old enough to be very disinclined to waste any of that time dealing with the crass stupidity of the young. Now be quiet until I tell you to speak.'

Farnor wilted a little under the unexpected force of Marken's manner.

'They spoke to me, Farnor,' Marken went on. 'Spoke to me directly.' A look of wonder came into his eyes. 'For all the strangeness of it, it was magical. Such depth, such meaning, such clarity. It was like the fulfilment of my every dream.' As suddenly as it had appeared however, the wonder faded and his face became grim and regretful. 'But that was the experience, for me, as a Hearer. The content of what they told me, though, held no magic. It was simple and blunt. Although they helped you, they fear you. They fear some power that you have, and some darkness within you. They told me to tell you that you're to go to the central mountains to stand amongst the most ancient of them so that you can be questioned and a decision made about your fate.'

Farnor felt panic rising in him again. Wide-eyed, he looked towards the window. A carved wooden shutter sealed out the night and the great, twisted labyrinth of swaying branches that lay beyond, but it seemed to Farnor that even now those branches were stretching towards him: innumerable, many-fingered hands reaching for him. His head began to fill with the noise of his own breathing, shallow and raucous, but through it he felt that he could hear purposeful scratchings and tappings at the glass on the far side of the shutter.

Marken bent forward and took hold of his arms, urgently, shaking him roughly. Sustained by this powerful grip, Farnor gradually regained control. He was determined to speak. 'I don't understand any of this,' he managed to gasp, eventually. Once more, he was about to deny any belief in the sentient will of the trees, but he knew that he could not. He understood about the vague, distant voices, but when he had first heard them himself he had been far away and secure in all things, with a life to live and a future ahead, knowing nothing of the great tree-filled land that was supposed to lie beyond the mountains to the north. Now, here, he had heard voices as clear and distinct as Marken's sitting before him now. And, as Marken had described, he had heard words filled with a meaning far beyond their immediate sounding.

And he had felt the power and determination of a terrible will. Whatever had happened when he was in the stables, he knew that he been unable to resist the force that had snatched back that mysterious part of him which, uncontrolled and unbidden, had been hurtling towards the valley with who could say what intent.

He set the memory aside with a slight inner shiver. He did not want to think about it.

The soft rumble of voices overhead percolated down into the silence around the two men.

Denial denied him. Farnor tried to plead his case. 'I've no – powers, Marken,' he said, in some desperation. 'Truly. I'm an ordinary person. A farmer. I know about sheep and cattle and . . . potatoes, and . . . all sorts of things, but I'm no . . .' A vision of Rannick came into his mind. He, too, had been an ordinary person, until something had woken within him the tainted legacy of his ancestors. And what was he now?

Farnor had no name for what Rannick had now become.

And too, as Gryss had said, ominously, the valley being the valley, self-contained and self-sufficient for generations, the blood of Rannick's ancestors probably ran in the veins of everyone in the community. 'I've no powers,' he repeated, twisting his hands together. 'At least none that I know of, or can use.'

Marken's face was troubled. He spoke again. 'I Heard what I Heard. At least, I think – there was such confusion, and—' He stopped abruptly. 'It's gone,' he said, softly, though with a hint of alarm. He looked around the room as if he expected something unusual to happen suddenly. 'I was so preoccupied with everything that I hadn't realized,' he muttered, half to himself. Then, thoughtfully. 'How long has it been . . .?' He looked at Farnor and held up his hand for silence. Farnor found himself holding his breath. 'There's not a vestige of a sound,' Marken whispered after a long moment. He nodded, realization in his eyes. 'Not a vestige. It's as if they're deliberately remaining silent around you.'

When he spoke again it was in a low soft voice, as if fearful of disturbing someone, or something. 'I think that I Heard a little about you that perhaps I wasn't meant to,' he said. 'Murmurs in the background, as it were, though, in truth, whether it was by chance or design that they reached me, I've no idea. But it was as I said. For some reason you frighten them.' He put his hand to his forehead as if to focus his thoughts. 'I Heard them say that you moved in the worlds that they moved in. Moved with great power and ease. A Hearer like none before, I Heard that, definitely. And more. Perhaps you were one that moved even in the worlds . . .' He shook his head and frowned unhappily. 'It's so

119

difficult to describe.' He paused. 'You moved in the worlds – between the worlds – the times between times. I'm sorry. My head's full of the images I Heard, flickering and dancing – whole worlds – universes even – shimmering in and out of existence. Now here, now there, in the instant . . . nothing in between, yet everything in between . . . and you, always you, moving between. Above, beyond, and through it all. I'm sorry, I'm sorry. It's so . . .' His voice tailed off and he slumped back in his chair.

Marken's patent distress did little to ease Farnor's increasingly fraught mood. Mixing with his fear came anger, and disbelief. Not, this time, disbelief in the reality of the trees and their will, but simply disbelief in their power to restrain him. He refused to accept it. Had he not escaped a truly monstrous and powerful creature to reach this place? And could these things move to seize him as that had moved? Of course not. The idea was ludicrous. The incident in the stables fluttered into his mind again but he crushed it ruthlessly. He had had no conscious part in whatever that had been so it was nothing to do with him. And he had to do something – anything.

He jumped to his feet impulsively. 'I'll go now,' he said, his face tense and determined.

Marken looked at him, startled. 'What do you mean?' he asked, standing up and reaching out to restrain him.

'I'll go now,' Farnor repeated. 'Right away. What can they do to stop me? They're plants, for pity's sake. Lumps of wood – stuck in the ground. How can they possibly prevent me from leaving?' He stopped as a thought occurred to him. Then he looked at Marken and gave it voice as he shook the old man's grip free. 'Except have you tell Derwyn and the others to hold me here by force,' he said slowly.

Marken turned away from him angrily, then his shoulders sagged and he sat down as if suddenly burdened by his age.

Again, the soft drone of voices from the room above, gently filled the room.

'We come from different worlds, Farnor,' Marken said. 'And even though we're both human beings, we have difficulty in understanding one another's ways.' He looked up at Farnor, who was still watching him, tense and suspicious. 'I can't begin to tell you how foolish – insulting – such words are. I don't know what laws you have in your land, or how you enforce them, but such an act here would be unthinkable. We're a free people. Save for the respect we freely give to those whose land this is, and the respect which we offer each other, we accept no constraint on this freedom. Even when a crime is proven we try to look to the causes and ways of rectifying them. And to reparation and conciliation.'

Farnor's lip curled in disdain. He pointed towards the ceiling. 'Derwyn himself told me that things were so confused that I might bring the hunt down on me, if I fled unexpectedly. Then he wouldn't answer me when I asked what would happen if I couldn't make the Congress understand what had happened with EmRan. And you yourself just said that my life was hanging by a thread. How much conciliation is there in that kind of talk?'

Marken put his head in his hands. 'I can't deny that not all causes can be put to rights, Farnor,' he said with a mixture of regret and impatience. 'Nor all misdeeds repaired. Sadly there are some individuals in our world, as doubtless in yours, who are just plain wicked, and who do wicked things seemingly for the joy of it. They're rare, thank the stars, very rare, but they appear from time to time and we have to deal with them. And, if need arises, they have to be sought out and brought back to face the consequences of their actions.'

'And by seeking out, you mean hunting them?' Farnor said. 'With dogs and bows and spears?'

Marken turned to him sharply. 'As need arises, yes,' he said, suddenly angry. 'And you can take the condemnation out of your voice until you're a damn sight better acquainted with how we conduct ourselves here. For one thing, we don't—'

Farnor was not listening. 'And *I* would have been treated as such a person,' he said heatedly, striking his chest with his fingertips. 'Hunted down like an animal, just for trying to return to my own home?'

Marken stood up, his fists clenched and his mouth working angrily. Farnor stood defiantly in front of him. For a long moment, the two men stared at one another, across both years and cultures. Marken forced himself to patience. 'Please try to understand,' he said, sitting down again and motioning Farnor to do the same. 'This has been an upheaval for everyone, not just for you and me. Derwyn and the others thought that I might have gone for good, as indeed, I might. It's not unheard of, and the loss of its Hearer is a serious problem for any lodge. Then this strange-looking outsider that we've taken in draws a weapon

121

against one of our own—' He waved his hand as Farnor made to speak. 'I heard your reasons,' he said, hastily. 'And so did everybody else.' He became stern again, as if ashamed of some momentary weakness. 'And that matter's finished.' He shouted angrily. 'Finished! Your story was confirmed and accepted, and you'll hear no more of it. That's the way we are. And too, much of the confusion's gone now that I've come back. And will you please stop hovering there and sit down.'

Farnor quailed before this outburst and, rather awkwardly, did as he was told.

Marken's manner became more gentle. 'Derwyn probably didn't answer you because he had no answer. Usually he's not a man to speak unless he's got something to say. He knew that if you left suddenly, it would make the existing confusion even worse. And it would certainly have given him all sorts of problems with EmRan.' He narrowed his eyes and shook his head as if that were a prospect that he did not remotely want to consider. 'And too, with me being gone, he'd be concerned about what *they* wanted in all this. After all, it was they who let you in and they'd already made their interest in you quite manifest.' He laid a reassuring hand on Farnor's arm. 'As for talking about the hunt, that would have been no more than an ill-considered comment when his thoughts were on other things. Your drawing against EmRan wasn't *that* serious, by any means.'

Farnor looked at the Hearer warily, far from being fully convinced by what he had heard.

'And you?' he said tartly. 'What about my life hanging by a thread? Or was that just another ill-considered remark while you were thinking about other things?'

Muffled footsteps overhead, and a low, resonant laugh, intruded into the silence that followed this question.

Marken conspicuously bit back an angry rejoinder to Farnor's sarcasm. 'No,' he said. 'At least, I don't think so. But the truth is that, as with much that's happening at the moment, I don't know. To be honest, as we talk I'm becoming increasingly loath to advise you. I'm beginning to suspect that your own instincts will serve you better than anything I can say.' He looked at Farnor shrewdly. 'I know that there are things you've not told me about yet.' He paused, but Farnor offered him no enlightenment. 'Still, I suppose I'm only an intermediary, a messenger of sorts,' he went on. 'And, I'll admit, perhaps a poor one. But the message I received, I've given you. You're to go to the central mountains to stand amongst the most ancient of them so that you can be questioned and a decision made about your fate.'

Anger welled up black and awful in Farnor. 'They can go to the devil,' he said grimly. 'I go where I want. How can *they* threaten me?'

'I might've misunderstood many things lately,' Marken said, his tones wilfully measured. 'But not that message. Nor the fear that hung about it. Many-layered, deep and complicated. And that's where the danger to you is Farnor. Their fear of you. That, and your defiance. True, they're not as we are, but I can't imagine such fear being far away from aggression . . . violence . . . in any thinking being.' He nodded to himself conclusively. 'As far as we're concerned, Derwyn and the rest of us, you can do what you want. You owe us nothing in any way, neither debt nor duty. If you want to head north, south, wherever, we'll help you on your way, but I couldn't begin to hazard a guess at the consequences of your disobeying them!'

Farnor gazed at him bleakly for a long time. Then suddenly his anger drained out of him, to be replaced by confusion and doubt. 'I don't know what to do,' he said, almost pleading. 'You're the one who talks to them, understands them. I know nothing. I'm lost in every way. Please help me.'

Marken smiled ruefully. 'I'm a Hearer, Farnor. I don't know why or how, I was just born to it.' He lifted his hands and delicately tapped his ears. 'And just as there's always noise about us, even at the quietest times—' There was an anonymous clunk above their heads by way of confirmation. Marken chuckled and, despite his anxiety, Farnor smiled weakly. The tension between them disappeared. '—So in me, and my ilk, there's always the sound of the trees to be Heard when all else is silent. Nothing distinct, just a low sighing – a murmuring. Like the sound of a large, quiet crowd in the distance.'

Farnor waited.

'But now, it's gone,' Marken continued. 'For the first time in my life I Hear nothing. Nothing at all.' He looked at Farnor. 'I think perhaps that you're the quiet place that I set out to find. And if you are, then perhaps I'm here for a reason.'

Farnor could not help but smile again. 'I've never been called anything quiet before,' he said. But no sooner had he spoken than the smile and the levity felt alien and offensive. The darkness within him rose to reproach him.

Marken looked at him thoughtfully. 'Perhaps they're remaining silent in your presence not for some benefit to me, but in order to listen to you better,' he said. His voice became almost cold as he reached a decision. 'My advice, I think, is, ask them yourself. We're fretting here in pathetic ignorance when a little knowledge would perhaps answer all our questions. The fear is theirs. The needs are theirs and yours. Ask them yourself.'

Farnor's face twitched, as Marken's simple statement of the obvious struck him like icy water.

'How?' he asked, uncertainly.

Marken waved his hands vaguely. 'Just ask,' he replied, unhelpfully. 'They're listening, I'm sure.'

'If they're – listening in my head, then they know that I don't belong here, that I came here by accident and that I want to leave,' Farnor replied, in some frustration. The faint sound of laughter drifted into the room from above. Farnor recognized it as Angwen's. It seemed to curl around his mind, subtly releasing it. 'When he was speaking at the Congress, Derwyn said that you'd been told to find me and make a judgement about me. Is that true?' he asked.

'Yes,' Marken conceded, somewhat defensively. 'But I think that was for us simply to decide what to do with you when we found you.'

Suddenly earnest, Farnor pointed to the room above again, and quoted Angwen. ' "They fear because they don't understand," ' he said. 'When I was a child, I once sneaked downstairs when Yonas the Teller was staying with us. I listened to one of his stories; one that he wouldn't have told to children. And for weeks after, at night, I lay under the sheets, afraid that all the shadows in my room were monsters and demons and evil magicians come to carry me away.'

Marken smiled and nodded, but there was an irritable note in his voice when he spoke. '*They* are not frightened children, Farnor,' he said.

'Aren't they?' Farnor said, rhetorically. 'Aren't we all children when we're afraid?'

Marken stared at him thoughtfully.

Farnor went on, 'You say, ask them. But I don't know how. You say, they're probably listening, but I can't speak to them, and I think they *won't* speak to me. I think they're hiding under the blankets from me.' There was an element of challenge in his voice, which made Marken look about nervously, as if expecting some retribution. But Farnor ploughed on. 'Make the judgement that they asked you for. Tell them what you think about me, Marken. Perhaps they're not listening to me. Perhaps they can hear me all too well. Perhaps they think I'm deceiving them in some way. Perhaps they're silent because it's *you* they're listening to, *you* they need to hear. You're the one they know, you're the one they trust. Tell them.'

Marken was pushing himself well back into his chair, as if to avoid this sudden determined outpouring. Farnor took his arm and nodded encouragingly at him. 'Do you have a special place where you do your listening?' he asked.

Marken stammered. 'Yes – no – well, when I'm dealing with one tree I stand near to it, but otherwise, I Hear best in my own lodge,' he said, eventually.

'We'll go there, then,' Farnor decided.

He began to regret his inspiration shortly afterwards, however, as he climbed painstakingly up ladder after ladder in leaden pursuit of the depressingly agile old Hearer. Insofar as he had considered the matter at all, he had imagined that Marken, being quite elderly, would have had a lodge that was somewhere below Derwyn's; somewhere much closer to the Forest floor.

Wrong, he mused bitterly, as they came to yet another ladder, and Marken began yet another effortless ascent.

'Wait a moment,' Farnor appealed, leaning his head on one of the rungs and waiting for his heart to stop pounding, his breath to stop rasping, and his legs to stop protesting. Marken released one hand and one foot and swung wide to look down. 'What's the matter?' he asked, without a tremor of breathlessness.

'Just wait a moment,' Farnor demanded this time, through clenched teeth.

Marken nodded and, to Farnor's horror, swung completely off the ladder and sat on a nearby branch. 'How much further is it to your lodge?' Farnor asked.

'Nearly there,' came the reply, with a hint of heartiness. 'You should relax more, you're terribly tense. It's going to make you awfully . . .'

'I know. I know,' Farnor interrupted sourly, and still through clenched teeth. Grimly, he began to force his legs up the ladder.

Being left standing by some trim young woman was one thing, but by this old beggar . . .!

A powerful hand reached out and supported him as he arrived at the top of the ladder and stepped on to the platform. Farnor could not muster the energy to shake it free. 'Thank you,' he said, gracelessly.

'My, you're puffing like a gnarl,' Marken said, half sympathetically, half mockingly.

Farnor did not reply.

'Anyway, we're here now,' Marken said, indicating a door a little way along the platform.

But Farnor's attention was elsewhere. He had straightened up and was gazing down at a panorama of brilliant lights, trailing through and between the tops of the trees in every direction. It was as if he was looking down on a star-filled sky rather than up at it. 'How high are we?' he asked, forgetting his fatigue.

'Oh, it's a nice spot,' Marken answered, with no small amount of pride. 'Good and high.' He leaned against the handrail next to Farnor and stared out over the scene. 'It took some building, this lodge, I can tell you. But it was worth it. I often come out here and just look.' He patted the handrail, then returned to the door and opened it. 'Of course, the lodge is quite small. Inevitable at this height, as you'll understand,' he said, stepping inside and holding the door open. 'But it's ideal for an old bachelor like me.' He turned and looked out over the lights again then raised an appreciative finger. 'You should see the sun come up.' His eyes were wide. 'Mingling with the sound of the dawn horns. Make you weep for joy.'

Farnor turned away from him sharply as he stepped past him.

Unlike Derwyn's lodge, the door of which opened into a long and spacious hallway off which stood several rooms and passageways, Marken's was served only by a short porch which, as far as Farnor could see, was purely to serve as a weather guard. As he followed Marken through the inner door, the room they entered filled with light. Almost immediately, Farnor's fatigue returned, and he slumped down into a nearby chair without invitation.

Marken snapped his fingers crossly, and motioned him to another one.

'That's mine,' he declared, possessively. 'You'll find that one's comfortable enough.

'I'd find a log comfortable,' Farnor muttered surlily, rubbing

126

his legs as he moved to the other chair.

'Bildar can give you something for your aches and pains, I'm sure,' Marken said, standing protectively by the seat he had just commandeered.

'He did,' Farnor replied, irritably. 'It's down at Derwyn's, and I'm damned if I'm trailing back for it. Even if I knew the way.'

Marken made a mildly sympathetic noise and went into an adjacent room. 'I suppose you're hungry?' he called.

Farnor grimaced guiltily to himself as the kindly voice contrasted itself with his own churlishness. 'Yes, I am, a little,' he said, reflexive politeness asserting itself. 'I had a meal at Bildar's this morning, but – it's been a long day.'

Marken came back into the room, chuckling. 'That's a considerable understatement for both of us,' he said, thrusting a plate full of thick slices of bread into Farnor's lap. A bowl of butter landed on a table by his elbow. Both plate and bowl were made out of finely joined and decorated wood. 'Make a start on that,' came the command, as Marken disappeared again. 'I've got some soup, or something, heating up.'

It was simple fare, but Farnor turned to it with relish. 'Thank you,' he said with genuine sincerity.

'I should warn you that I'm no Bildar when it comes to cooking,' Marken shouted. 'But I've not killed anyone yet.'

'I'm sure it'll be fine,' Farnor spluttered, spraying bread crumbs freely. Something fluttered in the corner of his vision, making him start violently and almost up-end the plate of bread. A large sparrow landed on his knee and began fussily picking up the crumbs he had spilt.

'Sod off, Roney,' Marken shouted, coming back into the room. 'Greedy fat beggar.' The sparrow looked up at him slowly, turned away with great dignity and then flew off, to a shelf at the far end of the room.

'See him off if he comes sponging around again,' Marken ordered, sitting down. 'He eats enough for a solstice turkey. He's supposed to be a messenger bird, but his wings can hardly lift him.'

Farnor responded with vague head movements, uncertain how to respond to this domestic revelation. From the shelf, the sparrow eyed the new arrival superciliously.

All immediate conversation seemingly spent, and Farnor busy eating, Marken drummed his fingers on the arm of his chair.

Then Farnor looked up and caught his gaze. 'I may well have told them what I think about you, Farnor,' Marken said, his face serious and his voice soft. 'I don't know. But I'll tell them again, now.' He closed his eyes.

Farnor gently laid the plate on the table and watched Marken intently. Outside, lights and tree tops swayed gently, and night hunting birds glided silently through the glistening darkness.

Farnor waited.

And waited.

The soft soughing of the trees seeped slowly into the deepening silence of the room.

And with it, came a voice.

Chapter 10

'Mover,' the voice said. Though it filled Farnor's mind totally, it was soft and very tentative. Yet too, it was hung about with many meanings, subtle and indefinable. Briefly, Farnor felt that he was watching himself, a child again, with Marna and his other friends, carefully dipping toes into the chilly lake where they would sometimes play; tensed and ready to snatch away should the trial be too fearful.

The long forgotten memory vanished.

'Mover.' Again the hesitancy.

'What do you want?' Farnor spoke the words out loud.

Marken, sitting opposite, started. Farnor raised a hand for silence before he could speak.

'What do you want?' he asked again. Marken drew a finger across his closed mouth and tapped his forehead then sagged theatrically in his chair.

Farnor looked at him blankly for a moment, then nodded and, frowning with concentration, thought, 'What do you want?' very loudly.

Marken shook his head, mouthed the word, 'Relax,' and sagged into his chair again.

Farnor scowled irritably then rested his elbow on the arm of his chair, closed his eyes and dropped his head on to his hand. 'How in Murral's name am I supposed to do this?' he thought to himself, in some despair.

A sound like a sigh pervaded him. It was laden with many emotions, not least among which was a sudden alarm. 'Not His name,' he thought he heard faintly. Then there was bewilderment, and excitement and even relief. Slowly, imperceptibly, it became the question, 'What are you, Mover?'

It was still anxious and tentative though, Farnor noted. Far removed from the stern purposefulness of the voice that had forced itself upon him in the stables. As this thought occurred to him, a confused clamour of images formed in his mind; trees bending and straining against a powerful wind, being torn from the ground by crashing rock slides and flooding rivers; being scorched into black ash and nothingness by fearful wind-blown fires. Involuntarily, he lifted his hands to his head, but even as he did so, the images, and the fear and panic that pervaded them, were fading, or rather, changing; twisting and swirling until they fashioned themselves into a rich weave that once again became a single voice.

'You ran amok, Mover. There was no choice. You brought great turmoil. You – frightened us. We had to stop you some-how.'

An apology formed in Farnor's mind, but he knew that he was not being listened to. The voice went on. 'The judgement of the Mover, Mar-ken, is that you are a sapling and no more tainted than any other Mover.'

Farnor opened his eyes. Marken was leaning forward, watching him intently. 'Do you Hear them?' the old Hearer asked. His voice was soft, but it sounded laboured, coarse, and inadequate in Farnor's ears. He nodded and, without thinking, reached out a branch to take Marken's hand.

A branch?

No, no. It was a hand.

And Marken's hand closed about it, firm and supportive, before Farnor had time to consider this eerie illusion. He shut his eyes again.

A sigh returned to fill his mind once more, though this time it was one of realization. And behind it, many voices debated.

'He is powerful . . .'

'He is strange . . .'

'He is dangerous . . .'

'And the seed of the Evil came in his wake . . .'

'He Hears, he Hears . . .'

A wilful silence descended.

The voice returned. 'But you are not as Mar-ken. He . . .' Farnor strained. Was the word sees? Knows? Understands? It was all three, and much more. '. . . that part of you which lies in his world. Yet we – see – you in our worlds, where he cannot reach. And you are not as he. Nor any Mover. You pass through our worlds without constraint. It has not been known before.'

The debate broke out again, loudly, but stopped almost immediately. 'It has not been known in many ages,' came the correction, with a faint tinge of injured dignity.

'I don't understand,' Farnor said silently. He clung to his oft-voiced vision of himself. 'I'm a person. A farmer. I know nothing about you, or your worlds, or why I can Hear you, and speak to you like this.'

There was a long pause, as if the reply were being considered. When the voice spoke, the caution that had pervaded it hitherto was a little less. 'This too, Mar-ken has told us. And we have Heard ourselves. Perhaps he is deceived, though he is many-ringed and not foolish – for a Mover. And perhaps we are deceived.'

Silence.

'But it was evil that came in your wake. The floating seed of the Great Evil that we had thought long passed away. Until . . .'

The silence came again, though it was full of a sense of unwanted change, and doubts and fears. Terrible images that Farnor could not begin to interpret hung about the words Great Evil. He remembered Marken's words earlier: 'as if something had happened somewhere that had unsettled the entire Forest.'

The voice did not pursue its reservation. 'And great was the – pain – of turning It from you.' It faltered.

Farnor waited, unexpectedly patient, now. Though he made no conscious effort, he felt the strains and tensions in his body slipping away. As they did so, the sounds of the debate reached him again, or rather, he had the impression that he was reaching them. The hubbub stopped abruptly amid a leaf-rustling hiss of alarm and surprise. 'He is here. He is here.'

'Perhaps you are as you seem,' the voice said, much clearer now. 'A sapling. And thus ignorant. Or perhaps indeed you deceive us all. Perhaps you do not flee from the Evil, but come as Its vanguard, as in the . . .' Ancient days? For the second time Farnor had a fleeting but giddying sensation of looking at aeons of time stretching back through shifting light and darkness, into – brightness? Heat?

It was gone.

'I deceive no one knowingly,' he replied. 'I want only to return to my home. The . . . evil . . . that pursued me here has done me great hurt and I must return to destroy It.'

Consternation broke around him. Around the word, home,

images formed of well-rooted security and safety. But following them came great waves of fear; unmistakable fear.

And denial!

Farnor felt anger stirring within him. 'I must go back,' he said, determinedly. 'I *shall* go back.'

'No!' The voice was nervous, but definite.

Farnor felt both of Marken's hands now gripping his, willing both strength and support to him.

'There is darkness within you, Far-nor. Darkness hidden from us and from Mar-ken. Perhaps hidden from you, too. Darkness that the Evil could possess, if It does not do so already. We cannot let you return until light has come to that darkness.'

'You cannot stop me,' Far-nor said angrily.

There was a nervous pause. Farnor sensed the debate being renewed.

'We can. We will,' the voice replied. It was quiet and undemonstrative and it bore both grim determination and fear in equal parts.

Farnor felt his will begin to yield before the naked openness of this revelation.

'I do not belong here,' he said, more quietly. 'Please let me go.'

'You belong in many places,' came the unhesitant reply. 'Many places. Until you learn, you are too dangerous.'

There was another long silence.

'What do you want of me?' Farnor asked eventually.

'Go to the mountains at our heart. Speak to us where we are most ancient,' the voice replied.

'And will you be able to see into this – darkness – this ignorance you fancy you see within me, at this place?' Farnor asked sarcastically.

'Perhaps. It is our best hope. But the darkness is the darkness. It may well be beyond us. We do not know.' The voice seemed reluctant to pursue the matter. Its tone changed. 'The ignorance is something else entirely. It is the ignorance of the sapling. Unlike stupidity, it is a curable condition.'

Was there a hint of humour in that answer? Distant parental laughter? Farnor frowned. 'And if I defy you?'

No humour now. Just reluctant, fearful determination. 'We have told you. We will oppose you, strong though you be. No matter what the cost. We have harmony with the Movers. It is not our way to touch their strange, brief lives, except where they touch ours. But you are more than a Mover.' There was another long silence, then Farnor sensed a decision being made. 'We . . .' Once again the word evaded Farnor. Was it feel? Fear? Know? Or all three, and more? '. . . that within perhaps a mere Mover's span past, there has been a stirring of the Great Evil once more, somewhere in this, His home world, and also, as ever, in the worlds between the worlds. It is seemingly ended, but, too, there is doubt.' Farnor had a momentary impression of consequence upon consequence flowing ever outwards, like ripples from a casually thrown stone spreading inexorably to lap at the farthest shores of a great, silent lake. 'We are afraid. And while the spawn of the Great Evil prowls at the boundary, and you, with your power, bear the darkness at your heart, you must remain here.'

'You have no right—'

'We have the right to be, Far-nor. All knowing things have the right to be. And your darkness, and the Evil beyond, threaten that right. If you oppose us then you leave us no alternative but to stand against you.'

Farnor opened his eyes. The voice slipped away from him, and Marken's spartan room closed about him, half welcomingly, half menacingly.

Marken was staring at him, wide-eyed. 'I Heard. I Heard,' he said, almost wildly. 'Such clarity. Such freedom . . .' He waved his hands excitedly then, catching Farnor's expression, clenched them guiltily. 'I'm sorry, Farnor,' he said. 'I didn't mean to – I wasn't excited about your problems – but – a lifetime, you see, listening, but never truly Hearing.'

Several times, he put his hands to his chest, and then to his head, made to stand up, then sat down again. Eventually he forced himself back into his chair, though he was still full of a restless excitement.

'I'm sorry,' he said again, with a very deliberate calmness in his voice. 'I think I Heard most of what was said, and I know it's serious, and even desperate for you, but . . .' He tapped his hands on the arms of his chair until he gained control of himself again. 'But . . . to Hear like that. I can scarcely believe it. What happened the other day was almost unbelievable, but this . . .' He shook his head.

His own mind whirling, Farnor watched him silently, growing increasingly irritated by his apparently unquenchable exhilaration. Then a smell reached him. He wrinkled his nose and said peevishly, 'Your soup's boiling over.'

Marken's rapture vanished. He swore and dashed unceremoniously into the other room. There was a considerable clattering and hissing accompanied by yet more swearing, but eventually Marken emerged bearing a steaming bowl and more chunks of bread.

'Here,' he said, dropping both bowl and bread on to the table, and blowing on his singed fingers. 'Eat.'

'For pity's sake, I can't eat now,' Farnor said, exasperated.

Marken levelled a finger at him. 'Just eat,' he commanded, with unexpected force. 'While I think. Whatever happens, you're going to need your strength.'

Farnor's appetite and his wiser nature bowed to Marken's authority and he did as he was bidden. The soup was very hot, and for the next few minutes, the tumbling confusion in his mind receded as, under Marken's stern supervision, he struggled to eat without burning himself.

'You've made it clear enough what you *want* to do,' Marken said, as Farnor spooned up the last of the soup. 'But what are you going to do?'

Farnor looked at him over the top of the bowl. Marken's food glowed through him, vying with his inner confusion for mastery of his mood. 'Do I have a choice?' he asked.

'Always,' Marken replied.

Farnor thought of the times when his mind had reached out to touch the creature, unbidden. And of the wind in the courtyard that had crashed the wicket door shut on his arm. And of Nilsson, casually beating him, tossing him to and fro as if he had been nothing more than some disobedient dog. He shook his head in denial. 'No,' he said. 'Not always.' Then he banged his clenched fist on the arm of the chair in frustration. 'If only I knew more about these things! About what they can do. About – oh, anything! Or, for that matter, what *I* can do, that makes them so nervous of me.'

'I can't help you,' Marken said, with some regret. 'It's generally thought that they can reach into the mind and turn it to whatever ends they wish. Our old stories are full of such tales. And there's no doubt that outsiders tend to wander about only in the fringes and then leave. They rarely come in deep, and they never set up home.'

Farnor looked at him. 'And what will you do?' he asked. 'You and Derwyn and the others?'

'Nothing's changed there. We'll help you to travel whichever way you choose insofar as we're able,' Marken replied without hesitation.

'But?' Farnor prompted, catching at the doubt in his voice.

'But if they're opposing you, I don't know what value we'd be to you,' Marken said flatly.

Rage rose up in Farnor again, bringing with it images of his slaughtered parents and the triumphant faces of Rannick and Nilsson. He felt like a caged animal.

He would not be so restrained!

Yet, what could he do?

Then, like a crafty wheedling child, an unexpected and dark thought came to him. A small, baleful light to illuminate his position. He could, after all, choose, as Marken had said. This apparent power of his that so disturbed the trees and which he could neither understand nor control. *They* understood it, thus *they* were the only ones from whom he could learn about it. The logic was inexorable. He must do as they wished, but he would study them as they studied him, and secretly ferret knowledge about the power from them. And once he had that, could they then restrain him? And could Rannick and the creature stand against him?

The long-cherished image of Rannick, dead at his feet, returned. More than ever before, now, he must cling to that to sustain him through whatever was about to follow. It would be his lodestar; his guiding light. While he held fast to that, nothing, nothing, could truly stand in the way of his bringing it about.

'I'll do as they ask,' he said, smiling slightly. 'I'll go to these mountains and do whatever they wish. It's not what I want to do, but it seems it'll cause a great many difficulties for everyone if I try to leave.'

Marken started at this abrupt change and looked at him uncertainly. Then he nodded slowly. 'It's probably the wisest decision,' he said.

'Will you help me?' Farnor asked, working up some enthusiasm for this new idea. 'Show me the way? Tell me where I can get food and supplies?'

'Of course,' Marken replied, relief showing on his face. 'I'm sure we'll be able to find someone who could act as a guide for you.' He hesitated. 'At least for most of the journey, anyway.'

Farnor looked at him questioningly. 'Most of it?' he asked.

Marken looked a little uneasy. 'The place they refer to near the central mountains is very special to them. No people live there, nor even go there to hunt, to gather fruits, barks, anything.'

'Why not? Is it dangerous?' Farnor asked in some alarm, seeing his new scheme floundering already.

Marken shrugged. 'I don't know,' he replied. 'It's just that it's *their* place. There are many such that they keep to themselves, but that place above all is their most precious, revered. There might be dangers, I suppose, to someone who wasn't invited.' His face brightened. 'But that obviously doesn't apply to you, does it?'

His intentions righted again, Farnor pondered Marken's offer. A guide would be very useful; he knew nothing of this land and very little of its people. Yet perhaps, too, a guide would hinder him if he was to discover the nature of his power and then use it to escape.

'I'll think about it,' Farnor replied. 'I don't know whether I want company or not.'

'As you wish,' Marken said.

A noisy, uncontrollable yawn seized Farnor. He clamped his hand to his mouth, guiltily, as the spasm finished. 'I'm sorry,' he said, colouring.

Marken smiled indulgently. 'It's late,' he said. 'And it's been a long day, not to say, a long two days. Almost a lifetime in fact. I think we'll both find our thoughts clearer after a good night's rest.' He stood up. 'I'll take you back to Derwyn's if you want,' he said, adding rhetorically, 'I presume you can't find your way back on your own, yet?'

As they stepped outside, the contrast between Marken's small and tidily functional room with its wholly masculine ambience, and the vast cool space above the tree tops struck Farnor forcefully. The stars strewn across the sky were dimmed by the brightness of the glittering sea of sunstones beneath, but they were still brilliant, and Farnor felt as if he were floating high in the night sky, calm and at peace.

On the city in the clouds, he thought, as the memory of one of Yonas's tales came back to him. For a moment it seemed to him that the perspective he had of himself, now, here, had a rightness about it by which he should measure all his future actions. He dashed the thought aside. It was heretical. His future actions were already determined. Or at least, the end to which they must lead him. 'What is the Great Evil?' he heard himself asking.

Marken stared out into the night. 'I don't know,' he said eventually. 'It's not something I've ever Heard before. It had a bad feeling to it.'

Farnor nodded. Bad feeling was a substantial understatement for the sensations that had hung about the phrase.

Marken turned to him, his face hidden in the shadow of an overhanging branch, save for the light of the sunstones reflecting in his eyes. 'I think you know something of it already. I know you haven't fully told us why and by whom – or what – you were pursued here, and I won't press you, much as I'd like to. That's your choice. But understand this: there *has* been some great disturbance somewhere, several years ago. Something that's unsettled the entire Forest. It's true it only began to dawn on me yesterday but I've been seeing it more and more clearly with each minute that passes. Just in the new perspective I have of what I've Heard over the years and independent of what we've Heard tonight. But you're caught up in it, Farnor. Perhaps we all are. It's not something we're going to be able to avoid.'

Farnor twisted his hand nervously around the rail that he was holding, but made no reply.

Marken shivered and folded his arms about himself. 'Come on,' he said, moving past Farnor. 'The night's chilly.'

The following morning old habits asserted themselves, and Farnor woke as soon as light began to filter into his room. There was a faint sound of distant activity in the lodge, and the smell of cooking. For a heart-rending moment he thought that he was back in his own room at the farmhouse. As realization dawned, he clenched his teeth and his fists, and stiffened his entire body in bitter rage. 'Rannick, Rannick, Rannick,' he muttered; a dark litany of hatred and intended vengeance, accompanied by the image of his enemy, slain, that he had chosen to guide himself by.

Dressed and brutally scrubbed, he eventually found his way to the kitchen where, somewhat to his surprise, he found a bleary-eyed Derwyn cooking.

'A good riser, I see,' Derwyn greeted him, smiling. 'Anxious to be off?'

'Marken told you, then?' Farnor replied.

Derwyn nodded. 'He certainly did. I've not seen him so excited in years. No . . .' He corrected himself. 'I've never seen him so excited, ever.' A stifled yawn twisted his face. 'He was here half the night, rambling on and on.' He became thoughtful. 'But no excitement for you though, was there?' he said, swinging out a chair from the table and motioning Farnor to sit down. 'Have you thought any more about what you want to do?'

'What did Marken tell you?' Farnor asked, bluntly.

Derwyn sat down opposite him, and began eating. 'That you're a Hearer,' he replied. 'A remarkable one at that, to put it mildly, judging by the way he was going on. And that perhaps you're something else, something that even you don't understand.'

'And that they're afraid of me?' Farnor said.

Derwyn nodded.

'And are you, now? Knowing what you know?' Farnor asked.

The lines in Derwyn's face deepened as he scrutinized his questioner. 'No,' he said dismissively, returning to his food. 'But then what do I know about such things? I just see a young man in pain. And even Marken doesn't know what they see.' He indicated a large bowl of fruit and cereal grains. 'Help yourself. There's no ceremony here. I just advise you to start before Edrien gets down, unless you're good at close-quarter fighting.'

Hesitantly Farnor filled his plate. The simplicity of the action and Derwyn's casual openness stirred uneasily within him. 'You've all been very kind and patient with me,' he said. 'I'm sorry if I've been difficult. Caused you such trouble.'

Derwyn shook his head, his face thoughtful. 'There's change in the air, Farnor,' he said. 'I don't know what, or when, but it's there, I can feel it.' He looked at Farnor, and began eating again. 'But I doubt you're the cause of it. I suspect you've just been caught up in it more than we have so far.'

Farnor wanted to ask him for advice, but instead he said, 'I'll leave as soon as I can. Marken said he'd tell me how to reach this place.'

'Don't you want a guide?' Derwyn asked.

Farnor shook his head. 'I don't think they'll let me get lost,' he said flatly.

Derwyn chuckled. 'I'm sorry,' he said. 'I shouldn't laugh. It was just your manner.' Then, more seriously, 'You're absolutely sure that this is what you want to do?' he asked. 'You're welcome to stay here, or we can try to take you back to your home, if you wish.'

Farnor shook his head. 'That might bring trouble down on you,' he replied. He looked down, ostensibly turning his attention to his food. 'I've made my mind up about what must be done, and I'll see it through.'

Derwyn watched him, his eyes narrowed and his face concerned. Farnor's hand shook momentarily under this searching gaze and his spoon rattled against the bowl. Derwyn saw him gritting his teeth and forcing the tremor from his hand. He opened his mouth to speak but then thought better of it.

Farnor looked up. His eyes were distressed. 'There's perhaps one thing you should do,' he said. Derwyn waited. 'Go south. Follow the tracks I made. Find my valley if you can.' Farnor seemed to be struggling with something. 'Guard yourselves against what's in there. Take your best hunters, well armed. And take Marken. You'll need a Hearer. And be very careful.'

Derwyn nodded slowly. 'I'll discuss it,' he said, unhappily, knowing that Farnor would not, or could not, tell him anything further.

They said little else for the remainder of the meal, Farnor pulling a deadening shield of politeness about him. He maintained it as Edrien entered, scratching ungenteelly, in marked contrast to her mother, whose movements were at once both profoundly earthbound and seemingly incapable of anything ungraceful.

It was only Angwen who penetrated Farnor's defences, and she did it with no more than a single glance. But she merely smiled enigmatically and did not press home her advantage. Marken too, emerged eventually, tousled, red-eyed, and stiff, having finally fallen asleep in a chair following his excited and protracted harangue of Derwyn.

It was scarcely two hours later that the momentum which Farnor's will had given to events bore him into the saddle. His well-tended horse with its well-packed saddle bags gave testimony to his increasing debt to Derwyn and his lodge, as too did a small but sturdy-looking pack pony standing sullenly beside the horse.

'Thank you,' Farnor said simply, as he looked down at Derwyn and the others who had gathered to see him on his way. In his hand was a crumpled piece of paper on which Marken had hastily attempted to draw a map of the route he should follow. It was covered with many crossings-out, and notes.

'Keep moving north,' the Hearer had said frequently, as a general nostrum for the flaws in his draughtsmanship. And he had given Farnor a lodespur, a fine needle which, when allowed to pivot freely, always pointed to the north. It was mounted in a robust but finely made wooden box.

At the last moment, Bildar appeared, pressing more jars of pungent ointment into Farnor's hands. 'For your aches and pains,' he said.

Farnor felt some twinges of regret as he made his farewells, but for the most part, his armour held. And it held too against the many cries of goodwill that came down to him from the surrounding trees. He acknowledged them with a wave and a smile, though a close observer would have noticed that the smile did not reach his eyes.

Then, following Marken's outstretched arm, he clicked his horse forwards.

Derwyn and the others stood watching him for some time as he rode slowly away, but he did not look back.

Chapter 11

'A more typical attendance today,' Derwyn said, with some irony, as he looked out over the empty clearing of the Synehal.

There was little mood for humour of any kind among those gathered for the meeting, however. Although it was several days since Farnor had left, his arrival and the turbulent events of his brief stay still formed the major part of talk about the lodge.

'It's just the weather,' Bildar said, looking at the grey rain streaming vertically down beyond the edge of the Synehal canopy.

Derwyn gave him a knowing look. There were only twelve of them sitting on one of the tiers at the rear of the Synehal platform. 'Even you don't believe that,' he said. 'It's good old-fashioned apathy, that's what it is. The lad's the sole topic of conversation at every hearthside, but when it comes to talking about him seriously, they can't be bothered stirring their roots.' He shook his head ruefully.

'It *is* only a shrub Congress meeting, Derwyn,' a yellow-haired young man said. 'We're lucky if all the members who're supposed to, turn up, let alone any observers.'

'I know, Melarn,' Derwyn replied. 'You must excuse me. Farnor's arrival might have given us some problems, but more than once he made me look at things I've known all my life and see them with new eyes. Not least here. The place, and what it means to us, as a lodge; as a people, even. I'm grateful for that. It's made me realize that perhaps we've become a little too staid in our ways. People should pay more heed to what happens here. Things haven't always been so peaceful and orderly, and there's no special reason to believe that they'll always be so.'

'You worry too much, Derwyn. Things have been the way they've been for generations. Why should they change? It doesn't do to go fretting about such matters.' The speaker was Melarn's father, Helgen. He was only a few years older than Derwyn, but bore himself as though he were several decades his senior.

Derwyn gave a discreet glance skywards. 'Yes, Helgen,' he replied, trying to keep the irritation from his voice. 'But you can't deny that it was good to see so many here the other night, such interest. The Synehal hasn't been that full in my memory and it was a splendid sight. It gave me a good feeling.'

'It gave me indigestion,' Helgen retorted, patting his chest. 'All that commotion and disturbance. Outsiders coming in, Marken disappearing; it was a bad business, and we're well rid of the lad. The sooner things get properly back to normal, the better. You should never have brought him here in the first place.'

. 'Indeed.' The support came from EmRan.

Derwyn held out a hand before EmRan could begin to amplify his objection. 'I know what you're going to say, EmRan,' he said. 'We all do. You've been saying it incessantly, even since the lad left, though what you think to gain by it I can't imagine.' A note of anger seeped into his voice. 'I did what I did, because I felt it right. And no one's offered me a realistic alternative. The Congress agreed with me. The lad's gone, Marken's back; and he also agrees with what I did . . .' He levelled his finger at EmRan. 'And the only person who behaved badly during the time Farnor was here, was you. Why don't you let it drop, for pity's sake?'

'Second, if I may.' Marken's voice forestalled any reply from EmRan, and his formal tone prevented Derwyn from continuing. 'We'd all prefer to be in our lodges. I suggest that we discuss what we came here for.'

With some reluctance, Derwyn nodded an apologetic acknowledgement. 'I think we already are, Marken,' he replied. 'But you're right. There's enough tittle-tattle buzzing through the branches without our adding to it.' He, too, became formal. 'I called this meeting because I wanted you to hear what Marken Heard when he was with Farnor the night before he left. And also to decide whether, in the light of what he had to say, we should try to find new hunting trails to the south.' He motioned Marken to proceed, before his companions had any chance to assimilate this last remark.

When the Hearer had finished, there was a stunned silence. Inevitably, EmRan was the first to speak. 'You're sure about all this?' he asked, frowning. 'I can't recall you, or any other Hearer for that matter, ever being so positive about anything before.'

'Oh, yes,' Marken replied quietly, despite EmRan's acid tone. 'I told you. I've never experienced anything remotely like it before myself. And there was much more than I've told you, though some of it was vague and difficult to understand, and quite a lot was beyond any words I can find. However, what I've told you was clear and beyond misinterpretation.'

EmRan grunted noncommittally, 'I thought he'd just decided to go on his way,' he said. 'So did everyone else.'

'Well, in a manner of speaking, he did,' Derwyn said. 'I offered to let him stay with us, or to help him go wherever he wanted, but he chose to go north, on his own.'

'It's as well,' EmRan declared. 'They let him in, they can deal with him.'

Derwyn looked at him angrily, but Marken caught his eye with a look that cautioned calmness. With an effort that brought tension to his jawline, Derwyn took the unspoken advice.

'Be that as it may,' he went on. 'Farnor's decision was his own to make, and he made it. We gave him hospitality and offered him help, so we did all that we reasonably could. What I think we have to do now is decide what to do about the problems in Farnor's land, to the south.'

'What!' EmRan exclaimed.

'I said, I think we . . .'

'I heard you,' EmRan interrupted. 'You said something before about opening trails to the south, didn't you? Now you're talking about doing something about, *the problems in his land!*' He slapped his forehead in disbelief. 'What in Imrel's name has his land to do with us?'

'Mind your language, EmRan,' Derwyn said angrily. 'This is a Congress meeting not a climbfest.'

EmRan's lip curled superciliously. 'Since when were you so sensitive, Derwyn? I don't know what's got into you since you brought that thing back—'

Fury lit Derwyn's face, but he managed to keep his voice measured. 'Don't you ever listen to anything, EmRan?' he said. 'You heard Marken telling how that young man was pursued here by some evil power. We don't even know what it was; people, or something else. Farnor wouldn't talk about it and Marken Heard nothing from them that would enlighten us. But the fact is, *they* let him in, as you're so fond of pointing out, and they turned whatever it was back. And, apparently, it was no easy task.

Indeed, it left them afraid and unsure. That, to me, signifies that there's a danger down there that we simply can't ignore.'

'The only danger we've got is certain parties getting over-excited,' EmRan said scornfully. He opened his arms and surveyed the others present. 'Evil powers, for pity's sake! I ask you. Fireside tales for children. Somehow this outsider's got in, caused a bit of a commotion, and now Derwyn wants us to start a war. What are we going to do, Derwyn? Raise the levy of ancient days? Launch ourselves like Athrys of old, against this . . . mystic . . . evil that's suddenly appeared from the south? You'll be seeing tree goblins next.'

His listeners were mixed in their reception of this outburst. Some laughed openly, but more of them frowned at EmRan's manner. He read the dominant mood and, lowering his voice, spoke in a more reasonable tone. 'It's not to be denied that we're very – parochial – down here,' he went on. 'No outsider's been seen here in generations, and when one arrives – a very strange one at that – we get ourselves in a great stir about it.' He became affable. 'Not least me, I'll admit.'

Derwyn watched him carefully. EmRan in this mood was far more difficult to deal with than when he was ranting and blowing.

'But if, by chance, we'd had friends from the north or the east visiting, they'd have taken it in their stride. They're used to outsiders. Some of them even trade with them, I've heard.' EmRan paused to assess the effect of his words. 'It's quite possible that there might be trouble in this lad's land. Forest knows, everyone has troubles from time to time.' He looked around the group significantly before casually adding, 'For all we know, he might have been the cause of it, just like he was here. He could be a bandit, a thief, anything.' Then with an airy gesture he dismissed this notion before Derwyn could protest. 'But, whatever the case, it's nothing to do with us.' He waved a finger towards the surrounding forest. 'This land is *theirs*. It's they who guard its boundaries, who keep outsiders outside. And for their own reasons, when all's said and done. It's not for us to go prowling into the fringes, arrogantly thinking we know best, taking on ourselves the job that they've been doing since ancient times.' He looked at Derwyn. 'I think we should all do our best to forget the disturbance that this lad's caused. He's gone on his way – made his choice, as Derwyn tells us – and I think the rest of us should do the same. We should choose to forget him and get back to normal as quickly as possible.'

There was some applause for this, and much nodding of heads, as EmRan sat back. Then all eyes turned towards Derwyn. He too, nodded as he looked at the familiar faces. The Synehal was empty, as it invariably was, EmRan was going on about something, as he invariably was, and even in himself, he felt the great momentum of his ordinary life seeking to reassert itself; to make him set aside this brief aberration and 'get back to normal'.

But the effects of his contact with Farnor could not be so lightly shaken off. It was like a log-weighted arrow in the side of a great stag. It would drag and drag, constantly wearing him down, until he collapsed with exhaustion, easy prey for the tracking hunters. He scowled. Bad analogy, he thought. His contact with Farnor was not without its grim concerns, but it had had more the feeling of release than capture.

He cast a glance at Marken. He could see that the Hearer was looking concerned after EmRan's speech. 'Before he left, I asked Farnor what he wanted,' he began quietly. 'Nothing, he said. He'd made up his mind what he had to do, and he was going to see it through. A good trait in a young man, I thought. Forest knows, we grumble often enough that our children rarely finish what they set out to do. It was the last of several things that he did that confirmed the opinion I'd already formed about him. Whatever else he was, he was no criminal. He was a lost and much troubled young man, plain and simple.'

EmRan conspicuously stifled a yawn.

'Then he said the most that he's ever said about what had driven him here,' Derwyn continued, ignoring the jibe. 'He said we should follow his tracks and try to find the valley that he'd come from, and then we should guard ourselves against what's in there. Odd phrase, that. We'd need our best hunters, and we'd need Marken. And above all, we should be very careful.' He leaned forward and lowered his voice. 'He didn't have to tell me anything. He'd decided to leave and he knew that I wouldn't interfere with him or question his decision. And he knew he'd probably never come back. But he wanted to warn us. For some reason he won't, perhaps can't, tell us what brought him here, but he knows that it's some kind of a threat to us.' He looked at each of the others in turn. 'EmRan likes to make fun of my concerns, talking about tree goblins and children's tales. But perhaps, like Farnor, EmRan's reluctant to talk even about what *might* be happening here. All this, let's get back to normal, do the things we've always done.' He allowed himself a little acidity. 'Stick our heads in the hollow tree,' he said, baring his teeth. 'Perhaps those are the real children's games.'

EmRan scowled.

Derwyn flicked his thumb towards Marken. 'You heard Marken tell you what he'd Heard,' he went on. 'An evil pursued Farnor here, they said. Spawn of the Great Evil, they called it. It means nothing to us, but those of you who were watching might have noticed that Marken went pale even as he spoke the words. Whatever he Heard, it had resonances about it that while he can't find the words to describe them, he can fear them here.' He struck his stomach forcefully, and his voice became stern.

'Now, unless we all decide that Marken's advice is no longer worth listening to, I suggest we pay heed to what he said, and to what Farnor said to me, and start preparing ourselves for the fact that our "normal" lives are perhaps not going to be quite the same in the future. And for the fact that change is on us whether we like it or not.'

EmRan slapped his knees noisily. 'No one's doubting what Marken's told us,' he said. 'Or that he had some profound experience as a result of helping this Farnor. All I'm saying is, whatever the truth of events, it's nothing to do with us. Nothing at all. We've got enough to do just tending our own. We can't go wandering about the southern fringe interfering with the affairs of outsiders, looking for whatever it was that chased him here and perhaps bringing it down on our own heads.' He lifted a cautionary finger. '*They'll* not thank us for that, if they've had such problems turning it away themselves.' He sat back again, smugly secure in the rightness of this last point.

Derwyn made no effort to assail this fortress, opting instead to move around it.

'I too, would like nothing more than to "get back to normal",' he said. 'But my every instinct tells me that change is coming.' Again he raised his hand to forestall an interruption from EmRan. 'Every so often, once every generation or so, a wind comes that shakes the Forest to its roots. A wind that brings down trees that have stood for tens of generations. A wind so strong that it splits open the walls of our lodges, sometimes even brings them down. I smell something like that brooding in the distance,

146

as does Marken, though perhaps for different reasons. EmRan says that they'll be less than pleased if we interfere with whatever it was they turned away from Farnor with such difficulty, but I'd put it the other way. I'd say that if they had such difficulty then we should look to help them, not just stand idly by. For two reasons. Firstly because it's simply the action of a good neighbour to help our friends – our hosts, I might add – if they're in trouble. We're all of us old enough to know there's no moral case for being a bystander in such circumstances. Secondly because *if* this thing returns, and this time they're unable to stop it, does EmRan think that we alone will be able to stand against it?'

An uncomfortable silence greeted this conclusion. Derwyn watched, and spoke just as he saw EmRan about to break it. He, too, now became affable. 'And as for disturbing anything, bringing it down upon us, simply by going to search the southern fringe, what are we? Drummers and players? Going in like climbfest dancers? We're hunters, for Forest's sake. We need no lessons in silence and stealth and caution. And with Marken helping us we'll soon know if we're going somewhere our presence isn't welcome.'

No one, not even EmRan, seemed inclined to pursue the matter further, so Derwyn placed his idea formally before the group: that a lodge hunting party be sent south, along such tracks as Farnor had left, to see if they could either find the valley from which he claimed to have fled, or find whatever it was that had driven him into the Forest. Somewhat to his surprise, the group agreed to vote on it immediately.

'EmRan had that log half sawn before you started,' Marken said sympathetically as he and Derwyn walked through the pouring rain after the meeting.

Derwyn snarled and then swore.

Marken looked at him askance. 'It's not the first time he's beaten you in a shrub Congress,' he said. 'You know how he is. He has to do something now and then to show how capable he is. Don't take it to heart. It's nothing serious. He'd never be able to sway the full Congress in advance.'

'Nine to three, Marken,' Derwyn said, in angry exasperation. 'Me, you and Melarn. And those other old stumps just trotted along behind him like message squirrels.'

Marken unsuccessfully tried to smother a laugh.

147

Derwyn bowed his head and shook it. 'No, Marken,' he said. 'I'm not in the mood.'

Marken took his arm, his face becoming more serious. 'It's only a shrub Congress, Derwyn. It's not that important.'

Derwyn stopped and hitched the hood of his cloak back a little. He glanced upwards into the falling rain. 'Marken, you're still up there, somewhere. Still buoyed up by what happened to you when you were with Farnor.' He looked at his friend. 'Don't misunderstand me. I celebrate your . . . excitement . . . or whatever it is; truly. But something's touched me, too. I look around here and see everything that I've known all my life, and I know it's going to change, and change for the worse if we don't do anything.'

Marken watched him unhappily. 'I respect your concerns, Derwyn,' he said. 'But nothing's really happened that can lead you to such a conclusion. It's—'

'No!' Derwyn's tone was unequivocal. 'I know what you're going to say. We've no facts. Angwen teases me for my hunter's intuition, but that's all it is, teasing. She accepts its reality. It's fed us often enough.' He patted his stomach noisily. 'But it's here, Marken,' he said. 'Just as sure as this rain's dripping down my neck. I sense things with more than my ears and my eyes and my nose. As do we all, if we but care to listen. Every part of me takes in something and pays heed to it. And it builds up, until . . .' He tapped his stomach with a solitary finger this time. '. . . I know. I know where a deer has passed, and how long ago. I know there's a boar in that bush, and a pheasant in that one. And when the weather's going to break. I know, Marken.' He tapped his head. 'I use this too, you know that, but in some things it's a poor laggard. It has to stumble on behind. And I *know* that bad things are hovering in the air, and that what we do will make a difference to them.'

Marken shrugged in a gesture of resignation. 'I can't argue with you. I do things that you don't understand, and I've seen you do things that I don't understand, many times. We just trust one another. But where does that leave us? And why the anger about EmRan's little piece of political trickery.' He offered Derwyn a reproachful look. 'It's not the first time he's done it. To be honest, I'd have thought you'd have seen it coming.'

Derwyn grimaced. 'You're right,' he replied. 'I was a bit naive. I just presumed that because I'd felt the events moving around

Farnor, everyone else would have.'

'EmRan wouldn't feel a log rolling over him,' Marken retorted caustically.

Derwyn smiled and gave a brief chuckle, but his face became grim again almost immediately. A gust of wind and a sudden splattering of heavy raindrops released from the leaves above sent the two men scurrying forward.

'Be that as it may,' Derwyn said, as they walked on, 'I can't let this decision stand. It's too serious. We must take Farnor's advice.'

Marken stopped and turned towards him. 'That would mean taking this to a full Congress meeting,' he said. 'And they'd be very reluctant to overturn a nine-to-three decision.' He stepped closer. 'You were right before when you said I was still floating in the air after that Hearing I had with Farnor. I can't help it. But I do know that the joy of experiencing the Hearing and the actual message it contained are two different things. I'm with you. I agree with your concerns . . .' He tapped his head and his stomach. '. . . however you've come by them. But the whole feeling of the lodge is as EmRan said. Let's all have a good gossip about this strange outsider, but let's get back to our comfortable, familiar ways while we're doing it. Head in a hollow tree it might be, but people prefer that to even considering that there might be a very unpleasant reality underlying it all. You couple that with the nine to three vote, and you having nothing . . . tangible . . . to offer, and EmRan will almost certainly win. And you can rest assured that he'll make the most of the fact that it was you who brought Farnor here. You could find your position as Second in jeopardy. And that *would* be serious.'

Derwyn's face was unreadable. 'Maybe EmRan should have the job,' he said, after a moment. 'I don't seem to be reading affairs particularly well at the moment.'

Marken made a disparaging noise. 'You're reading them too well,' he said. 'And you're reading them faster than everyone else, that's all. Don't reproach yourself.' He reached out and, taking Derwyn's arms, shook him. 'Come on,' he said earnestly. 'You know you can't defy the Congress. It's far too risky. Besides, the Congress is too slow to cope with what's happening now. And *you* need to know what's happening now. Just think of another way to get what you want.'

Derwyn looked at him solemnly for some time, then nodded

slowly. 'I suppose you want me to thank you for telling me the obvious, don't you?' he said, tapping his foot in a grassy puddle and watching the ripples flow from it.

'Of course,' Marken said, smiling.

The two set off again, Derwyn with his head lowered pensively. After a little while he straightened up. 'In that case,' he said, 'if you've no pressing business at the moment, I'd like to invite you to a small, private hunting trip I was thinking of making in the near future. I'll probably ask Melarn, too. He's a personable enough young man, and he'll come in handy if there's any heavy work to be done.'

'Sounds interesting,' Marken replied casually. 'It's a long time since I've been hunting, and I could do with a change after all this activity. Sharpen up my Forest lore. Where were you thinking of going?'

Derwyn affected a small debate with himself. 'Nowhere special,' he decided. 'South, probably.'

Chapter 12

Farnor was glad that he had chosen to ride on alone: it allowed him to give full rein to the dark and bloody thoughts that festered deep within him. For the most part these manifested themselves as a burning resentment at being compelled to head north instead of being allowed to return to his home, though his resolve to learn the secrets of his power from the trees held them in check to some degree. His senses drew in the sights and sounds of the Forest around him, and the rich and varied woodland odours, but his inner vision, focused as it was, almost totally, on his ultimate goal, forbade him any indulgence and he saw none of the profound beauty of the place nor felt any of its great peacefulness.

Only when the demands of his body or of circumstances drove him to such simple practical tasks as eating and sleeping and tending the horses, did he become the son of Garren and Katrin Yarrance once again. Not that he was aware of any such transition. Indeed, he approached such tasks with the same ill grace that he pursued his entire journey. But during their execution – making a small sunstone fire to cook his food, washing himself in a noisy stream, making and unmaking his camp, feeding the horses and checking their hooves and harness, a calmness came over him, and an occasional glimmer of light reached through to him. Just as the awful momentum of recent events carried him along relentlessly, so the quieter, but far greater, momentum of his entire life and upbringing, could not help but assert itself from time to time. The touch of the familiar objects that he brought with him, reached deep down into him, as too, did the unconditional kindness that he had received from the Valderen. Such strange people, he pondered, in his quieter moments, yet with so much in common with his own kind, with their care and concern for one another.

Not that he suffered many such quiet moments. Indeed, the unexpected similarities between the Valderen and his own people would often be the goad to the memory that prodded into wakefulness his grim vision of his future.

He was aware that the trees were 'keeping their distance' from him. There was none of the constant low murmur that Marken had referred to. Instead there was a deep, wilful silence. Were they watching him? Listening to him? Or were they simply afraid of him? He suspected that it was all three, and that, too, did little to improve his disposition.

He did however, reach out to *them* from time to time. As the dominant reason for his undertaking this journey was to discover more about the power that he apparently possessed, and as they were the ones who seemed to understand it, it was essential that he learn about them. His first approach was naively simple. Lying in the dry, warm darkness of the small tent that he had erected, he closed his eyes and shouted into the silence of his mind. 'Hello!'

Silence.

'Hello! I'm Farnor Yarrance. I'm here because the trees around Derwyn's lodge sent me. I'm to go north to the central mountains, to meet your most ancient.' Then, inspirationally, he told the truth. 'I need to know about you, and them, if I'm to understand what's happening.'

The quality of the silence shifted.

'I'm not Valderen,' he went on, probing. 'They call me an outsider. I know nothing of you. Nothing at all. Or of the power I'm supposed to possess. Speak to me, please.'

'This is not easy, Far-nor.' The reply formed in his mind. 'Your ignorance is profound.'

'Whoever spoke to me at the lodge said that ignorance is a curable condition,' Farnor replied. 'But I can't be cured if no one will speak to me.'

'We are afraid of you, Far-nor. You are indeed an outsider.' The word was loaded with many shades of meaning. 'And you do indeed possess great power. Much more is hidden about you than is seen.'

Farnor winced away from the stark honesty in the voice, then he snatched at a chance. 'You sound – feel – like the one who spoke to me at the lodge. How are you here? And why do you say, we, all the time?'

Bewilderment flowed into his mind.

'We don't understand,' came the reply, eventually. 'What is, we?'

Farnor put his hand to his forehead. 'We . . . all of us . . .' he managed, after some thought. 'As opposed to, I . . . me, on my own.'

More bewilderment followed this revelation. He sensed 'I' and 'we' tossing to and fro, in a distant debate.

'We can say I, if we causes offence,' the voice said, with a hint of apology about it.

Farnor frowned. 'There's no offence,' he said. 'I'm just puzzled. You say, we, when there's only you actually talking to me. Whoever you are.' He thought about the trees surrounding his tent and corrected himself. 'Whichever you are. Just you on your own. I presume you're speaking on behalf of the others. A spokestree, I suppose. Why don't you say, I?'

It occurred to him abruptly, that perhaps he was being rude. The trees were, after all, presumably speaking a foreign language. He reverted to his other question.

'And why do you sound like the one who spoke to me at Derwyn's lodge?' he asked. 'That's a long way away now.'

'We . . . I . . . don't understand,' the voice replied, patently confused.

Farnor grimaced. Foreign was foreign, but this was verging on stupidity.

He formed his words very slowly and, still with his eyes closed, made pointing gestures in the darkness of his tent. '*You* – were – *there*.' Point. 'Now – you – are – *here*.' Point. 'But – you – cannot – move. How – is – this?'

'You don't have to be patronizing,' a rush of injured voices swept into Farnor's mind. 'I'm doing our best.'

'We! We!' corrected an anxious chorus of voices that made Farnor start.

'We're doing my best,' the lone voice conceded.

Just as bewilderment had flowed into his mind, so now came a headache and his thoughts began to fill with images of dry, cracking, dead wood. Then he was drawn – or he drew himself – from one place to another, and the images became sap-filled and vibrant.

And as he moved, so his headache passed.

The bewilderment that followed this was quite definitely his own now!

'What's happening?' he demanded. 'What was that?'

The voice seemed to have recovered its composure. 'You are not as we are, Far-nor,' it said. 'But you move in our worlds. You touch us, and I touch you, without knowing. And there is much confusion and difficulty.'

'What are your worlds? Where are they? And how are you here when you are *there*, several days to the south?' Farnor persisted, pointing into the darkness again.

'Our worlds are where you are now, Mover. I do not understand here and there. They are perhaps in the world of our . . .' The word sounded to Farnor like roots, but it could have been trunks, branches, leaves, almost anything to do with a tree, and around it were intonations that filled his mind with a myriad interwoven images of joining and bonding, of infinite dividing and coming together, of yearning to the light, and feeding in the warm, damp darkness; and of home; yes, there was no debating *that* image. And too, there was a feeling of both wholeness and separateness, simultaneously known, and linked to a strange sense of direction that was neither up nor down nor sideways, but which made Farnor feel dizzily insecure, as though he were looking down from some great height or over some great panorama.

But, above all, there was throughout, a celebration in the word that had been formed; a celebration that was at once sensuous, ascetic, reasoning, and intuitive. Farnor turned away from it. It was too complex. And there was a joy in it that tore at him profoundly.

The images vanished as swiftly as they had appeared.

'It isn't there then, this here and there?' the voice said, almost incongruous after the breathtaking grandeur of the vision that it had just shown Farnor.

'Yes, I think it might be, actually,' Farnor replied.

'Aah!' Many voices formed the sigh of realization. Somewhere he Heard 'here' and 'there' being bandied about. And was that laughter he could Hear?

Despite the darkness, Farnor put his hands over his eyes as he pondered what he had just experienced. He was conscious of a discussion still going on at the edge of his awareness.

'We understand,' the voice said, eventually. 'I think. But it isn't easy. Movers have always presented us with a problem. It is difficult to talk to most Hearers.'

Farnor waited. And, seemingly from nowhere, a question came to him.

He asked it. 'Are you one or are you many?'

There was a long silence. Then came the answer. 'Yes.'

Farnor sighed. 'Yes, what?' he demanded impatiently. 'Are you one or are you many?'

'Yes,' came the reply, immediately this time. 'Of course we are one, and I am many.'

Farnor grimaced in frustration, then turned over and pushed his face into the rolled blanket that was serving as a pillow.

There was some disappointment in the voice when it spoke again. 'I see that you must be one, now, wandering the by-ways of your own world until the light returns. It is our way to respect such things, I shall withdraw.'

Rather than responding, Farnor found himself clinging to the last word as it began to fade away. It grew softer and softer but never seemed to disappear completely. Around it were wrapped the farewells of many friends. Farnor thought that he was still listening to its distant, restful waning as it gradually began to transform itself into the din of the dawn chorus.

The terrain was such that Farnor could not make the rapid progress that he would have wished. Nevertheless, he moved northwards steadily, using both the stars and his lodespur, sometimes riding, sometimes walking. He could not know it, but the step that carried him relentlessly towards his goal was that which had patiently carried his father, and generations of Yarrances before him, up and down the land at the head of the valley, moving sheep and cattle, sowing and harvesting crops, mending, tending, painstakingly measuring out a lifetime's endeavour; it was like a ringing, resonant echo through time.

He made no attempt to mark his trail for, despite the richness of the variety of the Forest, there were too many things that were too similar, and too few places where he could scan a broad panorama and select some feature to serve as a beacon. Instead, he placed a dull faith in the knowledge that as he now moved northwards to an unknown destination at the behest of others, so, in due course, he would return southwards, and his own will would carry him inexorably back home.

Such obstacles as he encountered, therefore, he greeted predominantly with anger; anything that stood in the way of his ultimate destiny could expect nothing else. At first he tried to enlist the help of the trees in finding a suitable route, but though they made obvious efforts to help him they still seemed to have little or no understanding of such matters as place and distance, and even less understanding of the problems he was experiencing.

In the end, those obstacles that could not be walked over or hacked through, had simply to be walked around. Even a wide, tumbling river that crossed his path received little more than a curled lip and a fatalistic scowl as he wandered its bank looking for a suitable place to cross. Yet the bridge that he eventually found evoked no prayer of thanks, not even to good fortune. This was, after all, hardly an uninhabited land, was it? He had crossed many well-beaten tracks confirming that, and had even been able to follow some of them for part of the way. That a river should be well bridged thus brought no surprise.

Had he paused to look at the bridge, however, he would have seen timbers large and small, trimmed, jointed, carved and decorated with a skill and knowledge far beyond those exhibited in the gate to the castle, which but weeks ago had held him awe-stricken with its massive solidity.

Apart from the tracks that he encountered from time to time, the main evidence of the Valderen was to be heard rather than seen. At dawn each morning he would hear horn calls ringing out in the distance. Sometimes two or three different calls would mingle in a confusing but not unpleasant clamour. The affirmation, the confident assuredness of the calls irked him.

Only once did he actually encounter people, finding himself one day passing through a lodge. It was oddly quiet after what he had experienced at Derwyn's, and such inhabitants as were to be seen, were all men, sitting, apparently casually on the lower branches of the trees. They watched him silently as he passed by, but for the most part he avoided their gaze, sensing that they would be only too ready to intervene should he show any sign of halting his journey there. Though he was not in any way menaced, the experience was frightening, renewing in him as it did, the fear of strangers that was his natural heritage and which had been so vividly justified by the arrival of Nilsson and his men.

Despite his dark preoccupation however, this reception offended him. 'Did they know who I am?' he asked of the trees that night in some indignation. 'And that I'm here because of your will, not my own?'

'Hearers Hear,' was the only response he got, despite several further askings.

He was still feeling puzzled, and not a little bruised by this encounter several days later, and he was reliving his surly march through the lodge as he stared into the flames of his campfire. He could not have said what whim made him go to the trouble of lighting a fire when the sunstones that Derwyn had given him would have been sufficient for such heat and light as he needed, but he had done it. Patiently he had searched around for dry twigs and branches, sorted them, broken them into convenient lengths and, with the flint that he had brought from home, eventually ignited them.

He had sensed whisperings of alarm from the trees as the flames had flared up and sent sparks wheeling and dancing into the night air. 'Not keen on fire, I suppose?' he had asked.

There had been no specific reply, but the whisperings became louder and began to fill with images which he could not understand, but which were distinctly unpleasant. His first inclination was to tell the trees to sod off, they'd brought him here, they could take the consequences, but instead he said, 'I understand. Don't be afraid. I'll cause you no harm.'

The whispering faded.

He sat for a long, timeless interval, staring into the fire. Memories of happier times hovered at the edges of his mind, just as the darkness hovered at the edges of the firelight. But he would not allow them closer. There was nothing to be gained in dwelling on such times; they were gone and could never be again.

Yet, paradoxically, it still disturbed him that he had not been greeted at the lodge he had passed through, as he had been by Derwyn and his family and friends. He could not see himself as the dark haired, lowering outsider that he so obviously was. Nor as the centre of a strange, unsettling upheaval. He was Farnor Yarrance, popular and loved by any who knew him, forced by cruel circumstance to do what he had to do. He was no man's enemy, save Rannick's. Why should anyone fear him, watch him as though he were a dangerous animal?

And it had been fear in that lodge, without a doubt, he realized, as he threw some more wood on the small blaze. And fear begets anger and hatred. He frowned. The firelight etched out the lines in his face, ageing him.

The silent watchfulness that had greeted him at the lodge lingered more menacingly with him than the open antagonism he had received from EmRan. They must be different from place to place, these Valderen, he thought. Just as someone from over the hill would be different from us.

He prodded the fire with a long branch. The darkness beyond the firelight seemed to deepen and his thoughts took an ominous turn. They were hunters, these people. Forest hunters. Silent, skilful movers through the shadows. And could not they, like he, decide that that which they feared should be destroyed?

Even as the thought occurred to him, a sound that was not a sound of the night, impinged on him. A soft rustling.

He moved his head slightly, idly turning the branch in his fingers. Then with a cry of terror he jumped to his feet and swung the branch at the dark shadow standing close behind him.

Harlen sat in the doorway of his cottage. One hand held a short-bladed knife while the other periodically reached down to pick up a willow rod from a bundle lying beside his chair. With swift, practised strokes he stripped the bark from each rod and transferred it to another bundle on the other side of his chair. He was scarcely watching what he was doing, and his progress gradually slowed as his attention settled on the lurid red sky that was filling the western horizon since the sun had dipped behind the mountains. It had been a fine warm day and it would be a fine warm evening, but the bloody sky and the jagged black teeth that the mountains had become seemed to make the day and its ending into a metaphor for his own life. He shivered slightly.

'Do you want any help with those?'

Marna's voice at once dispelled his momentary gloom and heightened his deeper concern. Gryss, Yakob and Jeorg were growing increasingly resolute in their determination to do something to bring Rannick down. And he, Harlen, a basket weaver, was helping. There were times when the enormity of what he was doing welled up inside him and threatened to choke him.

Surreptitiously, he was checking on the guards downland; their numbers, their routines. He noted the strengths of the armed columns that passed along the road a little way from his door, how long they were away, and how many returned, and, interestingly, were any of them injured. He had even taken to engaging in conversation some of the unsavoury characters who entered the valley with a view to joining Rannick's growing army. From such casual encounters he had learned a great deal about what was happening over the hill, and such knowledge he passed on to the others. This was consistently grim, though no clear picture of Rannick's intentions could yet be discerned.

But, worse than the implications of his own involvement, was that of Marna's. Dutifully she listened, as Gryss had asked her. Listened to the chatter of the women, of her friends, of the children. Listened, thought, told, so that the conspirators' knowledge could grow still further.

There was surely no risk in what she did?

But she was his daughter, a brightness in his life upon which he knew that he could not look and expect to see with true clarity, and without which he judged he would be nothing. And there was such awful darkness about . . .

And, too, if something happened to him, what then?

He twitched away from the question, and, almost angrily, tore the bark from the rod in his hand. 'No thanks,' he replied. 'I was just looking at the sunset.'

Marna moved to his side, and leaned against the door frame, her arms folded. Neither of them spoke for some time. Harlen continued to peel the rods, though now very slowly, absentmindedly, and Marna stared fixedly at the slowly darkening sky. Incongruously pink clouds were forming around some of the peaks.

Then Marna turned away and went back into the cottage. 'Nothing looks the same, nothing smells the same,' she said quietly, as she passed him. 'Everything's tainted.'

Harlen turned and looked back at his daughter. He wanted to find some words that would tell her that all was well, that everything would be again as it had been. But there were none. Nor could there ever be. Whatever the future held, be it either the rise or the fall of Rannick, Nilsson's intrusion from outside the valley and Rannick's corruption from inside it would leave a scar which no span of time could completely obliterate.

He looked down at the rod he had just stripped, as he had done year after year. Nothing *is* the same, he thought, inwardly echoing his daughter's words as he ran his hand along the smooth, damp wood. It looked the same, it felt and it smelt the same, but . . .?

Not the same.

Yet . . .

It was the same. How could it be otherwise?

In the texture under his hand he felt the willows growing before men had come to the valley, and growing perhaps when they had all gone. It was a long perspective.

'I'm afraid all that's happened is that we've learned more,' he said, laying the rod down. 'What we need to do now is become wise enough to live with our new knowledge. To see that Rannick and Nilsson touch *us*, not the sunset. And whether that touch is a taint or not depends only on us.'

There was a short silence. 'What we need to do is take that stripping knife of yours and cut Rannick's throat,' came the bitter reply from the shady interior of the cottage.

Harlen grimaced at the savagery in his daughter's voice, though his hand tightened about his knife compulsively. 'We're doing what we can,' he said.

'It's not enough,' Marna replied.

'We're doing what we can,' he said again.

Marna did not bother to reply this time, but he heard her fist come down on the table, and he knew what the expression on her face would be. A spasm of distress and anxiety shook him. Part of him said, 'Do as you're told. Don't make trouble. Co-operate. Don't attract attention.' But another part of him rejoiced at Marna's anger. 'Scream and shout. Slash and hack at the desecration they'd wrought to life in the valley. Let them know the same fear that they've brought with them.'

Cut Rannick's throat!

Again his hand tightened about the stripping knife.

Perhaps one day there would be such a chance . . .

But . . .

And for now? They must do what they could.

'Someone's coming.' Marna was by his side again, and pointing up the valley. Harlen lifted a hand to shield his eyes from the still-bright sky as he peered into the red-tinted dusk. Slowly his eyes adjusted, and the swaying figure of a rider emerged from the shadows. Unusual at this time of day, he thought. Whatever task it was that the occasional lone rider performed, they usually set out early in the day. Still, it was probably only a random visit to the guards downland. They happened quite frequently and their random character was a constant irritation to Gryss as he tried to

160

build up a picture of the men's routine. 'They've been proper soldiers in their time, these people,' he mused. 'Nilsson knows how to keep his men alert.'

And this time it was Nilsson in person, Harlen decided with a frisson of alarm as the figure came nearer. He was about to stand up and go into the cottage when it occurred to him that it would be a conspicuous act and might provoke the very contact he would rather avoid. 'Go inside, Marna,' he said quietly, bending over his work again.

Marna hesitated briefly then, sensing the seriousness of his mood, she slipped casually back into the cottage.

Harlen started to whistle softly to himself as he began peeling the rods again. Out of the corner of his eye he watched Nilsson drawing closer. By bending over the arm of his chair to pick up the rods, manifestly concentrating as he peeled them, and bending over the other arm to stack them, he should be able to avoid even casual eye contact with Nilsson as he passed along the road in front of him. Then he would be able to go into the cottage himself to avoid the same problem on Nilsson's return.

But Nilsson did not ride past. Instead he turned off the road and on to the pathway that led to the cottage. Harlen felt his throat tighten with fear. Had Gryss's scheming been discovered? With an effort he forced himself to look up. As if he had only just seen the new arrival, he stood up to greet him. Nilsson nodded to him as he reined his horse to a halt and dismounted. He looked down at the piles of willow rods and, with the toe of his boot, nudged the strips of damp bark that were littering the ground around Harlen's chair.

Harlen watched him nervously. Slip and break your neck, he thought.

Nilsson bent down and picked up one of the unstripped rods, then, without speaking, held out his hand and nodded towards the knife in Harlen's hand. Despite himself, Harlen's hand was trembling a little as he handed it over.

Nilsson took the knife and began peeling the bark from the rod. To Harlen's surprise he performed the task quite proficiently, though there was a quality in the way he worked that Harlen found oddly repellent.

'Interesting tree, the willow,' Nilsson said, flexing the now stripped rod. 'Fine, straight grain. Splits into the flimsiest strips with a good knife. Weave it damp and it stays that way when it's

161

dry.' He looked straight at Harlen. 'You know how the willow survives, don't you?' he asked, but he did not wait for an answer. 'It bends as need arises. This way. That way. Offers no opposition. Just accepts what's required of it, and thus lives on.' He bent the rod to and fro as he spoke. 'Of course, should it choose not to . . .' He slid his hands together along the rod, and bent it slowly until the white wood began to tear apart wetly.

Harlen swallowed. He knew that Nilsson could read the fear that his manner, even his presence, awoke in people, but he tried to keep his voice calm as he spoke. 'What can I do for you, Captain?' he asked.

Nilsson dropped the broken rod and kicked it casually to one side. He spun the knife in his hand and offered it back to Harlen, handle first.

Harlen saw that the blade was almost touching Nilsson's wrist. A sudden twist and slash, and Rannick's chief lieutenant would be mortally wounded; his arm opened from wrist to elbow. Images flooded over Harlen of the bull-like figure careening about his cottage, desperately trying to staunch the unstoppable flow that his very desperation would be pumping with increasing force from the long gaping wound. Flailing red skeins filled the air, splattering everything . . . everyone.

Harlen swallowed again and, involuntarily, his hand twitched to his face as if to wipe off the blood.

Yet there was such confidence in the man, standing there, proffering the weapon. Not the confidence of a young man daring a challenge, but the confidence of a man vastly experienced in imposing his will on others, and restrained by few, if any, physical fears or moral strictures.

Harlen reached out to take the knife. His hand was still trembling.

Casually, as if weary at the delay, Nilsson let his arm fall and dropped the knife on the chair. Harlen's hand hovered futilely in the space that the knife had occupied.

'Lord Rannick wants to see your daughter, weaver,' Nilsson said, looking into the cottage. 'Now.'

Chapter 13

As Farnor swung the branch around, the figure seemed to disappear. He felt a rush of air seize him. His campfire flew into the air, twisted round, and vanished from view, then two bone-shaking blows on his back knocked the wind out of him.

It took him some time to recover his breath, and quite a lot more to realize that he was on his back on the Forest turf some way away from the fire, and that the two body shaking blows had been him landing, and bouncing.

As the realization dawned however, he let out a panic-stricken cry, struggled unsteadily to his feet and looked around frantically. The figure, hooded and eerie, was crouching low, prodding the campfire with the branch that Farnor had just attacked it with. Farnor gave another cry and, wrenching the knife from his belt, charged wildly towards the silent ambusher.

The figure gave an impatient sigh as Farnor drew nearer, then casually lifted the branch and pointed it at his face. The timing of the movement was such that Farnor could neither focus on, nor dodge around the branch, and as his head flinched backwards to avoid the inevitable impact, so his legs and body continued forward, and he fell flat on his back again. The knife floated from his hand in a graceful arc, glittering in the firelight.

Some reflex in him struggled on, despite the lack of air in his lungs, and his hand banged petulantly about the turf in an attempt to recover his weapon. Noting this tattoo, the figure stretched out the branch and casually drew the knife towards its feet. A hand reached down and picked it up. Still gasping, Farnor made an effort to rise, but the branch flicked out and, with unexpected gentleness, brushed away his supporting arm, dropping him back on to the ground again.

'Do you always attack defenceless old women when they come

to your camp for a little warm, young man?' the figure asked, sitting down by the fire.

The words slowly penetrated the noise of Farnor's pounding heart and rasping breathing. The voice was that of an old woman, though it was remarkably free from any hint of frailty. Further, she was none too pleased, by her tone. As Farnor eventually managed to lift his head to examine his interrogator, the end of the branch hovering menacingly in front of his face confirmed this conclusion.

'Well?' the voice insisted. The figure's hood turned towards him, and he could feel himself being intensely scrutinized. Then there was a soft sigh of recognition, and the branch was withdrawn. 'You *are* the outsider, then,' the figure said, returning to poking the fire with the branch. 'I thought you must be, lighting a fire like that. It's unusual in the Forest. They don't like it, you know.'

Farnor watched the figure warily, but made no attempt to renew his attack. He had no idea how this . . . woman . . . had done what she had done, but she had tossed him through the air seemingly with even less effort than had Nilsson, and, the falls having apparently awakened every fading bruise in his body, he was loath to risk any more. And too, she now had his knife.

How had she come on him so quietly? Why hadn't the horses given some indication of her approach?

The woman motioned him to rise. 'I'm sorry if I startled you, approaching you like that,' she said. 'I didn't realize you were so engrossed. Are you all right?'

Farnor was still wide-eyed and panting as he clambered to his knees, however, and he ignored both the apology and the inquiry. He pointed to the spot where he had landed previously and asked the question that was uppermost in his mind. 'How did you do that?' he said, his voice hoarse.

The figure peered around him to examine the place at which he was pointing. 'What?' she asked.

'Throw me right over there like that,' Farnor amplified.

'Oh, that,' she said dismissively. 'I didn't. You did.' She chuckled softly. 'I put you down as gently as I could.'

'But—'

'Sit down – Far-nor, is it? What strange names you people have.'

Farnor had recovered his wits and breath sufficiently now to be a little indignant at this cavalier dismissal of his heritage. 'You have a name yourself, do you?' he asked caustically. The figure turned to him slowly, and the branch twitched slightly. Farnor flinched in anticipation.

'Mind your manners, young man,' came the authoritative reply, as she returned her attention to the fire. 'Round here they call me Uldaneth Ashstock,' she went on, her tone slightly conciliatory. Farnor frowned. The name was unexpectedly familiar, but where he had heard it eluded him. Then she was chuckling again. It was a warm, female sound, markedly at odds with the impact its owner had just delivered to Farnor and the way she was idly examining his knife in the firelight. 'Ashstock,' she repeated to herself, and the chuckle became a soft laugh as though in response to some inner amusement. Then she laid the branch across her knees and tested the blade of the knife with a tentative thumb. 'A good edge,' she concluded. There was genuine appreciation in her voice. 'In fact, a very good edge. Haven't seen the like of that in many a day. Where'd you learn to do that, young man?'

Farnor abandoned his search for the name, and shrugged. 'I don't know, I just do it now,' he said. 'I suppose my father showed me once but I always seem to have been able to do it.'

'Good,' Uldaneth said. 'That's very heartening. Don't forget to show other people how to do it, as well, though. Otherwise you'll lose the greater value of the skill, won't you?'

Farnor did not know what to say by way of reply, but before he could consider the problem, the knife had been gently tossed towards him, handle first. He caught it with a nervous scramble. When he recovered, he found that the hooded head was turned towards him again. Questions flooded into his mind. Awkwardly he thrust the knife back into his belt, 'Who—?'

'Why do you carry a kitchen knife, Farnor?' Uldaneth asked before he could continue.

The question seemed to surge out of nowhere and it felt to Farnor like yet another winding blow. Darkness and anger rose up within him, and simultaneously the many aches plaguing him suddenly began to throb. 'If you know my name, you know the answer to that as well,' he replied unpleasantly. Once again, he felt an almost imperious authority radiate from the shapeless black figure.

'Just answer me simply, we'll get on a lot better that way,' Uldaneth said.

Farnor gazed into the fire for a moment, his face taut and his jaw working. He could not move away from his pain and anger. 'Mind your own damn business, then. Is that simple enough?' he snarled, viciously. 'What I carry is what I carry, and I'll answer to no one for it, least of all to some strange old woman who sneaks up out of the darkness like a thief.' He braced himself determinedly for impact.

Uldaneth, however, turned back to the fire, prodded it once or twice, then laid the branch down and sat silent, staring into the flames. Farnor waited, still angry.

After a while, Uldaneth reached up and slowly drew back her hood. For a moment, Farnor thought he caught a glimpse of the proud, handsome face of a young woman but he dismissed it immediately as a trick of the firelight as Uldaneth turned towards him. As with Marken, Farnor found that he could not gauge the age of his new companion. She was certainly an old woman, but her face was that of a powerful and vigorous personality, and though its largest feature was a long nose it was her eyes that dominated; they seemed to look into the very depths of him.

'I apologized for that,' she said. 'And you're right. It is none of my business. I'm just naturally curious.'

The complete absence of any antagonism or even reproach in her voice and manner unbalanced Farnor almost as much as the throws that had tumbled him across the Forest floor, and his anger drained out of him instantly, leaving him feeling empty and not a little guilty. 'I'm sorry,' he mumbled, instinctively apologizing. Uldaneth nodded and returned to her contemplation of the fire again. Farnor looked at her intently then, as much for want of something to say as curiosity, he said, 'You've got black hair, haven't you? I thought none of the Valderen had black hair.'

'I'm not Valderen,' Uldaneth replied. 'I'm what they'd call an outsider these days, like you.' Farnor thought that he caught a flicker of a sad, lonely smile as she spoke, but it vanished into the firelit shadows playing over her face and the impetus of Farnor's curiosity swept it from his mind.

'But I thought that *they* usually kept outsiders out,' he said, lowering his voice and flicking a thumb towards the surrounding trees.

'Oh, they don't bother about me,' Uldaneth replied. 'I'm just an old teacher wandering from lodge to lodge. They're used to me. I've been doing it for . . . a very long time.'

A teacher! Much of her manner now made sense to Farnor. And he remembered where he had heard her name. 'Angwen,' he said, half to himself.

Uldaneth raised a quizzical eyebrow.

'Angwen told me about someone called Uldaneth,' Farnor went on. 'An old woman. An outsider. A teacher.' He paused. 'But she said that that was a long time ago.'

Uldaneth laughed. 'At your age, two weeks is a long time, Farnor. When you're mine, things tend to speed up a little.' Her laughter faded away and she shook her head pensively. 'It seems only yesterday I was teaching at Derwyn's lodge. Not that it was his lodge then, of course.' She let out a not unhappy sigh and fell silent. Farnor felt like an intruder.

Then she straightened up and slapped her knees noisily. 'But a lot's happened in the world since then, young man,' she said briskly. 'More even than any of the Valderen know.'

Farnor was uncertain of the relevance of this observation. 'But what are you doing wandering about on your own at night?' he asked, some concern in his voice as a feeling of companionship began to grow within him for this fellow outsider.

'I'm always on my own,' she replied. 'More to the point, what are you doing here?' Immediately, she gave an irritated click with her tongue and raised her hand to cut off the question. 'I'm sorry,' she said. 'None of my business that, is it?'

Once again, however, it was Farnor who felt apologetic. An earlier question returned to him. 'How do you know my name?' he asked.

'Derwyn told me,' Uldaneth replied.

Farnor wanted to ask how it was that she had come again to Derwyn's lodge after such a long time, but instead he asked, 'What else did he tell you?'

'Everything,' came the immediate answer. 'And so did Marken, Bildar, Angwen, Edrien, even that loudmouth EmRan.' Her forehead wrinkled. 'I should've taken my stick to that little beggar when I was here last. I might have known he'd turn out the way he has.'

Farnor ignored this digression. He was not sure that he enjoyed having his doings related to all and sundry, and it showed on his face.

Uldaneth smiled wryly. 'Don't be offended,' she said. 'I don't think you realize what a stir you've caused. And the Valderen are considerable gossips.' She became more serious. 'Besides, Derwyn wanted me to tell the other lodges about you. He'd sent message squirrels, of course, but as I was going your way he thought I might be able to explain a little better and perhaps help if you ran into any problems on the way.'

Farnor was only partly mollified by this. 'Derwyn told you why I was here?' he asked.

Uldaneth nodded. 'He told me what you'd told him about your parents,' she said. 'And that you're a Hearer of some considerable ability.' She smiled. 'Marken's still so up in the air with excitement, he scarcely needs a ladder to climb to his lodge.' Despite the humour in her voice, Farnor felt her sharp eyes watching his every response. 'But Derwyn's more concerned about what really brought you here – the thing that pursued you and alarmed the trees so much.'

'Is he . . .?' Farnor hesitated. 'Is he going to go south and – look for anything?' he asked finally.

Uldaneth nodded. 'Only on a private hunt, though,' she replied. 'EmRan got to the Shrub Congressim first, and they wouldn't support him with a full hunt.'

Farnor's eyes widened in dismay and he drove his fist into the palm of his hand. 'He mustn't go on his own,' he said, leaning forward and taking hold of Uldaneth's arm as if shaking her might unsay the news she had just given him. 'It's too dangerous. He's going to need a lot of good men. I did tell him.'

'Not clearly enough, apparently,' Uldaneth replied sternly.

Farnor dropped his head on to his hands, abruptly reliving again those moments when he had been at one with the creature. When he had seen – *felt* – the terror of its victims. And now Derwyn was seeking it out, perhaps on his own. 'Has he gone yet?' he asked, desperately shaking away the memory.

Uldaneth shrugged. 'I think he was intending to go after a first climb for one of Edrien's cousins. He's probably gone by now.'

'He won't have gone alone, will he?' Farnor asked.

Uldaneth shook her head. 'No. He was going to take Marken, and young Melarn. And I imagine Edrien will go with him; perhaps even Angwen.'

Farnor's anxiety turned to horror. 'Can't you stop them?' he gasped. 'It'll kill them all if they find it. It's attacked groups of armed men, for pity's sake. It'll . . .' He gave a cry of anguish and frustration and made to stand up.

Uldaneth laid a hand on his shoulder. Though her touch was not heavy, he could not move under its pressure. 'What's done is done, Farnor,' she said. 'Neither of us can do anything from here. But they're none of them foolish or reckless people. And at least they've got some measure of what it is they're dealing with. We'll—'

'They haven't the slightest measure!' Farnor burst in furiously. Then, scarcely realizing what he was doing, he poured out the whole saga of his strange encounters with the creature, ending with his panic-stricken flight into the Forest.

The telling was garbled and frantic, but, oddly, Uldaneth asked no questions; she simply watched and listened intently. 'Good,' she said softly, as the tale petered out and Farnor subsided into a morose silence.

'Good?' Farnor echoed savagely. 'Good? How can you say that? They might all be slaughtered. They should've stayed in their lodges and left me – everything – alone.'

'When people who see an ill thing stay in their lodges, they can look to lose them in time,' Uldaneth said with chilling calmness.

'Save your homilies for your pupils, old woman,' Farnor snapped angrily. He struck his chest. 'My parents neglected no ill thing. All their lives they worked to make the good better. But they lost everything, for all that – everything. Cut down like troublesome weeds.'

Uldaneth's eyes narrowed slightly. 'I know about losing parents, Farnor,' she said. 'Strange as it may seem to you, I've not that long lost my own father under less than happy circumstances. And I've few words of comfort for you. Sometimes – indeed, perhaps invariably – an ill deed begets ill consequences, and they travel on and on, far beyond the original cause, in both time and distance, until all sense of meaning has gone from them.'

'And the good deeds?' Farnor's voice was bleak and cynical.

'The same,' Uldaneth replied, with crushing assuredness. 'The same.'

Farnor could not argue. Uldaneth looked at him as if she was waiting for something. But he remained motionless, his head buried in his hands.

For all his stillness however, Farnor's thoughts were twisting and turning, like caged creatures scrabbling frantically for escape.

Images of Derwyn and the others, perhaps now to be slaughtered through his neglect, joined those of his parents, massacred on some mindless whim. This stupid old woman might ramble on about causes and effects travelling on and on, but *he* knew the single cause of all these happenings; all these brutal pointless deaths. It was Rannick. And only Rannick. And when he had killed Rannick, then . . .

Then . . .

But that was of no concern. All that mattered now was to kill the man. Put an end to the horrors he had begun. The image of Rannick's dead body rose to fill his entire being. It would sustain him, carry him forward. And nothing must be allowed to stand in the way of his achieving this: not surly, watching Valderen, rivers, mountains, trees, ancient or sapling . . .

As this reaffirmation gathered strength, he felt himself reaching out; reaching back towards the south, to the valley where he belonged, his home; and Rannick. Vaguely he felt a nervous fluttering about him. A myriad tiny cries of, 'No!' clung around him, binding him, straining to hold him here.

He would not be opposed thus! His will turned angrily towards the voices – began to move . . .

'No!' Uldaneth's voice and her hand on his shoulder drew him back to himself with a force that left him breathless, as if he had suddenly jerked himself violently awake from that uneasy gloaming between waking and sleeping. 'You nearly fell into the fire,' she said gently, still holding his shoulder. 'Perhaps you should go to your tent. You look very tired.' She looked into his eyes intently. 'And you've a long way to go yet.'

Her voice was very soothing, and as she spoke she gently moved her hand on his shoulder. The jagged, vivid edges of the awareness to which he had just returned began to fade, and drowsiness began to seep over him. He struggled for a moment to keep his anger alive, but it slipped away from him. 'You're probably right,' he said weakly, his head starting to droop. Then, somehow, he was on his feet, being guided back to his tent, and gentle hands were pulling a blanket up around his neck. A remnant of his true character rose to the surface through the mounting weariness. 'But where are you going to sleep?' he mumbled. 'And the fire? The trees don't like the fire . . .'

'Don't worry about me,' Uldaneth said. 'Or them. I'll tend the fire. They know that.' As she walked away from the sleeping figure she spoke softly to herself. 'And what would *I* do with sleep?'

Curious images floated through Farnor's dreams; if dreams they were. Images that were vague and undefined, but full of calmness: a softly stirring treescape, or was it a motionless lake, echoing faithfully the sunlit mountains and sky above; or the campfire gently glowing . . . The calmness went deeper and deeper, yet always beneath it, as if deliberately hiding, lay something else. Something that festered and brooded, dark and ominous. Something that waited . . .

'Strange . . .'

A murmuring drifted out of the nothingness. A tale was being told. A tale of a great and ancient evil, arisen again, and defeated again.

Realization. Then denial. A voice, or voices, jumbled and distant. 'But it is here . . .'

Silence. Despair? Resignation?

'It would seem so . . .'

'And the sapling? The Mover?'

Doubt.

'His power is great . . . But wild.'

Certainty. And fear.

'Can you help?'

'It may be but an echo. Pebbles after the avalanche.'

'But you have been drawn here, too.'

Reluctance.

'He cannot have returned again so soon, surely. But . . .'

Doubt.

'I belong elsewhere. Most urgently. You know this.'

Acceptance.

'But the sapling?'

Silence.

'He is sound . . .'

'You doubt.'

'We are all flawed. I sense his choices, but he alone can choose.'

'But . . .?'

'He alone. This, too, you know.'

A red and golden light danced and fluttered in front of Farnor's eyes, until it gradually became the campfire. A huddled figure

171

was silhouetted, night dark, in front of it. 'Uldaneth,' he said softly.

The darkness shifted slightly. 'Go back to sleep, Farnor. Have no fear, I'll tend the fire.' The voice, full of resonances that assured and supported, weighed down his eyes, and returned him to the darkness.

And the voices.

'Then I must judge him?'

Dark humour. 'Judge not lest ye be judged.'

Bewilderment. 'But . . .?'

'*He* will choose. That is beyond doubt. And who can say which falling leaf will tilt him hither or thither? And what are we in the path of that which his forebears have led him along?'

'But . . .?'

'Teach, old ones. As I do. Teach and trust. Bring light into the darkness of his ignorance. We should be wise enough to know the limits of our wisdom.'

Resignation.

Silence. Long and deep.

The following morning Farnor felt as though a smile were suffusing him as he woke. On the instant he was wide awake, and profoundly rested. Out of recently acquired habit however, he moved very cautiously, but though his many aches and pains were still there, they were much easier.

He turned towards the open mouth of his tent. A watery dawn light filled the small clearing and there were grey wisps of mist lingering here and there. The sound of horns, distant and faint, floated to him. Uldaneth was sitting as she had been the previous night in front of the dully smoking fire. She was quite motionless. Farnor sat up, suddenly alarmed, nearly bringing the tent down about him. 'Are you all right?' he called out anxiously, scrambling hurriedly out of the tent.

Before he reached her, however, he saw that his concern was unfounded. The fire was barely smoking because it was glowing hot, and Uldaneth was pushing some slices of hissing meat about a metal dish, her long nose wrinkling in distaste.

Farnor smiled. 'Shall I do that?' he asked, bending down beside her. 'You seem to be having some trouble.'

Uldaneth gave him a narrow-eyed look and then relinquished the task to him. A few minutes – and two burnt fingers – later,

Farnor was eating his unexpected breakfast, having wedged the slices of meat between two unevenly hacked slices of the bread that still remained from the supplies that Derwyn had given him. 'It's a bit stale now, but it's edible,' he said, speaking with his mouth full. 'Are you sure you don't want any?' He held out his bulky sandwich.

Uldaneth edged away slightly and shook her head. 'I've eaten,' she said.

Farnor looked at her uncertainly and then continued eating. 'I thought I heard you talking last night,' he said, between mouthfuls.

Uldaneth's eyes fixed on his. They were blue and piercing. 'Quite possibly,' she replied acidly. 'I frequently talk to myself. It's often the only intelligent audience I can find.'

Farnor turned away from her gaze. She was a strange one, this old woman. He was convinced that she had sat by the fire all night without sleeping and that, despite her protestations, she had not eaten this morning: apart from the meat, nothing had been taken from his supplies, and she did not seem to have a pack of her own. And when she moved, she did not really move like an old woman. A twinge as he adjusted his position, reminded him too that on their first meeting, she had effortlessly defended herself against an extremely violent attack.

He wanted to ask her about all these things, but something told him that it would be either foolish or impertinent. And too, he realized that he did not want to enter into a cross-examination that might lead her to question him further about the creature. He did not know why he had told her what he had the previous night, and he did not know why she had not pursued it, but he was grateful.

'You teach the Valderen?' he asked eventually.

Uldaneth nodded slowly. 'Their young,' she said. 'They teach the parents.'

'Tell me about the trees,' Farnor said, somewhat to his own surprise.

Uldaneth tilted her head a little as she looked at him, as if she were listening for some distant sound. 'Tell me the history of the world,' she mimicked, raising her eyebrows in gentle mockery.

'Tell me about the trees,' Farnor asked again, unabashed. 'As you seem to know, I – talk – to them. I Hear them. But there's so much I don't understand about them.'

'Nor ever will, other than slightly,' Uldaneth said, looking at the trees around them. 'Nor they us. We are too different. You'd understand a bird or a fish more easily.'

Farnor persisted. 'I've never spoken to a bird or a fish,' he said. 'Let alone have one give me orders or call me ignorant. But if you've lived with the Valderen you must know more about the trees than I do.' Urgency filled him. He leaned forward. 'You said you'd spoken to Marken, didn't you?' he asked.

'Yes.'

'Then you'll know that I've things to do elsewhere, and that these hold me here.' He waved a hand at the surrounding trees, his mood becoming angry.

'Against your will?'

Farnor shrugged awkwardly. 'They say they're afraid of me because I possess some strange power, and they'll oppose me if I try to leave. Yet when I talk with them, I get so many confusing impressions. Sometimes they're like children, at others they're stern, even fierce. Sometimes there's one, always the same one, somehow, and sometimes there's many. And they seem to have so little idea of place and distance.'

Uldaneth sniffed, then stood up. 'Break camp,' she said. 'We'll talk as we walk.'

Farnor's eyes widened. 'You'll come with me?' he asked hopefully, the prospect of company on his journey suddenly shining through his anger like a bright ray of sunlight through the Forest canopy.

'Our paths lie together a little way,' Uldaneth replied. 'I'll tell you what I can, but I too have important matters to be dealt with elsewhere.'

Farnor's simple camp was soon dismantled and packed away. Uldaneth watched him carefully ensuring that the fire was completely extinguished. 'They don't like it,' he said, half apologetically. 'I can understand, I suppose.'

Uldaneth nodded.

Then, catching her apparently talking to his horse, Farnor asked if she would like to ride in preference to walking. By way of reply however, he received only an unexpectedly suspicious glare and he decided not to press the matter.

As they walked away from the camp site Farnor, leading the horses, was surprised at how quickly he had to walk to keep up with the stooping form of his companion. 'You said last night that

I'd a long way to go yet,' he said, after they had been walking for some time. 'How many days is it to these central mountains and this special place of theirs?'

Uldaneth did not answer immediately. Instead, she stopped and gazed about her. Then she nodded. 'You *do* have a long way to go yet, Farnor,' she said, striding out again. 'But the mountains . . .' She took his elbow and ushered him away from the trail they had been following.

Within a few minutes Farnor, flushed and breathless at the pace that had been set, found himself emerging on to a sloping grassy knoll. It was higher than much of the immediate Forest, and offered an extensive view over the rich, many-greened canopy.

Uldaneth, still holding his elbow, twisted him round and pointed.

Chapter 14

As Marna looked about her, she tried to keep her nervousness from showing in her manner. It was almost impossible. Time ticked by, heartbeat by heartbeat, pounding achingly in her stomach. This fearful clock had begun the instant that Nilsson had spoken his message, 'Lord Rannick wants to see your daughter, weaver,' and Marna had the feeling that she had not breathed out since his final, emphatic, 'Now.'

Her immediate impulse had been to flee, but that had scarcely had chance to form in her mind before it faded. Not so much because she knew that it would have been futile, but because of the look on her father's face. There had not even been an initial expression of shock. Instead an eerie deadness had come over it, as though he had suddenly donned a strange mask. Only his eyes were alive, searching deeply into this intruder with his appalling news.

It was because she could not read what was in them, except that it was terrible, that she stepped forward immediately.

'What does he want me for?' she had asked before her father could speak.

It was not possible that she could know it, but Nilsson was as relieved at this intervention as she was concerned about his message. For he could read what was in Harlen's eyes. His nerves were jangling with the shock of a man whose mind is far away from any thought of threat and who suddenly finds the blade of a frantic assassin at his throat, or his hand resting upon a poisonous snake.

Almost out of habit, he had quietly tormented the slightly built weaver with his stripping knife, and he had been routinely prepared to knock him to the ground had he chosen to protest and bluster at the taking of his daughter. But this was different. Nilsson had seen such a look only a few times before, but it had been enough to teach him that he might not survive the next few moments, even though he were to kill his opponent. For though Harlen made no threatening movement, the eyes with which he was now watching Nilsson came from a part so deep within him as to be scarcely human: they were the eyes of an animal guarding its young. Harlen was beyond any possibility of fear because his own death was now of no account to him. Nilsson had the vision that but seconds before, Harlen had had; of being torn open by that short bladed but lethally sharp stripping knife. It could happen in the blink of an eye, and he knew that he would not have the reflexes to stop Harlen seizing the knife from the chair should he so decide.

Thus, at Marna's approach and her question, he took the opportunity to step back a little, ready to leap clear of the confines of the doorway to where space might give him a chance to defend himself. At the same time he muttered a hasty reassurance to Harlen, before addressing himself to Marna. 'She'll be all right,' he said, man to man.

'He asked me to fetch you to him,' he replied to Marna. 'I don't know why he wants to see you.'

'And if I choose not to go with you?' Marna asked.

Nilsson shrugged and surreptitiously edged a little further away from Harlen. He tried to put a little lightheartedness into his voice. 'I don't argue about my orders, young lady,' he replied. 'I suppose I'd have to throw you over my saddle and carry you to him that way.'

Marna moved between him and her father, who, to Nilsson's considerable alarm, bent forward to pick up the knife. When he stood up his eyes were fixed on Nilsson and he laid a quiet hand on his daughter's arm as if to move her to one side. She turned towards him and looked into that fearful gaze. 'I'll be all right,' she said simply, though her voice was far from steady. Harlen's grip tightened, but she gently prised it loose and moved across to Nilsson. 'I'll be all right,' she said again, more emphatically.

Nilsson nodded, as if in confirmation, though, as with his previous assurance, he had no notion of what Rannick intended with the girl. Casually, but unashamedly he kept Marna between himself and her father as he led her towards his horse.

Only when he was mounted, with Marna behind him, and moving away from the isolated cottage did he begin to recover his inner composure.

Bad mistake, he thought, with considerable and genuine self-reproach. He, above all people, should know the dangers of such a mission. Though not one to dwell excessively on death avoided, he knew that it would be some time before he was totally at ease again. Still, he mused, on his way to that state, at least he'd survived. And the incident had certainly woken him up! The occasional lesson like that was no bad thing.

Then curiosity returned. What *did* Rannick want this girl for? Probably the obvious, he decided, as he had decided several times on his outward journey. She was not unattractive, he supposed, though from what he'd seen of her in the past, she could be a surly looking bitch at times. Yet Rannick had shown no interest in such matters with any of the women who had been brought back from the raids. Then, again, he had sent him to collect her with the simple but menacing caveat, 'She's not to be hurt, captain.'

He let the question go. Accurately anticipating Rannick was virtually impossible. His main concern was to be alert enough to follow wherever Rannick chose to lead. Doubtless he would find out why the girl was wanted in due course.

Still, best be reasonably polite to her, he decided. Just in case. Women were natural and treacherous string-pullers once they fastened on to a man. And she might yet end up as Rannick's consort.

Then they were entering the castle courtyard. A noisy clamour greeted them. Marna took in such of her surroundings as she could as Nilsson guided his horse through the confused activity. There were guards at the gate and patrolling the battlements, and men everywhere: some lounging about idly, others apparently busy, and still others – fastened with chains? – unloading wagons and unharnessing horses. And there were women too. Unhappy, miserable looking women for the most part, presumably brought in from wherever the raids had been made. Her stomach turned over. Was that to be her fate? She began to shake but somehow she crushed the thought. She'd known Rannick all her life, surely he wouldn't . . .

But old memories held few comforts for her. Rannick had always been coldly formal to her after she had finally rebuffed him.

Reining his horse to a halt, Nilsson swung his leg over its head to dismount and then reached up to help Marna. She ignored his outstretched arms and jumped down beside him. He caught her as she missed her footing and staggered, but she yanked herself free.

'I'd be a bit pleasanter than that with Lord Rannick if I were you,' Nilsson offered, though not ungently. 'Whatever he used to be around here, he's very different now. Just do as he tells you.'

Rather than let her fears show, Marna glowered at him.

He gave a shrug of indifference. 'You'll learn, one way or another,' he said. 'Come with me.'

They walked only a short distance across the courtyard, but Marna felt as though she were the focus of the attention of everyone there. Clenching her fists, she drove her fingernails into her palms and fixed her gaze resolutely on Nilsson's retreating back. The shaking began to return and her legs began to feel weak.

She heard some comments being made to Nilsson. They were spoken in his own language, but their content was unmistakable and she coloured. She took some relief however from the fact that his terse response silenced the enquirers immediately.

'Enjoy yourself, dear,' a lecherous voice said, close by, as she reached a door. Someone else laughed.

The tone of the voice snapped Marna's brittle control and she spun round furiously to face her taunter. It was a mistake, she realized, even as she did it. The speaker's leering mouth became O-shaped in mock surprise, as did his companion's. Then they both laughed raucously. 'That one's mine when he's finished with her, definitely,' one of them said.

'She'll be everyone's,' another voice called out, to further, spreading, laughter.

'Come on, girl.' Nilsson's abrupt command was almost welcome. She stepped through the door with the laughter ringing about her. For a moment she stood motionless, struggling in vain to control her shaking body. The laughter seemed to go on for ever.

'Come on!' Nilsson had stopped at the far end of the passage and was beckoning impatiently to her. With a monumental effort, she forced herself forward.

For a while, her feet clattered along stone floors and steps, then, after they had walked up a wide stairway, the sound disappeared. Glancing down, she saw that the floor was now carpeted. She stopped and looked at it, puzzled. Whatever state the castle might have been in after being closed for so long, it was not possible that any fabrics could have survived. The truth dawned on her. Like the women she had seen in the courtyard, the carpet must have been stolen on one of the raids that were being made beyond the valley. Suddenly she shuddered; a different shaking from the tremors that she had been fighting against since she left her father's cottage; this was deeper, and colder. This carpet had been torn from some ordinary house somewhere far away. Perhaps a family had been slaughtered like Garren and Katrin just to obtain it, or, somehow worse, slaughtered and then robbed as an afterthought. Her toes curled within her shoes as she tried to shrink away from it. What rich memories in that woven fabric were marred for ever now?

She shuddered again, and then ran after Nilsson. He was standing at the foot of a flight of winding stairs.

'Up there,' he said, with a flick of his head. 'Don't dawdle. He knows you're here now.'

There was a quality in his voice that made her look at him. 'How?' she asked, somewhat to her own surprise.

Nilsson returned her gaze, though she could read nothing in his eyes but indifference. 'He *knows*,' he said starkly. Then he motioned her towards the stairs again.

The stairs were quite narrow and steep and not easy to negotiate. Like the passageway she had just left, they were carpeted, though here the close proximity of the rough stone walls made any decorative effect incongruous. Nevertheless, the thoughts about where, and how, the carpet had come there lingered. Her earlier conversation with her father returned to fill her with guilt. How could she complain about life in the valley when she compared to it what must be happening elsewhere?

Other considerations however, rose to spare her as she paused to catch her breath. Used only to simple cottage stairs, the long, steep flight of spiral steps unsteadily lit by tiny lanterns made her feel at once oppressively closed in and vertiginously exposed. She fought back her momentary panic but only to find herself assailed by other, equally fearful, and more tangible thoughts about the immediate future. She struggled to reassure herself again. She knew Rannick, for pity's sake, she could handle him. But Nilsson's words tolled like a knell. 'Whatever he used to be around here, he's very different now. Just do as he tells you.'

Do as he tells you.

Her legs threatening to fold under her again she reached out and pressed her hands against the curved walls of the stairwell. The hard stone, cold and gritty, reminded her that no matter what she felt, there was no way but forward for her.

At last she reached the top of the stairs. There was a small landing and a solitary door. Hesitantly she knocked on it.

It opened with a sound like a soft, sighing breeze.

'Come in, Marna,' said a familiar voice. Tensing her stomach muscles she forced herself to move forward.

Farnor started as he followed Uldaneth's pointing hand. The mountains to which he had been journeying rose up ahead of him, seemingly only a few hours' walk away. Though perhaps no higher than those which hemmed in his home valley, peculiarly jagged, broken peaks and sheer cliff faces gave them an ominous, brooding quality. The effect was heightened by the trees which swept up the ramping sides then petered out as though exhausted. It was as if the mountains had suddenly burst through the Forest and the trees had attempted vainly to restrain them.

From where he was standing, Farnor could not see much of the northern horizon, but what he could see was filled by the mountains.

'I'd no idea I was so close,' he said, a little awe-stricken by the suddenness of this revelation.

Uldaneth nodded. 'Woodland terrain's very deceptive. But you'd have found out within the day,' she said, with some amusement.

'How far do they go?' he asked, gesticulating towards the mountains, vaguely.

'A long way,' Uldaneth replied unhelpfully. 'Like your own mountains, they're part of the same upheaval that caused the great ranges to the north.'

Farnor looked at her, startled. 'You *know* where I come from?' he asked.

'I like to get around,' Uldaneth replied offhandedly. 'But it's a long time since I've been there. A very long time.' She pointed again before he could pursue any enquiry. 'That's where you need to go,' she said. 'That's the place where they're most ancient. That valley.'

Farnor looked at the gap between two mountains to which she was pointing. From this vantage, it seemed in no way unusual.

'It's a strange place,' she went on, nodding pensively to herself. 'Very strange. Haunting, beautiful.'

'I thought they didn't allow anyone in there,' Farnor said suspiciously.

'Nor do they,' Uldaneth admitted. 'But no one bothers about a wandering old teacher.'

Abruptly Farnor asked as he had before, 'Tell me about the trees.'

Uldaneth looked at him and then at the mountains. 'I can't tell you anything that will be of value to you,' she said reluctantly.

'I think you can,' Farnor said, quietly but resolutely. 'You're an outsider, like me, but you know both the Valderen and the trees well enough to be allowed to come and go freely. You've learned a lot about me, but I know nothing about you except that there's a damned sight more to you than meets the eye. Just tell me what you can, teacher, I'll judge its value. You're bound to tell me more than I know at the moment.'

Uldaneth's hand twitched a little, as if she was about to dismiss him, then she pursed her lips and smiled a brief, enigmatic smile.

Farnor sensed an advantage and pursued it. 'You're here of your own choosing,' he went on insistently. '*I'm* here because they left me no choice. They say they want to question me, whatever that means.' Despite his endeavours to remain calm, he bared his teeth angrily. 'Personally, I'd like to take an axe to them, to be frank about it, but I don't know what – who – I'm dealing with.'

Uldaneth gave a conceding nod. 'The trees are the trees,' she said. 'All I truly know is what I've gleaned from various Hearers through the years.'

Farnor looked at her both doubtfully and expectantly. She turned and began to walk back towards the trees, motioning him to follow her. He took a final look at the mountains then, tugging the horses away from their grazing, set off after her.

Within a few paces the trees had closed about him, but although the mountains could no longer be seen Farnor could now feel their dark, brooding presence colouring the stillness of the Forest.

Uldaneth was well into her stride again by the time he caught up with her. And she was answering his question. 'They're very old, the trees,' she was saying. 'It's even said that deep in their memories is knowledge of the world that was before this world;

182

before the great heat from which all we know came to be.'

She had an inflexion to her voice that reminded Farnor of Yonas the Teller, but he was in no mood for a fireside tale. 'I'm not interested in myths and fairy tales,' he said. 'I till soil, sow seed, reap crops, tend animals.' He held out his hands, clawlike. 'I'm a simple farmer, a practical man. I've simple, practical matters to attend to far away from here and I want simple practical advice about these – things – that'll enable me to get away from here as quickly as possible and get on with them.' With an effort he forced himself to be a little more polite. 'I need to know what they want, how they think, how they talk to me the way they do, why in Murrel's name they're afraid of me, and what I can say to make them leave me alone.'

Uldaneth's eyes became cold. 'Don't mention that name here, or in my hearing again,' she said with chilling authority. 'Not until you know Who you're talking about.'

It was only a tiny part of Farnor that bridled and sought to respond to this rebuke, so powerful was it. The bulk of him hastily forced a brief and self-conscious apology out of his suddenly dry mouth.

'As I was saying,' Uldaneth continued icily and without acknowledgement. 'They're old beyond our imagining. They're one and they're many, though the distinction's far from clear, not least to themselves, as you've already discovered. As many, they live here.' She waved her hand at the surrounding trees. 'In this world. Living, growing, dying, heir to the ills of this world like the rest of us, and for the most part in some harmony with it and its creatures.' She gave Farnor a stern glance. 'Certainly more in harmony than we are, for sure.' She grunted to herself, then continued. 'As one, they're immortal in a way. They live in the world – the worlds – that are both here *and* beyond – that the strength they gain here enables them either to reach – or to create.'

Farnor's head started to reel as he clung to Uldaneth's words and tried to make sense of them. He wanted to repeat his appeal for practical simplicity, but she forestalled him. 'Don't ask me any hows and whys,' she said. 'I'm only telling you what I've been told. Make of it what you will.'

He tried to protest, but again she gave him no opportunity.

'You might imagine that I know more, or that you need more,' she went on. 'But do you? You sow your seed and you reap the

183

crop that you know must surely grow from it, because it's grown thus always. But, simple farmer, could you lie under the cold sod for a few months and grow into a single stalk of corn?' Suddenly angry, she seized his hands in a powerful grip, causing him to drop the reins to the horses. Instinctively he tried to jerk free, but as he moved, he found that he was having difficulty in keeping his balance, and could not gain any purchase.

'Could you grow a fingernail on your own, young man?' she demanded crossly, shaking his hands vigorously. 'Grow a hair on your head? Water your eyes when the dust blows in them? Sweat when you're hot? Turn your breakfast into the stuff of brains and backsides? No! But you get by well enough without giving any of it a thought, don't you? And doubtless will do for many years yet.'

There was such an ominous crescendo growing through this diatribe that, for a moment, Farnor thought he was about to be cuffed around the ears like a child whose latest offence has unleashed punishment for the last dozen such which were thought forgotten or forgiven. Instead, however, Uldaneth threw his hands down and stalked off.

In some turmoil, Farnor gathered up the horses and hurried after her. As he came alongside, she turned to him again. He flinched. But her anger seemed to have spent itself. This time she patted his arm gently. 'And some people can do even stranger, more miraculous-seeming things than any of those, Farnor,' she said. Her gaze seemed to look into his deepest thoughts.

'Me,' he said hesitantly.

She nodded. 'Yes,' she said. 'I suspect so.' She looked down, as if for a moment it was she who could not hold *his* gaze. 'No,' she said, looking up again. 'You deserve honesty. You need honesty, if you're going to make the right decisions. I don't suspect, I *know*.'

Fear suddenly curled around Farnor's stomach. 'Who are you?' he asked shakily.

'Just a teacher,' she replied. 'Truly. I look, I listen, I learn, and what I learn I pass on to others as well as I'm able.'

'But—'

'No buts, Farnor,' she said, as he hesitated. 'Teacher I am. And from what I've seen and heard of late, I've learned enough to know that I should be elsewhere, imparting my knowledge to others. I can guide you most of the way to the valley where the

184

trees are their most ancient, but there we part.'

'I'm frightened,' Farnor heard himself blurting out.

Uldaneth seemed relieved. 'I know,' she said, taking his arm again, though gently this time. 'It's a small measure of your growing wisdom that you can tell me of it. You'd be a fool indeed if you weren't frightened after all that's happened to you. But you're well founded in your life, and stronger than you know.'

Farnor looked at her, his eyes, full of doubt, searching her face.

'You'll be burdened with no more than you can bear,' she said, turning away. 'Come on, let's be on our way.'

They walked in silence for a long time. The early-morning air was damp and clear, and rich with the promise of a fine summer's day. And it was alive with bird song, chiming through golden light.

The two walkers, however, seemed to be oblivious to this great celebration. Uldaneth was bowed and preoccupied, while Farnor was nervous and fretful. Occasionally he would become calm, serene almost, as the ringing, mote-filled sunlight and the soft turf springing under his feet conspired to disperse the dark vapours that wreathed through his mind. Vapours that rose from the fear and rage which was bubbling inside him like some foul broth.

At such times however, he dashed the tranquillity angrily from his mind, though now, he felt a sense of vandalism in the act. But it was unimportant. What mattered was to reach the end of this journey, learn about this power he was supposed to possess, and then return south as quickly as he could. The image of the dead Rannick rose repeatedly before him, solid and alluring. He clung to it more tenaciously than ever.

The terrain that Farnor had been travelling over for several days had been much more uneven than that around the more southerly part of the Forest, and he realized now that he had been walking through the foothills that fringed the central mountains. The present surroundings began to emphasize this observation as, increasingly, large rocky outcrops began to disrupt the tree-filled landscape. They opened the leafy canopy to reveal great swathes of blue sky overhead and, at times, the sharp edges of the ever-nearing mountain peaks. The ground also became relentlessly steep. Not that this seemed to distress Uldaneth in any way, for she maintained the same steady pace independently of whether she was walking uphill or downhill.

Then they were on top of a broad grassy knoll, once again above much of the surrounding Forest. A solitary peak loomed above them, its hulking shoulders hiding its neighbours and giving the impression that it stood almost alone amid the Forest. Uldaneth pointed. 'That way,' she said.

Farnor looked at her blankly.

'That way,' she said again, very gently. 'It'll lead you to the valley of the most ancient.'

'You're not coming any further with me?' he asked, knowing the answer.

Uldaneth shook her head. 'I go eastward,' she said simply. 'I've urgent tidings to carry now. I can't delay further.'

For a moment Farnor felt desolated. He wanted to take the old woman's hand and implore her to stay with him, to help him deal with these strange . . . beings . . . that had brought him here for who could say what purpose. But, even as the thoughts came to him, his inner anger rose up and tried ruthlessly to scatter them. 'Go if you must then, you stupid old woman. But what can possibly be as urgent as my needs?' it wanted him to shout, but instead he said, 'I'm sorry. It's been good to have another – outsider – to talk to.' He looked down. 'And to help me. I wish you could stay with me. Tell me who you are, where you come from – all sorts of things. I think there's a lot of questions I should've asked you, but . . .' His voice tailed off.

'Who I am and where I come from are tales for another time, another place,' Uldaneth replied kindly. 'And long tales at that. As for the rest of your questions, there's others will answer them for you when you're ready, have no fear. And you'll answer more than a few on your own.' She smiled. 'But don't forget, although seeking answers is the only way to go, the answer to each question is apt to bring two more questions in its wake. There are times when you need to sit on top of a mountain and just gaze around.'

Farnor jerked his hands nervously, uncertain what to say next. 'Selfish bitch. Leaving me here on my own,' part of him still cried. 'Do you want any supplies?' he actually said. 'Or . . . or, one of the horses, perhaps?'

Uldaneth's mouth tightened uncertainly for a moment, then relaxed. She patted the pack pony. 'I've had many an offer of a fine horse in my time, Farnor, but this is perhaps the kindest.' She patted the pony again. 'Thank you, but no. I make better progress on my old two feet than many men do on a horse. And besides, much of my journey isn't through good riding country and I've no burdens that a horse can help me carry.' She looked at him earnestly. 'And your need is more pressing than mine.'

Farnor looked over his shoulder towards the gloomy trees that Uldaneth had indicated. 'How shall I find them?' he asked.

'They'll guide you from here, I'm sure,' Uldaneth replied. 'Believe me, they wouldn't have invited you here to have you flounder about lost.'

'I wasn't invited,' Farnor's angry inner self muttered.

'What shall I do when I . . . meet . . . them?' he asked hesitantly.

'The right thing,' Uldaneth replied immediately and with great confidence. 'Just tell the truth as you see it. Whatever it is.' She paused. 'And, above all, be yourself.'

Briefly her arms came up as if she were going to embrace him, but then she jerked them back awkwardly and turned the gesture into one motioning him away. 'Go on now,' she said briskly. 'Don't dawdle any longer. Goodbyes don't become easier with time and, in my experience, the quicker they're made, the better.'

Farnor fluttered helplessly for a moment. He'd never known such a parting. Then he turned to the pack pony and began struggling with its load. 'Well, will you take this, then, as a small gift?' he said. 'It's the branch I tried to hit you with. It's a good piece of wood. Strong, straight-grained. I've cut it to length and shaped the ends a little. It'll make an excellent stick for rough ground.'

Uldaneth smiled broadly as she accepted the branch. 'Yes, this I *will* take,' she said. Then she squinted along it knowingly, attempted unsuccessfully to flex it, nodded approvingly, and finally swung it round to land with a menacing smack in the palm of her hand. 'A good stick is always handy. And they seem to expect one of me where I'm going. Thank you, Farnor. It couldn't have been a finer gift if it had been encrusted in gems.'

Her hand flicked out again, in the direction he was to take. 'Now, on your way, and don't delay me any further.' Her voice was hoarse and strained.

Farnor found himself bowing to her awkwardly, then he took the reins of his horse and set off. He turned round after a little way. Uldaneth was still standing there, motioning him on. Her manner was vigorous and confident, but had Farnor been close enough he would have seen a deep anxiety, even fear, in those bright, penetrating tear-filled eyes. 'Light be with you, Farnor Yarrance,' he heard her call.

It was a farewell he had never heard before, but somehow the words reached into him and buoyed him up. 'And with you, Uldaneth Ashstock,' he shouted back, without knowing why.

Then she turned and stalked off, leaning on her newly acquired stick. Farnor continued on until he was at the edge of the trees. There, he stopped and turned again. Uldaneth was also by the edge of the trees at the far side of the knoll, and she too had turned.

He raised his hand in a final salute, and smiled as he saw the stick raised in reply.

Then the two figures turned and disappeared into the darkness of the Forest.

Chapter 15

As she entered the room, Marna heard the door closing behind her with the same soft sigh that had accompanied its opening. Momentarily she felt a breeze lightly touch her cheek.

She stepped away from the door and looked around the room. It was circular, and she found that she had emerged from what was a broad pillar at its centre. The long-shadowed light pervading the room was eerie and disconcerting though she realized quite quickly that this was simply because it was sunset. There were arched windows all around the room, and those facing east were displaying a purpling night sky, while those facing west let in the blood red remains of the dying sun from a sky streaked now with thin black lines of cloud. As she looked round, however, she could see no sign of Rannick.

'It's very high up here.'

His voice made her start. She turned sharply towards it, to see Rannick emerging from the other side of the central pillar.

'It's an odd feeling, being high up in a building after having lived all your life in a cottage, isn't it?' he said, moving over to one of the windows. 'And quite different from being high up the side of a mountain.'

Marna clutched at the everyday normality in his voice. 'Yes,' she replied as casually as she could manage. 'It does feel strange.' Then, for want of something to say, 'And it's always hard to know when to light a lantern at this time of the day.'

Rannick, silhouetted now against the red sky, nodded, but did not speak.

Marna looked around the room again, still searching for something that might help her reach through to the reason for this unwelcome summons. Like the passages through which Nilsson had led her below, the room was an odd mixture of carpeted floor, and grim, grey stone walls, though in places, there were pictures hanging. She squinted at some of them intently. And tapestries?

Yet neither pictures nor tapestries were such as might be found anywhere in the village; nor was any of the furniture. It must all have been looted from places over the hill. Once again she felt the alien character of everything about her. It cried out that it did not belong here. Not because it was unattractive, or ill made – indeed she could see that many of the pieces were extremely fine, and there was an unexpected order, even dignity, about the way the room had been furnished – but because it belonged to others. Each item brought with it to this high tower room, the aura of the place from which it had been torn. It resonated with the cries of those to whom it truly belonged.

Marna forced herself to stop shaking. She had more pressing problems than concerning herself with the fate of the unknown people who had unknowingly furnished this place. Again she clung to the prosaic. 'How in the world did you get some of these things up that narrow stair?' she asked, running her hand along the delicately carved edge of a large, finely polished table.

Rannick laughed; a sound that was a ghastly mixture of inhuman glee and an all too human relief at being able to speak to end the fraught silence. 'Nilsson's men have many talents amongst them,' he said. 'They were just ordinary men, pursuing their ordinary skills before they chose the way that brought them here.' Again the laugh, but this time it was almost totally inhuman. 'And what they can't provide' – he raised his hand in an airy gesture – 'we find elsewhere.' He turned and looked out at the fading red sky. 'There are many, many things over the hill, Marna,' he said. 'You've truly no idea.'

'I know there are villages and towns,' Marna responded, a little defensively, in spite of herself. 'And even cities. Like the capital. Where the king lives.'

Rannick nodded slightly. 'Yes,' he said, though seemingly to himself. 'The king. And his capital. And his great army.' There was scorn in his voice. 'But even beyond that,' he went on. 'There are lands and peoples. Spread across the whole world.'

'Oh,' Marna replied dully.

Rannick turned back towards her. 'Lands and peoples that will be mine, Marna,' he said softly but with great intensity, his hand coming forward and closing, clawlike, to make a bony, knuckled fist.

His face was in complete shadow, while her own, Marna knew, would be clearly visible even in the fading light. Desperately, she fought to keep her inner alarm from reaching her eyes. She let some of her fear force her face into a puzzled frown. 'I don't understand,' she said, walking to the window adjacent to the one where Rannick was standing. She could see part of the battlements below, but very little of the courtyard. And beyond, she could see far down the valley, familiar shapes and landmarks fading into the shadows of the western mountains. It was, as Rannick had said, an odd feeling looking down from this high, yet confined vantage.

Rannick watched her as she gazed out of the window. 'It needs very little understanding, Marna,' he said. 'My imprisonment in this miserable place is ended. I now have the power that was always destined for me, and these mountains, these petty village huts, can confine me no longer.'

Marna wanted to argue. Wanted to defend her village, her community. Wanted to ask what it was that had held him here against his will thus far in his life. But there was a note in his voice that warned her away from such a debate. Lingering somewhere in her mind were always the deaths of Garren and Katrin Yarrance. 'Power?' she queried.

Rannick moved towards her. He put his hand on her shoulder and turned her towards him. She tried not to stiffen under his touch. 'The power given to me by my ancestors, and released by . . .' He closed his eyes briefly, and gently tightened his grip, fingers and thumb probing intimately. He left the sentence unfinished, however. 'Power to draw men such as Nilsson and his band to my side and make them blindly obedient to my will. Power to sweep aside whatever stands in my way, be it forests, rivers, locks and bolts, walls of stone . . .' He paused and looked at her intently, his hand still rhythmically caressing her shoulder. 'People,' he said, significantly. 'Anything.'

Marna's mouth was dry. Her eyes were drawn reluctantly to his. She saw there what she heard in his voice. Manic obsession, mingling with an almost pathetic yearning for—

For what?

Praise? Acceptance?

Her?

She felt her hands shaking, and she pressed them tightly against the sides of her legs to still them. Little surprise in that, of course, she reasoned carefully to herself. Reason however, held little comfort for her, for though she had fended off more than a few unwanted embraces in her time, this was very different. Different not only because of the circumstances but because amid the waves of fear that threatened to possess her, the repulsion that she felt was entwined around another, unexpected and contradictory emotion.

Desire.

It held her eyes on his lean, shadowed face and tried to lift her hand to cover his, to tighten further that grip on her shoulder. 'What's this to do with me?' she managed to reply, forcing her hand tighter against her leg.

His hand drew her a little closer, though there was uncertainty in it as well as an almost irresistible strength. 'Soon, kings and princes will be bending the knee to me,' he said a little hoarsely. 'They will bring their wealth and their power to increase my own, and no ambition will be beyond my achieving.'

Marna felt herself going pale.

'Share it with me, Marna,' he said very softly. 'Share *everything* with me.'

Memories of their early, awkward and distant friendship, with its sudden conclusion, flooded over Marna as she looked up at him. It did not seem possible to her that his eyes could contain the confusion of emotions that she read there. A confusion that was echoed within herself. But dominant in her confusion now was fear. She must get away from him. But how. A blow? A push? A laugh? A kindly smile? None of these would suffice.

'I don't understand,' she prevaricated, tearing her gaze away from him as casually as she could.

'You *do*,' Rannick said, still softly but emphatically. 'You know you do. You belong by my side, Marna. You always have.' He waved his hand across the darkening valley. 'All this is nothing. All that has been before has been nothing. Just a waiting time. And now it's finished; gone, vanished. Now we go to take our true inheritance.'

And what about Garren and Katrin, slaughtered, and their farm burnt? she suddenly wanted to scream. And Farnor, wherever he is? And Jeorg, beaten senseless? And all those people from over the hill brought back in chains?

And then, her mind was clear. The confusion and the desire retreated. 'I'm confused,' she lied, this time making no attempt to stop her voice from trembling. 'It's all so sudden.' She brought up her hand and laid it over his. Forcing a plaintive bewilderment into her eyes, she looked at him. He returned her gaze uncertainly. Terrifyingly, she could see rage bubbling beneath his doubt. She must be very careful. Fear lay cold inside her, but she held Rannick's gaze. Then she shrugged her shoulders and at the same time turned away slowly so that his hand naturally slipped from both her shoulder and her grip.

Free of his touch, the desire retreated further. She spoke quickly, before he could take command again. 'One minute I'm in the cottage helping my father, like I've done for years. Then, all of a sudden' – she clapped her hands together, and moved a little further away from him – 'I'm here. High above everything. Just that is making me giddy. And I'm listening to you talking about being – a king, or something.' She put her hands to her head.

'You doubt me?' Rannick said suddenly, his head craning forward.

'No!' Marna said, a little too hastily.

'See!'

A breeze suddenly caught Marna's hair, blowing it across her face. She cried out, startled. Rannick held up his hand, both for silence, and as reassurance.

As she swept the hair from her face Marna saw a blurred light floating in the air some way in front of her. Abruptly, it was a flame. Despite Rannick's assurance, Marna cried out again, and stepped back.

'Ssh. You're safe with me,' Rannick said.

The flame moved from side to side, like a hunting dog impatiently waiting to be unleashed. There was little light coming from the windows now, making the flame virtually the only source of illumination in the tower room. Marna glanced rapidly at Rannick. Now there was no ambivalence in his face. The flame etched dark shadows into it, and glistened in his eyes. Uncertain how she herself would look, Marna fought to compose her features.

But her efforts were unnecessary. Rannick's total attention was on the flame. It grew, it shrank, it divided and came together again, it danced into a myriad shapes, like trees and bright golden flowers, and scattering stars, and things that had no name, all the time moving hither and thither to its master's unseen commands.

At its touch, wild shadows from the plundered furniture danced desperately about the walls of the room as if, empowered by the spirits of their erstwhile owners, they were attempting to flee this terrible place.

Marna watched in fearful fascination. It must have been something like this that Gryss and the others had been shown on the day of Farnor's disappearance. She clung to such calmness as she could, but she was becoming increasingly uncertain about the outcome of this frightening demonstration.

Then the flame drew near to her, stopping scarcely an arm's length away from her. She could feel the heat of it, and she cringed away, only to find the wall at her back. Rannick turned towards her but the flame was too bright for her to see his face, and she saw only the reflections of the flame in his eyes, gleaming out of his dark silhouette.

'Touch it, touch it,' he said, a strange, expectant tension in his voice.

She looked into the two bright lights that were his eyes. 'Touch it,' he repeated, adding softly, 'Trust me, Marna. Trust me.'

She had no choice, she knew. Holding her breath, and tensed to jerk her hand back on the instant, she reached out hesitantly. Her fingers curled into a loose fist involuntarily.

'Go on. Go on.' Rannick's encouragement was urgent.

In the jagged silence of the room, she heard the flame fluttering and hissing. It was like the gloating breath of some primitive animal. A faint but bitingly acrid smell struck at the back of her throat, and for an instant a sense of the dreadful unnaturalness of Rannick's creation almost overwhelmed her. She fought the sensation back and somehow pushed her hand nearer to the flickering flame.

'Yes,' Rannick whispered, drawing out the word to mingle with the sound of the flame. 'Touch it.'

Gritting her teeth, Marna willed her fingers to open. Her hand flinched back as it neared the flame, but, fearful of Rannick's response, she forced it forward.

Abruptly, although she did not see it move, the flame was around her hand. Frantically, she tried to jerk it back, but it would not respond. Her throat would not form the scream ringing inside her as she stared in horror at her hand, pale and distant, and shimmering with cascades of light that flowed round and round it before tumbling away into some unknown place.

Yet even though she could still feel the heat of the flame on her face she realized that there was no burning. Instead there was a sensation that she could hardly describe. It was as if her hand were somewhere else, somewhere different in every way from where she was, not only to this flickering circular room, but to the whole castle; the whole valley; everything. Again, the unnaturalness of what was happening rose like gorge inside her, threatening to disorientate her completely.

'Aah!' Rannick's rapturous sigh saved her teetering awareness and she tore her eyes away from her transfigured hand to look at the shadowy form of her captor. 'I knew you could,' he said, before she could speak. 'I knew you'd understand.'

'What have you done, Rannick?' Her throat throbbed with the pain of speaking, it was so taut and parched.

'See . . .' was the reply.

Marna turned again to her hand. Abruptly the flame shrank, and the room filled with a soft, high-pitched whistling that to Marna seemed, like her hand, to be in some other place.

Then there was only her hand, the flame flickering about it as though it were a many-jewelled glove caught in a great blaze of light. She moved and flexed her hand, fascination gradually replacing her terror. Unlike a glove however, the flame was caressing her hand gently and rhythmically, just as Rannick had done to her shoulder.

And again she was at once repelled and attracted.

Slowly the flame continued to shrink, until there was only a dazzlingly bright ring about her third finger. It was achingly beautiful and, without thinking, she reached out to touch it with her other hand. Before she reached it, however, the ring floated from her finger and moved towards Rannick.

As his outstretched hand closed about it, the bright circle sent out shafts of white light between his fingers to divide the gloomy darkness of the room. Then, as if further escape were impossible, it seemed to spread through his entire body so that, for a brief instant, he stood like some eerie, translucent, inner-lit statue, with an almost unbearable brightness shining from his eyes and his slightly opened mouth.

Then it was gone, and an empty silence hung in the room.

'There is no limit to what can be now,' Rannick said very softly. 'And you will share it with me, Marna. We shall rule *all*.' His voice became urgent and earnest. 'Marna, we can do such things together. We *will* do such things.'

Do as he tells you!

Never!

Her eyes adjusting to the gloom, Marna saw his hands rising to take hold of her again. Desperately she seized his wrists. 'You must give me more time, Rannick,' she said breathlessly, reverting to her earlier plea. 'I'm more bewildered than ever now. Everything's happened so quickly. Only a few minutes ago I couldn't even have imagined what I've just seen. Now I'm just . . .' She stopped, her head drooping.

'The merest toy,' Rannick interjected quickly. 'I can do countless such tricks. But my true power lies far far beyond such trifles as that.'

Inspiration coming to her, Marna nodded, and shook his arms insistently both to acknowledge this boast and to press home her own concerns. 'Yes,' she said. 'But with this – power – that you have, you can choose your own time for everything you want to do. No one can tell you when this must be, or that must be. You are total master of events. You've grown used to all this over months – years, for all I know. You can surely allow me a little time to' – she smiled self-deprecatingly – 'to get my breath back.'

For a moment, she felt that she was standing next to the old Rannick: the much-despised Rannick for whom she had felt sorry and in whom she thought she had seen glimpses of a nobler nature. There was a tense silence. She released his wrists.

'Yes, I suppose so,' Rannick replied eventually, though there was an uneasy tension in his voice.

Marna drove her fingernails into her palms savagely, to prevent her sudden elation from reaching her eyes.

The familiar Rannick vanished, to be replaced by this alien figure clothed in his form, who had brought such horror to the valley. 'Tell Nilsson to take you home,' he said, as if he had suddenly lost interest. 'I'll send him for you tomorrow evening. Be ready then.'

He laid his hand on her cheek affectionately. The interest had returned in full measure. 'Tomorrow will be a rare night, Marna. A rare night.' He bent forward and kissed her on the mouth.

His lips were unexpectedly soft and their touch gentle . . .

As he drew further away from Uldaneth and deeper into the trees, Farnor's darker preoccupations began to hold sway over him again. Increasingly, his anger at the futility of this whole journey was held in check only by his desire to discover more about the power that he apparently possessed. Despite this however, the aura of his surroundings began to impinge on him. The trees were larger than any he had ever seen before, massive in girth and stretching up into a canopy higher by far than he would have believed possible. And although he could see little of the sky, yet the place was remarkably light.

Such part of him as whispered in awe in the presence of such magnificence however, was the merest sigh amid the turbulence of his feelings.

After a while, he stopped and took out his lodespur. 'Which way do you want me to go?' he asked sourly.

The silence which had hovered about him for so much of his journey, changed in texture. He knew that they were close about him again, though this time the silent presence was different. It was as though some deep bass note were sounding, far below anything that could be heard. It seemed to resonate through his entire body.

'We do not understand, Far-nor,' a voice replied. It was at once similar and very different from the voice that had spoken to him before.

A caustic rejoinder began to form in his mind, but instead he said, 'Uldaneth tells me you are one and many. Perhaps those of you who are many know where they are and where I am. You brought me here to question me, but I wish to question you too, and I wish to speak to those among you who lead.'

Bewilderment washed around him, then he sensed a decision being made.

'Touch,' the voice said.

Farnor frowned.

'Touch,' the voice repeated a little impatiently. 'Touch one of the many.'

Farnor shook his head to rid himself of the plethora of complex images that formed in his mind around the word many. The meaning of the instruction, however, was quite clear. He walked to the nearest tree and rested his hand against it.

'Ah. I have him,' said a quite distinct voice that he had never heard before. Farnor snatched his hand away then, a little shamefacedly, replaced it.

'Stop that, please,' said the voice crossly. 'You're confusing

197

me. You're not the only one, you know. I've got Movers all over me and it's not easy to tell them apart. Just stay where you are for a moment.'

Farnor did as he was bidden.

'Hm. Very interesting,' the voice said after a while. 'Go across to . . .'

Farnor could make nothing of the word that followed, but his gaze was drawn to another tree some distance away.

'Bye bye,' the voice said incongruously, as he began to pull his hand away. Farnor found himself mouthing the words in reply and waving his fingers vaguely. He coughed self-consciously and walked over to the other tree. As he touched it, there was a short pause and then he heard another voice say, 'Ah, yes. Very . . . unusual.' It was speaking to someone else, he could tell, even before it said to him, in a brisk, matronly fashion, 'Go over to . . .' and he found himself being once again directed towards another tree nearby.

He travelled for quite some time in this manner, encountering a bewildering range of voices and responses, ranging from kindly affection to irritable brusqueness and including one or two that gave him an impression not dissimilar to what his own usually was on finding that he had trodden in something unpleasant.

And between these many encounters, was the distant, unheard rumble of the watching silence.

As he walked on, the trees became taller and more massive still, and the silence pervading them deeper and more profound. And though he could not see it, he could feel the looming presence of the mountain which he and Uldaneth had stood before when they parted.

'Is this the place of the most ancient?' he asked as he laid his hand on the rugged bark of the next tree.

'You will know,' came a gentle reply as he was directed again to another tree.

He began to walk more slowly. And even the horses seemed to be losing interest in their predominant occupation of grazing whenever Farnor paused. They were gazing around in a subdued manner.

The light was still remarkably good for all that he could scarcely see any sign of the sky even when he looked directly upwards. But it was growing dimmer; he was walking through a deepening gloaming. The long, straight trunks of the trees soared upwards, their size and height overawing him almost completely and robbing him of all sense of scale. Even the smallest were far larger than the largest he had seen at Derwyn's lodge. He began to imagine that he was walking through a great building: one that had been built by an ancient and wise people to celebrate some truth too profound to be expressed in mere words. Lichens and climbers patterned the trunks and long, tumbling strands of mosses hung down motionless like venerable beards. It was as though no wind had ever reached in to disturb this deep calm. The soft sound of his footfalls and those of the horses on the ancient litter seemed almost like a desecration.

When he spoke in the silence of his mind to the trees that were guiding him, he felt as though he were whispering. Eventually he stopped and gazed around. I am so small, he thought. My concerns are so trivial.

But even as these thoughts formed, his inner anger, held at bay by his encounters with the trees that had guided him here, bubbled to the surface. He had allowed himself to be brought here to learn about the power that he possessed so that he could return home and kill Rannick; avenge his slaughtered parents. He must not allow anything to distract him further from this.

'You are not ready, Far-nor.'

The voice, familiar yet unfamiliar, clear and sonorous in his mind, made Farnor start. There was judgement in it. 'Ready for what?' he demanded vehemently.

'For whatever it is you desire.'

Farnor's lip curled angrily. 'And what might that be, pray?' he asked, acidly.

The silence around him filled with distress and concern. 'We are not as you are, Farnor. We touch such as you only a little, and we understand still less. We are more apart than we are together, by far. Always the greater part of you will be beyond us, as the greater part of us will be beyond you. And what you desire lies deep, deep within you. Close to the heart of what it is to be – a Mover.'

The words filled Farnor's mind with such subtle meanings that he involuntarily lifted his hands to his head. 'If you do not know what my desire is, how do you know that I'm not ready for it?' he managed to ask after the confusion had passed.

'Because you are dangerous,' came the unhesitant reply.

'So I've been told,' Farnor said. 'But I threaten no one here, nor ever have. I wanted to leave, and *you* brought me on this journey against my will under threat of – assault.'

Farnor suddenly felt as though he were peering down some dizzying height, as he had in Marken's room. There was a slightly apologetic note in the voice when it spoke again. 'You awaken memories from the times when the sires of the sires of these . . .' – Homes? Bodies? – 'were but saplings themselves. Not since then has a Mover moved so freely amongst our worlds. And they too possessed the power . . .'

Fear and consternation broke around Farnor, though it was not his own. It stopped abruptly.

'Tell me about this power,' Farnor said, as ingenuously as he could manage.

'The power is.'

Farnor plunged on. 'But I don't understand. I know that I – see – feel – things that others don't, but I feel no power within myself. Nor can I control these feelings'

'You have strange minds, you Movers. So layered, so devious, so much torn within themselves. And so separate.'

Farnor scowled. 'Such as you can see of us,' he retorted sharply, and somewhat to his own surprise.

There was a faint hint of realization in the voice. 'True,' it conceded.

'The power,' Farnor reminded his questioner.

'The power is, Far-nor. As the sky is. As the earth is. As all things are. It is in the fabric of all things.' The voice became awed, fearful, almost. 'And such as can wield it as you can reach through and beyond, and into the worlds between the worlds. Drawing from them . . .'

The voice faded – in horror, Farnor thought; and his mind filled with images of intrusion and unfettered, unbalanced disorder, carrying terrible destruction in its wake. They were shadows of what he had felt as he had charged across the fields to his burning home, and when he had been an apparently passive witness to Rannick's fiery demonstration before Gryss and the others in the castle courtyard.

'Those who came before, in the most ancient of times, both wrought and mended such damage; both rent and sealed the fabric.'

'Why?' Farnor asked.

'It lay beyond us then, Far-nor, as it does still. They warred.

200

Like your desire, it lies deep within the heart of what it is to be a Mover.'

Farnor felt his anger stirring again. 'Why did you bring me here? If you knew enough to know that I possessed this – power – then you must have known that I was no danger to you—'

'You are a danger to all things, Far-nor.' The voice crushed his protest ruthlessly. 'Know this. Within even your short span we had felt the presence of a great disturbance. Now we learn that the unthinkable had happened. The Great Evil had wakened again, though this time It was ringed and hedged by stern foes and seemingly defeated before It could spread forth.' Momentarily the voice faltered, as if it were gathering resources with which to tell its tale. 'Yet tremors of It reverberate still. Its defeat is perhaps questionable. And it was beyond a doubt a seed of the Great Evil that pursued you here—'

'I've heard all this,' Farnor interrupted. 'Why don't you answer my question?'

There was irritation in the reply. 'It cost us dear to lead your pursuer astray, Far-nor. It had great power.' The tone softened. 'But we had touched you before, and were – intrigued – by such an unusual Hearer. And we had sensed no more evil in you than in most Movers. We protected you out of both curiosity and concern, and perhaps for reasons that are beyond us. But when you were amongst us, we felt your power growing, and we came to fear the darkness that we knew lay at your heart.' It concluded starkly, 'We were afraid.'

Farnor looked round at the great trees surrounding him.

'I mean you no harm,' he said simply. 'I wish only to be away from here.'

'No. You wish for more than that, though there is great pain and confusion in you. Yet you have the power, and while there is the darkness in you that lies beyond us, we cannot know the truth of your wishing.'

There was a long silence.

'Why have you brought me here?' Farnor asked again.

There was another long silence. Farnor felt a debate going on about him, then, 'You are to remain here, Far-nor.'

'What!'

'You are to remain here.'

'I heard that. What do you mean?'

'You are to remain amongst us until we know whether you are

what you seem, or a more subtle seed of the Great Evil come to strike at us from within.'

Part of Farnor wanted to reassure, to help, to co-operate, but a black wave of rage rose to submerge it.

'No!' he cried out, both in his mind and out loud. The two horses started, and somewhere a bird fluttered away in alarm. 'Why won't you listen to me? Why won't you believe me?'

'We have decided.'

'You can't do this. I won't allow it.' Farnor turned round and round, crouching, as if expecting human assailants to appear suddenly from amongst the vast trunks.

'We do not wish to oppose you, Far-nor. But we have no choice. If you are Its spawn, then we must hold you as best we can, no matter what the cost.' There was fear in the voice, but a greater proportion of grim determination.

Farnor saw the trees about him begin to shimmer and change. 'Get out of my head!' he roared. Desperately he seized the reins of his horse, swung himself up into the saddle, and drove his heels into the horse's flanks. The animal trembled, but did not move. He swore and kicked it again. Still it did not move.

Farnor snarled and dismounted. Looking around, he saw that his vision was clear again. But he could feel dispute all about him; restraint and tolerance mingling with fear and the need for desperate and swift action.

'Move, damn you!' he screamed at the horse, but it looked at him helplessly. With an oath he struck it viciously across the head, but still it did not move. 'Damn you all!' he screamed at the top of his voice. 'Damn you all! I will not be opposed.'

Then, it seemed to him that all the trees were bowing over and reaching down to him. He started to run.

Chapter 16

'With your permission, I'll escort you back to your home, ma'am,' Nilsson said very politely as Marna emerged unsteadily from the spiral staircase that led down from Rannick's eyrie. As he spoke, he casually brushed his forefinger across his lips, and, with an incongruously paternal gesture, touched a wisp of her hair that was being disturbed by a draught from somewhere. Then he cast a significant glance up the stairs.

It was then that Marna realized that the persistent draught that had been ruffling her hair and causing the lanterns along the unnervingly steep stairs to flicker was more than it seemed. It was a lingering touch from her would-be lord and lover. Or, if she understood Nilsson correctly, was it perhaps a spy?

Whatever the truth, its irksome, spider's-web touch was still with her when she emerged into the now torchlit courtyard.

'See, you made the sparks fly, girl,' came the same lecherous voice that had addressed her earlier. Even as she turned to look at the speaker she saw Nilsson's arm snapping out. There was a dull, ground-shaking thud and a rasping gasp of air and the culprit went staggering backwards with considerable force until he crashed into a wall and slithered to the floor.

Marna looked up at Nilsson to thank him, but his finger touched his lips again and then flicked towards the waiting horse. The incident swept Marna's dominant concerns to one side for a moment. Nilsson's swift, yet almost casual, dispatch of the offender had struck deeply into her. Disturbingly, it had a quality about it not dissimilar to one she had often seen in her father as he practised his craft: a complete ease and effortlessness and yet an overwhelming focus of intent. She had learned something important, something she had known all her life, but she was not sure what.

They were some way from the castle before the faint breeze

that was playing about them faded away. She felt Nilsson relax, though he gave no outward sign. After that, their silence became almost companionable.

A little way from her home, Marna asked to be put down. 'I need to walk for a while,' she told him. 'You're to come for me tomorrow evening, he said.'

Nilsson nodded, but she could not see his expression in the darkness. Then he brought his horse around and gently urged it forward. Marna stood looking after him until his dark silhouette merged into the night.

'Are you all right, Marna?' The anxious voice startled her. A lantern was uncovered to reveal her father. 'I've been waiting and waiting,' he said. 'Wondering what to do. I didn't know whether to stay here. Or dash up to the castle. I didn't—'

'I'm all right, Father,' Marna said quickly, taking his arm and squeezing it reassuringly. 'Nothing happened. Nothing happened.'

Questions began to tumble out of Harlen. 'What did he want you for? What did he say? What did he do? Why—'

As they walked back towards the cottage, Marna told her father what had happened, though she said nothing about her own unexpectedly ambivalent feelings. Harlen gradually became less agitated, but as she told of Nilsson's intended visit the following evening to take her to the castle permanently, he froze.

'No!' he hissed into the darkness. 'I'll cut his throat sooner.'

Marna's eyes widened in alarm. 'Father, no, please,' she said, shaking his arm anxiously. 'Whatever happens, promise me you'll do nothing foolish. He is *so* powerful. He can do such – strange things. You mustn't even try to approach him.'

Harlen was silent.

'Promise me,' Marna demanded, suddenly stern. 'I'm not a child. I'll find a way of dealing with – whatever happens, somehow. But it'll be important to me to know that you're still here, safe. And the cottage. Please don't do anything. He'll kill you without giving it a moment's thought, I'm sure. Just like he did Garren and Katrin.'

Again Harlen did not reply, but Marna heard him taking a deep unsteady breath. Only when they reached the cottage and stepped into its familiar lighted heart did she see that his face was drawn and his eyes were gleaming wet. She could not meet his gaze.

204

'I was so afraid for you,' he said. 'I didn't know what to do. I nearly attacked that . . . Nilsson . . . when he first said what he'd come for. Then you were there, standing between us, so calm. And I thought, what good would that do? He might be dead, but the valley would be sealed, his men would be everywhere. And where could we run to? You'd be taken anyway. Then, you were riding off with him. I couldn't move. I felt so useless, so . . .' His voice faded away. 'I'm sorry, Marna,' he finished weakly.

Pity overwhelmed her and she put her arms around him. 'Don't be, don't be, you couldn't have done anything,' she said, fighting back tears. 'You've always looked after me, and you've brought me up to look after myself as well. We'll manage between us, somehow. All that's really important now is to stay alive. We've seen enough of what he can do to know we can't deal with him like a normal person. There has to be another way. And we'll only find it if we keep watching and listening.'

They stood for some time in silence, each supporting and sustaining the other. Then Harlen gently pulled Marna's arms from around him and straightened up. 'You put me to shame, daughter,' he said. 'Your mother would've been proud of you. But I don't know if I can sit idly by while that man comes to collect you tomorrow – like just another piece of furniture.'

Unexpectedly the comparison made Marna laugh, though it was a strained and humourless sound. 'Rannick has some – affection – for me, Father,' she said. 'I think I—'

'I know what he has for you well enough, girl,' Harlen replied bluntly before she could finish.

Marna held up her hand to prevent him continuing. 'Yes, and I know that, too,' she said. 'But I told you, I'll manage somehow, if I know all's well here.' She faltered, and her lower lip trembled momentarily. 'There are women up there putting up with far worse right now. Women far from home who don't even know what's happened to their men, or worse, have probably seen them killed. I'll manage, I know.' Her face became determined. 'And it will bring me close to him. Closer than anyone else could possibly be. Opportunities will arise.'

Harlen lifted his hands as if to sweep aside the implications of what he was hearing, then they fell limply by his side. 'We're trapped, aren't we?' he said.

Marna sank into a chair. 'Yes,' she said starkly. She gripped the arms of the chair to prevent her hands from shaking. Harlen caught the movement. He knelt down beside her, urgently. 'No, Father,' she said, looking with wide eyes into his distraught face and reaching out gently to fend him off. 'No more. Don't touch me again. Just let me know that you'll be here, like you've always been, ready to pick up the pieces.'

Harlen looked at her steadily for a long time, then his face tense, he stood up. 'I understand,' he said softly.

An uncertain silence hung between them until finally Harlen said, 'I'll leave you alone to get your thoughts clear. I'll go for a walk. To do the same.' He smiled slightly. 'I won't be long. And I won't do anything foolish.'

Marna nodded, unable to risk speaking. She knew that he needed to weep, somewhere out of sight and out of hearing. He wanted to rave into the night, to bend with the terrible wind that had suddenly blown through his life. Then he would be upright again, and strong. For all his gentleness and seeming weakness, he would sustain her unfailingly.

Later that night she lay in bed staring up at the familiar beamed ceiling lit by a dim lantern that, for some reason, she did not want to extinguish. Despite her best endeavours she had been unable to control and order her thoughts as she had hoped: not while she had sat alone in the house while her father grieved into the night, nor in the hours since his return.

Heading away from the castle, clinging to Nilsson's bulk, and nestling in the comfort of her father's love, she had boasted that she could cope with anything that might happen. But alone, in the quiet hours of the night, her resolve wavered. The strange, alien character of what Rannick had created both fascinated and repelled her. Nervously she twitched a strand of hair from her face as she remembered the breath that had fluttered around her head as she had left the castle. That, with its secretive intimacy, had, if anything, been worse than the eerie, dancing flames he had created.

Yet the proximity of Rannick, his will, his intention – his touch – all so focused on her, made her reluctant body ache with an unexpected need. But the images that came with the need and its fulfilling, were tainted with the cruelty that she was all too aware of: the dull-eyed women that she had seen in the court-yard; the strange response she had had to the plundered furniture in Rannick's tower room; the memory of Jeorg's beaten body, and, underscoring all, like a bloody harmony note, the brutal slaying of Garren and Katrin Yarrance.

Suddenly frantic, she swept the blankets from her and swung round to sit on the edge of her bed. Seizing her pillow, she pressed her flushed face into its cool underside. She could not do it. Whatever benefits might come to the valley by her being Rannick's woman, she could not pay the price. It was too much to ask. She did not have the courage to lie with him and to lie to him, still less to plunge a knife into him as he embraced her.

Yet how could her fate be avoided? The darkness around her would yield to the daylight, and the daylight would wear into the evening, and the solitary form of Nilsson would appear along the road, as surely as the sun would rise and set. Her chest tightened with fear as, in as many heartbeats, she lived through those hours. It tightened and tightened until she thought she would have to scream out loud for release.

Then the tension evaporated, and another, longer-held resolve reasserted itself. She tossed the pillow to one side and walked quietly across the room to a chest of drawers. Kneeling, she cautiously opened the bottom-drawer and pushed her hand underneath the neatly arranged contents. After a brief search, she took out a small bundle wrapped loosely in an embroidered kerchief. Unfolding the kerchief, she withdrew the finely made leather wallet that contained Gryss's maps and notes showing the route to the capital; the wallet that she had stolen from Jeorg's pack, having carefully substituted a handful of old rags neatly wrapped in the waxed paper.

Like Jeorg before her, she had spent a great deal of time quietly memorizing the contents of this wallet.

Farnor ran and ran. He gave no thought either to direction or destination; he just ran. He must escape from these – trees, beings, whatever they were before they could bring to bear against him whatever resource it was they possessed.

His mind rang with defiance. He should never have come to this place. He would not be bound. He would not be restrained. He would not be denied his vengeance upon Rannick and his hell-spawned familiar, or any who stood beside him.

At times, breaking through the swirling turmoil filling his mind, he Heard the voice – voices? – of the trees calling out to him. They were full of fear. Fear of the consequences of attempting to restrain him, fear of the consequences of allowing him to escape. Agonizing doubt mingled with confusion and anger and reproach.

Every part of Farnor trembled under the images of pursuit. Snarling dogs were scenting after him, foaming horses were being spurred recklessly forward, sharpened edges and points glinted in the forest light. And always the towering trees seemed to be bending forward, their branches flailing wildly down to entangle and ensnare him in an embrace that would hold him there for ever. 'Leave me alone!' he cried out repeatedly as he crashed blindly through the Forest.

Dissension washed over him furiously. Now loud, now soft, now one, now many. But he had not the wit to listen.

'He is Its spawn. He has come here to destroy us from our heart, as before.'

'No, he is a sapling, ill-formed and foolish.'

'He moves in the worlds beyond this world, and in the places between the worlds.'

Fear.

'He is a shaper, a sealer. He could make whole that which is rent.'

'And he could rend also. He could destroy us. The darkness in him is beyond our reach. We cannot know.'

'We must defeat him.'

'No. We must trust.'

'Trust in what?'

Fear returned to swamp the broken discourse. Fear of the ancient evil, the Great Evil, returned again.

There *had* been truth in the signs they had Heard. She had confirmed it. And her word was beyond any gainsaying.

Fear. Crueller than the bitterest winter.

And self-reproach at a vigilance long-neglected; at an age-spanning complacency.

And such ignorance; such appalling lack of knowledge.

And all the time, Farnor ran and ran.

'We must trust.' A resonant, persistent declamation.

Doubt.

'What can be said that has not been said? The Hearer Mar-ken judged him sound—'

Scorn. 'He has not this one's power. He is only a—'

'A Mover. And many-ringed by their lights. Skilled in their ways. However dimly, he sees where we cannot. We must trust.'

There was a sudden silence.

'And she too bade us trust.'

Realization.

Resignation.

Farnor burst through into sunlight. A rocky slope lay in front of him. With scarcely a pause he began to scramble up it.

Silence now, save for the sound of Farnor's rasping breath and his scrabbling feet as he clambered higher and higher.

'We will trust.'

'But his darkness is terrifying.'

'We can do no other. We shall watch him still. Do not despair.'

And the debate faded, dwindling fainter and fainter into an unknowable distance.

But the conclusion was unnoted by Farnor. His only need was escape. Escape from the great soaring temple of trees where their ancient spirit tried to bind him. Upwards, upwards he went, over the thinly grassed turf until it was no more and, knees and hands bruised and skinned, he was clambering over rocks.

Then he could go no further. Through his sweat-blurred vision, he saw a sheer rock face ahead of him. He fell against it. His hands came up to beat a brief and futile tattoo, then exhaustion, physical, emotional, total, seeped up through him like a black cloud, and with a plaintive, almost animal whimper, he slithered to the ground.

Silence.

Time, now, was nothing. Nor place. Nor how he had come here, nor how he would leave. Some instinct had drawn him into the lee of a long, tumbled slab that leaned against the rock face, and in this narrow lair the world had become a tight drawn, nameless knot of aching limbs and tortured thoughts, the one indistinguishable from the other.

And in the darkness dreadful things stirred. Fearful, crushed and oppressed things that had long been prowling in the shadows and which should not be shown the light, nor heard, nor felt, for fear of what would come in their wake.

Things that disturbed and distorted the sustaining, pain-branded images of the dying and dead Rannick; blurred their edges; questioned them . . .

Memories, simultaneous and separate, ordered and random, came and went. Sustaining hands and voices. Scents – of flowers, of cooking, of cattle and hay and grass, of soft embracing, and comforting clothes. And hands that tended, and mended; made whole that which was broken, made new from that which was old; repaired and healed, and nursed with tender sorrow where they could not do either; strove endlessly and without question to weave order from disorder, because that was how it should be.

Memories that ripped open and probed deep into his pain.

And through all, threading unbreakable, that which no words could encompass. That which showed, 'This is wrong, because . . .' and, 'This is right, because . . .' And too, 'This is both right and wrong, because . . . and there will be pain in the judging, but it is not to be shunned.'

Kindness and gentleness. And love: love that was not afraid to be stern and to reproach and restrain.

But mingled with this remembering came also the darkness: the anger, the hatred, the desires. They too tore and wracked, treading these gentle memories, these deep and gentle learnings, under iron-shod feet, lest they rise up and bring the light, the truth, with them.

Knees pulled tight against his chest, arms wrapped about his head, Farnor wedged himself harder and harder against the ancient rock, as if this painful immobility would halt what seemed to be rolling inexorably towards him. Yet though his body was motionless, his inner self tossed and turned, swayed hither and thither, tormented by the boiling mixture that his conflicting emotions both formed and stirred.

Faster and faster his thoughts began to whirl, a terrifying, churning conflict beyond any possibility of reconciliation or control.

Then, with a momentum like that of a tumbling boulder, the release crashed through the remains of his fading resistance, a great cry, filling his mind, filling his whole body. A great wordless cry of agony at the cruel, untimely death of his parents.

And through the breach, like vomit, poured all that had been dammed there; the guilt that he had not been by their side when they died, but tending to his own trivial concerns; guilt that he had not died with them, and guilt that he was glad that he had not died, but lived and breathed still, and did not want to die, ever. Then anger at his guilt; and familiar well-worn anger at Rannick and Nilsson and the creature, and the blind chance that had brought about their fateful alignment; and unfamiliar anger at Gryss and Marna and all his friends for not being there to save his parents, or to help him in his pain.

Then, an awful climax in this fearful torrent; bitter, choking reproach for his parents for having died and abandoned him, and shown him the wretched frailty of his own mortality. And, in its wake, yet more guilt at this treacherous betrayal of everything his parents had ever been to him.

Farnor's hands clawed at the cold, unyielding rock, his body racked with sobs, his eyes blinded, his face sodden.

The flood ebbed and flowed, but it could not be stemmed. Not one part of it took form but it came back a score of times.

But weaker . . .

And weaker . . .

Until there was only a husk, filled with a cold, black emptiness, and surrounded by a cold, black, empty night. A husk that waited and waited for it knew not what, until an older wisdom within it gave it sleep; dreamless, restful sleep, far below the wreckage of the turmoil on which such indulgence would surely have foundered.

A trembling penetrated the darkness, and with it, a greyness.

Slowly; very slowly; it came to Farnor who he was, and where he was. Cold struck through to the core of him, and wretched, dragging pain filled his joints and muscles. It focused what little consciousness he had and, with painstaking slowness, he eased each limb into life and crawled from the narrow cleft that had been his shelter for the night. As his awareness grew, so did his discomfort.

But something had changed.

He did not pursue this vague realization. Instead he concentrated on gradually, painfully bringing himself upright and attempting to rub some of the juddering cold out of his bones. His every movement felt alien, inappropriate.

He looked around at his surroundings. The sky was grey with the light of the coming dawn, and in front of him was the rock face that had barred his reckless upward progress an eternity ago. It was not so large as it had been and to one side it fell away to reveal a gentler slope. For no reason that he could clearly form, except perhaps to distance himself further from the trees, though even these now seemed to be of little import to him, Farnor turned and began slowly walking up the slope.

As he walked he gave no thought to where he was going, though vaguely he began to feel that he needed to be on a high place, where he could just . . .

He needed to be on a high place.

The journey passed unheeded, but had it been ten times the length, Farnor would not have noticed. All was a grey emptiness. Time, distance, effort, were naught.

He reached the jagged summit.

Neighbouring mountains, hidden by their fellow from its foot, now looked down upon it, bleakly indifferent.

Farnor stared out over the Great Forest, though little was to be seen except for the tops of some of the trees reaching up above a thin, damp, summer morning mist.

He sat down and dropped his head into his hands.

And waited.

Faint echoes of the dreadful turmoil of the previous night still sounded through him, reverberating to and fro. But they were distant now, no longer such a part of him. All feeling seemed to have gone from him.

Yet something had changed. His pain was different. It was the pain of healing rather than the pain of injury.

Still he waited, his head buried in his hands, staring at the rocky ground between his feet, though scarcely seeing it. Occasionally he shuddered, as his body responded to the chill that his mind was not noting.

Then a vibration ran through him that was different; finer, more delicate, longer.

And the light around his feet changed.

And there was a sound in the air; distant, but ordered.

As though he were waking from a long sleep he leaned forward into the sound, his head still bent low.

It was a horn call. Indeed, a series of horn calls. Calls such as he had heard almost every morning since he had left Derwyn's lodge, and to which he had paid no heed. Others rose out of the Forest to mingle with the first.

There was a joyous quality about them that but the previous day would have jarred and offended, stirred him to black anger. But no longer. Now the sounds passed into him unhindered, ringing, and sonorous, moving amid the grey emptiness that waited there.

The light around him grew brighter and, still gazing down, he became aware of every small detail of his soiled and scuffed boots. The sight unfolded before him their entire history, commonplace and familiar, yet poignant and intense. His vision blurred as the memories mingled with the sound of the horns and brought unforced tears to his eyes.

'Mother, Father,' he heard himself saying, softly and hoarsely, through an aching throat, and out into the morning stillness.

A warmth touched him.

He looked up.

Into the full glory of the rising sun.

He could do no other than stand as the dazzling sea of light washed over the vastness of the Forest to engulf him. His eyes blurred again, splintering the sunlight into bright, shifting shafts as tears ran down his face.

And, though they were distant, and should have been faint, the echoing horn calls became part of the light and rose up to fill his entire world with a tumultuous paean of thanksgiving; of joy at being.

And he was one with it.

'Thank you, Mother, Father,' every part of him cried out over and over.

Over and over.

Slowly, and in the natural way of things, the exaltation faded, leaving in its wake only golden echoes that would probably ring on for ever, and a young man alone on a mountain top aching and stiff, not untroubled, but more whole. And, though transformed, himself again.

Farnor held out his arms wide to embrace the risen sun.

Then he turned and began to walk down the mountain.

213

Chapter 17

Uncharacteristically, Nilsson swallowed as he took the sealed note from Harlen. It needed no great perception to read the messenger's demeanour: fear and distress radiated from him, shot through with a raging anger that was struggling against its enforced silence.

That damned girl's run away, Nilsson diagnosed. He felt his stomach churning.

Rannick's power and ambition he could live with and, with care, use to his own ends. It followed a simple, brutal logic. But a woman on the scene was like a crazed horse in a cavalry charge; capable of causing unknown mayhem. Who could say which way Rannick's dark malice would strike if he'd truly become infatuated with this stupid bitch?

Harlen's fear leaked directly into him as he fingered the letter. Whoever delivered *this* message was at no small risk. But equally, it was not a message that he could give to some underling. 'When did she go?' he demanded.

Harlen started. He had said nothing about Marna's flight, merely confining himself to delivering the letter which had greeted him when he rose that morning, together with a note saying what she intended to do and to the general effect that he should, 'Not worry, and please take this letter to Rannick.'

'I – I don't know,' he stammered. 'Sometime during the night. I was awake a long time myself, but I didn't hear her go.' Despite himself, his anger tore through. 'What in Murrel's name did that—?'

'Shut up,' Nilsson snapped savagely, but it was the look on his face that stopped Harlen. 'Your life's hanging on the thinnest of threads. Ask no questions, make no demands, if you value it in the slightest.' He looked about the courtyard, his forehead furrowed and his eyes narrowed in concentration. 'Lord

Rannick's not here,' he said, almost offhandedly. 'He went riding . . . north . . . after your daughter left last night. There's no telling when he'll be back, but it'll be this evening at the latest, I'd imagine.' He turned sharply back to Harlen. 'It's in both our interests to find your daughter and have her ready and amenable for him whenever he chooses to return.'

Harlen's jaw tightened and his eyes blazed, but Nilsson seized the front of his shirt with a single hand and, lifting him casually up on to his toes, pushed him violently against the castle gate. 'Spare me your fatherly wrath, weaver,' he said. 'I've seen it too often to waste my time discussing it other than with the edge of my sword. Understand this, Lord Rannick will have whatever he wants. And nothing you or any of us can do will stop him. He wants your daughter, and whether you're alive or dead means even less to him than it does to me. The choice is yours. Stay silent and helpful, and perhaps you'll be there for her when he's finished. Argue the point, and you certainly won't. Now, where's she likely to have gone? The valley can't have that many hiding places.'

'She's not in the valley, damn you,' Harlen shouted, shaking himself free from Nilsson's grip. 'She's gone over the hill. I've no idea where she is.' He retrieved a crumpled paper from his pocket and thrust it under Nilsson's face.

Nilsson took it and read it. Harlen stepped back, appalled by the emotions that surged into Nilsson's face and by the ruthless cruelty that crushed them.

'She's gone to the capital?' Nilsson asked rhetorically. 'Gone to tell the king about us?' He held up the sealed letter. 'And she's told Lord Rannick as well? Is this some kind of a joke?'

Harlen shook his head. 'I doubt it,' he replied unnecessarily. 'She knows there's nowhere to hide here. And she's taken plenty of food and clothing.'

Again a range of emotions fought for control of Nilsson's face, and again he crushed them until he was left with a vicious, humourless grimace, his lips curled to reveal his clenched teeth. He looked at Harlen. 'I've seen things and faced dangers that you couldn't begin to imagine, weaver. And I can't begin to tell you what I feel at having my life jeopardized by some ignorant farm girl who's so stupid she thinks she can escape from this valley, and, even stupider, leaves a note saying what she's going to do.' Then, menacingly, 'I presume you've had no part in this?'

Harlen quailed at the restrained fury in Nilsson's voice, and though somehow he held his ground, he could not reply except to shake his head weakly. Contrary to Marna's instructions, he had in fact spent some time searching for her, shocked and stunned, and then he had delayed even longer before carrying her message to the castle. In the end, however, he had realized that he had been left with no alternative but to deliver the message. And, in honesty, despite his love for his daughter, and his distress at her sudden, foolish flight, he had not been without some reproach for her for leaving him in that position.

Now, however, he could do no more. He was frankly relieved that Rannick was away, envisioning more accurately than his daughter what his probable response would be. And, for the rest of this day at least, he had a common interest with this foreign captain. Though he could not have admitted it, he felt the strange companionship of the co-conspirator.

'Saddre! Dessane! To me!' Nilsson's booming voice rose above the noise in the courtyard. Within minutes, some twenty or more riders burst through the castle gates and galloped off towards the village.

Harlen, waiting, forgotten, watched them until they were out of sight, his face unreadable. Then he turned and began to walk after them.

Marna breathed a sigh of relief. She was through. She dropped down on to the ground heavily and leaned back against a tree. As Gryss had suspected, Marna had been quietly plotting 'some foolishness', for some time. She had studied the maps and notes that she had stolen from the bottom of Jeorg's pack and, accompanying her father on his trips downland she had reacquainted herself with the now heavily guarded terrain that had once been her solitary childhood playground.

Jeorg had ventured to leave the valley in cautious openness, hoping to be able to plead his way out should he be challenged. Marna planned for complete concealment. Dull, colourless clothes hid her in the palely lit night, and would help to conceal her too, in the daylight. A carefully acquired knowledge of the routines of the men who guarded the valley told her that only a few would be abroad patrolling so late. This, coupled with their not being truly prepared for anyone trying to escape, her own knowledge of the terrain, and her grim, fear-driven determination, carried her successfully along stream beds, though shrub and fern, over rocky outcrops, until finally she had passed around the guarded line and reached the woods that fringed the valley's sides. Now, surely, only ill-fortune, or gross carelessness on her part would see her captured.

The thought reminded her that she was still quite close to the guarded line and she allowed herself only a few minutes' respite before she clambered to her feet and cautiously set off again.

She looked up through the trees. The sky was greying a little. Soon it would be dawn, then her father would wake to find her message. She felt an uneasy twinge about the errand she had left him, but she did not dwell on it. She must do what she had to do. Someone had to reach the capital and bring some form of lawful retribution down on Rannick and these people, and she could do it, she knew. Besides, fathers were invulnerable, weren't they?

She shook her head as the memory of Garren and Katrin Yarrance threatened to return, and strode out as quickly as the darkness and the need for silence would allow.

She pondered the journey ahead of her as she walked. There was no way of knowing how far abroad Rannick's depradations had been carried, but if she used the night for the greater part of her journeying and the daytime for careful sheltering and rest, she must surely come eventually to a place that was beyond his reach, and then what could possibly prevent her from reaching the capital?

She looked up at the greying sky again. Each step she made was carrying her further away from Rannick and Nilsson and it would be a long time after daybreak before her father could deliver her letter and some form of search for her be set in train. She must make the most of this interlude.

After a while, she paused and looked back. She was far enough away from the guards not to be too concerned about travelling quietly. All she had to do now was walk, and listen for any kind of pursuit coming along the road below. Then, and only then, need she consider searching for somewhere to conceal herself for the day.

She strode out, through the lightening wood.

She was still striding purposefully forward when something wrapped around her ankle and brought her crashing down heavily. As she struggled desperately to regain her breath, she felt the grip on her ankle tightening.

'Well, well. What have we here, charging through the trees and

217

disturbing our sleep?' said a voice.

Startled by the voice, Marna kicked out violently with her free leg. She struck something and there was an oath as she was abruptly released. Still gasping for breath, and encumbered by her pack, she scrabbled awkwardly to her feet.

At the same time, two figures rose up out of the shadowy ground. 'You should look where you're going, my friend,' said one of them. The accent was strange. Whoever was speaking was not from the valley, but neither was he one of Nilsson's men. Apart from a note of irritation in the voice, Marna took some reassurance from this.

'First you barge into our little camp, making us think you were a bandit or suchlike. Then you nearly kick me in the face.'

'I'm sorry,' Marna gasped, as she flexed her ankles and legs, instinctively testing for damage after the winding fall. 'Who are you?'

There was no immediate reply, but she could make out the two figures turning to look at one another in the gloom. 'Who are we?' came the mimicking, high-pitched echo, after a moment. 'Bless me if we haven't stumbled upon a lady, no less.'

'No, no. She stumbled on us, don't forget.'

'True. True.' There was a pause. 'I thought that ankle felt – interesting.'

There was a short, unpleasant laugh, then. 'Talking about – feeling . . .'

'Who are you?' Marna asked again, sufficiently recovered from her fall now to begin to be frightened by the tone of the conversation she was hearing.

'Just two travellers come to join Lord Rannick's army. We were spending a cold, lonely night in the woods until—' The figure shrugged and came a little nearer.

'But who are you, my dear, wandering the woods all alone?' he asked.

'I'm not alone,' Marna said, increasingly alarmed. 'And I'm one of Lord Rannick's women.'

But on the instant, she knew that the tremor in her voice had exposed the lie in this announcement. There was another short pause in which the two men seemed to consult one another silently, then they stepped forward simultaneously. A hand was clamped across her mouth, and she felt hands grasping for her legs, seeking to destroy her balance and bring her down again.

She lashed out wildly and staggered backward. In the mêlée, her pack slipped off her back on to the floor and one of the men went sprawling over it. The other, however, still held her firmly and she found herself being spun around roughly. A stunning slap across the face exploded in her head and sent her reeling.

A terrible fear rose up inside her. She had never been struck before – not like that – not with malice and power and awful, focused intent. She remembered Nilsson felling the man in the courtyard, and knew now how he had felt. The strings of her adulthood began to unloose and childhood began to reassert itself.

As she floundered under the numbing impact of the blow, she was seized from behind, powerful arms pinioning hers by her sides. Ironically, the continued assault galvanized her. She began to struggle violently.

There was a grunt of effort from her captor as he tried to restrain her. 'Whack her again, she's strong, this one,' he gasped to his companion.

Marna saw the figure in front of her draw back his arm. Yoked together, fear and anger screamed defiance. She wouldn't be hit like that again! Wildly, she lashed out with her foot in the general direction of her attacker's groin. Insofar as she had been aiming, she missed, but her stout walking boot connected solidly with his knee.

The man cried out and staggered backwards, swearing foully. His partner tightened his grip around Marna, making her gasp with pain. 'You all right?' he called out breathlessly.

A further stream of abuse greeted this enquiry as the injured man crouched low, hugging his knee. 'I'll teach you, you bitch,' he concluded, straightening up slowly.

As he limped towards her, Marna saw the glint of a knife blade in the growing light. A pounding terror rose to paralyse her, like a rabbit before a stoat. In the far distance she was aware of a voice calling out, 'No. Don't spoil her. We can do that after.'

The man with the knife hesitated, and Marna felt waves of gratitude towards her captor mingling with her terror. Then the man took another step forward. He lurched violently as his injured knee gave way under him. His hesitation vanished and the clear intent that rang in his cry of pain and fury brought Marna back vividly and brutally to this dawn-lit woodland and what lay ahead for her.

The knife drew nearer, with wilful, taunting slowness.

Marna began to struggle even more frantically than before. Then, as the knife was drawn back, she made a desperate final effort, and by blind chance did what any trained fighter would have told her to do. Her heel crashed down on to the foot of the man holding her, and her head jerked back viciously, hitting him full in the face. The grip on her slackened and with fear-bred strength, she twisted away from the lunging knife. Her arms came up wildly and she collided with the advancing attacker as she found herself staggering forward, suddenly free. Stumbling to her knees, she landed on her pack. In the midst of the tumbling horror of what was happening, the familiar contact was incongruously reassuring.

There was a strangled cry behind her, and as she clambered to her feet she saw the two men bending low and staring at one another. The knife-wielder turned towards her. She could see his eyes, wide and savage. His mouth gaped to form a silent scream.

Without thinking, she swung her pack at him as he lurched towards her. It did not strike him particularly hard, but it unbalanced him and he fell to the ground with a cry of rage and pain as once again his knee collapsed. The knife bounced from his hand.

Unbalanced herself by her effort, Marna tumbled almost on top of him. Arms and legs flailing, she rolled away, intent now on seizing the fallen knife. As her hand closed about it, a great weight fell across her, forcing her face into the soft, damp forest litter. She gagged as she felt twigs and clinging soil being pushed into her mouth. Powerful hands twisted her over on to her back and she looked up to see her attacker sitting astride her, in a dreadful mockery of a childhood wrestling game. His weight crushed the breath out of her.

Then, those same powerful hands closed around her throat, thumbs hard, purposeful and practised, against her windpipe. All thoughts left her as a choking blackness instantly swept over her, but a screaming reflex thrust her hands upwards in an attempt to beat off this fearful assault. There was an interminable, timeless, moment, then the awful blackness was gone. Through her trembling, painful breathing, Marna saw light. As her vision cleared, she made out her attacker. He was still astride her. But he was motionless.

And there was something else . . .

On her hands. Warm. Unpleasant.

Slowly her eyes moved from the figure above her to her hands. Her face contorted in horror. One of the hands that had thrust up to beat off that final, murderous attack had held the knife. She felt it in her hand, but she could not see it. It had passed upwards, underneath the man's ribcage, killing him almost immediately. Blood was running dark down her hands.

She could not release the knife.

As she watched, the now untenanted form above her toppled very slowly to one side. With her grip still reflex-tight around the handle of the knife, Marna was drawn upwards by it, until with a blood-spurting sigh it tore free from the body, and she dropped on to one elbow. The corpse rolled away from her and lay still like a spent lover.

Marna was shaking uncontrollably. Something in her mind was crying out to warn her that this was not yet finished. She struggled to listen to it, knowing that it was important.

The other man!

She jerked her head around in sudden fear of a renewed attack. He was there! Only a few paces away. Leaning against a tree, and staring at her.

With a strange, animal whine, Marna scrambled desperately to her feet and, retreating, levelled the shaking knife at him. But he did not move. Then she saw that he was clutching his side, and a broad stain was colouring his loose, ragged tunic. Realization dawned. He must have received the knife blow intended for her when she fought free.

They stared at one another for a long moment, then the man, grimacing with pain, and his eyes fearful, turned and staggered off into the trees on a path that would carry him down the side of the valley and towards the road.

Marna stood staring after him for a long time after he had disappeared. She was motionless, except for the trembling which was still racking her. Then, with a cry of disgust, she spat the bitter twigs and leaves from her mouth and, dropping to her knees, vomited violently.

As the retching spasms faded, so others began, and she began to sob equally violently. At intervals she gasped, 'I'm sorry,' to the corpse of her would-be murderer. She crawled to his side and knelt by him, the knife still in her hand; for some reason she still could not let it go.

How long had it all taken? Perhaps only seconds, she thought. And how was it possible that so much could change so quickly? For many things *had* changed. For one, her carefully planned journey to the capital was in ruins. She was a practical woman. She had allowed for fatigue and discomfort, for hunger and thirst, for weather, bad and good, but she had not allowed for events such as this; dangers from other people who were not Rannick's people. Such people would have been friendly and helpful, because that's the way people were. Now it came to her that Nilsson's band might perhaps be no more than the vanguard of a great army of such people, scattered all over the land.

And, too, was gone her confidence in her own ability to complete her journey. That was the truly appalling loss, and the one that most of her tears mourned. Part of her knew her for a foolish young girl, whose reckless actions would probably bring great harm to her father and perhaps many others in the valley when Rannick found out that she had fled. And too, they had led her to the killing of a man.

And in her folly she had told Rannick what she was going to do! She drew in a sour breath through clenched teeth and looked up at the brightening sky. Was there no folly of which she was not capable? She should run back to her father, ask his forgiveness. Ask – no, beg – Rannick's forgiveness. Be strong by remaining in the valley and being close to him. Whatever he did to her could be no worse than her two assailants had intended. There was at least some affection in him, and who could say how he might change under her influence?

Yet still, another part of her told her that she was alive; that she had fought back against greater strength and prevailed. And that not only could she complete this journey, she must. How else could Rannick be stopped? For stopped he must be. Affection or no, he was a murderer, and he drew his own kind to him, like an open sore drew infection.

As the word murderer came to her however, she looked down at the bloodstained knife in her hands. Again, her response was disturbingly confused. She should throw the hideous, life-stopping thing away. Yet she knew that it was no more than an artifact. She was the life-stopping thing, not it. And she might well need a good knife again on this journey . . .

Her mind cleared quite suddenly, as if a cloud had moved from in front of the sun. And indeed, as her way ahead formed itself

222

anew, long, bright shafts of sunlight began to cut through the wooded gloom, transforming it into a myriad greens and browns, shot through with the yellows and reds of countless woodland flowers. She began to hear the birds singing.

She looked down at the dead body. She could not leave it lying there; it was unthinkable. The forest creatures would . . .

She turned away from the thought.

Yet she could do no other than leave it.

Her resolution finally determined, she was about to stand up when a noise made her turn. She drew in a long, trembling breath, and the knife slipped from her hand.

Moving slowly towards her, ominous and long-shadowed in the dusty, leaf-dappled rays of the rising sun, were four riders.

Chapter 18

'Of the true beginning, the beginning of the time that was before this time, nothing is truly known, though we sense that the world that was then is remembered, albeit dimly, at the heart of our knowledge. And too, by some others, though they are strange, and elsewhere.

'But from the forming of this time, from the time of the fading of the great heat and the great remaking, we remember much. The shaping of the valleys and the mountains by those who were formed of the essence of the beginning, we remember. The filling of the rivers and the lakes and the oceans, we remember. The coming of the Movers in their many forms, we remember.

'And the Great Evil, we remember. For that, too, was of the essence of the beginning.'

There was a long silence. Many of the words that came to Farnor were so hung about with subtle shades of meaning that he could scarcely begin to grasp them. He could grasp the pain and distress permeating them, however, and he made no interruption.

'And there was great suffering. Amongst ourselves, and the Movers of every form. Even the land itself was torn and racked. And the air and the seas and all the waters. All were tainted and foul. But perhaps above all, the greatest suffering was among the vast tribes of Movers such as yourselves, for such was the form that the Great Evil had chosen in which to exercise Its will.'

'Because that was Its true form from the time before the beginning,' Farnor said. It was part statement and part question and he could not have said from where the idea came.

There was a pause, heavy with shock and wonder which gradually turned into awe. 'You Hear further into our meanings than we could have believed possible, Far-nor.'

Farnor did not reply, but simply waited for the tale to continue. He stroked his horse's head gently, still remorseful at having struck it in his angry frustration and fear. His first act on returning down the mountain had been to ask the animal's forgiveness.

The voice continued. 'That is indeed a most ancient belief, though it is not truly known, and what we speak of here, *is* truly known.

'And it *is* known that the Great Evil was overcome. Overcome utterly by a Great Alliance of many powers. Overcome for ever, it was thought, though Its taint was spread wide and deep, touching all things, and ever to be seen by those who chose to look.

'Now, what had been, of late, little more than a suggestion of dark happenings far away, a deep unease, has been revealed to us as a terrible truth. The Great Evil has come again, even within the span of your brief life, Farnor. Come, and been confronted, and overcome again.'

Farnor frowned slightly, there was such fear in the voice that he had no wish to make light of this revelation, but he could ask no other than, 'If It's been overcome, why are you concerned?'

The fear flooded into his mind, primordial and terrible. It forced a sharp breath into his lungs, and his hands came to his ears as if in some way that would end this silent distress. And there was another fear, deeper yet, far deeper. 'What was that?' he gasped, horrified.

The fear vanished, to be replaced by regret and dismay. But there was no reply. Then he sensed again a debate being held somewhere away from him. 'Tell me,' he demanded, intruding into it forcefully. 'Share this with me. Or do you now consider ignorance to be preferable to knowledge?'

The debate ended, though there was great reluctance in the voice when it spoke again. 'You must understand, Far-nor, this is not known. It is – sensed – felt. But deeply, for all that.'

Farnor waited.

'It is thought that that which ended the time before and formed this one was – flawed. That in the remaking of that which had been, an error was wrought, an error so deep that it may doom us all unless some great wisdom is found to repair it.'

'I don't understand,' Farnor said.

'Nor do we. But thus we feel, and thus we have now told you.' The voice became almost casual, anxious to return to matters of more pressing moment. 'And until we *know*, then there can be no righting such an error, so we should not concern ourselves with it.'

'But—'

'No, Far-nor. You asked and we answered. But this – fear – this great doubt – may be no more than idle fancy, for all it is deep-rooted and ancient.' Farnor made to interrupt again, but the voice overrode him. 'And if it were not idle fancy but cruel truth, then it would be a task well beyond your means to undertake, sapling. Or, for that matter, ours, unaided.' The voice faded a little, suddenly pensive. 'Though, perhaps indeed we are already undertaking it. Perhaps as we each tend to those problems that confront us, we are fulfilling some greater need.'

For an instant Farnor felt a sense of revelation all about him, and indeed, there were tinges of excitement in the voice when it spoke again. 'But, whatever the reason, we must face what we must face, here and now, with what allies come our way. We must survive the moment if we are to survive the whole, mustn't we?'

Farnor however, was given no time to answer.

'And the moment we face is grim enough,' the voice continued, sweeping on now. 'Why are we concerned that the Great Evil came again if It has once again been overcome, you asked. True, whatever happened was far away, and, by our lights, brief.' The voice became grim and dark with meaning. 'But we cannot begin to give you the true measure of what the Great Evil was, Far-nor, nor what Its defeat cost. Nor would we wish to. But you have had some small measure already in Hearing of our darkest fears. Long-forgotten fears, brought anew to us by the merest hint of Its being amongst us again.

'And Its recent defeat is perhaps not as certain as has been believed. That which pursued you here is ancient and of Its making, beyond a doubt. But there is another. A Mover. As you are, powerful but, unlike you, deeply tainted with Its touch. Touched by Its spawn, he has arisen from nothingness, like a ringing echo, crying out in faithful copy of the terrible sound it has heard.'

'Rannick,' Farnor said simply.

'He is beyond all help that we can give. But he must be – restrained.'

Farnor did not reply for a moment as a reproach formed in his mind: That's what I was going to do when you brought me here. But he left it unspoken. It was a lie. His intention had not been restraint, it had been mindless murder; an act perhaps worse than Rannick's in that, had he succeeded, it would have betrayed all that his parents had meant to him.

Now, though he could not deny that a strand of bloody vengeance still rose from some dark source deep within him, to weave serpentine, through his thoughts, it was but one of the many that formed the pattern of his present intentions. They were far from clear, but he knew that, if possible, Rannick should be confronted and defeated so that he could be brought to account for what he had done before some ordered forum of law. He should be allowed the opportunity to speak for himself, to turn away from his present course, to make some attempt at righting that which he had marred.

In that need however, Farnor's intentions came full circle. For he knew Rannick too well. Touched as he had been by his appalling familiar, Rannick could no more be returned to his old self than a full-blooming flower could be made a solitary bud again. His malice and desire came from the same dark depths as Farnor's bloodlust, but they were wholly unfettered and ruled him utterly.

'Rannick can neither be restrained nor contained,' he said. 'He must be given choice, but I fear his very nature determines his destruction.'

'He is your kind. That knowledge lies beyond us. The power is yours. The judgement is yours.'

Farnor looked up at the silent trees. 'Yes,' he said, tears coming to his eyes unexpectedly. 'I couldn't protect my parents as they had protected me. But to honour them I must try to – restrain – him, or at least protect those who lie across his future path.'

His lust had become his duty. It was no joyous realization.

'But I know nothing of this power I have; neither what it is nor how to use it. Will you help me?' he asked, almost plaintively.

'We cannot,' came the stark reply. 'It is a power, a gift, close to the heart of a Mover. Like the knowledge that orders your judgement in this, it is beyond us.'

Desperation began to seep into the quiet euphoria that Farnor had brought with him down the mountain. 'Then who can?' he asked.

'None here,' the voice answered, though Farnor caught a fleeting glimpse of Uldaneth in the words. It vanished instantly, however, leaving him knowing only that, in some way, Uldaneth's task was more important even than his. And it lay elsewhere.

'Then what can I do?' he asked, memories returning to him of his frantic dash across the fields towards his destroyed home, and his terrified flight through the forest. 'Rannick and the creature are far more skilled in the use of their power than I am.'

'Not so. Not now. You are not what you were. Much of the darkness is gone from you. You are freer than you were, and your true self can guide you more now. And you are indeed well rooted. Mar-ken judged you well, and we were right to aid you.'

Farnor left his considerable doubts unspoken, and mounted his horse. He looked about him, and then began searching through his pockets for his lodespur.

'We will guide your Mover,' the voice said.

There was a strangeness in the word Mover that made Farnor frown in puzzlement until he sensed an image of his horse in it. 'Oh, the horse is a Mover too, is it?' he said. 'I thought it was just people you called Movers.'

Amusement filled him. 'Your separateness breeds such arrogance, Far-nor. There are many Movers, large and small. They fly, they crawl, they walk. Where we are here, they live in us, on us, under us. They feed off us, they serve us. They protect us, and sometimes they destroy us, but that is the way of this place and they do this to return us to ourselves. We touch each in different ways. People, as you call them, are but one such.'

The perspective disturbed Farnor. 'Brighter than most, I hope,' he said defensively.

'Oh yes. And darker than most too. As you yourself said, perhaps your form is the true form of the Great Evil.'

Suitably diminished, Farnor urged his horse forward. Without any further instruction from him, and to his considerable surprise, it set off at a gentle trot.

Riding the horse thus was a strange experience, and it took Farnor some time to get used to it. After a short while, however, he reined the horse to a halt and dismounted. He gazed around at the great trees towering above him. Their majestic, silent stillness permeated him, making him, for a timeless interval, one of them. One and many, and truly vast. And without end, through all time. 'Thank you,' he said softly, as he gradually became himself again.

228

'Thank *you*, Farnor,' the voice replied. 'It has been so long since such as you has moved amongst us. You awaken memories that should not have slept, and you have renewed and deepened our insight into the nature of what it is to be a Mover. And other things.' A great sorrow came into the voice. 'We understand a little better, your own darkness now – your pain at the striking down of those you call your parents.' Then, with a poignancy that Farnor could hardly bear, 'Your separateness is truly a terrible thing. It is small wonder that at times your kind are so demented.'

The voice did not speak again for a long time. The horse, guided by commands that Farnor could not hear, carried him steadily south, sometimes walking, sometimes cantering, but must of the time just trotting. With some considerable regret Farnor moved away from the place where the trees were most ancient, passing over the knoll where he and Uldaneth had parted, and thence the small clearing where he had been camping when they met.

He frowned as he remembered that encounter. Amongst other things, he had forgotten to find out how she had managed to throw him so far so effortlessly. He remembered her chuckle. 'I didn't. You did,' she had said. He swore to himself. He had missed something important there. He should have asked. But then he should have asked Uldaneth many questions, he realized. Still, that was a long time ago. And something that happened to a different person. Even so – he'd have to think about that throw. And he wished she were here now.

As he was carried through the Forest, Farnor began to see for the first time the true splendour of the place. Not only the trees which, though lacking that quality that marked the most ancient, were nonetheless huge and majestic in their own right, but also the countless flowering shrubs and the rich, teeming undergrowth, the whole shot through with bright dappling sunshine, dancing to the endless rhythm of the wind-stirred branches.

And he could do no other than stop and gaze in wonder at the flower-lined banks and clearings which burst upon him from time to time. He remembered Gryss's gentle reproaches about the yellow Sun's Eyes that bloomed outside his cottage. 'How many petals do the flowers have? What shape are the leaves?' and so on, concluding with, 'Not looked at them as much as you'd thought, have you?' It was such a long time ago. And so true.

'No,' Farnor mouthed softly to himself. 'But I'm beginning to now.'

Although the horse was making no great haste, Farnor knew that his progress was quicker by far than when he had been travelling northwards. There were fewer places where he had to dismount and walk the horses, fewer detours around heavily overgrown areas, fewer places full of cold, dank shadows.

It came as little surprise to him therefore when, the following day, he found himself riding into the lodge that had greeted him so sullenly on his outward journey.

Somewhat to his alarm however, there was a large crowd waiting to greet him this time. He reined his horse to a halt and looked at them uncertainly.

A figure detached itself from the group and came towards him, an elderly, frail-looking man. 'I am Marrin Beechstock, Hearer to this lodge,' he said, as he reached Farnor. He held out both hands.

Farnor nodded an acknowledgement, still warily eyeing the crowd blocking his way.

Marrin shrugged apologetically. Farnor looked at him carefully. His eyes were bright with exhilaration. Farnor smiled as he recognized the expression. 'They've spoken to you about me, haven't they?' he said.

Marrin's head came forward and his hands shook excitedly. 'As never before,' he said, briefly a young man again. 'Marken's messages hinted at it, but . . .' He waved his hands ecstatically and made no effort to finish what he was saying.

'What do you – they – want of me?' Farnor asked, indicating the waiting crowd.

Marrin looked a little guilty. 'Just to offer you food, and anything else you might need for your journey. And our apologies for the way we greeted you when you passed through before.'

Farnor nodded. 'It was a wise greeting, I fear. I wasn't fit company for any civilized hearth.'

He dismounted and gripped Marrin's arms. The Hearer returned the gesture. Farnor remembered just in time to tense his arms to resist the inevitably powerful grip. There was some applause and cheering from the crowd, which immediately surged forward and surrounded them both. Marrin, however, smiling broadly, beat them back. 'We must remember that our guest is on an important journey,' he shouted. 'We mustn't delay him. Give him your gifts and then let him be on his way.'

Before he could offer any resistance to this suggestion, Farnor found himself the recipient of several baskets laden with bread, pies and fruit, and bottles. 'Just water,' Marrin said paternally. 'We know you'll be needing your wits about you. And you're already quite a faller from what we've heard.'

Farnor could do no other than laugh at the old man's tone. The action felt strange to him, almost hurting his face. 'I'm afraid I am,' he agreed, as he turned to the packhorse and began searching for space for the gifts.

The crowd, happy and smiling, milled around him, holding things for him, offering him things, and generally making his task last twice as long as it would have if he had been left alone. Several times he had to pause while he was introduced to various people, whose strange names he immediately forgot, and several times, too, he had to bend low in order to let young children touch his black hair before they ran away giggling.

Eventually, however, he finished. The crowd parted as he mounted, but just as he was about to move off, Marrin emerged again. He was holding a staff. 'Take this, Farnor,' he said. 'It's good ash. Tight, straight grain. Very strong. Very old. It might even have come from . . .' He left the sentence unfinished, but inclined his head significantly towards the north. 'It's been in my family for years.'

The last remark made Farnor withdraw his hand from the offered staff. 'You've all been very generous to me,' he said. 'But I can't take this if it's precious to you. I may never be back here.'

Marrin shook his head, and thrust the staff under a strap on the packhorse's back. 'Take it,' he said briskly, slapping the pack. 'Let's have no foolishness, sapling. It's only a good sturdy staff. And you being such a faller and all . . .' He pursed his lips and looked knowingly at Farnor. 'Besides,' he said. 'You'll be back. Without a doubt.'

His manner allowed no argument, and Farnor gave a rather self-conscious nod of acceptance. Then, as he was searching for the words with which to make an appropriate farewell, his horse set off without any command, obliging Farnor to grab the reins hastily and bring it to a halt. 'A moment, if you don't mind,' he said indignantly, but silently, to the trees. A faint air of apology surrounded him and the horse became still again. He turned to Marrin. 'They're anxious for me to be on my way,' he said.

231

'Yes, I can feel it,' Marrin replied, excited again. 'I'm sorry you can't stay. I've so many questions to ask you.' A look of sadness passed briefly over his face but with a little shake he transformed it into a smile. 'But there'll be some other time, I'm sure.' He slapped Farnor's horse. 'Travel well, Hearer. As Uldaneth would say, light be with you.'

The horse set off again, walking for a little way, then breaking into a trot. Farnor turned in the saddle and waved to the watching crowd.

As he rode through the lodge, many other people appeared out of the trees to encourage him on his way, some of the younger ones running alongside him for a while. The crowd around Marrin, however, remained stationary, as if waiting for something.

Farnor had scarcely disappeared from view when Marrin's smiling face sobered. Nodding grimly to himself he raised his hand and beckoned. Several riders emerged from the trees; they were all heavily armed. At another signal from Marrin, they turned and rode in the direction that Farnor had taken.

Spared much of the effort of his journey by the silent guidance being given to his mount, Farnor found himself almost hypnotized by the steady drumming of its hooves over the forest turf. The release he had found on the mountain was still with him, but though much of his inner torment had gone, the way ahead remained ominous and forbidding, and he was reluctant to dwell on it too deeply.

But it could not be avoided. Each step of the horse took him nearer to whatever destiny lay in wait for him and when he considered his position it gave him no comfort. Now, despite the pain he felt at the loss of his parents, and his determination to see that some kind of justice was done, he had no desire to die at Rannick's hands – and still less at the jaws of that fearful creature – as a result of some reckless confrontation. The lofty declarations he had made when he returned down the mountain seemed to be increasingly hollow as vivid memories of his beating by Nilsson and his pursuit by the creature returned to give him a measure of his skill as a fighter. It was a measure that turned his stomach to lead.

'You must help me,' he said eventually to the trees. 'Tell me what you *do* know about the power that Rannick has, that I have.

You speak of worlds between worlds, but I've had only giddy visions of what you mean. Tell me clearly.'

There was an amused despair in the voice that answered. 'I would if we could, Farnor,' it said. Despite his grim preoccupation, Farnor smiled as he noted the return of the confusion between the one and the many now that he was some distance from the place of the most ancient.

'What are these worlds of yours that I – walk – in, then?' he asked.

'They are what they are,' came the unhelpful, but apologetic reply. 'You are there now. They lie at the edges of the world where we are many. And because we are many, and there, we have the strength to reach them to become one. But how you reach them to be with us, is beyond us.'

At the edges of the world? Farnor frowned. The words made no sense to him, nor did the strange, flickering images that hung about them. He returned to his first question. 'The worlds between the worlds. What are they?' he insisted. 'And why are you so afraid of them?'

'This you know.'

Farnor felt the power of the most ancient reaching out to him in this reply. The words drew from his mind his memories of the wrongness he had felt in his contact with Rannick and the creature. The wrongness of something brought to this world from another place; something that did not belong here and which, by virtue of that alone, could be ferociously destructive. There were also fleeting images of a terrible imbalance and appalling chaos, but they were torn from his mind with such force that his hand came to his head as if he had been struck. He knew that to pursue this would be futile.

'The worlds lie between the worlds. Lie in the infinite spaces between the . . .' Farnor strained for the word. Again a strange flickering pervaded it. Was it heartbeats? '. . . of this world. As we lie between the . . .' Again the word eluded him. '. . . of theirs. And they are beyond number. But they do not belong here, nor our world there.'

'But the fabric can be rent,' Farnor heard himself saying.

There was a great sigh of relief. Farnor felt again the fear of some terrible ancient and profound flaw bubbling to the surface of his mind, but again it was taken from him.

'Yes,' came the simple answer. 'But that which is torn can be

233

sealed; can be made whole again.'

'And this I can do?' Farnor asked.

'This you have done,' the voice replied.

Farnor recognized the truth in this declaration, and the memory of his inadvertent interference with Rannick's fiery demonstration in the courtyard returned to him. As, too, did the sense of complete inadequacy that he had felt in the face of the torrent of wrongness that had swept over him as he had dashed across the fields to find his parents slaughtered and his home destroyed. What could he possibly do against such as that? 'But how?' he demanded. 'How do I do it?'

Silence.

Farnor clenched his teeth. 'You realize that I might get killed if I oppose Rannick?' he said angrily.

'We know a little of the pain of separateness, but it is not as yours. We grieve for you.'

'Thanks a lot!'

'But you will die a different, crueller death if you turn away from him. This you know too.'

There were so many meanings in this that Farnor's only response was to swear. 'I have to face him – him and that creature – on my own, then?' he asked.

There was a hint of amusement in the answer. 'You're not that separate, Far-nor. We will be there. And we will help where I can.' The amusement faded. 'But where it is Mover against Mover, you are correct. There is little we can do. But you are stronger than you know. Have no fear.'

A caustic reply began to form in Farnor's mind, but he kept it to himself. 'Fear will keep me alive,' he said, without thinking.

There was a pensive silence. 'I shall think about that,' the voice replied eventually.

Farnor rode on.

Behind him, the armed men from Marrin's lodge followed, silent as only Valderen hunters could be.

Chapter 19

Marna stood motionless, gaping at the approaching riders. For a moment, the sight of them approaching, with long, leaf-strewn shadows cutting through the sunlit air ahead of them, held her spellbound. They looked magnificent; they might have been riding straight out of some magic fireside tale by Yonas.

Only when they were almost upon her did she recover her wits. Nilsson's men!

Her heart jolted. Hastily she bent down to pick up the knife.

'Leave it, girl,' one of the riders said, stopping a little way in front of her. Marna, crouching, tightened her grip on the knife despite the command. She squinted up into the streaming light in an attempt to see the features of the speaker but she was unsuccessful. The rider seemed almost to blend with the shadows. Her thoughts raced; this couldn't be a search party looking for her, surely? Not so soon. It must be a random patrol of some kind, though she'd never noted such being undertaken before. But it didn't matter. What mattered was that she must get away. Should she slash out at this man and flee? She'd probably make better progress on foot through these trees than the others would on horseback. And they'd have to tend their injured companion, wouldn't they? Or should she stay and hover near the truth? She had been out looking for special woods for her father when she had been attacked by this man, and so on . . .

No, there were too many problems with this, she decided quickly. Too many questions to be answered later. Why was she out so early? Why was she carrying such a well stocked pack? And the maps? And, though she was too agitated to see its irrelevance, there were few woods about here that her father could use.

She would have more chance if she fled. Affecting a casualness she did not feel, she stood up.

Even as she made her decision, however, one of the other riders edged a little closer and said simply, but in a tone that was beyond argument, 'Don't.'

Marna's eyes widened in both alarm and surprise. Not so much at this seeming anticipation of her actions, but because though, like the rider who had spoken first, the voice was heavy with the accent that characterized Nilsson's men, this speaker was a woman.

She dismounted, and Marna felt herself being examined by searching eyes, even though she still could not make out the woman's features with the low sun shining in her face. The eyes moved to the disturbed ground, the dead man, and the steaming vomit.

'What happened?' the woman asked, returning her gaze to Marna. There was an unexpected gentleness in the voice.

'They attacked me,' Marna replied, without pausing to consider anything more elaborate.

'They?' There was an urgent edge to the first speaker's voice, and he leaned forward in his saddle anxiously.

'Two men,' Marna said, looking up at him. 'Outsiders. On their way to the castle. They—'

'Where's the other one?' the man demanded sternly before she could finish.

'He ran off,' Marna said. She waved a hand vaguely towards the dead man. 'He stabbed him by accident when I was struggling with him, then I did – that. Then he ran off.'

The other two riders dismounted rapidly. 'Which way?' one of them asked. It was another woman. Marna pointed. Her hand was shaking.

'There's blood here. And a trail,' said the fourth rider, a man. He was bending down by the tree that the injured man had leaned against.

There was no further talk, but the two of them disappeared silently into the trees in the direction that Marna had indicated. Their sudden departure seemed to cut through Marna's bewilderment. Questions tumbled through her mind, not the least of which was how women came to be riding with Nilsson's men, but she pushed them to one side. Whoever they were and however they came to be there, there were only two of them now. She must make her dash for freedom quickly, before the others returned.

Yet somehow she could not blindly lash out with the knife at another woman.

But she could push her into the rider. That would cause enough confusion for her to escape. And they wouldn't abandon the other horses to give chase.

As inconspicuously as she could, she took several deep breaths to steel herself to this venture.

Then, as she thought, without warning, she spun round and with a cry, hurled herself at the unsuspecting woman. The impact she anticipated, however, did not happen. Instead she found herself caught up in some way and spinning round a great deal more than she had intended. Then, abruptly, she was once more firmly pinned face downwards on the ground, gasping for breath. Before she could properly register what had happened, she felt the knife being gently prised from her grip.

A low chuckle came down to her from the rider above, and a word she did not understand, but which was plainly an oath, hissed out softly under the breath of the woman who had effected this sudden change in her posture. The chuckle became a laugh. 'Language, language, Aaren,' the man said.

Then she was being helped up. She was shaking. 'Stay where you are,' Aaren said, her voice firm but not unkind. 'No one's going to hurt you, providing you don't do anything silly like that again.' She pointed towards the dead man with the knife. 'Do you want to tell me what happened?' she asked.

'I didn't mean to kill him,' Marna blurted out.

Aaren glanced at the vomit and nodded. 'It happens,' she said, though her tone was far from casual. 'And he *was* trying to strangle you.'

'How—'

'You've got muddy handprints around your neck,' Aaren answered, before the question was asked, her hands reaching out in a motherly gesture to brush the offending stains. 'Don't fret. People who do things like that can expect to be killed.'

The strange mixture of callousness and compassion in the woman's voice seemed to unhinge Marna, and suddenly she was sobbing again, while at the same time cursing herself for her weakness.

Supporting arms lowered her gently to the ground. She covered her face with her hands. No one spoke as Marna's sobs ran their course. 'I keep thinking, maybe he had parents somewhere, a wife, children. It's awful. I can see their faces. What've I done?' she said eventually.

'Is any of this blood yours?' Aaren asked, crouching down and taking one of Marna's crimsoned hands.

A little bewildered by this question, Marna looked at her interrogator as if she had misheard, before she shook her head.

'Then you've survived,' Aaren said bluntly, returning Marna's gaze intently. 'He may well have had people unfortunate enough to love him, somewhere. But so do you, I'm sure. And I doubt you came into these woods to kill him, did you? He was the one who brought death here, not you. It was him or you. His loved ones or yours. Take a deep breath. Be glad you're alive. For yourself and for them.'

Marna turned away from her as if cold water had been dashed in her face. 'That's just – words,' she said, gasping and wrapping her arms about herself.

Aaren reached out and took Marna's face in her hands. Turning her head she looked into her eyes. 'I understand,' she said. 'Believe me, I do. You must feel as you feel. Deny nothing. But after that, words are all we've got. Be thankful at least that they're true.'

Marna met her captor's gaze uncertainly. 'Who are you?' she asked.

The return of the other two however, prevented any answer to this question. 'We couldn't catch him,' the man said. 'We'd have had to go out of the trees. But he's bleeding badly. I doubt he's going to last long.'

The rider nodded. 'Even so, we'll have to move this.' He pointed to the dead man. 'And the camp they'd made. Take it all well down, and cover the tracks. Give him the knife, Aaren. Make it look like a quarrel between the two of them. We don't want to encourage anyone to come prowling about up here.' He turned to Marna. 'You did say they were outsiders, didn't you, girl?'

Caught in a momentary spasm of self-pity, Marna snapped angrily. 'Don't call me girl.'

The two women looked up at the rider and smiled knowingly. He cast a brief glance upwards and tried again. 'They're not – Nilsson's men, are they, young woman?' he said.

Marna stared at him, her face puzzled. 'No,' she replied,

repenting her outburst a little. 'They said they'd come here to join Rannick's army.'

The rider nodded to his companions and they set about gathering together the remains of the camp. 'No, that's my pack,' Marna cried out, as the man took hold of it. He watched her as she stood up and walked towards him, arm extended. While there was no animosity in his gaze, there was a quality about him that made her want to shiver. 'Thank you,' she managed to say as she took the pack from him. Then he was picking up the dead man.

As the two disappeared once more into the trees, the man carrying his dreadful burden, Marna turned back to the rider. Increasingly bewildered by what was happening, she asked again, 'Who are you?'

'More importantly, who are you?' Aaren asked her. 'And what are you doing in the woods at dawn with a large travelling pack, when there's a perfectly good road along the bottom of the valley?'

Marna considered a variety of answers, then forced herself to ask another question. 'Are *you* with Nilsson?'

Aaren and the rider exchanged glances. 'No,' the rider replied after a pause.

'But you're from the same country,' Marna said, an inadvertent note of accusation in her voice. 'You speak the same way as he does.'

'That's nearly true,' the rider acknowledged. 'And that's why we're here. But we're not with him, believe me. Now tell me why *you're* here. It's important. We don't want to stay here too long, it's dangerous for us.'

Marna looked from him to Aaren standing beside her. Aaren nodded encouragingly. She took the chance. 'I was trying to get to the capital to tell the king about what was happening here. About Nilsson, and Rannick and – everything.'

The rider nodded. Though his face revealed little, Marna felt his approval in this acknowledgement. 'I'd like you to come with us, Marna,' he said. 'We've a camp higher up, and we could use your help.'

'I – I don't know,' Marna stammered. 'I don't know who you are or . . .' Her voice tailed off.

The rider looked at her thoughtfully then he bent forward and spoke in a kindly voice. 'You're right to be uncertain,' he said. 'Especially after what's just happened to you.' He pointed south.

'That's the way you need to go to get out of the valley. It won't be easy to reach the capital. Your . . . Rannick . . . has done a great deal of harm hereabouts, and there are a great many unpleasant people gravitating to this place as a consequence. You might be able to make it, judging by how you've handled yourself here. But it won't be easy.' He paused. 'The choice is yours, Marna. We need your help here, but if you want to go on, we'll give you what advice we can, and we've got messages of our own that we'd like you to carry to the king for us.'

Marna was torn. The encounter with the two men had shaken her profoundly, and the hint about conditions beyond the valley that she had just been given had a truthful and unwelcome ring about it. She turned to Aaren, but this time the woman's face was expressionless. 'Your choice,' it said.

The journey ahead unfolded before her, as she had so often studied it, though now the uncertainties that had hovered about it had doubled and trebled and they had an all too real vividness about them. And these people intrigued her. There was something disturbing . . . frightening even . . . about their quiet, purposeful intensity, and their seeming indifference to what had happened. And they were from Nilsson's country, without a doubt. Yet . . .?

If they'd wanted to kill her they'd have done it by now; she had no idea how she had finished up helpless on the ground after she had attacked Aaren, but she knew that she could have done nothing to prevent it.

Then her practical nature advised her that she could always sneak away from them later if need be. 'I'll come with you,' she said.

'Good,' the rider said. 'I'm glad. There's a great deal we need to know about this place and what's been happening here. Give Aaren your pack and mount up behind me.'

As Aaren cupped her hands to help her on to the horse, Marna noticed that the tip of one of her fingers was missing. It was another small question to add to those that were still tumbling around her head.

'What about your friends?' she asked, as she wriggled herself comfortable.

'They'll follow us,' the rider replied. 'And they'll hide our tracks. Don't worry.'

Marna raised her eyebrows in surprise. It had never occurred to her to consider hiding her tracks.

A little while later, after a silent and predominantly uphill journey, Marna found herself in the strangers' camp. To her, it seemed that they came upon it very suddenly, and it was only when she looked around that she realized how simply and yet how cunningly it had been hidden by the careful positioning of a few branches.

The rider introduced himself. 'I'm Engir,' he said. 'This is Aaren. The others are Levrik and Yehna.' He motioned her towards a grassy bank. 'Do you want anything to eat?'

Marna shook her head. 'I'm thirsty, though,' she said, taking the water bottle from her pack.

'Eat,' Aaren ordered, when Marna had finished drinking. An apple was thrust into her hand. 'You'll need it, you left most of your breakfast back there.'

Marna looked at the apple for a moment, her stomach rumbling, before hesitantly biting into it. Only then did she realize that she had not eaten since some time before Nilsson had made his fateful visit the previous day. She finished it noisily.

As she ate, Aaren and Engir talked, in their own language. Marna listened unashamedly, though she could understand nothing of what was said. There was a sonorous beauty about their speech that enthralled her, however. Could these people really be from the same country as Nilsson and his men? 'Why are you here?' she asked abruptly, interrupting them.

'There's a little stream just over there,' Aaren said, ignoring the question, and pointing. 'Go and clean yourself up, you look a mess.'

Slightly affronted, Marna did as she was bidden. It took her some time to wash all the blood from her hands in the cold water and she was shivering when she returned to sit on the grassy embankment. She looked at her new companions. Both of them were lying idly on the sunlit grass as though they were on some leisurely picnic. It appeared, however, that they were simply waiting for the return of their companions, for as Levrik and Yehna arrived, Marna found herself the focus of their attention. 'Tell us about Nilsson, Marna,' Engir asked, smiling. 'And this . . . Rannick . . . person we've been hearing about.'

Marna would rather they had told her about themselves first, but she could not but respond to this pleasant albeit determined asking. A little self-consciously at first, she told them what had happened since the arrival of Nilsson and his men on Dalmas Morrow. Even as she spoke, she found it hard to imagine that so much had occurred in so short a time. She also found her listeners almost disconcertingly attentive. They sat still and silent throughout, only interrupting on those occasions when she knew herself that she was repeating herself or rambling.

The atmosphere in the small camp changed as she spoke, however, becoming noticeably more uneasy particularly as she spoke about Rannick and his strange metamorphosis. And when she concluded with the details of her own decision to flee the valley, the unease became open concern.

Engir put his hand to his forehead, while the two women both spoke at once, in their own language. Levrik leaned back on the grass, but Marna could feel a tension in him.

After a moment Engir spoke to the two women and nodded towards Marna. Yehna protested a little, but Engir replied, 'No. Speak her language. If we're going to ask her to trust us, then we'll have to trust her.'

'What's the matter?' Marna asked, concerned by this sudden agitation.

'Will this Rannick come looking for you?' Engir asked.

Marna did not get an opportunity to reply. 'We must assume he will, no matter what she thinks, and act accordingly,' Levrik said.

Engir nodded. 'You're right, of course. Yehna, put on her boots, get back to where we found her and lay a false trail. Don't take too long, just' – he shrugged – 'take it up towards that escarpment we passed and lose it in the rocks. We'll move up to the lookout we set up yesterday.'

Swept along, rather than agreeing with this idea, Marna found herself exchanging boots with Yehna and, despite Engir's earlier request, surrounded by the native language of these mysterious travellers. Then Yehna was gone, and Marna was left walking with the others to some unknown destination and peering down at her temporary new boots. They were a little small for her and squashed her toes, but she could walk well enough. In fact she was not a little pleased to be wearing such fine boots. For they were indeed of a remarkable quality and beautifully made.

The observation prompted her to look at her new companions more closely. Their clothes were travel-stained but, like Yehna's boots, they were well made and of a high quality. So, too, was the equipment on the horses that they were leading. And the horses themselves were finer than any she had ever seen before.

She took hold of Engir's arm as they trudged silently along.
'Who are you?' she asked, yet again. 'Where do you come from?
What are you doing here? Why—'

'We're Nilsson's countrymen,' Engir replied, before she could
continue. 'At least Levrik and I have that dubious pleasure.
Yehna and Aaren come from a neighbouring country. But both
are a long way from here.'

'What have you come here for?' Marna persisted.

'To find Nilsson, and his men. To see if they can be brought
to account for something they did,' Engir replied straightforwardly.

Marna remembered Engir's reference to messages for the king.
'You're from the king, aren't you?' she burst out, clapping her
hands together. 'Are you' – she snapped her fingers excitedly as
she struggled for the word – 'mercenaries? Paid by the king to
free us all?' As suddenly as her hopes had risen, however, they
fell. 'What can four of you hope to do?'

Even Levrik smiled at the tone of her voice. Engir raised his
hand a little to indicate that she should not make so much noise.
'We're here with your king's authority,' he said. 'But we're not
mercenaries. We're professional soldiers owing our first alle-
giance to the peoples of our homelands. And you're quite
correct, there's very little four of us can do against Nilsson's band
as it is now.' His expression became anxious. 'Especially with this
Rannick appearing on the scene.' He fell silent, and Marna felt
loath to press him further.

Then, without any spoken command, the horses were left in a
small clearing, and the walkers continued, moving always higher
up the tree-lined sides of the valley. Eventually they stopped at
another carefully concealed camp. From this one, however, a gap
between the trees enabled them to see along the valley without
making themselves visible. Marna stared at a small, isolated
cottage in the distance until she eventually recognized it as her
home. Looking at it from this unusual vantage made her feel very
strange.

'When Yehna gets back, I'd like you to tell us about Rannick
again.' Engir's voice broke into her reverie. 'And the boy,
Farnor. The one who disappeared.'

Marna turned to him. 'He's not a boy,' she said flatly. 'He's as
near a man as makes no difference. And he's my friend.' Her face

twisted in distress but she did not weep as she added, 'And he might well be dead by now.'

Engir nodded sympathetically. 'I meant no offence,' he said, quietly. 'And I'm afraid there are many people dead in the wake of Nilsson and his men. But please tell us your story again. I know it'll be painful, but it's very important.'

Marna made no answer, but turned to look along the valley towards her home again. Engir did not press his request.

It was some time before Yehna returned, and though she thanked Marna for the loan of her boots, she took them off and put on her own with conspicuous relief, at the same time shooting a sour glance at the two men, both of whom were grinning.

Although she had been treated courteously, even kindly, Marna could not help but feel like a gawky outsider as she watched the subtle interplay between the four companions. They seemed always to know what each needed of the other, even though they rarely spoke. And there were equally subtle things about the way they moved; a studied effortlessness. Yehna, for example, was barely flushed when she returned, even though she must have walked a considerable distance.

Marna had little time to ponder these observations however, as shortly after Yehna's return, Engir looked at her significantly.

She told her tale again.

This time however, she found herself being frequently interrupted and closely questioned about various details which she had passed over as being inconsequential: what Farnor had said about his mysterious contact with the creature, what Gryss had said about the fiery column that Rannick had conjured up, and what she had felt when she saw and touched the flame in the tower room. And too, they probed into the few words that Rannick had uttered about his future plans. Only their politeness prevented her from losing her temper at this meticulous attention.

However, as her tale unfolded, she noticed as she had at its first telling that a tension began to pervade the group. Aaren spoke softly and rapidly in her own language. Engir frowned and nodded towards Marna. 'Their language, Aaren,' he said, with some reproach. 'All the time now, unless we run into difficulties.'

Aaren cast an irritable look at no one in particular, then spoke again. 'It's so,' she said, still softly, as if afraid of eavesdroppers. 'I've smelt it for days. Ever since we began to hear about this Lord Rannick. Ever since we learned that that broken troop we were closing with had suddenly miraculously recovered and begun raiding the countryside.' She levelled a finger at Engir. 'And so have you, if you'd only own up to it.'

Engir turned away from her and slapped his thighs agitatedly, as if both anxious and reluctant to deny this accusation. 'I . . .' he began, but his voice tailed off almost immediately.

'Riders.' Levrik's whisper silenced any further debate. He was pointing up the valley. The others turned to follow his gaze. It took Marna some time to see the tiny, distant dots, but when she did, she stood up and craned forward to get a better view. Yehna gently pulled her down again.

'They can't possibly see me from here, through all these trees,' Marna protested.

Yehna merely placed a finger to her lips. 'Be still, be silent,' she said softly, but with irresistible command.

There was a long silence, broken only by birdsong and the sound of the trees moving in the breeze. Marna found herself almost holding her breath. Then she drew it in sharply. The riders had stopped by her cottage.

'What's the matter?' Engir asked, without turning round.

Marna told him.

The riders began to spread out. 'They'll find her tracks in minutes,' Aaren said.

Engir nodded. 'Between us, we saw all three of them die,' he said. Marna looked at him, puzzled by the remark. But the others seemed to understand. 'And He was destroyed too.' He struck his chest. 'And we *knew* they'd gone.' He laid a heavy emphasis on the word, knew.

'But they're back,' Aaren said urgently. 'Or one of them, at least.'

Engir's eyes narrowed and he shook his head. 'It couldn't be,' he said.

Aaren took his arm and shook him. 'Damn you, I know,' she hissed. 'But it is. What's got into you? You're not going to tell me you haven't felt it in everything we've seen these past days. And now there's this girl's tale. Face it or we're all finished.'

Engir turned on her. 'They're all dead,' he said angrily and unequivocally.

The two of them glared at one another. Marna watched this bizarre turn of events in both bewilderment and trepidation.

'*They're* dead. But *it's* here.' Levrik, still watching the now-

245

scattering riders, ended the confrontation with this softly spoken, enigmatic comment. Engir looked at him sharply, but did not speak.

'It was so focused in those three and Him that you've forgotten what it is,' Levrik went on. 'It's everywhere. All around us, all the time. Available for those who know how to use it, for good or ill. Unfortunately, someone here – this Rannick – has learned how to use it and is using it for considerable ill.' He turned to Engir. 'And, equally unfortunately, it leaves us with something of a problem.'

'That's an understatement,' Aaren said caustically.

'What's the matter?' Marna asked, unable to remain silent in the middle of all this strange concern.

The four exchanged glances, then Engir spoke to her, his voice gentle, but full of grim resignation. 'We understand a little about the power that your Rannick uses, Marna. We've – met it before. I was reluctant to accept that it was here again, but . . .' He shrugged regretfully. 'It's a terrible thing,' he went on. 'Not something any of us would willingly meet again. And not something that can necessarily be dealt with by simple force of arms. It needs someone with the same skill.' He cast a sidelong glance at Levrik. 'The problem that Levrik spoke of is that none of us here has that skill, nor can we bring such a person here without a journey of many months.'

Marna's commonsense completed his tale, unbidden. 'But he's getting stronger every day,' she said forcefully. 'All manner of people are coming to join him, and raiding parties are going out every few days. We can't wait months before we do something.'

'They've found them.' Levrik's voice again broke into the discussion.

Marna looked back up towards her home. She could see the tiny dots converging. 'Will they find us?' she asked, suddenly fearful, her mind filling with images of the man she had just killed.

Engir shook his head. 'Probably not,' he said. 'But you must do everything we tell you, immediately and without question, do you understand?' Marna nodded, now not so much the gawky outsider as a nervous waif.

While Levrik continued his relentless watch on the approaching riders, the newcomers returned again to their wider difficulties.

'I can carry on with my journey to the capital,' Marna offered.

'Take your messages with me. The king could send the army.' She brightened. 'Or we could all go. If you can't do anything here on your own, there's not much point staying, is there?'

There was another exchange of glances amongst her listeners.

'I wish you'd all stop doing that,' Marna flared indignantly. 'Looking at one another as though I'm some kind of idiot.'

Engir raised his hands appeasingly. 'I'm sorry, Marna,' he said. 'It's just that you seem to have led such a sheltered life here. There's so much—'

'It's not sheltered any more,' Marna retorted angrily, before he could continue. 'Foulness has come from the north, from the south, and from within. These last two months or so might as well have been twenty years. Now tell me what's bothering you, straight out, and how I can help, or let me get on my way, and I'll help myself and my friends as best I can.'

Levrik cast her a brief, unreadable glance, the two women looked awkwardly at one another, and Engir nodded his head, genuinely chastened by this outburst. 'You're right, Marna,' he said. 'You'll have to make allowances for our strange ways, and the strange times. The past couple of months might have been bad for you, but over the last few days we've had to come to terms with facing something – something truly awful, that we'd all thought finished and gone for ever years ago.'

Marna was in no mood to make concessions. 'Shall we go to the king, then?' she demanded.

This time there was no debate amongst the four, silent or otherwise. 'Your land has been very prosperous for a long time, Marna,' Engir replied. 'A peaceful place, as I imagine your own valley has been. Your king is a just and kindly man. But . . .' He hesitated, as if what he had to say were deeply distasteful. 'Because of the very peacefulness, there's been no need, no inclination, for your people to bear arms, to maintain the military skills that helped your forebears to build and sustain this very peace. Whatever army the king ever had is little more than a ceremonial guard now.' He leaned forward. 'It was only fear of the pursuers they knew were following that kept Nilsson and his troop moving on.'

'They fled from four of you?' Marna said disbelievingly.

Engir smiled weakly. 'They fled from what they'd done and the accounting that they knew would be demanded of them sooner or later. Just a whiff of our very existence in the wind was enough to galvanize them. To rob them of any peace.'

'And now?' Marna asked.

Engir looked at the distant riders. 'And now, somehow, they've regained their confidence, their morale, and the whole land . . . perhaps more . . . lies hostage to what's happening here. Nilsson's a military man, a capable and ambitious one. He can and will use terror as a weapon of power. He's had a rare instructor. He knows that it'll take very little to subdue this entire country. And with Rannick behind him he won't hesitate to move even further afield.' He had to force his final words out. 'He understands those who can use the power better even than we do. And what we shake and tremble before, he'll have opened his arms to and embraced.'

Chapter 20

Marna felt herself go cold at the almost fatalistic acceptance in Engir's words. The mountains that had sheltered and held secure the only home she had ever known seemed now to be like the walls of a cruel prison, and the warm sunlight pervading the high lookout mocked her with its bright contrast to her dark fears. 'We can't just do – nothing,' she said, more plaintively than she had intended.

For a long time no one answered, then, as if they had reached a conclusion after holding a prolonged debate, Levrik said, 'We kill him then?'

Marna started at this unexpected and blunt announcement, though none of the others showed any signs of surprise.

'I can't see any other alternative,' Yehna said after a while. 'If he wants . . . Marna . . . here, then he's got plenty of down-to-earth appetites left. And that means he's a long way short of being totally consumed by the power yet.'

'And thus vulnerable,' Aaren concluded, a knife appearing in her hand.

Marna suddenly felt herself the centre of attention again. It took her a little while to appreciate the message she was being given. When she did she waved her hands in denial. 'No, no!' she said emphatically. 'I couldn't do it. Last night I thought perhaps I could, but I was wrong.'

'You've killed one man already,' Aaren said starkly.

Marna's mouth dropped open as she drew in a sharp breath. Her shocked reaction was reflected, albeit less visibly, in Levrik and Engir. They glanced at one another to confirm that they could play no part in what was to follow.

Marna blasted out her response in a voice full of both anger and reproach. 'That was an accident, for mercy's sake.'

Aaren shook her head. 'It was your better judgement,' she said calmly. 'Your life was threatened and you did what was necessary, quickly and efficiently.'

'No!'

'You didn't kill him?' Aaren said, eyebrows raised.

The two men watched, helpless as Marna looked from side to side, as if for some way to escape this unexpected assault. 'You know I did, you bitch,' she snarled, finding none. 'But it was an accident. I didn't mean—'

'That's twice you've said that, and twice you've been wrong,' Aaren interrupted, making no response to the abuse. 'I'm not saying you enjoyed it, or that you weren't sickened by it, but don't keep blaming it on some chance happening. Face what you did, girl, you'll survive it, and while it's unlikely you'll ever be happy about it, you'll be the better for it. Just thank your ancestors for breeding wits enough into you to make sure you could do the right thing when you had to.' She levelled a finger at Marna. 'And you don't need me to tell you that you *did* do the right thing, do you?' she said. 'Or that you'd do it again if you had to.'

The two women stared at one another. Levrik and Engir waited. Then Marna let out a noisy breath, and sagged. 'I don't know, I don't know,' she said unconvincingly. 'I – I couldn't do it to Rannick, all the same.'

'Fancy him, do you?' Aaren asked.

Surprisingly, Marna replied without either hesitation or rancour. 'Up here, no,' she said. 'But close to . . .' She shook her head, and coloured a little. 'I don't know.' She paused for a moment, then suddenly, she was once more on her back, fighting against a choking blackness and thrusting her hands up into the figure straddled over her. The vision, intense though it was, passed as suddenly as it had come, leaving her shivering and nauseous. A hand came forward to help her, but she brushed it aside almost angrily and forced herself to speak. 'Anyway,' she managed, 'doing something in the heat of the moment is one thing. Doing it—' She gritted her teeth. 'Killing someone in – cold blood – is another. Even Rannick, and knowing what he's done. I couldn't do it. I've known him too long. Part of me still – feels sorry for him.'

Engir interrupted. 'He killed your friend's parents and was quite prepared to take you as his woman by force—'

'I know that,' Marna snapped, rounding on him viciously. 'I

didn't say it wouldn't be the best thing for us all if he were dead, or even that I'd be particularly unhappy about it. But *I* couldn't do it. Least of all, posing as his – lover.' She waved her hand towards Aaren and Yehna as she turned away from him. 'They understand,' she said, adding under her breath, 'You stupid man!'

There was a long silence, during which only Levrik seemed to be watching the distant riders. His three companions sat in silent preoccupation.

As the heat of her unexpected confrontation faded, other thoughts came to Marna. 'Is there nothing else that can be done?' she asked hesitantly. 'Four of you can't do anything against him. He's got men, his own powers – and perhaps this creature.'

Engir shook his head. 'No,' he replied. 'You said it yourself in all innocence. There isn't time. We're too far from any kind of help, and this place is like a festering boil. If we don't lance it, and fast, what you've seen so far will seem like a pleasant dream compared to what will happen next.'

'You seem very sure about it,' Marna retorted.

Engir looked at her. 'I'm afraid I am,' he said. 'Absolutely sure.'

Marna turned to the others. 'But – you'll be killed if you try to attack him,' she protested, her voice a mixture of exasperation and distress.

'We're soldiers, that's always a risk,' Engir replied.

'But . . .'

'No buts,' Engir said, before Marna could continue. 'It's the way it is. We none of us wanted to walk into this, I can assure you. But we're trapped here now, just like everyone in your village.'

'You sneaked in, you can sneak out,' Marna said. 'Surely the king has some semblance of an army. What about people in nearby towns and villages, can't they—'

Engir took her arm. His grip was gentle, but there was a hint of impatience in his voice. 'Once more, I'll tell you, Marna. Grasp it, whether you like it or not, and don't cloud your mind with ifs and buts: they'll kill you. Nilsson's men are our countrymen. They're trained in many of our ways. They're battle-hardened, disciplined after a fashion, far from badly led, and murderers to a man. Even without Rannick and his burgeoning skills, your king and what passes for his army would be hard pressed to stand

251

against them, and any civilian militia would be massacred out of hand. You're quite right, we *can* sneak out and try to find help. But this place and this time will haunt us always. By the time we could muster any real help, this land would be long fallen, and the cost in human life and suffering in facing the forces that'd be in play by then, are truly beyond your imagining. We none of us want to be here. We've all got firesides we'd rather be sitting by. But we *are* here, we know what we know, and we are what we are. Getting killed is a risk in our profession, a calculated risk, not a certainty, and you can rest assured that whatever we do it'll be with a view to being able to ride away from this place successful and intact.'

Engir's words dropped into Marna's tumbling thoughts like shards of ice. Her doubts and fears tossed to and fro, but beat themselves to nothing against both his reasoning and his resolution. She looked at the others, but saw that they were only waiting for her to understand. Until she did, she realized, she was a burden; just another risk to them.

She put her hand to her head. How long ago was it since she had stood by her father as he stripped the willow poles last night? Ten years? Twenty? A lifetime? Her eyes suddenly filled with tears of rage at the rape of her life. She swore violently, and dashed the tears away angrily with her hand. 'I'm not a soldier,' she said, sobbing and hoarse. 'I can't fight.' She shot a savage look at Aaren. 'For all I killed someone. But it's my valley, my village; my country, I suppose; and certainly my friends. Just tell me what to do to help.'

Nilsson quailed inwardly. Rannick must surely return soon. And when he did . . .? He breathed slowly and deeply to ease the griping in his stomach. Once again, he wished that damned girl into every hall of hell. Talk about an empire lost for want of a nail!

He brought his fist down on the table, then stood up and arched his back in an attempt to ease his discomfort. Not for the first time, his ambitions – not to mention his life – were balanced on an unsteady and precarious edge, and there was nothing he could do but watch and wait and hope that he could ride out the avalanche that must inevitably be coming. His thoughts oscillated between a profound wish for a quiet, simple existence somewhere far away from all this turbulence, and a driving desire for the kind of life that only Rannick's power, coupled to his own military skill, could give. Invariably, he kept returning to his oft reached conclusion that only the latter could now give him the former. It did nothing however, to stop his thoughts from setting off on the entire cycle again.

He swore at the recurrent vision of Marna. That surly bitch! There'd been not a sign of her after she'd reached those rocks. Even Storran and Yeorson had shaken their heads, though he could tell they'd been unhappy about the tracks in some way. But he'd had no time for niceties, they'd had to press on, search as far as they could as quickly as they could.

In the end he had had to give up. She could be anywhere up there. She probably knew the area as well as she knew her own miserable little cottage, for all these villagers affected never to travel so far downland, or whatever it was they called it. He sneered to himself at the ludicrously restricted vision of these pathetic little people.

Not that those who were being drawn to join his growing army were much better, he reflected, as he thought again about the two bodies they had found. Imbeciles! Killing one another. Ye gods, the materials he had to work with! They were never going to be more than arrow fodder, but on the whole they would be of greater value if they waited for their opponents to kill them rather than doing it themselves.

He shook the thoughts from his head. They were an irrelevant distraction. He must, above all, concentrate on composing himself to face his lord when he returned. And where the devil was he anyway? It had been hours since sundown. Hours since the time appointed for the bringing of this girl to him. Nilsson sat down again, as other thoughts returned to plague him. Had Rannick had an accident? Had he fled for some reason?

He scowled. He could not envisage either possibility, not with Rannick's power growing as it was, and with their plans moving forward so well. Besides, he had read his lord well enough to know that he had been hot for this girl when he had ridden out of the castle earlier that day.

A clamorous banging brought him to his feet again with a heart-stopping jerk. 'What?' he bellowed furiously, as he tore the door open.

'The Lord, Captain,' stammered a figure, stepping back hastily from this blast. 'He's returning.'

Nilsson sent the man reeling against the opposite wall of the passage as he stormed past him. Whatever was going to happen, his every instinct told him that it was better that he go out to meet it. As he strode along passageways and clattered down stairs, his mind became completely clear. Now, he must respond heartbeat by heartbeat to events as they unfolded. If anyone could survive the coming storm, it was he, but he must not burden his thinking with a teetering pile of possibilities.

The castle gates were swinging open as he emerged into the torchlit courtyard. He noticed the gate guards standing well back as Rannick entered. He was mounted on the horse that he invariably used, and which was becoming increasingly like him in its vicious, erratic temperament. As Nilsson walked forward to greet him, it seemed to him that Rannick and his sinister mount were not simply moving towards him through the long, wavering shadows of the torchlight but were entering into this world from some other place, alien and frightful. He stopped, as if to go further forward would be to plunge himself into that world and be lost forever.

Rannick came slowly but relentlessly nearer. His horse stared at Nilsson, its eyes glittering red in the torchlight and its head and neck moving from side to side. It was an unnatural, serpentine movement, and it chilled Nilsson. He prepared to step to one side, but the horse halted without command, and Rannick dismounted. A nervous groom came forward and took the reins of the horse, which stared at him balefully as he hesitantly tugged at it. Rannick laid a hand on its neck, and it loped off after the groom, its head bowed close to the ground but still swaying, this way, that way, as if searching for something.

Rannick had the hood of his cloak pulled forward and Nilsson could see nothing of his face, while being all too aware that his own face was clearly visible in the torchlight. Slowly, however, Rannick pulled back the hood. Though he could not have identified any specific change, Nilsson knew that his master was not the same as he had been when he left the castle the previous evening. He risked the initiative. 'Are you well, Lord?' he asked, not without some genuine concern.

Rannick nodded slowly. 'Yes, Captain,' he replied. 'I am well. Why do you ask?'

His voice was subtly different too; distant, more sonorous. Nilsson's mind was drawn inexorably back to the lord that he had followed in the past. Rannick was but a pale shadow of what he had been, but he was beyond dispute, following in his steps. For no reason that he could immediately discern, Nilsson felt the balance of his concerns shift favourably. He reaffirmed his ambition. He must survive this coming danger, and then . . .?

'You seem – different, Lord,' he said, keeping from his voice any hint of either concern or criticism.

Rannick's gaze seemed to pass straight through him. 'You are a shrewd and ambitious man, Captain,' he said, his voice leisurely yet, like his eyes, penetrating. Nilsson felt as though every part of his body were being spoken to. 'It makes you an attentive as well as a loyal servant. You, above all, have the vision to see . . . to know . . . that I change each day, that my skill in the use of the power grows each day. But you are right. This day has been a day beyond all others.' Then, out of the shadows, like an assassin's knife: 'Where is the girl?'

Despite himself, Nilsson flinched a little at the suddenness of the question. He steeled himself. 'She is not here, Lord. She has fled.'

Rannick inclined his head slightly, as if he were listening to a voice speaking very softly, or at a great distance. Nilsson felt his own body's defences marshalling themselves: He became aware of every movement, every sound, in the entire courtyard, yet it was as though he were alone in a silent, motionless world that existed only for him and for this moment. And from this world, he saw his lord's face slowly change. His reactions, racing, followed the change, nuance within nuance, as they searched for the probable outcome of his message.

There was anger there. That he had expected, of course: and feared. Feared deeply. He had had enough experience of men thus stricken to know the murderous insanity that could follow such rejection. And with Rannick's power . . .?

In the blink of an eye he oversaw the alternatives before him. They ranged from prostrating himself and begging for mercy, to a sudden knife thrust that would slay at once both his lord and the future that his rekindled ambition had built for him.

And yet there was something else vying with the anger, something deeper, yet in a way pettier. Irritation? Annoyance at an unwelcome distraction?

Nilsson watched. And waited.

'Fled?' Rannick echoed, after an interminable interval.

'Yes, Lord,' Nilsson heard himself replying.

The subtle battle for control within Rannick was perceptible only to Nilsson's heightened awareness. The anger came and went until, abruptly, it was transmuted, and when it eventually came to rest in Rannick's eyes it was cold and malevolent but quite free from the wild dementia that Nilsson had expected. It was no less terrible for that.

'That is not acceptable, is it, Captain?' Rannick said, his voice eerily distant. 'But I shall deal with it in due course.' He closed his eyes and turned his face upwards. Slowly, his flame-shadowed expression became ecstatic, then he smiled slightly as he opened his eyes again and looked at Nilsson. He reached out and closed his hand around Nilsson's shoulder. 'You seem abstracted, Captain,' he said, the concern in his voice set at naught by the coldness in his eyes. 'Doubtless you feared my return?'

Experience had taught Nilsson many years ago that at such times, telling the truth was invariably the wisest course. 'I was concerned when I heard of the girl's flight,' he replied. He was about to begin describing the search that he had mounted, and the plans he had made for further, more thorough searches beyond the valley the next day, but Rannick was nodding and his grip was tightening about Nilsson's shoulder. He began walking across the courtyard, moving Nilsson ahead of him.

'A wise concern,' Rannick conceded. 'And an understandable one. But as I went in exultation to commune with – myself – in the silence of the woods, to prepare myself, it was revealed to me that this could not be. To squander myself on such transient pleasures, to spend my greatness on a single female, especially one who was, in truth, unsuitable, would be to jeopardize my greater destiny, and with it the true pleasures that lie ahead.'

Nilsson moved forward under the pressure of the guiding hand, still uncertain about the outcome of this unexpected turn of events. 'A hard decision, Lord,' he risked.

The hand tightened further about his shoulder until, his knees almost buckling, he was obliged to gasp in pain.

Rannick's grip eased, though he did not remove his hand 'You can have no conception how hard, Captain,' he replied. 'For my appetites are great.'

They reached a door which a guard threw open for them. As Rannick's hand left his shoulder, Nilsson felt suddenly so light and disorientated that for a moment he thought that the least breeze might have lifted him off his feet.

Rannick looked around the circular hallway that they had entered. He nodded to himself several times, and very slowly. Then he straightened up. 'I must meditate further on what has happened today, Captain,' he said. 'For it is much more than it seems. But the time is come. We begin the preparations for our conquest of this land in earnest.' He paused. 'Tomorrow. See that everyone is ready to move, as we planned.'

Even as he was speaking this last, terse order, he was walking away. Nilsson saluted. He stood motionless until his lord was out of sight, and for some time after that. Elation filled him. He had flown close to the flame again, closer than ever before. And he had survived! Nothing, *nothing*, could stand in his way now. Rannick's dangerous aberration had passed. And he would turn to no other woman in the future; his obsession with his skills was total and all-consuming, now. Nilsson could not begin to surmise what unholy communion had passed between Rannick and his creature that day, but he knew intuitively that Rannick had felt a lessening of his power when he had turned his mind to someone other than himself. And it was the essence of the power that it could not see itself depleted; it could only lust to grow greater and greater. Rannick was trapped utterly.

Chapter 21

Farnor's homeward journey continued to be both quicker and easier than his outward one. But though he was more at ease with himself, many thoughts about the future disturbed him. Not least among these were the practicalities of what he was intending to do.

How should he confront Rannick? He couldn't simply ride up to the castle and announce himself. Whatever power he might possess, he had learned nothing about either its nature or its use from the Forest, despite his original intentions, and he was loath to assume that it would suddenly manifest itself as need required. And, mementoes of beating, climbing, and riding, the intermittent aches and pains in his body reminded him that he was not proof against fleshly distress. He could thus not sensibly oppose himself against point and edge, still less bone-crushing teeth.

The memory of the creature's malevolent and powerful presence chilled him.

Gradually he came to the conclusion that he had reached before he had been drawn on his strange journey through the Great Forest. He would hide in the woods beyond the castle, watching and listening silently, until he could encounter Rannick alone. He had little doubt that, given the element of surprise, he could seize and overpower him. His darker vision of the future might have turned from Rannick's death but he would nevertheless relish subduing him by main force. And this time he would sound no challenge that might bring the creature down on him. And too, he was no longer alone. The trees would be watching and listening with him.

His mood was unsettled, however. Despite all his plans, confronting Rannick was still a stomach-turning prospect which became more frightening with each southbound stride. Yet, it also had a familiar quality of inevitability about it, not unlike that which preceded a trip to Gryss with toothache, though worse by far. What was upsetting him more were his thoughts about Derwyn and his family. True, he had advised Derwyn simply to search for the valley and prepare to defend his people against what might come from there. But he had been vague; he had not warned him as he should other than to tell him to take his best men. He cursed himself roundly for his dark folly every time he thought of his last meeting with Derwyn. It gave him no consolation that not for a moment had it occurred to him at the time that Derwyn would undertake such an expedition with a small family hunting party.

That, through his neglect, he might have brought to Derwyn's kin the pain of loss that he himself had suffered, troubled him greatly. And the trees could not help. He had asked about Derwyn's fate only once.

'We are frightened where we are near your home, Far-nor, the power there grows apace. It is terrible. And the fear clouds all. Mar-ken and his company passed into the spreading nightfall and I could not Hear him further.'

Farnor did not need to be told this last; fear and confusion permeated the words, jagged and frightful, and layered through with apologies and regret – and shame. 'I understand,' he said, though he added sternly, 'But we must both of us struggle to face our fears if they're not to bring us down.' Then he had tried another approach. 'Are Marken or the others back at their lodge?'

The answer was starkly clear. 'No.'

Farnor swore to himself, and unthinkingly urged his horse forward. It took no notice, however, continuing resolutely at the pace that it presumably found most suitable.

There had been such distress in the voice of the trees that, despite his concern, he had not been able to bring himself to pursue the matter. 'They're none of them foolish or reckless people,' Uldaneth had said, but that too gave him little consolation. Though as the words came back to him he heard her saying again, 'What's done is done, Farnor. Neither of us can do anything from here.' Oddly, that *had* helped. Some quality in her voice had told him that destroying himself with gnawing anxieties about matters beyond his control was to compound one folly with another. He began trying to quieten himself by becoming absorbed in the gentle, drumming rhythm of his journey, and the tranquillity of the Forest about him.

And tranquil it was. The nights were cool, scented and dreamless, and each morning he was awake, refreshed and alive, before the sound of the dawn horns floated over the treetops to greet him. He found streams to drink from and to bathe in, and the food from Marrin's lodge left him no need either to economize or to hunt.

And sometimes, the trees sang.

Though he met no other Valderen on the way, he noted now their presence in many things to which previously he had been oblivious. He came upon carvings unexpectedly. One in particular struck him forcibly; a great bird, twice his own height, wings widespread, had been carved from the crown of a dead tree in the middle of a clearing. Its glistening, varnished eye fixed itself on him so realistically as he dismounted and walked around it in wonder, that he was almost afraid to go near it for fear it would suddenly lunge down at him. And there were many others: strange man-like creatures with comical faces squatted in families on low branches; large insects peered at him from the undergrowth; faces were carved into trunks, and sometimes he came across shapes, polished and smooth and resembling nothing, yet beautiful both to look at and to touch. And too there were trees whose branches had been shaped and formed in ways that could not have been natural but which yet celebrated life and nature.

Frequently he touched individual trees and talked to them. It was a strange experience, quite different from his contact with their collective voice. They were at once prosaic and intriguing, full of local gossip about matters that he could not begin to understand – subtle images involving branches and roots, sunlight and warm darkness, and, with unmistakable and quite disconcerting delight, seeds!

And yet they were full of tales of distant places and distant times as well. 'They made a magical carving of me in a great castle far away from here, once,' was a common tale, though he could make little sense of that either except that it was obviously a source of some pride.

Then, quite unexpectedly, one bright morning, he was riding into Derwyn's lodge. Voices called out to him from above and people began to appear; some walking and running towards him, others bouncing perilously down ladders, touching scarcely one rung in ten. He reined his horse back to a walk as his worries crashed in upon him. 'Is Derwyn here?' he asked the first person he came to.

Before he received any answer, EmRan appeared by his side. 'What have you come back for?' he demanded. 'You caused enough trouble the first time.'

Farnor's mood curdled into violence at this greeting. He rounded on EmRan angrily. 'Why did you prevent the Congress from helping Derwyn when he wanted to go south and find the route to my valley?'

EmRan started at this unexpected response, then bridled, but Farnor gave him no opportunity to speak. 'I told him it was dangerous,' he went on. 'And that he should take the best men he could. And travel carefully and quietly.' He leaned down towards EmRan, and his pent-up concerns of the last few days hissed out. 'It was no expedition for old men, women and girls, you meddling buffoon—'

'Don't let Marken, Angwen and least of all Edrien hear you say that.'

Farnor spun round. Standing on the other side of his horse was Derwyn, his arms extended. Farnor almost tumbled out of his saddle in his relief. He took his erstwhile host's arms in the Valderen manner.

Derwyn smiled. 'You still have a faller's grip, Farnor, but it's good to see you.'

'It's good to see *you*, Derwyn,' Farnor replied. 'I was so afraid for you when Uldaneth told me what EmRan had done.'

Derwyn chuckled. 'EmRan did nothing I shouldn't have expected,' he said. 'It was my fault. I was so preoccupied with you and Marken and everything that I just didn't look what I was doing.' He put his arm around Farnor's shoulder. 'Besides, did you take us for fools, young man?' he asked mockingly. 'Did you think we'd go charging around like fleeing deer? You told me clearly enough that it was dangerous.'

Farnor waved his arms vaguely. 'No – of course not,' he said, embarrassed. 'But—'

Derwyn released him. 'It's all right,' he said. 'I understand, and I thank you for your concern.'

A little later however, having exchanged the crowd gathering on the Forest floor for the smaller one which had gathered in Derwyn's lodge, Farnor told his hosts of the events that had driven him from the valley. And, predominantly at Marken's pressing, he told something of his encounter with the most ancient amid the great trees around the central mountains.

There was an almost reverent silence when he had finished. 'Your story answers many questions, Farnor,' Derwyn said. 'I'm glad you felt able to tell us now.' He nodded towards Marken. 'We'd been told that you'd changed greatly. I hope you'll not be offended if I say it's a considerable improvement.'

Farnor smiled, a little sadly. 'No,' he replied simply. 'I met some rare teachers on my journey.' He leaned forward and, massaging his legs, added ruefully, 'But none who could teach me to climb your ladders easily.'

The atmosphere in the room lightened. 'But what did *you* find on your journey?' he asked.

'Well, we'd very little trouble finding the trail you'd made,' Derwyn replied, to some laughter. 'And we were able to follow it until we came to the entrance to your valley.'

'And?' Farnor prompted.

'And nothing,' Derwyn replied, with an unhappy frown. 'Marken said that all he could Hear was alarm and confusion, and that it was getting worse. And I wasn't happy about the place, anyway. There was a bad feeling about it. Really bad.' He hesitated. 'And we heard something – your creature, probably – howling one night. Only the once. But it was horrible. It seemed to cut right through me.' He shivered and finished his tale rapidly. 'So we just marked the trail and left.'

'Can you take me there?' Farnor asked.

Derwyn looked at him carefully. 'Yes,' he said. 'But do you really want to go? Are you still intent upon vengeance for your parents?'

Farnor lowered his eyes. The room darkened as a cloud drifted in front of the sun. 'A little,' he said eventually, looking up again. 'But not like before. I've better ways to honour my parents now. I want to live. But if I'm going to have a life, then I have to go back. I have to do something to free the valley of Rannick and Nilsson and the creature.' He paused and looked round at the other watching faces: Angwen, Edrien, Marken, Bildar, and a yellow-haired young man he had seen at the Synehal but whose name he did not know. 'I don't want to. To be honest, I'm very frightened. But it seems . . . that I have . . .' He looked at his hands, 'the same – gift' – he almost spat the word – 'as Rannick, and that I'm perhaps the only person who can stop him.' He looked up at Derwyn. 'And if I don't, if someone doesn't, then he'll go on to hurt more and more people.'

Derwyn reached out and took Farnor's arm. 'You'll have all the help we can give you,' he said quietly.

Farnor smiled ruefully. 'I'd like to ask you for a few score armed men,' he said. 'But it'll be help enough if you'll show me the way.'

Derwyn leaned back in his chair and looked a little smug. 'You'll have plenty of hunters at your back, Farnor,' he said. 'There's well over a score of them just come down from Marrin's lodge alone. They were travelling close behind you all the way.'

Farnor looked at him in disbelief. 'Close behind? No. I heard no riders,' he said.

'I should think not,' Derwyn exclaimed.

Farnor frowned. 'I don't understand,' he said. 'If they were coming here, why didn't they ride with me?'

Derwyn looked away from him a little uncomfortably. 'We hear what we hear from our Hearers. And we listen carefully. But we're responsible for our own actions, and we're a cautious people. We like to find things out for ourselves, as well.' His eyes were full of concern. 'And there was such darkness in you when you left, Farnor. Such anger, such hatred. After what I – we all – felt in your valley, I had the same fear as they did about you, despite what they'd told Marken about their judgement. I couldn't know whether you were a victim of some evil – or its vanguard. So I asked Marrin's people to give you every courtesy and help, but otherwise to keep away from you until we'd spoken.'

Farnor felt a spasm of anger forming, but it faltered and he gave it no voice. 'And now?' he asked.

'Now we've spoken, and the doubts are gone,' Derwyn replied.

'All of them?' Farnor twitched inwardly as he tried to snatch back the question.

Derwyn laughed softly and shook his head. 'To be without all doubt is not to be human, Farnor,' he said. 'But I'm as free of them as I can expect to be.' He glanced at Angwen and patted his stomach. 'And apart from what my stomach tells me, the difference in you when you rode back into the lodge was visible to everyone.'

'Not to EmRan,' Farnor retorted.

'EmRan's EmRan,' Derwyn said. 'He invariably stands in his

own light. And he did himself no favours by denying me the lodge hunt. A lot of people were very angry with him when they found we'd gone as family.' He chuckled to himself then waved a dismissive hand. 'But that's by the by. It's just . . .'

Farnor however, was not listening. The reference to the hunt had thrust an ominous thought into his mind. His eyes widened in alarm. 'Why were Marrin's hunters coming here?' he asked. He gripped the arms of his chair and his voice became urgent. 'It's not been here, has it? Into the Forest, hunting?'

Derwyn shook his head reassuringly. 'No,' he replied. 'But we're Valderen, Farnor. We protect and provide for the Forest, as it protects and provides for us. Now we know for certain that some menace lies to the south, we must seek it out. Hunters have come from all over to join us.' He laughed. 'Even EmRan's not spoken out against it.'

Farnor, however, was gazing about him anxiously. There was a self-satisfied – excited, even – quality in Derwyn's manner that disturbed him in some way. 'But you can't just hunt the creature,' he said. 'It's like nothing you've ever imagined.' Memories flooded over him and his words began to tumble out. 'Why do you think the trees themselves are frightened? You mustn't go after it as if it were just another – fierce animal.' He tapped his head. 'In all its evil traits, it's human. It thinks. If you enter its territory – my land – then *it* will hunt *you*. It attacked and routed a column of Nilsson's men. Hard fighting men, all armed. It—'

Unsettled by Farnor's passion, Derwyn held up his hand to stop the flow. 'We're in the same position as you are,' he said forcefully. 'We can't do otherwise. We must protect the Forest or we're nothing.' He became defensive. 'Besides, we're not children. We've experience in hunting every kind of—'

'You heard its voice. You heard it howl,' Farnor said significantly, cutting him short.

Derwyn pursed his lips and frowned. An uneasy tension filled the room. 'Yes, you're right,' he replied eventually. 'I did hear it howl. And I've no desire to meet whatever made that noise. But my feelings don't come into it. I told you. We can't do otherwise. No matter what that creature is, we must use what skills we have to track it down, just as you must track down this Rannick.'

Farnor looked round at the watching faces again. 'I'm sorry,' he said unhappily, after a moment. 'I didn't mean to offend you. But I know what this thing's like. It's no natural creature. It sends terror before it.' His voice fell. 'It *feeds* on terror. Don't let *anyone* go anywhere alone – or – even in small groups. And never unarmed.' He snatched a phrase from one of Yonas's tale. 'Stack your night fires high and ring your camps with guards for a great army is seeking you.' The seriousness of his tone removed any incongruity from his words.

'We'll do as you say,' Derwyn replied simply. 'And we'll ride with you until we have to part, if you'll allow us.'

Farnor met his gaze. 'You'll go your own way, no matter what I say,' he replied. 'But I'd be lying if I said I'd be anything other than glad of your company.'

For the rest of the day Farnor wandered about the lodge with Edrien as his guide. At Edrien's prompting they ate at Bildar's, where the old Mender insisted on giving Farnor 'A quick lookover. Just to set my own mind at ease.'

'Thanks a lot, for that,' Farnor said to Edrien acidly as they left. 'Was that your father's idea, or your stomach's?'

Edrien smirked.

Then, at Farnor's request, they climbed up to Marken's giddy eyrie. When they arrived, Marken was leaning on the handrail, staring out over the vast treescape below. Roney was perched on his shoulder. 'Thinking about giving him flying lessons?' Edrien asked irreverently.

Marken gave her a narrow look, then lifted Roney from his shoulder and held him out to her. 'Take him for a walk for a few minutes,' he said. 'I want to talk to Farnor.'

Edrien placed the bird gently on her shoulder. 'Take him for a walk!' she muttered to herself, affecting a withering sneer. 'Fat old sod.' Roney eyed her beadily. 'You're in the pot, come solstice, you know,' Edrien added, but Roney turned away disdainfully and flapped his wings, ruffling her hair.

Marken smiled as Edrien walked off. 'I think Angwen must have been frightened by a gall wasp when she was carrying that one,' he said reflectively. 'She's got a natural charm that's really quite – elusive.' Then he chuckled. 'Mind you, she's changed lately. Watches her tongue a lot more. I think your arrival made her think about a great many things she'd taken for granted before.'

Before Farnor could offer any comment on this he found himself being scrutinized intently. Taken aback, he ventured, 'I suppose you want to know what it was *really* like, meeting the most ancient?'

'Oh yes,' Marken replied passionately, but without lessening his scrutiny. 'But not now. We can talk on the hunt.'

Farnor had a momentary vision of Marken among the Valderen hunters, being scattered like fallen leaves by the creature just as Nilsson's men had been.

'What's the matter?' Marken asked.

Farnor looked away from him. 'Nothing. Nothing much,' he said. Then, 'I'm frightened. Frightened for you, and everyone who's going on this hunt.' He tightened his grip on the handrail and shook his head violently, before turning his gaze back to Marken. 'I shouldn't be, should I?' He echoed Derwyn's phrase. 'After all, you're not children. You're experienced hunters and I'm not, and nor were Nilsson's men. I must trust. I must trust.'

Marken took his arm.

'It's not easy, is it?' Farnor said, looking out over the trees again.

'No,' Marken replied simply. 'Trusting the ability of people you're fond of to face danger is profoundly difficult, but we all have to do it sooner or later.' He nodded pensively to himself as if he had reached a decision. 'I'm truly glad to see that Edrien's not the only one who's changed.' Farnor turned back to him. 'Your eyes are still haunted and full of fear, but where there was anger – perhaps even madness – now there's determination – resolution.' He looked as if he wanted to say much more, but he simply patted Farnor's arm paternally.

The next day, after a pleasant but slightly self-conscious breakfast with Derwyn and his family, Farnor was led down to a Forest floor awash with people and horses. And rain. A fine steady rain.

As Derwyn led him from group to group of waiting hunters, he did his best to cope with the confusion of introductions. There were not only given names, but lodge names and family names, elaborate lineages, convoluted relationships and, not infrequently, trades became involved in some way: climbers, slingers, rootmen, splicers, and many others, equally unfamiliar. In the end he was utterly bewildered and confined himself to nodding and smiling and holding his arms tight against his sides to minimize the effect of the many crushing greetings he was receiving.

After each meeting, however, he noted that the hunters faded into the surrounding trees, and when eventually all the introductions were complete and he was riding towards the place where he had first been discovered, he was surprised to find himself accompanied only by Derwyn, Marken, Melarn, Edrien and Angwen. 'Where is everyone?' he asked.

'They're here,' Derwyn said, waving an arm airily.

Farnor peered earnestly into the dripping trees. Here and there he caught sight of an occasional rider, but he could see nothing of the great crowd that had gathered in Derwyn's lodge. 'They're very well hidden,' he remarked.

Derwyn merely smiled, smug again, and the party continued in silence.

Farnor examined his companions as they rode on. Melarn's bright yellow hair held his attention. He had never seen hair that colour, ever, even though many of the valley people were fair-haired. He cast his mind back to the gathering of the hunters. With their bobbing heads, red, yellow, brown, and every rich and subtle combination of these colours, they had reminded him of wind-ruffled autumn leaves. It brought home to him vividly for the first time how strange he must seem to them with his black mop. He was smiling at his whimsy when Marken brought his horse alongside. 'Now you can tell me what it was like, Farnor,' he said. 'Hearing the most ancient. I've heard that the trees there are truly huge and that the silence is almost tangible.'

Farnor looked at him. The Hearer's brown eyes were full of youthful excitement and curiosity. 'Give me your hand,' Farnor said, extending his own. Marken's hand shot out and seized it enthusiastically. 'Show him,' Farnor said silently to the trees, closing his eyes, 'Reach out. Learn and teach.'

There was a brief hesitation and then abruptly the fear pervading the surrounding trees washed over him. He felt Marken's grip tighten in alarm and he tightened his own in a reassuring response. 'Show him,' he insisted. And as if he were some great centre to which all must be drawn, the deep silence of the most ancient entered him, setting aside the fear. Deliberately Farnor filled his mind with his memory of the soaring splendour of the great trees and the awe which he had felt in their presence. Marken made no sound as they rode on.

After a timeless interval, Farnor felt the Hearer's hand slipping away from him, and gradually he became aware of the Forest about them. He looked at Marken. The old man's eyes were shining with tears. Farnor remained silent.

Throughout the rest of that day, Farnor and the Valderen hunters moved unseen and silent through the trees, drawing inexorably further away from the heart of the Forest, and nearer to their unknown and fearful destination.

Gryss started violently as he heard the door of his cottage open and close quickly. It had been his sad practice of late to lock his door at night, but it was far from being a habit yet. There was an uncertain rumbling from the dog and some rustling in the hallway while, with no small trepidation, he levered himself up out of his chair. Before he could reach the door, however, it opened. 'Marna!' he exclaimed, as she stepped hastily inside and closed the door behind her. 'Where have you been? What's been happening? Why—'

Marna waved him silent and motioned him vigorously back towards his chair. Gryss retreated under this assault, but he was not so lightly silenced. 'Your father's frantic with worry, Marna,' he said in a low, urgent whisper, for some reason feeling the need to keep his voice down. 'What—' His chair nudged him behind the knees and he sat down abruptly.

Marna dropped to her knees in front of him and seized his hands. 'There are people here, Gryss. People from over the hill. Come to kill Rannick,' she announced.

Gryss gaped at her, but before he could speak she was recounting the story of her decision to flee the valley and her meeting with the four strangers, though she made no mention of the man she had killed. When she had finished, Gryss closed his eyes and put his hands to his head. For an awful moment, Marna thought that her impetuous entry had been too severe a shock for the old man.

But his eyes were sharp and attentive when he opened them. 'Tell me all that again, but more slowly,' he said, lifting her up from her knees and pointing her to a chair opposite.

For a little while the room was filled with the soft murmur of her half-whispered tale and Gryss's intermittent questions. The two of them leaned towards one another, their faces almost touching, like an tentative arch. When she had finished her second telling, Gryss closed his eyes again and leaned back in his chair. 'This will take me a moment or two, Marna,' he said.

Marna tapped her fingers impatiently on her knee as she waited. 'How did you get here?' Gryss demanded suddenly.

'They watched until the search party went back to the castle, then they brought me to where I could reach the top fields on my own,' Marna replied.

'Where are they now?' Gryss asked.

Marna shook her head. 'I don't know,' she said. 'They wouldn't tell me. They said it was in case Nilsson found me and I told him about them.'

Gryss looked at her closely. 'You don't seem too offended by that,' he said, gently taunting.

Marna grimaced. 'A day or two ago I might have been, but not now,' she said. Then, with an effort, 'More's happened than I've told you about.'

Gryss frowned. The comment confirmed the pain that he could feel underlying her every word. 'Do you want to tell me about it?' he asked.

Marna shook her head vigorously. 'Perhaps one day,' she said. 'When this is all over.'

'Whenever you want,' Gryss said. 'But it may be some time before that happens. What can four people do against Rannick and Nilsson? Storm the castle?'

Marna's manner changed, and she looked at him like a parent about to admonish a child for an offence that was so serious that shouting and summary punishment were out of the question. 'I was with them, Gryss,' she said. 'They're *real* soldiers. Real.' She slapped her stomach to confirm the depth of her inner certainty about this declaration. 'And they move like shadows. They brought me, and the horses, through ways over the tops that I never dreamed existed. And they'd never been here before. They just – see things. And they pay attention to such details.' She nodded reflectively to herself, then, with quiet, but deep assurance, 'I told you, they know about the power that Rannick has. It frightened them more than it ever has us, and still they've gone on to fight him. Gone, on their own, because they knew they hadn't the time to get the help they needed. But they'll do something that'll be neither foolish nor futile, and, at the least, they'll hurt him badly in some way.' She leaned forward and her voice became urgent. 'And they'll do it soon. Very soon.'

'I don't suppose they told you what they were going to do, either, did they?' Gryss said.

Marna shook her head. 'No, but they were very interested when I told them that Rannick sometimes rides out alone to the north. I think if they get the chance, they'll try to ambush him.'

'They made quite an impression on you, I gather,' Gryss said.

'Yes,' Marna replied simply.

'And?' Gryss caught the note in her voice.

'And whatever it is they're going to do, we can't let them do it alone,' she said.

Gryss looked at her, almost fearfully. There was no youthful petulance or impatience here. He could still sense the presence of a frightened and lost young girl, but this was fluttering at the edges of a stern resolve. She was unequivocally not the Marna of even a few days ago. He resisted the temptation to question her about those parts of her journey that he knew she had kept from him. 'What can we do?' he asked, trying to keep any hint of defeatism from his voice.

Despair flared into Marna's eyes momentarily, only to be swept aside. 'Be ready,' she said, clenching her fists. 'Just be ready to help them, protect them, if anything starts to happen. Not be frightened of the unknown.' Before Gryss could interject any reservations, she ploughed on. 'I've been thinking. Everyone who we're certain is with us can go up to Farnor's place tomorrow. If we're asked, we can say we're starting to rebuild it for whoever it's to be granted to. There's plenty to do there that'll warrant a crowd carrying axes and hammers and the like, without causing any alarm. And from there, we can arrange to watch the castle. And to move, if we have to, if anything starts to happen. We don't even need to tell anyone why we're really there.' She hesitated. 'In fact we *mustn't* tell anyone else why we're there. We've too few good liars.' She frowned thoughtfully. 'We'll tell everyone it's just what it is. A ploy to watch the castle. To see if we can find out how well they guard it, how many new people are arriving, whether they ever send patrols to the north; anything that might be useful later on!' She nodded her head, satisfied.

Gryss's eyes widened in surprise. His mind filled with doubts and hesitations but they foundered against both Marna's determination and the simple practicality of her suggestion. He felt a long-suppressed anger and resentment bubbling up through the confusion of his thoughts. And too, guilt. Had he acted with such plain common sense at the very outset and, say, questioned Nilsson and his troop, perhaps none of this horror would ever have come to pass. It was no new thought, but it tormented him no less for that. Indeed it had grown worse with time, as, rippling out from that first wrong action, had come so many others; small, day by day acts of appeasement and quiet acquiescence to Nilsson's and thus Rannick's will. Even though such deeds were done ostensibly as a cover for the organizing of more forthright action, they distressed him profoundly, not least because of the example they set to the other villagers.

'Yes,' he said. 'You're right. It's a good idea. I'm sick of doing nothing except fret over ever more futile plans.' He stood up. 'Jeorg, I think, should know what's happened. But I agree, none of the others. I'll tell your father you're safe but not where you are. And you'd better keep well out of sight.' He lifted down his cloak from a hook. 'I'll start things moving right away. Delays have won us nothing in the past, and with a bit of effort I should be able to get a . . . working party . . . to the farm before noon tomorrow.'

When he had gone, Marna locked the door behind him and doused all the lanterns. Then she curled up in the chair and waited.

Chapter 22

The following day was cloudy and overcast, but to Marna's considerable relief it did not rain. Where a group of people working in the sunshine might not have been unduly conspicuous, a group working in the pouring rain would be highly so.

She was awake before dawn after a night tormented by confused desire-laden dreams of Rannick and terrifyingly vivid images of her struggle with the man she had killed. The latter in particular had started her upright, sweating and gasping, and they came sometimes even when she simply closed her eyes. It helped only a little that Aaren had told her to expect such a reaction to her ordeal.

Moving silently about the cottage, she packed some food, left a note for Gryss, and then used the morning twilight to cover her journey to the Yarrance farm. Studiously she tried to move the way that the four newcomers moved, for despite the danger and urgency of their mission, they had made a point of instructing her where they could.

While her endeavours were hardly skilled, she had instinctively picked up some of their sense of inner stillness, and she found that she both saw and heard many things on the short, familiar journey that she had never noted before.

Despite the horror of the destruction of the Yarrance farm, the ancient momentum of the valley's ways had seen the livestock rapidly moved to several different farms for care until such time as Farnor might return, or a decision be made by the Council about the disposition of the property and goods. No one, however, had known what to do with the various household items that were immediately salvageable from the wreckage of the farmhouse, and, with a strange mixture of embarrassed haste and care, they had been put into one of the undamaged store sheds.

Marna paused as she reached the open gate to the farmyard. In the dawn gloaming, the scarred and broken farmhouse looked both sinister and vengeful, with its charred rafters dark against the dull sky and its shadowed windows like sightless eyes. She hesitated for a moment, nervously, then, avoiding looking at the house, she slipped quietly across the yard to the shed.

Her nervousness eased a little as, after a little struggle with the wooden latch, she closed the door behind her, gently. The interior of the shed was dark, and it took some time for her eyes to adjust.

Though she had chosen dull and nondescript clothing for her journey, she felt the need now for clothes that would disguise her even more effectively. Then she would need some weapons. One thing that she had noticed while she had been with the four outsiders was the extent to which they were armed. And, she was sure, what she had seen was by no means all that they carried.

Tentatively, she had touched on the subject of carrying a knife . . . or something . . . for her protection, in the vague hope of receiving advice of some kind about how she should use one. Aaren's comments, however, had come from a deeper insight. 'You don't carry a weapon unless you're fully prepared both to use it and to account for using it,' she had said quietly, but with a look that transfixed Marna. 'And you don't ever rely on it, or you'll be robbed of your will if it fails you, and it'll probably be taken from you and used against you.' Naked doubt had filled Marna's face but Aaren had continued. 'Someone once told me that being a true warrior did not lie in knowing how to use weapons, but *when* to use them. And that relying on weapons and technique can stop you learning how to watch and to listen and develop the wisdom to judge that moment truly. Very wise advice, I realize now, though I didn't take it with too good a grace at the time.'

'I don't understand,' Marna had replied, herself a little miffed at this unexpected lecture.

'You understand better than you realize,' Aaren had said encouragingly. 'You've never been trained to fight, I imagine, but when you needed to today, you – your body – acted as wisely as any hardened soldier.'

The remark had torn at Marna for some reason. Of the many thoughts she had had about the slaying of her attacker, not one had identified it as an act of wisdom.

And yet . . .?

Aaren had become purposeful. 'Still, these are dangerous times and this is a particularly dangerous place now, whatever it's been in the past. If you must arm yourself, get yourself a good sharp knife, one that's comfortable to wear and to handle. Make sure you can draw it easily but not so easily that it'll tumble out of its scabbard if you have to jump over anything, or roll about. But,' she had been emphatic, 'above all, *don't* rely on it. Just think about what wearing it means, and think about it honestly. And don't be afraid of whatever conclusions you reach. Trust your judgement, Marna. It's very sound, I know.'

'How should I use it?' she had asked.

Aaren's brow had furrowed in distress, but her voice was calm as she replied, 'Straight, fast and without warning, when your decision's been made.' Her hand had come up. 'No more,' she had said. 'Just think about what I've said.'

The brief conversation kept returning to Marna, at once a warning and a guiding light.

The clothes took little finding. A loose, rather bulky tunic would hide her shape, and scruffy cap would contain her hair and obscure her face. The knife presented more of a problem, though only because she was spoilt for choice. This particular store shed was the one which housed Farnor's grinding bench, and over this hung a large array of very sharp knives in their leather and stiff cloth scabbards.

Marna's hands closed about a machete and she hefted it menacingly so that its blade glinted silver wet in the dull morning light that was coming through the window. It was comfortable all right, but not something she could reasonably conceal, let alone carry easily. With some reluctance, she put it aside. Eventually she decided on carrying three in her belt: one either side and a short one at the back, as she had noted Yehna wearing. She tried one up her sleeve like the one she had seen Engir carrying, but it kept tumbling out. And her attempt to wedge one into the top of her boot proved not only unsuccessful but also quite painful.

She frowned. There was a great deal she had missed when she had thought she was studying those soldiers and their weapons. She could have learned much more had she had the wit to watch and listen more carefully. Still, all being well, they would meet again soon and she would be more attentive next time. She slid over the interim period.

'Are you comfortable?' she muttered to herself, giving her

clothes and weapons a final check. A little self-consciously she jumped up and down twice to see if any of her knives bounced out of their hastily rigged scabbards. Then, as quietly as she had come, she was across the farmyard and moving over the fields towards a tree-lined hillock from which, as she had agreed with Gryss, she would be able to watch both the farm and the castle.

Her immediate instinct had been to keep to the edge of the fields, but it was much lighter now and, should anyone be observing, she knew that a figure skulking along the hedgerows would be more conspicuous than one wandering leisurely across the fields. It proved a little more nerve-racking than she had envisaged, however, and as soon as she reached the trees, she scurried to find herself a good, well-hidden vantage point.

As she waited, she tried again to emulate the quiet stillness of the four soldiers. It was not easy. She found herself drifting off into daydreams, or seized with cramp brought on through sitting too stiffly. Also, on occasions, as during the night, she was once again suddenly, horribly, back in the woods, fending off her attacker, her hands warm and sticky. 'Don't be afraid,' Aaren had said. 'It's got to come out of your system one way or another. Just remember that you won.' The words helped, but the incidents still left her shivering and wiping her hands down her tunic.

However, the forging of the last few days also began to make itself felt and, without realizing it, she achieved a quietness that would have been quite beyond her only a week previously, as she turned her mind to the needs of the valley and its four would-be deliverers, and forced herself to watch the castle attentively.

As usual, little seemed to be happening, except for the guards, whom she could just make out, patrolling the walls. Occasionally however, her eye was drawn to the tallest of the towers, as strange lights flashed from the windows of its highest room. It was Rannick's room, she knew, with its plundered furniture and its ambivalent memories for her. As the lights came and went, she eased herself further into the shade, as if they were in some way seeking her out.

She tried to ignore a part of her which felt slightly injured that, following her unequivocal rebuff of his proposal, an infuriated Rannick had not come looking for her in person, or at least sent out a larger, more determined, search party. She was sure that he had been hot enough for some such precipitate action. On the other hand, she was relieved that neither of these had happened. She remembered Nilsson's surreptitious warning about the eerie, clinging, little breeze that had fluttered about her head as she had left the castle, and her stomach tightened as she thought about what it implied.

As she recalled this gossamer touch, something brushed lightly against her cheek. She started violently and almost cried out. But it was only a leafy branch touched by the breeze. She dashed it aside angrily, and returned to her vigil scowling grimly.

As the morning wore on, people began to arrive at the farm below, a few, unusually, on horseback. They milled around for a little while, then eventually, and at a very leisurely pace, began cleaning up the debris in the farmyard.

Marna watched them idly for some time and then turned back to the castle. Even as she turned, the castle gates swung open and a column of men began to emerge. Her heart started to pound with both fear and anticipation. A search party was being sent to look for her, after all. Or was it just another raiding party? Other thoughts came. Would whoever was leading them notice the crowd at the farm? Would they start asking questions? She was glad that Gryss had decided to tell no one about her apart from Jeorg.

She frowned. The column was turning away. It was heading north. Count, girl, count, came an urgent thought from somewhere; an echo of the frequent questions from Engir and the others about the numbers of men, and horses, and wagons, and prisoners, and . . . everything . . . that was currently inside the castle: questions that for the most part she had been able to answer only vaguely.

The column kept on coming. There were a few mounted men, several loose horses, and what, she decided, must be nearly all their wagons. Her frown deepened. What was happening? She knew that Nilsson had expressed an interest in the north when he had first arrived, but there hadn't even been any talk in the village of a raiding party in that direction.

'Marna!'

The soft voice made her freeze.

'Marna,' it came again.

Cautiously she peered around the trunk of the tree she had been leaning against. It was Gryss, gazing around rather vaguely.

'You frightened me to death,' she hissed, stepping out from behind the tree.

Gryss started violently. 'And you, me, Marna,' he snapped back, banging his fist on his chest. 'Jumping out like that. I didn't see you.'

Marna, still shaking a little, was about to argue the point when she recalled why she was there. 'I'm sorry,' she said, taking Gryss's arm. 'Look.' She pointed towards the castle. As Gryss leaned forward, the end of the column emerged from the gate, which slowly closed.

As Marna had done, Gryss frowned. 'Where are they going?' he asked.

Marna shrugged. 'I haven't the faintest idea,' she said. 'But I think they've taken all the wagons, most of their horses and nearly all the men.'

'And Rannick, has he gone as well?' Gryss asked.

As if in answer to that question, a light flared livid in the upper window of the tower. 'No,' Marna answered coldly.

Slowly the column disappeared from view around the shoulder of the hill. Gryss shook his head. 'They must have learned about your friends,' he said. 'They're going hunting for them.'

Marna clenched her fists. 'No, no,' she said despairingly. 'No one knew. No one knew. It can't be.'

Gryss did not reply. Marna turned on him. 'You didn't tell anyone else, did you?' she demanded.

Gryss shook his head. 'Only Jeorg, that's all,' he said. 'And Jeorg'd have his tongue cut out before he'd give away such knowledge.'

Marna looked at him questioningly for a moment, then put her hand to her head. 'Then what's happened?' she said futilely. 'And what can we do?'

Gryss reached out to put a supporting arm around her shoulder as he had done many times in the past. Then he lowered it. It seemed to be an inappropriate gesture now. This girl – woman – did not need that kind of support now. 'What we set out to do,' he said. 'Watch and be ready for whatever happens. We've enough work down at the farm to keep us looking busy for some time if we take it easy. We mustn't be impatient. We've no idea what your . . . friends . . . are intending, for all they seem to think the matter's urgent.' He nodded towards the castle. 'And there's no point even conjecturing what's going on up there now. Perhaps they're looking for these people, perhaps not. We'll just have to wait and see.' He let out a noisy breath. 'I'll send our "official" watchers to that copse over there as we agreed, but I'll come back every now and then, to see if you're all right. Or I'll send Jeorg; it's a bit of a pull for me.' He paused, then took out a kerchief. 'If you see anything unusual, hang this' – he searched around for a moment – 'there, on that branch, and one of us will come up straight away. It'll take a little time as we're going round the back so that no one'll notice.' He looked at her. 'You're sure you're all right up here on your own?' he asked uncertainly.

Marna smiled and nodded. 'Yes,' she said. 'I've got a lot to think about.' Then she lowered her eyes. 'How's my father?' she asked.

A look of reproach passed over Gryss's face, but there was none in his reply. 'He's better for knowing you're well and still in the valley,' he said. 'But it wasn't easy refusing to tell him where you were.' He looked as if he wanted to say more, but instead he clenched his fist and waved it at the castle. 'Damn you, Rannick,' he said. 'Damn you to hell.' Then he turned and left.

The day passed without anything else of note happening other than Gryss meticulously changing his 'official' watchers to lend credence to the ostensible purpose of the activity at the farm-house. Marna spent the time thinking, with varying degrees of agitation, about everything that had happened since Dalmas. And, at times, daydreaming. And trying not to fall asleep.

She was more than thankful when Jeorg appeared towards evening and declared that he would watch through the night. Rather than risk being seen walking back to Gryss's cottage, she surreptitiously made her way back to the now-deserted farm, and made herself comfortable in a corner of the barn.

Ironically, unlike the previous night when she had been restless after an exhausting day, following her motionless day watching the castle she went to sleep almost the moment she lay down and scarcely moved during the night.

Some instinct woke her before dawn again and, after splashing herself into shivering wakefulness at one of the water butts, she returned up the hill through the cold morning darkness to take up her vigil.

Jeorg, unshaven, stiff and surly, relinquished his post without any expression of regret.

'Anything happened?' Marna asked.

Jeorg shook his head. 'Only lights coming and going at that tower window,' he replied.

'Rannick,' Marna said.

Jeorg glowered at the tower. 'They felt bad,' he said. 'Unnatural, somehow. I've never seen a lantern that could make light like that.'

Marna confined herself to nodding at this observation. There was nothing to be gained by adding her own comments about the possible nature of that light. Jeorg needed no further incentive to focus his anger against Rannick. She commandeered some food that he had left.

'If you're not going home, don't sleep in the barn,' she said, with a mocking smile, as Jeorg yawned noisily and picked up his bag. 'That's my room.'

Jeorg pulled the brim of her hat down over her face and left with a grunt. He was soon lost in the gloom and, straightening her hat, Marna turned her attention once again to the castle. It was barely visible against the bulk of the mountains, although a few torches in the courtyard illuminated its interior dully and threw a feeble and sickly yellow light part way up the walls of the towers, making them look jagged and incomplete. The upper window of the highest tower continued to flicker alive with light from time to time, however; waxing and waning to some unheard rhythm and giving the impression of a malevolent, watching and inconstant star floating above the tainted remains of some noxious pit. Marna stared at it fixedly for some time and then deliberately pulled her gaze away from it. There was a quality in it that stirred something deep within her, which she knew, instinctively, would only serve to hinder her, though whether it repelled or attracted her she could not have said.

The day passed largely as had the previous one. Figures appeared down in the farmyard, and pairs of lookouts began their own observation of the castle at Gryss's command. Marna watched and waited fretfully, her mood more uncertain than before, but still dominated by a feeling of urgent expectation. Yet nothing happened. The mysterious column that had moved off to the north did not return, and there was little or no activity around the castle itself. 'Where are you? What are you doing?' she began to mutter to herself from time to time.

Towards midday, sheets of fine rain began to blow across the valley. Shifting and changing like a thin grey mist, they now revealed the castle, now obscured it. Marna swore softly. The tree under which she had lodged herself would keep the rain off her for some time, but eventually it would come seeping through and she could look forward to a damp and chilly afternoon.

Her enthusiasm drained to its lowest point as the thought of a warm haven at home rose to tempt her. Then she swore loudly and angrily into the damp air and banged her fist against the rough bark of the tree. There was no haven in this valley for her now. Her father's house could no longer protect her, nor could anyone else's. She had taken herself beyond the pale with her defiance and flight. Her place was here, no matter how grim and dismal it became. She had chosen sides. Chosen the side of those who had come in pursuit of Nilsson but who stayed now in order to make an attempt to slay Rannick and free the valley. They would be as cold and miserable as she, but she knew that they would stay here, in this alien valley, far from their own homes, until that attempt had been made and they were either successful or dead.

Her lips curled back and exposed her clenched teeth in unconscious mimicry of Nilsson's familiar tic as her resolve renewed itself. She stamped her feet and rubbed her hands together, not so much because they were cold, but to remind herself to be alert, to let no part of her fall asleep.

And the action did indeed seem to clear her mind. The scents in the air became sharper, the noises of the dripping trees about her more distinct. As she took a deep breath she caught a slight movement in the corner of her eye. She turned towards it. A powerful hand clamped over her mouth, silencing her cry.

Nilsson looked around sourly as he emerged from his tent into the dull morning. He would have preferred to leave this task to Saddre or Dessane but Rannick had insisted that he oversee it personally, so he could look forward to at least the next few days under canvas and living off camp fare.

He smiled grimly to himself. Had he really adjusted to his changed circumstances so quickly? Only a few weeks ago, such a life had been all that he had known in years, and was all that he could look forward to until some random fortune favoured him, or one of his own men ended his concerns with a silent knife blade. And while that prospect had lain ahead of him, behind him had lurked the will of those against whom he and his men had fought. Fought cruelly, treacherously, and treasonably. And that will would be seeking for them always, he knew. It was the way of his people. All must account for their misdeeds, and neither distance, time, nor the shielding hand of others would diminish the demand for that accounting, or the resolution with which it would be sought.

The reflection made him feel better. No one would dare to test his right to leadership now; he had brought his men prosperity, and, too, as he had been before, he was the only one who truly had the ear of the power that underwrote their ambitions. And as for those who pursued him, let them come. They were as naught now. They would soon discover that events had come full circle and that what they had thought conquered was risen to challenge them again.

He looked up at the trees. These would do splendidly. Tall, large-girthed and straight, they would provide ideal timbers for the siege machines, the wagons, the barracks, the fortifications, and all the other paraphernalia that would be needed for the army that was already forming about the nucleus of his own men. The army which, with him at its head and Rannick at its heart, would strike out from the valley to sweep aside the distant king and his feeble rump of an army and thence use the entire land as a base for the conquest of its neighbours and beyond.

The camp was already alive with noise and clamour, not to mention the smoke and smell of cooking fires. 'A good site, Captain.' Nilsson turned. The speaker was Yeorson, his naturally supercilious expression heightened by a crooked smile. 'Plenty of fine trees here. It'll be some time before we've stripped this place bare. And it'll only take a week or so to cut a decent road back to the castle.'

Nilsson nodded. 'We'll use our new recruits to do most of the dirty work. We can make it part of their . . . initial training. It'll also get the men used to command again. We've a long way to go in every sense and we've been neglectful of discipline lately. These new people need to learn our ways if they're going to be any use to us.'

Yeorson's smiled broadened. 'I'll set them to making a gallows, then,' he said. Nilsson chuckled darkly. This was going to be a good day.

There being nothing to be gained by delay, working parties

were busy clearing the camp site and preparing it for more permanent occupation within the hour, while others were set to work on removing the trees that stood in the way of an easier route back to the castle. The woods rang to the sounds of axes and saws, the groaning crashes of falling trees, and the cries of raucous, commanding voices. The smoke of a dozen or more fires blowing hither and thither, like frightened animals, before finally finding escape out into the dull morning air, gave testimony to the destruction of undergrowth and leafy branches and other unwanted timbers.

Within that same hour, Nilsson also casually stretched two of the new 'recruits' full length on the ground as that part of their 'initial training' that related to injudicious remarks about the distribution of labour within the hierarchy that he was beginning to build.

He breathed in the smoky air, listened to the ringing din about him, and pensively rubbed his bruised knuckles. It was going to be a good day, indeed.

Chapter 23

'Don't scream,' a voice whispered commandingly in Marna's ear. 'It's me, Aaren. Do you understand?'

Marna nodded and mumbled behind the hand clamped over her mouth. Aaren slowly released her. Marna turned on her. 'What did you do that for?' she demanded. 'You frightened me to death.' She held out her hands; they were trembling. 'And what are you doing here, anyway? Aaren? I thought you were up past the castle somewhere. Did Nilsson's men find you?'

Aaren offered no apology, and answered only one of the questions. 'I didn't know it was you until I was on top of you,' she said. 'It's the old man, Gryss, I wanted to see. He's on his way up now and I couldn't risk you – whoever you were – raising an alarm if I suddenly appeared. It is Gryss coming, isn't it?'

'Yes, probably, but—'

Aaren waved her silent. 'Answers when he arrives,' she said curtly, lifting a finger to her lips. 'Right now, I need a little rest. That charade at the farm cost me some heart-searching before I saw what you were up to, I can tell you. It was well done.' She crouched down and leaned back against the tree. She closed her eyes, and Marna saw her wilfully relaxing. 'Keep watch,' she said.

'But—'

'Ssh . . .'

Marna snorted and, still trembling a little, leaned back against the tree next to the resting figure. After a moment, she realized that she was pouting and made a deliberate effort to compose her features. Then all was quiet for a while save for the splashing of the rain through the trees.

Aaren's eyes opened abruptly. 'Someone's coming,' she said, cocking her head on one side. 'It'll be the old man.' She stood up. 'Introduce me to him.' A gentle but definite push propelled Marna from the shelter of the tree.

'Ah. You won't make me jump this time, young woman,' Gryss said, smiling.

Marna held out her arm towards the emerging Aaren. 'This is Aaren, one of the four soldiers from Nilsson's country,' she blurted out, without preamble. 'She – wants to meet you.'

Gryss gaped while he took in this unexpected development, then his natural courtesy carried him forward. He extended his hand and smiled.

Aaren stepped forward and took his hand in both of hers. She bowed slightly. 'We need your help, sir,' she said, before Gryss could speak.

Gryss, still recovering himself, stammered slightly. 'Of course,' he said unthinkingly. 'Marna's told me everything about you. But I thought – Marna thought – you'd gone up past the castle to catch Rannick alone.'

Aaren gave a little smile and nodded an acknowledgement to Marna. Then she flicked an enquiring glance towards one of the knives visible in Marna's belt. 'Everything?' her eyes enquired. Marna gave a slight, fearful, shake of her head. No, not everything. Not that she was a murderer. Aaren understood.

'So we had, sir,' she said, turning back to Gryss. 'But matters have—'

Gryss wrapped his other hand about both of hers. 'Please don't call me sir,' he said. 'I feel old enough as it is. Just call me Gryss, like everyone else.'

Aaren's smile broadened, but, if anything, it highlighted the strain on her face. 'As you wish,' she said.

Gryss released her. 'We're none of us fighters . . . Aaren . . . but we'll help you if we can,' he said.

Aaren looked back towards the castle as she spoke. 'Marna was right,' she began. 'We *were* going to wait for Rannick to make one of his lone trips to the north. But circumstances have changed. Nilsson and almost all of the troop have moved out and are setting up a work camp in the woods.'

'A work camp?' Marna echoed, puzzled.

Aaren nodded. 'They're felling trees.' She gesticulated vaguely. 'Almost certainly it's for the equipment and machinery that they'll need as an army on the move. It means that they're getting ready to move out on a major expedition.'

'And you want to get Rannick before they start?' Marna interjected excitedly.

'Yes,' Aaren replied coldly. 'But mainly we want to kill him while we can.'

Her blunt, but casual use of the word, kill, cut through Marna's momentary exhilaration. The proprietorial glow she had felt in presenting this strange woman to Gryss evaporated, and she was brought back to her damp look-out post and the cruel circumstances of the valley.

'What do you mean?' Gryss asked unhappily.

Aaren hesitated. 'We have some experience of the power that Rannick uses,' she said eventually. 'A great deal, unfortunately. Having seen what we've seen these last couple of nights, and – felt what we've felt, we think that Rannick may be reaching a stage where his skill will render him almost invulnerable to a normal physical assault.'

She looked into Gryss's openly doubting face. 'It's true,' she said. 'Marna's told me what you've seen yourself: the wind that was guarding the castle yard, the fire that he conjured out of nothingness. We think that by now he's probably passed far beyond such tricks. And the greater his skill becomes, the faster it will grow.' She paused, as if she did not want to continue. 'Soon, he'll be scarcely human, and beyond anything we might be able to do to him.' She turned to Marna. 'I think you've got some measure of this in that he didn't come looking for you particularly hard after you rejected him.'

Marna tried to meet her gaze with studied indifference, but she had to turn away from the pain in it. 'I was – surprised,' she conceded uncomfortably. 'He was all too – human – when I parted from him.' She felt herself colouring at the memory of Rannick's last gentle kiss and the promise that had lain behind it. 'But he was like two people when he drew that strange fire out of nowhere.'

Aaren turned to Gryss again. 'If he reaches that stage, then nothing – nothing in *this* land – can stop him. And by the time we could marshal resources against him, his power, his following, and his conquests would be a hundred times what they are now.'

Gryss shook his head in bewilderment. 'I can't begin to take all this in.' He wanted to ask why all this should be happening to him, to the valley. Why Rannick? Why now? Why . . .? But he had asked the questions many times and he knew that, for all her knowledge, this woman would have no answers for him. 'Just tell me what you want us to do,' he said, clinging to the simplicity of practicalities.

'What we have to do, Gryss, is kill him as quickly as possible,' Aaren said starkly. 'We can't risk waiting until he decides to come out on his own. There's no saying when that might be.' She hesitated, then, 'We're going to try and get into the castle tonight. While most of the men are away. And—'

'Do you have to kill him?' Gryss interrupted. His voice was as full of judgement as it was question. In spite of all that had happened, he had known Rannick all his life and he found Aaren's quiet purposefulness cutting through him.

Momentarily however, Aaren's emotions broke through on to her face. Gryss started back at the mixture of anger, fear and desperation he read there. 'Yes,' she said, through clenched teeth, as she struggled to control herself. 'The power corrupts and will tolerate no restraint. It's him or us.' She waved a hand across the rainswept valley. 'All of us. All of you. And beyond. Be under no illusions about that.'

'But—'

'No buts, Gryss,' Aaren said, angrily wiping a tear from her eye. 'Knowing what we know, we've no choice. While he can still be stopped by such as us, we have to try. If we fail – then—' She stopped and let out a nervous breath. 'The future you have now will probably be unchanged.' She looked at Marna. 'But we'll leave you with messages to carry to the king – in case . . .'

Gryss closed his eyes. Arguments tumbled through his head. And questions; still so many questions. And Aaren's doubts were contagious. But there was one certainty, above all: he must not betray the valley and its people again. The memory came to him of the cruelly slaughtered bodies of Garren and Katrin Yarrance. There lay the future as sure as it was the past. And Farnor, wherever he might be now. And all the pain that had come to his friends, his charges. And could he accept the responsibility of this being repeated over and over?

He remembered Farnor fingering the simple iron ring that swung from its chain by his door. A memento of his youth, of times and places far away. A memento finely and skilfully carved with lines of warriors, waiting.

For what, did not matter. They were a people prepared.

He opened his eyes and looked at Aaren. She was one such, surely. Armed with knowledge to see what had to be done, and perhaps the skill to do it. And there was Marna too: Marna Harlenkind; made by circumstance into a grim-faced fugitive, with knives in her belt.

And they were both waiting. 'What do you want me to do?' he asked.

'Is none of this familiar to you?' Derwyn asked, trying to keep the incredulity from his voice.

Farnor shook his head. 'No,' he replied. 'All the Forest north of the castle was unfamiliar, and when I came through here, it was at some speed and for most of the way with my eyes closed.'

This answer, uttered with exaggerated self-deprecation, caused a little more laughter than it should have done, reflecting the growing nervousness of the Valderen as they moved steadily into what they kept referring to as the fringe.

'The trees are – smaller – more compact – less happy,' Derwyn had explained uncertainly, when Farnor had asked what they meant.

'They look fine to me,' Farnor replied, a little defensively. 'But I don't suppose I've got your eye for such things. I've always thought that all trees were fascinating.'

Derwyn had beamed. 'Your eye's fine, Farnor. And so are your trees,' he said, without patronizing. 'They're just different.' He looked at Farnor archly. 'And you've probably got Valderen blood in your veins somewhere. Perhaps there used to be a lot more movement between the valley and the Forest once upon a time.' And he had laughed.

But it had been a different sound to that which greeted the admission that Farnor just made. Indeed, everything about the group seemed to be different now. Farnor had the impression that they were riding into a deepening darkness. In part, this was actually true: the weather was overcast and gloomy, and the enclosing mountains made their shading presence felt even when they could not be seen through the canopy. Sunset would come earlier and dawn later. But also, he sensed an inner darkness beginning to pervade the group; a darkness that brought the riders closer together and made them even more silent than usual.

It came from the trees, he was sure. 'Everyone Hears a little,' he remembered someone saying, and they would not have to Hear much to be affected by the fear and uncertainty that was quivering through the trees all around them. He himself was having to exert a continuous effort to keep the din from his mind.

As if sensing his concerns, Marken came alongside him. 'It's dreadful, isn't it?' he whispered. 'I've never Heard anything like it. It's bad enough during a fire, but at least then they seem to understand in some way, seem to be able to cope. Here, it's like a mindless panic. What can we do?'

Farnor puffed out his cheeks. The Hearer, wiser than him by far, was looking to him for help. It was a strange sensation, both frightening and exciting. 'Stay by me. And listen,' he said on impulse.

Reluctantly, he opened his mind to the trees. A fearful confusion cascaded over and through him and for a moment he swayed in his saddle. Then, suddenly angry, he shouted at them furiously. 'Shut up!'

The noise faltered.

He shouted again, his anger growing. 'Shut up, damn you! You cloud all our minds with your clamour. If you want our help you must ride with us, not against us.'

The noise faded, and Farnor felt as though he were in the presence of a group of children caught in some misdeed; both guilt and relief filled the silence. In the distance he could Hear the noise continuing, and he realized that his command had somehow made a pool of calm amid a torrent of confusion.

Having obtained this calm, however, he was uncertain what to do with it. He could sense the single presence of the Forest, but it was fragmented into a myriad individual voices. Abruptly he had an image of himself as a child, looking at a piece of metal lying on the anvil in the village forge. What had been a magically glowing yellow had faded through orange and red into a dull grey brown even as he watched it, and he had wanted to know why. He remembered how he had reached out to touch it and how his fingers had snatched themselves away almost before he felt the dreadful pain.

He remembered, too, Gofhern the blacksmith lifting him bodily away from the anvil and plunging his hand into a bucket of cold water in one swinging, head-spinning arc. 'Your fingers have more sense than your head, young Farnor,' he had chuckled, though only after he had determined that the injury was not too serious.

And was it thus here? Were the individual trees responding to some pain that he could not feel, and confusing his perception of the will of the whole? 'What do you do when there's a fire?' he asked without thinking why.

The listening silence shifted awkwardly. He had the feeling that he had asked an embarrassing question.

'Well?' he insisted.

'If I have the time, then we move,' came a slightly injured reply, eventually.

'Explain,' Farnor persisted.

Then he felt the presence of the most ancient; distant, but quite distinct. It coloured the answering voice. 'I withdraw that which is private to each – home – and it remains amongst us, sharing – homes – until the seedlings come again and a new – home – can be made.' The images that filled Farnor's mind with each mention of the word home were deep, personal and intimate, with a poignancy far beyond even the feelings that he had for his own home. 'But the pain is great, Far-nor, and the leaving of a – home – is no light thing. There is always pain in the loss of what we are attached to. Even to speak thus distresses us.'

Farnor became more gentle. 'I'm sorry,' he said. 'But we must learn to understand such things. What happens when your . . . homes . . . die, or are felled by the Valderen to make their lodges and to fulfil their other needs?'

He could feel puzzlement and debate at this question, then an amused realization. 'I do not – die, Far-nor. This we told you.' Again Farnor felt a brief touch of the dizzying, time-spanning perspective that he had felt on occasions before. 'But our – homes – change, and fall back to whence they came, to become eventually – homes – again, renewed. These we leave at our leisure. It is the way of things. As for the Valderen, they perceive our needs, albeit dimly, and they respect them. They ask, and time is granted for the leaving. And *their* needs are slight within the endless falling and renewing that occurs within our vastness. We can withstand a little pain for the sake of our friends from time to time.' There was almost a chuckle. 'Besides I do not dwell too deeply in those – homes – that lie near to the Valderen.'

Farnor rode on in silence for a while, thinking about the words and the nuances behind and beyond them. 'But this fear around me is not the fear of fire?' he asked tentatively, after a while.

'Fire is both ancient and frequent, Far-nor. It is not welcomed, but it is known and understood and thus not *truly* feared. It, too, is in the way of things and a part of my nature. But the power that

289

threatens here, though known and ancient, is nevertheless not understood. And it is unfettered and greater by far than when you first came. We fear to stay, and we fear to leave.' The voice was full of regret, shame even.

'I understand,' Farnor said. 'So it is with us also. But your fear clouds our vision. Though they do not know it, it touches the hearts of the Valderen and darkens them, weakens them. You must be our ally or you aid our common foe.' He spoke sternly. 'Prepare yourself for fire, or accept the pain of leaving and go from your homes here, now.'

There was a long silence. Marken glanced nervously at Farnor, uncertain about the consequences of his making this unexpected demand so resolutely.

'We accept your rebuke, Far-nor,' came the answer eventually. 'We can do no less than you do. We are with you. We shall prepare ourselves for fire.'

That evening, as they camped, Farnor spoke to a gathering of the hunters and told of his discourse with the trees. He was listened to with great attentiveness and there was much head nodding. 'There *is* a different feeling in the air, something that's not just the mountains and these fringe trees,' was the consensus.

Farnor was pleased with what he had achieved as he lay down in his tent that night, though he found being the focus of the Valderen's attention whenever he spoke, disturbing.

When he woke the following morning he felt refreshed and alert, although at the edges of his mind were vague, troubling images. They slipped away from him as he tried to recall them, vanishing into the clamour of the awakening camp.

Throughout the day, the group moved on as noiselessly as before, but in better heart. Yet the watchful silence that now pervaded the trees was unsettled. 'What's the matter?' Farnor asked eventually.

'The power grows,' came the reply, with undertones that once again verged on panic.

And then, like an elusive but unpleasant smell in the air, Farnor sensed the presence of the creature. He reined his horse to a halt and looked about him carefully. He felt part of him reaching out to touch the creature, but somehow he restrained it. The creature was sleeping, or in some other way dormant. He must not touch it. It must remain thus.

Derwyn looked at him questioningly, but did not speak.

Farnor edged his horse over to him. 'I think we may have to go our separate ways soon,' he whispered. 'Move quietly from here, and take great care. We're in its territory, for sure, though it's not hunting at the moment.' He took Derwyn's arm and gripped it strongly. 'I can't tell you too strongly. Don't underestimate this thing,' he said. 'It's no wild boar or bear. It's human malevolence made into tooth and claw, and far more savage than anything you've ever known. It's a thing of nightmare. It'll kill you and those with you with greater ease and far greater relish than a fox kills chickens in a coop if it's given the slightest chance.' Then, for some reason he did not understand, he said, 'Expect to be afraid, but don't fear your fear.'

Though the message was not new to him, Farnor's intensity disturbed Derwyn as much as his forthright manner surprised him. He made a gesture and the hunters began to string their bows and untip their lances.

And then they were moving again.

Despite Farnor's warning, however, nothing untoward happened during the remainder of that day, nor during the following night, although a little while after he had first noticed it he began to sense the presence of the creature constantly. Again, he felt himself restraining some urge to reach out to it. That night, without comment, Derwyn placed an extensive guard about the camp.

'You must warn us if it wakes,' Farnor instructed the trees. An unspoken acceptance filled his mind.

Knowing that the trees would watch unsleepingly for any stirring by the creature reassured him greatly as he lay alone in his small tent. But despite this, and though fatigued from the day's riding, he was unable to sleep. As he drew inexorably nearer to his own land and the source of his troubles, so the need to make clear and definite plans became more pressing. Yet, still he could not; at least no more than he had been able to do hitherto. All he could do was hide in the forest, watch the castle and wait for the time when Rannick would emerge alone again to ride north and . . .

Then, for the first time, he realized that the goals which he and the Valderen were pursuing were inextricably linked. That such an obvious fact had not occurred to him before chilled him and brought him upright, breathing shallowly. What else had he missed? Not for the first time in the quiet of the night, he asked himself what he was doing here. He felt again the eyes of the listening Valderen watching him, trusting him, relying on him. Men and women older than he. It was frightening.

As he lay back again, he searched instinctively for an excuse for this negligence. Throughout his journey to the central mountains and back, his hesitant advice to Derwyn had been locked tight into his mind. *Guard* your southern border. *Protect* yourself. In his thoughts had been images of defence; images of an attack being repelled by a static, impenetrable barrier of some kind; people, traps, . . . whatever. Indeed, it seemed to him, such ideas pervaded the whole thinking of the Valderen themselves, with their talk of the fringes of the Forest and outsiders.

Yet these people were hunters. It could not be in their nature to tolerate persistent danger from an animal. A threat of the moment might be averted by flight, or noise, or fire, and was acceptable; but a further threat – an expression of wilful intent – was surely a death sentence for the offending animal.

And, of course, it was death that they intended for the creature. Perhaps it was the fact that it had scarcely been voiced in so many words that had kept the consequences from presenting themselves clearly before him until now; had kept him thinking, in so far as he had thought about it at all, that he and they were merely riding together; they to seek out the creature with a view to – keeping it from the Forest – and he to seek out Rannick.

But of course, Rannick and the creature were effectively one. To attack either would be to bring the other down in furious response. He swore angrily at himself for his foolishness in not appreciating this earlier. 'Obvious, obvious, obvious,' he muttered to himself. Then abruptly, and somewhat to his surprise, he became calm and resolute, and oddly relieved, as if something had just fallen into place.

It was, after all, only a matter of tactics. The affair was no longer one of his personal revenge. As he had told the trees, they all shared a common enemy and it did not matter who defeated which, just so long as the enemy was defeated. His eyes closed.

He must discuss this with Derwyn in the morning. The obvious . . . he clenched his fists at the word, then used it again . . . the obvious thing to do would be for the Valderen to seek out and, if possible, destroy the creature, and then await the arrival of Rannick. He yawned. He must discuss this with Derwyn . . . in the morning . . . no, immediately. Even as he made this decision, however, he fell asleep.

Nevertheless, this same train of thought was still with him when he woke the next morning, and he was still dressing himself as he walked sleepily across to Derwyn's tent with the intention of discussing it. He stopped suddenly as a jolting tremor of panic ran through him.

Fire!

The fear in it jerked him so violently into wakefulness that he almost stumbled even though he knew immediately that the response was not his own.

'What's the matter?' he asked silently.

'Movers. Fire. Felling,' came the immediate response. It was a mixture of one and many voices and it was full of fear and pain. And was that screaming in the distance?

'Marken!' Farnor roared across the gentle hubbub of the waking camp.

'Save yourselves,' he said to the voices with a calmness and authority that surprised him. 'But show me. Take me there.'

'But—'

'DO IT!'

And on the instant, he was transformed.

There was darkness. Or rather, there was no sight. Nor was there hearing, nor touch. But what had been these things was now a myriad other senses, each telling him of the many worlds about him. He was at once vast and but an infinite part of that vastness. And where that infinite part lay, the pain lay also. The terrible pain. And the deeds of the Movers. And their will. That unmistakable will: callous, indifferent, killing . . .

And there were many threads within it. A great many threads. Some dull and lifeless, others sharp and . . .

Nilsson!

The part of the Forest that was Farnor recognized *that* thread woven among the will of the Movers. It was Nilsson who had entered to wreak havoc amongst the . . . homes.

A searing pain swept through him.

'This is too dangerous, Far-nor.' The voice of the Forest, though distant, was determined. 'You are not as we are. You must return.'

'Are you all right? Are you all right?'

Farnor's eyes focused with agonizing slowness on Marken's

anxious face. 'Yes, yes,' he stammered, his voice alien in his own ears. 'Did you Hear their calls?'

Marken nodded. 'Fire,' he said. 'And something worse. What's happening, Farnor?'

Derwyn emerged out of the circle forming around them.

'I must speak to you right away,' Farnor said, but as he stepped forward he staggered. It seemed to him that his feet were rooted deep into the earth, and their sudden moving caused him to cry out in pain. But only the trees heard the cry. Farnor's fellow Movers, knowing him to be a faller, merely caught him. He shook them off roughly. 'I'm all right. It's just cramp,' he lied.

'Come into my tent,' Derwyn said, taking his arm firmly.

With an effort, Farnor cleared himself of the residue of his strange transformation and forced his feet forward carefully. He was grateful for Derwyn's supporting hand however, for the first few paces.

He offered no explanation of what had happened as he halted by Derwyn's tent. He simply blurted out, 'Nilsson and his men have come into the woods and are cutting and burning the trees. We must—'

He stopped. The effect of his announcement on Derwyn and those around him had been staggering and immediate. First disbelief, then an unbelievable fury, coloured all their faces and suddenly there was uproar. For a moment he was afraid. It dawned on him that he had not the remotest measure of what the trees truly meant to these people. Derwyn, patently struggling to control his own emotions, stood in front of him and closed a powerful hand about his shoulder. 'Cutting and *burning*, you say?' he asked. '*Our* Forest?'

'There's fire,' Marken intruded by way of confirmation of what Farnor had said. 'I can feel it. And something else.'

Farnor nodded. 'It's – it's Nilsson and his men,' he managed to say, increasingly concerned about what he might have inadvertently unleashed.

There was barely a flicker of reason in Derwyn's ferocious gaze as he asked, 'How can you know that?'

Briefly Farnor sought for an explanation, but there were no words that could begin to encompass the experience. 'I know,' he said simply. Yanking himself free from Derwyn's hand, he stepped away. Though he had no idea what forces he had let loose with his rash announcement, he knew that it was more important than ever now that he give voice to his thoughts on what must be done next. 'Whatever's happening ahead, we must deal with the creature first,' he shouted determinedly into the din. 'Its lair is within a day's ride, I'm sure. We must—'

'We must deal with these intruders,' Derwyn said grimly. 'The animal can wait.' He began giving orders to the people standing about him.

'No!' Farnor cried, seizing his arm. 'Listen to me! It's asleep now. It may be possible to find and kill it before it wakens. If it wakes, then' – he waved an arm over the now hectic camp – 'everyone's life here will be at risk from it.'

Derwyn looked at him intently. It was a strange gaze, full of a terrible passion, but Farnor could see indulgence and patience vying there. There was a forced calmness in Derwyn's voice when he spoke. 'I feel your concern, Farnor, and I respect it. But you don't understand what it is to be Valderen. We must rid the Forest of these intruders before we do anything else. On your own admission, you're no hunter. I've no doubt that this – thing – this creature – is something very dangerous. Or that it gave you a severe fright when it chased you into the Forest.' He tapped himself on the chest. 'But we *are* hunters. We know about animals. Truly. There's none as bad and treacherous as man, and we'll deal with those first. Then we'll return for the creature, have no fear.'

Farnor released him and looked around frantically as he felt events slipping away from him. Somewhere, ill-formed and unclear though the thoughts were, he knew that Derwyn and the others were using this unexpected development to take refuge from the strangeness of this whole eerie, alien hunt. There was, after all, nothing strange in protecting the Forest from the depredations of outsiders. It was the Valderen's ancient duty, and even though they had not been called on to exercise it for countless generations, it was none the less a fundamental measure for them of their worth as a people.

Farnor's every instinct told him that he could not overcome the momentum of this ancient will, but he could do no other than try. 'If your old tales are anything like ours, with battles full of glory and excitement, then this will be nothing like them,' he shouted, again seizing Derwyn's arm as he was turning away. 'Nilsson's men aren't casual intruders. They're brutal fighting men, and they're doing whatever they're doing to fulfil some purpose of

Rannick's. If you go against them like this, rashly, they'll hack you down without a thought.' He pointed up towards the mountains. 'And if that thing smells blood, it'll awaken. You could end up with Nilsson's men *and* Rannick to your front, and that creature at your back.'

Derwyn faltered before Farnor's grim purposefulness, but the deeply ingrained history of his people carried him forward. 'We'll drive these people out, Farnor, return to hunt the creature, and then help you to deal with this Rannick,' he said, though the reassurance in his voice was denied by the impatience with which he pulled himself free from Farnor's grip.

'In the name of sanity, tell them!' Farnor roared silently at the trees.

'The Valderen are the Valderen,' came the reply. 'As you are you. Your pain is that of a Mover. It is beyond us.'

Farnor swore at them viciously and turned to Marken. 'Tell him, for pity's sake,' he said, waving towards Derwyn's retreating back as he walked through the camp issuing instructions.

'I can't,' the Hearer replied, his face pained. 'I'm torn myself. I understand what you say. I feel the truth of it. But I'm Valderen. I . . .' His voice faded and he made a helpless gesture.

Farnor looked around desperately. He saw Angwen and Edrien standing nearby, watching. Edrien's face was distressed, but Angwen's had become like a mask and was beyond any reading by him. He went over to them.

'Do Valderen women fight?' he asked Angwen brutally, his eyes glaring into hers.

'We hunt,' she replied, very quietly, touching the bow that Edrien was carrying.

'Fight?' Farnor insisted, baring his teeth and raising a clenched fist in front of her face. 'Kill people?'

Angwen shook her head.

'You've a few hours to school yourselves to the idea then,' Farnor went on, his voice harsh. 'You and the other women, pack this camp, arm yourselves, and wait. If things go badly for your husbands – *and they probably will* – be prepared to kill as many of the pursuers as you can. Show no mercy; it's not the time, and they don't deserve it. But above all, make sure that some of you get back to your lodges and spread the word of what's happened here, because this will be only a beginning. Do you understand me?'

Angwen nodded slightly, but her face was still unreadable. Edrien laid a shaking hand on her mother's arm. 'And what will you do, Farnor?' Angwen asked, her voice almost icily calm.

Farnor put his hand to his head, then dropped it limply. He looked from side to side, as if for some way of escape. His thoughts were in turmoil. How could things have gone so horribly wrong so suddenly? 'I don't know,' he said eventually.

'You seem to know what my father should be doing, though, don't you?' Edrien burst out furiously. Angwen raised a gentle hand to silence her.

Farnor glowered at her, a vicious response forming in his mind. Then he felt Angwen's eyes on him, and Edrien became a daughter; someone little different from himself in that soon she might well be cruelly, pointlessly, orphaned. He turned on his heel and strode off without replying.

Chapter 24

As soon as Gryss had left them, Marna turned to Aaren. 'Take me with you,' she said.

'No,' Aaren replied unequivocally and without hesitation. 'It's too dangerous.'

'*Here* is dangerous,' Marna retorted. 'Everywhere in the valley's dangerous now, especially for me. I can't go with Gryss and the others, can I? And there's nothing useful I can do here.'

Aaren's reply was impatient. 'Just stay here. Stay hidden until it's all over.'

'The hell I will,' Marna blazed. 'This is *my* valley, woman, and most of what you know about it is because of me!'

'No! You're not trained. You couldn't—'

'I killed that man.' Shame filled her at the boast, but she held Aaren's gaze.

'You got lucky. Be told. Stay here. You're no use to us.'

The shame became a livid rage as Marna took in this remark and its scornful utterance. Furiously she swung her hand up to strike Aaren's face. A contemptuous flick deflected it effortlessly and she suddenly felt Aaren's hand closing about her throat. The pressure was not great, but almost immediately she felt everything around her begin to swim and darken. Somehow she lifted her hands to take Aaren's wrist, though there was no strength in them. 'My valley, my people, you bitch,' she heard herself saying in the distance.

Then the darkness was gone and two strong arms were wrapped around her, supporting her. 'I'm sorry, Marna,' Aaren said, her voice hoarse and unsteady. 'You're right, and I'm wrong. It *is* your valley and it's not up to me to stop you fighting for it. We'll find something useful for you to do. You can come.'

Her embrace fell away. Marna straightened up and looked at her erstwhile antagonist. Her anger vanished at what she saw.

'You're a long way from home, and frightened, aren't you?' she said with a sudden, heartbreaking insight.

Aaren's lips tightened briefly, then her features composed themselves and she raised an ironic eyebrow. 'And you, young woman, are too much like I used to be.' She became purposeful. 'But understand, as you've already been told, if you come with us you keep quiet and do *exactly* what you're told, immediately and without question.' She shook her head. 'I hope I'm not going to regret this. Let's hope your luck holds.'

The next few hours saw the two women making a stealthy journey through the woods and across the rainswept landscape until they were in the woods to the north of the castle. There they were met by Engir, Levrik and Yehna.

Engir threw a quick glance at Marna and spoke sharply to Aaren in their own language.

'I've come to help,' Marna said, before Aaren could reply. Engir started in surprise. 'I don't need to know your language to understand *that* remark,' Marna went on. 'And I've had this argument once. I mightn't be trained but I'm not stupid. Just tell me what to do and I'll do it, because I'm not leaving.'

There was an uncertain pause, then Levrik said to her, 'You can mind the horses. We might need them quickly when we come out and it'll be pitch dark then. It could save a lot of time, not to mention our necks.'

Marna was both surprised and pleased by this intervention from the most silent of the group, but despite a feeling of gratitude towards him there was still a quality about the man that disturbed her.

His suggestion was accepted however, and some time was spent introducing Marna to the horses and giving her detailed instructions for their tending, followed by further instructions on how to respond to the different signals that she might hear once the attack had begun. For the remainder of the day the four continued their own preparations; checking and rechecking their weapons and equipment, and repeatedly going over their plan and its various contingencies. Then there was a strange, tense interlude when all was completed and there was nothing to do but wait until the night came and they could venture forth.

It stopped raining, and the air filled with rich, damp forest perfumes, and the sound of the soft dripping of the rain still held in the leaves above. As she watched her new companions, Marna wondered at their quietness and stillness, though she sensed that only Levrik was truly relaxed, truly here. Some part, at least, of each of the others was elsewhere. She herself felt as though she were holding her breath continuously.

Unable to cope with the waiting, she wandered over to Aaren and spoke to her softly, asking about the attack they planned, even though she had heard it described a dozen or more times. Aaren seemed quite willing, even anxious, to speak about it yet again. She concluded almost in a whisper, 'You know what you've got to do, but if things don't appear to be working out as we intend, don't be afraid to use your own judgement.' She paused and looked straight at Marna. '*I* trust it. And so does Levrik.'

Marna had no reply. She glanced over at the motionless figure of her other sponsor into this mysterious group. 'He frightens me,' she heard herself whispering. She clamped her hand over her mouth as her mind raced to find an apology.

Aaren looked at her. 'So he should,' she said, a strange flatness in her tone. 'As should I. As should all of us.' The light caught her eyes, making them glint as she peered through the leafy shade, and Marna's hands began to shake. Aaren reached out and took them. 'Above all, Levrik should frighten you. But in what we do, believe me, Levrik guarding your back is worth a score of the rest of us.'

Unnerved by the turn of the conversation and anxious to end it, Marna staggered into another blunder. 'How did you lose the end of your finger?' she asked.

There was a slight pause, and then Aaren's noiseless laugh reached her. A maternal hand patted her face. 'A friend bit it off,' came the reply, and the soft laughter renewed itself.

'A friend!' Marna exclaimed softly.

'There are times when you get to know who your real friends are, Marna,' Aaren said, still laughing. 'But that's enough. I'll tell you some other time. When this day's behind us as well.'

Marna held her peace, far from certain what folly she might commit next. For some time she heard Aaren chuckling to herself, but even in the failing light she could see that the woman was nervously squeezing the end of her damaged finger.

Then, unseen behind the grey clouds, the sun dipped behind the mountains and darkness began to seep into the valley. There was a terse command from Engir, and with a last-minute check that Marna knew her signals and what she was to do, the four were gone, soft and silent as shadows.

Marna stood for some time in the deepening gloom, then, carefully checking that the horses were securely tethered, she cautiously followed a thin guideline down to what was to be her post at the edge of the trees. In the near distance, she could make out the castle. As on the previous night, torches in the courtyard were illuminating the walls of the various towers, and from Rannick's eyrie the sickly and unnatural light pulsed erratically.

She shivered, though whether it was the light from Rannick's window, the evening dampness, or the cold fear that was tugging at her stomach, she could not have said. Now she must watch and wait and, above all, as Aaren had emphasized at the last, 'Be aware.'

Farnor dropped down on to a grassy bank and wiped his forehead. He had been walking uphill steadily for some time and, despite the rain that had started, he was sweating and his shirt was sticking unpleasantly to his back.

Somewhere below, he knew that Derwyn and the Valderen would be advancing through the woods towards Nilsson and his men. He rested his head in his hands and tried to shake off his vexation at what he still saw to be the folly of this action. His anger, he knew, would serve no useful end, and, he suspected, might well cloud his judgement; indeed, it might well already have done so. In so far as I've got any judgement, he sneered to himself as he recalled his part in what had happened.

Seeing the futility of his appeals to Derwyn, he had stood for some time watching the Valderen frenziedly preparing to leave, then he had packed his own few things, taken his two horses, and quietly slipped away. He must stay with the realization that had come to him in the night. The creature, Rannick and Nilsson were enemies to both the Valderen and the people of the valley, and they must be seen as such. If Derwyn, for whatever reason, could not accept the threat that the creature posed, then to quarrel with him beyond a certain point was merely to serve the enemy's ends. He, Farnor, must act so as to make good what he saw to be the folly of his ally. He must kill the creature on his own.

And so far, all had been with him. The presence of the creature hung in the damp air like a miasma, but it was still dormant, as if it were sleeping or, more sinisterly, absent in some other way.

Farnor let his feet guide him. As well as the presence of the creature, he could feel the trees around him, resolutely watchful. In the distance he could sense the pain that Nilsson's assault was causing them and he knew that they were deliberately keeping it from him. Occasionally however, a thin, piercing shriek would tear through to him, making him stop in his tracks and stiffen in distress as it faded into the interminable distance. He remained silent, though. Their true pain was beyond his understanding, and nothing he could say would lessen it. All that he could do, he was doing, and this they knew and accepted.

He looked up at the darkening sky and frowned. Soon it would be pitch black and he would be wandering about the woods with only a small sunstone lantern to guide him. Not only would he not be able to see very far, he would also be very conspicuous. He swore silently to himself, then stood up and set off again. He must make what progress he could, while he could, though that in its turn begged the question as to what progress was, for he had no specific idea where he was going.

Occasionally, as he had started to do on his journey back from the most ancient, he would touch a tree to see if, as individuals, they could offer him any guidance. But their responses were weak and varied, and he sensed that much of whatever spirit lay in these . . . homes . . . had already withdrawn, and that his touch tended to lure them back and was thus painful. After a while he stopped.

Eventually he came to the edge of the trees to find himself on the arm of a great cwm which swept away from him into the gloom, dark and ominous. In what was left of the light, he could just make out a rocky slope rising up from the tree line.

The presence of the creature was growing stronger. He looked at his two horses. They would be no further use to him now, clattering and unsteady across the rain-slicked rocks. And, not knowing when, or if, he would be back, he could not tether them somewhere, like sacrifices. He would have to abandon them and carry such as he needed himself. Besides, they were becoming increasingly unhappy, as if they too could sense the nearness of the creature.

Wiping the rain from his eyes, he went over to the pack pony to remove the various weapons he had snatched up for this expedition. There was a Valderen bow, quite unlike anything he had

302

ever seen in the valley; not big, but very powerful – if he could draw it. And there were the vicious, barbed-headed arrows. He was no bowman, but he was sure he could hit a large animal at a range that would be safely out of jaws' reach, and that was where he intended to remain. Nevertheless, he had chosen also a large machete on which he had managed to hone a reasonable edge.

As he began loosening the straps that secured its pack, the pony slithered sideways into him nervously, knocking him off balance. He grabbed at it hastily but missed his footing on the wet rocks and staggered heavily against it. With a startled neigh, the pony began prancing anxiously. The noise of its scrabbling hooves on the rocks rose into the silent air to startle it further.

Still unbalanced, Farnor flailed out blindly in an attempt to catch hold of the pony and restrain it. His hand closed around something just as the pony decided to bolt. Panicking as he felt himself beginning to be dragged along, Farnor tightened his grip but, fortunately for him, the object tore free from the loosened straps as the animal gathered speed. He was still gripping it tightly as he went sprawling painfully on the rocky ground.

He lay there for some time, absorbed in the new discomforts that were putting fresh life into his older aches and pains. Then, as his senses began to clear, he realized that he was listening to the flight not only of the pony but of his horse as well: it had seemingly concurred with its fellow's judgement and also fled.

Struggling to his feet, he stared into the darkness in dismay, until the last faint echoes of the fleeing horses had died away completely. For a moment rage overcame him. He wanted to rant and scream after the demented animals, to hurl rocks into the darkness, to rend the very air with his fury. But the mood faded as quickly as it had come, displaced by an odd fatalism. Briefly, the memory of Uldaneth returned to him. What had happened had happened and nothing he could do would remedy it now. And he still had no alternative but to go on and to deal with events as they developed and with whatever came to hand.

He reached into his pocket and retrieved the small sunstone lantern that Angwen had given him as a gift. Carefully he checked that the shutter was closed before he struck it, then he eased it open very slightly; he still had sufficient wit to realize that the last thing he needed now was his night vision destroyed for minutes on end by the lantern's brightness.

With the aid of the thin, rain-streaked sliver of light he

examined himself to see if any serious damage had been done in his fall. Eventually satisfied that he had suffered only yet more bruising, he sat down on a rock to think. As he did so, the faint light from the lantern caught the object that he had grabbed hold of when the pony bolted. It was the staff that Marrin had given him.

He clicked the lantern shut as he bent to pick up the staff. This was going to be invaluable, he thought caustically as he hefted it. He felt a hint of disapproval about him, but it was gone almost before he noted it, and he did not pursue it. Then the fatalism that had quietened him earlier gave-way to anger and despair. What use was he going to be now even if he found the creature; alone, unarmed and benighted.

'Not alone, Far-nor.' The voice of the trees filled his head. He waved a pointless acknowledgement. 'No,' he conceded. 'But unless you've suddenly learned to walk and fight, then I'm afraid you're going to be nothing more than a silent witness to what happens if that creature awakes.'

'No. We can touch it a little. We did before. Turned it from you in confusion.' There was a plaintive quality in the voice that did not inspire confidence, however.

I was on a desperate, charging horse then, Farnor thought, but he did not articulate it so that the trees could Hear.

What a mess! Some rearguard he was going to make for Derwyn now. What had possessed him to think he could tackle the creature on his own? What was he, after all? Just a stupid boy, stuck up a mountain with an ornamental lantern, his mother's carving knife in his belt, and an old man's stick. He sneered at the image.

Then, the atmosphere about him changed. 'Far-nor,' the trees whispered fearfully. 'It wakes.'

Derwyn's mood shifted violently as he rode steadily southwards through the fine, damping, rain. The ancient mistrust of the Valderen of outsiders was deep and powerful. It provoked a response that could not easily be set aside by reason, least of all by the Koyden-dae, with their almost total inexperience in dealing with such people. And these outsiders were doing that which, said tradition, outsiders had always done; they were wantonly, cruelly, destroying the Forest. It was, beyond a doubt, the duty of the Valderen to drive away such people.

And yet, Farnor's response disturbed him. The young man was seemingly a Hearer such as there had never been before; one before whom Marken bowed without reserve. He should be accorded respect and, above all, listened to. But too, he was barely a man yet. He could not possibly have the soundness of judgement of an older man, an experienced leader of men. And he was not Valderen.

But he had been called to the place of the most ancient – a hitherto unknown occurrence. And that strange old bird Uldaneth had expressed a great interest in him. Uldaneth; an unrepentant outsider, who knew more about the Valderen than they themselves, who vanished for years on end and then just appeared again, wandering freely from lodge to lodge. He shook his head. He had problems enough without fretting about Uldaneth. She was an enigma even deeper than Farnor.

'You're troubled.'

Marken's voice broke into Derwyn's milling thoughts. He nodded. 'Farnor's troubling me,' he replied. 'He seemed so certain. And so angry. And sneaking off on his own like that. I can't help wondering if I should've listened to him more.'

Marken put his hand to his head, his face troubled. He could barely keep from his mind the terrible sound of the trees struggling to escape the depredations of Nilsson and his men. And he, too, was torn. Farnor's leaving had drawn a cloudy veil over his own newfound contact with the trees. He wanted to go after him, find out what was happening, ask him what he was going to do. Yet he was the lodge's Hearer. His place was here, by Derwyn, riding to destroy these invaders. And whether the decision to ride against them was right or not, it had been made, and Derwyn had to be supported. Doubt would serve only to cripple him. 'He's not Valderen,' he said. 'He doesn't truly understand. Your judgement's sound in this, Derwyn. But he can be trusted too. Don't forget, this is more his land than ours, and these raiders more his problem, until now. Wherever he's gone and whatever he's doing, it'll be to help us.'

'I hope so,' Derwyn called out ruefully as their horses drifted apart. But Marken's words had heartened him. This *was* Farnor's land and whatever he had chosen to do, it would be as an ally. He would do no harm, even though he might do little good. For a moment he heard Farnor warning him again about the creature. He shrugged the memory aside. For all his own unease about this strange animal, he'd always thought Farnor's concerns exaggerated; a farmer's response, not a hunter's.

He could have been right about this Nilsson and his men, though. Men who would hack down trees without due ceremony and delay were vicious and savage beyond doubt. And as for *burning* them . . .

Anger filled him.

Still, it would be folly to go charging among them, knowing nothing of how many there were, or how they were situated. What was it Farnor had said about them? 'They're brutal fighting men . . . If you go against them rashly, they'll hack you down without a thought.'

The light was fading. They should slow down, send out scouts to see where these people where, and how many. Yet these thoughts merely bubbled and frothed on top of the great swell of his Valderen heritage. Though unHeard by him, the small skill in Hearing that he possessed in common with all the Valderen was responding to the panic and terror of the trees about him and clouding the rational thought that normally ordered his judgement. His hands twitched uncertainly at the reins of his horse.

The branch sailed over the battlements again. It was wrapped in a cloth to reduce the noise that it would make against the stonework. For the third time, Levrik cautiously pulled the rope that was attached to it, ready to jump back quickly if it suddenly went slack. This time, however, the branch wedged in the embrasure. Levrik pulled on it again and then allowed it to take his full weight. There was a springiness in it that disturbed him a little; the branch was not as strong as he would have liked, but had it been any stouter it would have been almost impossible to throw it high enough.

He nodded to Yehna, the lightest of the group. Taking the rope from him, she tested it herself and then, satisfied, began clambering up it. The other three looked up into the darkness after her, even when she had disappeared from view. Eventually, the rope stopped shaking. They waited for a signal.

Instead, an angry, challenging voice floated down to them. Before any of them could react, however, there was a thud, and the voice stopped abruptly.

There was a brief, tense pause, then the signal came. Aaren

went up the rope next, to help Yehna support the branch while the two men climbed after her.

Jeorg lurched towards the castle gate and began to bang on it. 'Open up. Open up,' he shouted, his speech slurred.

After a while, and more banging, the wicket gate opened and a guard emerged, torch in hand. Jeorg gazed at the flickering flame and swayed uncertainly. 'It's here,' he said, smiling inanely and pointing into the darkness.

'What's here?' the guard demanded, scowling angrily.

Jeorg bent towards him precariously. The guard turned away from his breath with a grimace. 'The wood,' Jeorg said, pointing again into the darkness.

The guard followed the wavering hand. He was just debating whether to give Jeorg a beating for this disturbance when a shape as unsteady as its herald formed in the darkness and moved towards him. He stepped back, alarmed, but as the shape neared, it became a horse-drawn cart. Leading the horse was Gryss, and there were a few men behind it. Gryss stepped up to the guard and cast an apologetic look at Jeorg. 'I'm sorry about this,' he said confidentially. 'I'm afraid he's been celebrating Whistler's Day a little too well.' He beamed suddenly and waved an arm towards the men by the cart. 'In fact we've all been celebrating a little.' He swayed slightly.

'What?' the guard asked, frowning. 'Celebrating? What the devil are you blathering about? And what's all this?' He gestured towards the cart.

Gryss looked at him in exaggerated surprise. 'Celebrating. Whistler's Day,' he said, as if stating the obvious. 'You know, the Whistler who comes from over the hill.' The guard stared at him vacantly. 'Lures all the ills of the valley away with his playing. Plies them with drink then dances them up into the mountains.'

'I whistle away – oops!' Jeorg's tuneless song ended as he bumped into the gate and slithered to the ground. He laughed ridiculously.

'I don't know what you're talking about, you old fool,' the guard shouted, pushing Gryss aside roughly. 'Get this clown out of here unless you want me to run him through. And this as well.' He waved his torch at the cart.

'It's the wood the captain asked for,' Gryss said, taken aback.

'Said he wanted it urgently. That's why we worked on Whistler's Day to get it for you. It's supposed to be a holiday, you know. And I've brought some lads to unload it as well.'

'No one's told me anything about any wood,' the guard said. Others were emerging from the wicket gate. 'Do you know anything about this?' he asked, turning to them. There was universal denial.

Gryss shrugged. 'All I know is that the captain said he wanted this lot urgently. So it's here. It's taken some work, I can tell you. Do you want to ask him about it or shall we take it back?'

The guard hesitated. 'It's urgent, you say?' he asked.

Gryss nodded.

The guard blew out a resigned and fretful breath then he motioned the others back through the wicket gate and stepped after them. After a muffled but obviously heated debate, there came the sound of bolts being drawn and the two great leaves of the gate began to open, causing Jeorg to tumble over backwards. This was greeted by raucous applause and cheering from the men who had accompanied the cart.

Gryss, still smiling broadly, began to lead the horse slowly forward. The cart creaked ominously as the horse took the strain. The guard cast an impatient glance skyward. 'Come on, come on. Move it,' he urged.

As the cart reached the gate however, there was a pause while Jeorg struggled uncertainly to his feet. Several of the men stepped forward to help him up and guide him out of harm's way. They were milling about the cart as Gryss began to drag the horse forward again.

Suddenly there was an ominous crack and those around the cart jumped back with cries of alarm, tumbling over one another. With a weary creak, followed by another crack, one of the cart's wheels fell off, narrowly missing the watching guard. The cart crashed down on one side bringing the horse with it, and the bundles of staves that it was carrying slid off and blocked the gateway.

Four shadows moved silently along the battlements at the north end of the castle, leaving a second dead sentry behind them. Coming to the top of one of the stairways they paused, studying the buildings about them and looking in particular at those from which the highest tower rose. Then they moved down into the dimly lit courtyard and headed towards a doorway. A clamour from the far end of the castle held their attention momentarily, then they were through the door.

It opened into a passageway lit by a few, widely spaced lanterns. The only information the four had about the interior of the castle had been gleaned from Marna and, to some extent, from Gryss. It had not been particularly helpful, however. Both Gryss and Marna knew only cottages and houses, and were confused by the complexity of the passages and stairways along which they had been led on their few visits to the castle.

The consequences of this had thus been discussed and faced by the four attackers before their present venture had been set in train and they scarcely spoke as they moved quickly and silently along the passage.

'We'll follow our noses, reduce the odds on the way, if we can, and hack our way out if we have to,' was the agreed summary.

And there were two less already.

Some of the doors along the passage stood open, revealing disordered and deserted living quarters, and at the end was a stair well. Steps went both up and down, and Engir signalled upwards. Just as they were about to move, however, a sound drifted up the other flight. Yehna signalled a halt then, without speaking, seized one of the wall lanterns and ran down the steps. Engir threw a nervous, enquiring glance at Aaren, who shrugged and set off after her.

At the foot of the stairs was a single door barred on the outside. Yehna held the lantern by her face and, shading her eyes, peered through a small grill. Then, with a grimace of anger, she thrust the lantern into Aaren's hands, lifted the timber balk that secured the door, and pushed it wide open. Snatching back the lantern, she stepped inside.

The light illuminated what must once have been a storeroom but was now a dormitory. A women's dormitory. Bodies lying on crude bunks turned to look at the intruders and the faint sobbing that had caught Yehna's ear redoubled itself fearfully. Aaren's eyes widened in dismay, but Yehna's narrowed and her lip curled viciously. She put the lantern on the floor. 'Most of the men have gone for the time being,' she said, her voice icy with restraint, and her accent heavy. 'You'll probably find some weapons in the rooms along the passage at the top of these stairs.' Then, almost as an afterthought, she added, 'Some of the villagers are doing their best to hold the gate open. They're as much captives here as you are. Mind you don't kill any of them on your way out.'

Then she and Aaren were running up the stairs and motioning the two men forward with gestures that forbade any questions. As they reached the top of the stairs, the sound of voices and shuffling feet came up from below, followed by the crash of breaking glass. They were a long way away before the fire started by the broken lantern began to send smoke up the stairs.

Though the guard was speaking predominantly in his own language, it was quite apparent that he was deeply dismayed by what had happened. Gryss was both flustered and placatory, fussing around him, picking up odd pieces of timber here and there and then dropping them again, promising to have the gateway cleared immediately and asking where the staves should be stacked.

The other villagers, after having, amid a great deal of confusion and noise, righted the horse and calmed it, were wandering around equally vaguely. Some were examining with much head shaking, the broken cart and its scattered contents while others were hurling recriminations at no one in particular about why the cart had been so heavily loaded, and how it should have been stacked this way, not that, and how two carts would have been better . . .

Jeorg remained leaning against the gate mumbling happily to himself.

Attracted by the noise, more of Nilsson's men began to gather. The jeering from some of them increased the guard's agitation to the point where he began to lash out at those villagers nearest to him. Those who were half-heartedly beginning to move the staves dropped them and scattered, causing further mockery from the watchers.

Infuriated, the guard drew his sword and waved it menacingly. 'Get this lot moved, now!' he bellowed. 'Put them over there. Now! Move!'

The villagers stared at him, wide-eyed and fearful. 'Move, move.' The guard's command was echoed drunkenly by Jeorg.

The guard strode over to him and, seizing him by the front of his loose tunic, dragged him to his feet and pushed him violently on to the tumbled heap of staves. 'Start moving them now,' he shouted, levelling his sword at Jeorg's throat.

Jeorg blinked and nodded. 'All right, all right,' he muttered several times, as he clambered unsteadily to his feet. 'Don't get angry. It is Whistler's Day, you know. We're only trying to help.' He took hold of two staves at once and yanked at them. One of them came loose suddenly and he staggered backwards waving it wildly. The guard stepped back to avoid this flailing confusion. As he did so, Jeorg abruptly recovered his balance and, swinging the stave round, struck him a stunning blow on the side of the head.

The four slipped across a darkened hall and paused by a closed door. Light streamed underneath it and voices could be heard. Engir listened intently and then silently signalled, 'Two.' Very slowly, he eased the latch and began to pull open the door. It creaked immediately. Without hesitating he yanked the door open and strode through. Levrik and the two women followed right behind him. Almost before the brief screech of the door had died away, a savage blow from Levrik's iron-protected knuckles had silenced one of the two startled speakers while Engir's knife had finished another.

'Attack! Attack! Atta—' The cry rent open the breathless silence in the brightly lit passage. It came from a man just emerging from a room nearby and it cracked as he saw Aaren hurling herself towards him. None of Nilsson's men were such as would readily flee the threat of personal violence, but the knowledge that he was being attacked by a woman, together with the unhesitant ferocity of her approach and the shock of realizing who she must be, conspired to make Aaren's intended victim falter as he reached for his knife.

Aaren seized his fumbling knife hand and, swinging round, drove her knee into his groin. As he lurched forward, she stepped aside and pushed him head first into the opposite wall of the passage. He slumped to the ground.

As Aaren turned away from him, she saw the door being pushed shut. A massive kick from Levrik sent it crashing open and he was dragging the prostrated occupant to his feet as Aaren entered the room. 'Saddre!' she heard, as the figure was drawn up on to his toes and thrust against the wall, Levrik's hand tight about his throat. 'No!' she hissed, laying her hand on Levrik's free arm as it drew his knife.

Levrik paused at the touch but did not take his cold, unread-able eyes from Saddre's face. Saddre's eyes, by contrast, showed his every emotion as they flicked from his would-be executioner to his unexpected saviour. Fear and cunning mixed equally, but terrified recognition overrode all. 'You can't kill me,' he gasped. 'You've no authority. You have to take me back.'

Levrik's eyes flashed fiendishly alive for an instant, and his knife came up under Saddre's chin. Aaren's hand still rested gently on Levrik's arm, but she made no apparent effort to stop him. 'Exigencies of the situation are all the authority we need now, Saddre,' she said. 'If we kill your new master, then you'll get your accounting, have no fear. Failing that . . .' She shrugged. 'Now, take us to him.'

Despite the threat to his own life, Saddre's eyes opened in scorn. 'Kill him? You're insane. You'll not even get near him. He's probably already as powerful as—'

Levrik's grip tightened about his throat, choking off his reply. 'Don't even say that name,' he said very quietly, but with such intensity that Aaren let her hand slide from his arm. 'Just take us to him if you want to live long enough for your accounting.'

Saddre, his hands wrapped futilely about Levrik's wrist and his face contorted with pain, managed a flickering and desperate nod. As Levrik eased his grip, an angry voice reached them from the passage.

Chapter 25

'Riders coming! Riders coming!'

The cry galvanized the resting camp. Nilsson burst out of his tent and almost collided with the frantic messenger. Before he could ask any questions, the man answered them. 'Dozens of them,' he gasped, pointing northwards. 'Armed. Coming fast.'

With uncharacteristic gentleness, Nilsson eased the man to one side, then bellowed out, 'Arm up. Take close positions.' The order was unnecessary, however, for his men needed no urging. Even as he shouted, Nilsson saw they were gathering up weapons and forming defensive groups.

A torrent of thoughts swept over him. He had no doubt about who these riders could be. They'd come at last to demand an accounting from him and his men. It puzzled him a little that they'd come from such an unexpected direction. They could only have come to the valley from the south, but how had they managed to move around him in force, unnoticed? And what were they thinking of, using cavalry in this terrain? Was there an infantry force somewhere? But he dwelt on none of these questions. He was content to thank the old habits that had made him place seemingly unnecessary lookouts about the camp. His lips curled back to reveal his teeth, predatory in the firelight that lit the camp. Good discipline on his part meant that the attackers had lost the element of surprise they were obviously relying on, and now it was they who would be surprised.

Suddenly he felt exhilarated. For years, the fear and the rumour of pursuit had debilitated his troops, and to some extent even himself. And even though the fear had dwindled greatly over these last months, it had been with them too long to be banished utterly. If his men could now destroy this force, then the threat would be gone for ever, and morale would be enhanced tenfold.

He plunged back into his tent and emerged, sword in hand, just as Derwyn's men, shouting and screaming, and borne along by their ancient fury, galloped into the camp. They made a formidable sight and, skilled horsemen and lancers that they were, they brought down several men with their initial rush. These however, were mainly new recruits, who panicked and ran. The bulk of Nilsson's men had faced true cavalry in the past, and though they wavered at the first onslaught, they held their ground in tight groups, spiky with menacing swords and alive with blazing brands.

Then, as the impetus of the Valderen's charge was lost and the riders began to mill about, obstructing one another and uncertain how they should attack these unexpected enclaves, Nilsson's men attacked in their turn. The tightknit groups became suddenly mobile. Selecting a rider they would surge forward, some to hack at the horse's legs while others menaced the rider, who could do little but wave his lance futilely until his horse collapsed under him, or he himself was struck from his blind side.

Derwyn, one of the first riders into the camp and now at the edge of the mêlée, turned to look at the scene. His eyes widened in horror at what he saw, but it was the terrible noises that were beginning to ring through the silent trees that struck to his heart and froze him into immobility: the dreadful screaming of men and horses and the savage, triumphant cries of Nilsson's men. Farnor's words formed cruelly in his mind. 'They're brutal fighting men. If you go against them rashly, they'll hack you down without a thought.' And in his careless fury he had moved against them rashly indeed.

As Nilsson watched, however, his reaction was one of growing disbelief. Who were these people? Certainly they weren't his own countrymen, as he had assumed. In fact, though they were good riders, they weren't even cavalrymen. What he had anticipated being a long-awaited confrontation, a bloody and testing battle, promised now to be a bloody and amusing rout. The suddenly remembered old fears, evaporated. He shrugged and chuckled to himself. No doubt a few of the attackers would be taken alive for entertainment later on, and he could have his questions answered then.

'Derwyn!' Marken's voice, soft but desperately urgent, penetrated into Derwyn's guilt and horror.

He started violently. 'What have I done, Marken?' he said, his voice trembling.

'Your horn, man, your horn. Call them to you. Get them out of there,' Marken shouted.

Derwyn hesitated for a moment then, with shaking hands, unhooked the hunting horn from his saddle. As he raised it to his lips he faltered. His mouth was too dry and his breathing shallow and unsteady.

'Spit, for pity's sake. Take a deep breath, and don't let the others see you like this, or we're all dead,' Marken hissed, seizing his arm and shaking him ferociously.

Derwyn nodded automatically. Somehow, he managed to moisten his lips and steady his breath. The first note was harsh and discordant, but the very sound of it started to lift him out of his paralysis. Marken raised and sounded his own horn, then others gathering around them did the same, until the calls finally rose above the din of the battle.

Farnor needed no warning from the trees. The presence of the creature grew in intensity, although it was not as if it were waking. Rather, it seemed to be returning from somewhere; somewhere that was not in this place. It was a terrifying sensation. His own words to Derwyn returned to him mockingly. 'Expect to be afraid, but don't fear your fear.' Well, he was afraid, all right, but that said, what was he to do next?

He put the lantern back into his pocket, then he tightened his grip about the staff. Perhaps the creature wouldn't see him, or scent him. But he knew that these were vain hopes even as they came to him. The creature knew him as he knew it, and it would smell his fear both drifting through the night air and trembling through that mysterious bond that he had with it. No. There would be no place secure enough, or flight fast enough, to save him from it when it emerged to hunt.

His mouth filled suddenly with acrid saliva, and his body was possessed with a terrible longing. Blood and terror were in the air, rich and desirable.

Good . . .

Farnor spat in disgust and denial. In the distance he heard horn calls. Though their note was rapid, desperate even, he was once again staring over the ancient Forest, washed in the bright dawn sunlight, his heart crying out its prayer of thanksgiving to his parents for the gift of life that they had given him. And, he realized now, thanksgiving for the other gifts that they had given him: the love that had sustained him and brought him thus far, scathed but whole; and himself, knowing better both the light and the darkness of his nature. And as he had accepted and enjoyed these gifts, so now he must accept that other gift, the one they had given him unknowingly, the one that had twisted and turned its way through the generations of lives in the valley until it had become his; the gift to oppose this creature and the foulness that it had guided Rannick to.

He opened and closed his hands about Marrin's staff fitfully. He could feel the spirit of the most ancient still held in it. Oddly, it gave him more comfort than had the machete and the bow and the vicious arrows that he had just lost. But it was not going to be much use as a weapon.

He peered up into the darkness. The presence of the creature was becoming more intense. It was drawing nearer. The horns were still calling. Derwyn and Nilsson must have met and, whatever the outcome, blood had been spilt. And soon the creature would leave its lair to range through the woods, slaughtering and feeding amongst whomsoever Rannick decreed. Derwyn's people. 'No,' he said. Not knowing how he did it, he reached out and touched the creature. 'I understand you more now. Your darkness holds no greater terrors or knowledge than my own. But the light I bring you will destroy you and your master.'

A terrible, high-pitched scream tore open the night. Farnor flinched away from it, but using Marrin's staff to test the ground ahead of him, he forced himself to walk on towards the heart of the malevolence that he could now feel oozing down the mountainside towards him. He felt, too, the creature's claws scrabbling over the rock-strewn ground as it raced frenziedly to reach him. And its pounding heart, its rasping breath, its foul desires. And he could feel its lust for the fear that was soaking through him. Then, most terrifying of all, he felt the rift through which, with Rannick, it drew its awful powers. That mysterious rent in this reality that opened into those worlds that did not belong here; could not belong here without terrible havoc following.

For a fleeting instant, Farnor had a vision of the Forest's great and ancient fear: fear that a flaw lay in the very nature of all things in this age. But it left him – was torn away from him? – almost before he could note it, and his fear became more prosaic

– a fear of the power that was emerging to overwhelm him.

Scarcely realizing what he was doing, he leaned on his staff and, looking into the darkness, let the shaking and trembling that he was struggling to restrain take complete possession of him.

After a timeless time, he was still, and all about him was still. The wound torn by the creature filled his consciousness. He reached out, and with his quietness, made it whole.

The scream that the creature had made before was as nothing to that which it uttered now. It seemed to Farnor that the whole of creation rang with its fury and desperation as it strove to tear open that which he had sealed.

But Farnor held.

Though this would not be enough, he knew. The creature still had power enough to kill him and return to undo his work. It had to be destroyed utterly.

He stepped forward into the darkness.

'What in His name is all the noise?'

Engir and Yehna turned to face the inquisitor, who had just emerged from a doorway at the far end of the passage. He came towards them, head craning forward, eyes narrowed.

'Lord Rannick?' Engir almost whispered his question. His mouth and throat had suddenly become dry, and he was shaking.

'Who else, you dolt?' Rannick replied. He stopped some distance away, his hand pointing towards the fallen man, but his eyes flickering from Yehna to Engir.

'We're new recruits to Captain Nilsson,' Engir managed to say.

Again Rannick craned forward. 'No,' he said, very softly. 'You're his kind, but there's a foulness about you that he'd choke on, just as I am now.'

'No, Lord,' Engir said, stepping forward.

With a cry of rage, Rannick extended his hand towards him. Engir cried out and clutched at his throat. His mouth working desperately for air, he staggered into the open doorway. He collapsed part way into the room, his eyes signalling frantically to Levrik and his right hand circling strangely. Yehna drew her knife and rushed at Rannick, but she had scarcely taken two paces when the same fate befell her.

'No need to take you to him. He's here,' Saddre gasped to Levrik as Engir tumbled across the threshold. Saddre's eyes were gloating, despite the hand and the knife at his throat. 'Your turn to account now, I think. I'll enjoy this.'

'Saddre!' Rannick's voice rasped along the passage.

A vicious blow in the stomach doubled Saddre up before he could reply, though Levrik stopped him from collapsing to the floor. He thrust the gasping figure to Aaren then pulled a leather thong from his belt and took a stone from a pocket.

Long schooled in each other's fighting techniques, a brief hand signal told Aaren of his intention. She was very pale, and her eyes were unashamedly fearful, but she nodded. Then, seizing the gasping Saddre by the scruff of the neck, she yanked him upright and charged with him to the open doorway. He tripped over the choking Engir but Aaren kept up their joint momentum, and as they burst into the passage she swung him round and, using him as a shield, charged at Rannick, screaming.

Taken unawares by this explosive response, Rannick instinctively held out his hands to prevent the collision. He was partly successful in that he deflected Saddre with a sweep of his arm, but in doing so he lost his balance and staggered heavily into the wall.

Yehna and Engir were released. 'Down, now,' Levrik's terse command rose above the frantic gasping of his recovering companions as he stepped into the passage. In his right hand he was spinning the leather thong. Before Rannick could react, Levrik's arm came forward and he released the sling. The stone flew from its soft leather saddle towards Rannick's throat.

Levrik had dropped the sling and was drawing a knife even as Rannick's hands came up again to protect himself. The stone caught his wrist and, bouncing up, struck him on the temple. With a cry of pain, he stumbled backwards.

Levrik was moving forward when suddenly Rannick's eyes seemed to burst into light. At the same time Levrik saw his own shadow leaping violently ahead of him. Then something hit him powerfully in the back, lifting him off his feet. Reflexes curled him up, rolled him over and brought him upright almost immediately to face his unexpected assailant. But there was no one there except his three companions. Aaren was dragging Yehna and Engir to their feet. At the end of the corridor however, bright flames were pouring out of the doorway they had passed through only minutes before. Black, flame-filled smoke was rolling along the ceiling of the passage.

As Levrik took this in, he became aware of Aaren pointing. She was shouting, too, though her voice was hardly audible above

318

the noise of the flames. He spun round, recalling their true enemy. Saddre was reeling around drunkenly, and Rannick, too, had been knocked over by the concussion from the now blazing hall.

Simultaneously the four moved towards him; dark, menacing and swift against the roaring flames, black knives glinting. But it was too late. Rannick may have been downed but he was sufficiently recovered to defend himself once more. He held out his hand. 'No!' he roared. 'Whoever you are, I shall show you what happens to blasphemers.' The firelight shone in his eyes again, making it seem as if some internal fire were rising up in response to that now consuming the castle.

The four hesitated.

'I shall show you the true fire,' Rannick cried. A thin, nerve-wrenching screech rose above the noise, and in front of Rannick a shimmering light appeared. 'Thus starts your death,' he said, clambering to his feet, his arm still extended. He turned to Levrik, the light growing ever more brilliant. Abruptly a figure lurched between them. It was Saddre, still stunned from his fall. As he stepped in front of Rannick, the light streamed forward, enveloping him.

He burst into flames.

For a moment there was silence. Then Saddre was screaming. The four watchers stared, unable to move, so horrific was the sight.

And, just as suddenly the screaming stopped. Saddre pivoted with an eerie grace to face Rannick. 'Lord?' he said, his voice oddly calm through the clamouring flames.

Rannick's face contorted with rage. His arm swung out and struck the blazing figure sideways with appalling force. The floor shook with the impact as Saddre struck the wall, and the flames about him flared angrily. Then he crashed forward on to the floor and lay still.

Staring through the flames still rising from his erstwhile lieutenant, Rannick's appearance was hypnotically terrifying. The four warriors stood, still transfixed.

The shimmering light appeared once more, but, abruptly, it flickered uneasily. Rannick cocked his head on one side, as if he had heard a far-distant sound. The action seemed to waken the watchers. 'He's only a man!' Engir shouted hoarsely. 'And there are four—'

Before he could finish however, a furious cry of rage and desperation filled the passage. It was Rannick. He made a wild gesture and, with a great roar, the shimmering light burst along the ceiling of the passage to join the flames in the blazing hall. The four hurled themselves flat on the floor as the flames passed over them, but, the immediate danger passed, Engir's command still carried them forward, intent on the destruction of Rannick at any cost.

But Rannick was gone. The sounds of his screaming flight echoed up the staircase as the four reached it. 'What happened?' Yehna shouted.

'It doesn't matter,' Levrik replied. 'It's not finished yet.' Then his eyes widened in horror and he pointed along the passage. As the others turned, it was to see the flames that Rannick had released, licking over the walls and ceiling like living creatures.

They were consuming the very stones.

When he had arranged with Aaren a diversion to keep the castle gates open, Gryss had deemed blundering incompetence to be their best ally. It had certainly not been his intention to have his few trustworthy volunteers become involved in actual combat with Nilsson's men. There were several reasons for this, not least being the fact that none of them were fighters, and most of them were past their most vigorous youth.

Jeorg however had precipitated events, when the weeks of simmering anger could be contained no more and he felled the gate guard. Two more swift blows had stunned two other men, and, to their credit, Gryss's impromptu force had read the situation with considerable alacrity; rage is not the sole province of the young man. Soon the courtyard around the gate was a mass of struggling bodies and flailing wooden staves.

Nilsson's men however, were experienced enough not to be afraid to retreat when caught by surprise, and this they did remarkably quickly. A lull developed. Gryss managed to keep his men together, blocking the gate and waving their staves menacingly, while Nilsson's men were strung out in a thin semi-circle at a safe distance. Some of them were calling out abuse, but most of them were just watching silently. Gryss had seen several of them run towards the buildings across the courtyard. They'll be armed when they come back, he thought. We won't stand a chance.

He looked up anxiously at the tower that housed Rannick's

eyrie. The high window was black and dead. Had Aaren and the others succeeded in killing him? Or had he killed them and was even now coming to take vengeance on those who had abetted the attempted assassination?

Before he could ponder these alternatives however, a cry brought his attention back to the immediate fray. His heart sank. Several figures were emerging from the darker reaches of the courtyard. Sheer weight of numbers could overwhelm them now, even without weapons, or Rannick's aid. 'Keep together,' he shouted to his companions. 'It's our only chance.'

But there was something unusual about these new arrivals. 'They're women,' a surprised voice said nearby, answering Gryss's unspoken question.

And, as if in confirmation, a shrill voice rang out, and the women released by Yehna began to launch themselves at Nilsson's men. Gryss and the others watched in bewilderment for a moment until they realized that many of the women were armed and that several of the men, taken by surprise again, had been badly injured.

Impulsively Gryss's impromptu force broke ranks and charged forward into the battle. No combat was engaged, however, for even as they were running forward, part of the castle roof burst open with a tumultuous crash, and blazing timbers were hurled high into the night sky. All fighting in the courtyard ceased, as friend and enemy stood open-mouthed, gazing at this spectacle.

But terrifying though it was, this was as nothing compared to what followed. For as further sections of the roof burst into flames, a terrible screaming began to fill the air.

Someone struck Gryss's arm. He turned to see Yakob, dishevelled and bleeding, his eyes wide and his hand pointing. He was shouting too, but even standing so close, Gryss could scarcely hear him above the noise. He looked in the direction that Yakob was pointing.

Galloping towards them across the courtyard was Rannick on his demented steed. His mouth was gaping wide but the scream that was coming from it seemed too awful to have been created inside any living thing. Worse than the noise, though, were the bright flames flowing around him and dancing in his wake. They ran like dust devils along the ground, leaving glowing, smouldering trails until they struck the walls and blossomed upwards and outwards like grotesque flowers.

Gryss, however, barely noted this. His dominant concern was the dreadful focus of Rannick's will that he could feel. 'Run,' he shouted, unheard and unnecessarily, for even the oldest among them had suddenly rediscovered the agility of their youth at the sight of this monstrous charge.

But Rannick's intent lay elsewhere, and he ignored the scattering figures as he rode through them. At the gate, his horse leapt over the broken cart effortlessly, flames tracing out his passing, arcing behind him like some fearful rainbow.

As his scream faded into the distance, it was overtopped by the noise of the flames in the courtyard. Almost the entire castle roof was now ablaze, flames and smoke cascading up into the night. But so too, it seemed, were the very walls of the castle, as flames which should have spluttered into nothingness against their cold stone clambered eagerly over them, their sinister light spreading and devouring.

None of the combatants lingered to watch however. Those who were still standing, dashed past the cart and through the gate to form a silent, watching group out in the darkness, all of them too stunned to pursue their original intentions. As they watched, the cart and its scattered contents in the gateway burst into flames, but this was of little note against the sight of Rannick's unnatural fire, crawling along the walls and rising up the towers.

Something buffeted Gryss. 'Where are they?' an urgent voice shouted at him. He turned round to find himself looking into Marna's distraught face as she leaned forward from the saddle of a large horse. She was holding three other horses by a long rein.

'Who?' he said.

'Aaren and the others,' Marna shouted angrily. 'This wasn't meant to happen. Where are they?'

The other wheel of the cart collapsed, sending up a great shower of sparks. Gryss gesticulated helplessly. 'I don't know,' he shouted back. 'I haven't seen them. If they got in, then . . .' He waved towards the inferno.

'And Rannick?' Marna shouted, reaching out and shaking Gryss's shoulder as if he were some inattentive child. 'Is he dead?'

Gryss pointed. 'No. He rode off. It was awful. Didn't you hear him?'

Marna straightened up and gazed at the blazing gateway, flame-shadowed lines of pain and doubt etched deep into her face. Then she leaned forward again and put her arm around Gryss's neck dragging him off balance with a passionate embrace. 'Tell my father I love him, and I'm sorry,' she said, then with a loud cry she drove her heels into the horse.

Before Gryss could protest, the four horses had leapt past him and were charging towards the burning gateway, Marna frantically urging them on. He found voice only as he saw them silhouetted against the flames lighting the gateway. 'Marna! No!' he cried, though his voice cracked as all four horses leapt the blazing remains of the cart and disappeared into the brightness beyond.

Scarcely a horsewoman, let alone a jumper, Marna released the rein leading the other three horses, and clung on to her own mount with both arms as it leapt through the gateway. The impact of the landing jolted her, but the sight that greeted her set such discomfort at naught. The light in the courtyard was brighter than a summer's day, and it seemed that not one part of the castle's stonework was free from the clamouring flames. The heat was suffocating and terrifying. She felt herself gasping for breath.

Even as she gazed about her, the walls of one of the buildings collapsed with a ground shaking impact, amid a triumphant roar of flames. Somehow she recovered the leading rein of the three horses before their burgeoning panic overcame whatever will it was she had inspired them with. She gazed around desperately, calling out at the top of her voice. But she could hardly hear herself above the din.

Her horse spun round and round and began to rear, almost unseating her, but she managed to cling on to both it and the rein of the others. She could feel the heat scorching her skin however, worse than anything she had ever known through working too long in the summer fields, and it came to her that she had committed a folly that would probably kill her.

But despite the awful scream forming inside her, she couldn't leave. Not yet. Surely, they couldn't be dead. Not such people . . .

Then through the glaring heat she saw four figures come tumbling out of a doorway. Without any bidding from her, the horses turned towards them. Faces blackened, and clothes smouldering, the four warriors clambered on to their horses, Levrik mounting Marna's horse and taking the reins. She offered no resistance.

As she looked at the gateway however, she saw that the flames were all around it and that it was changing shape.

She knew that Levrik's horse was driving forward, urged on by the enigmatic soldier's cold unhindering will and she was aware of the other three beside them, moving as one. But as they galloped towards the gate it seemed to her that it was retreating from them, so slow was their progress. Then they were leaping over the remains of the burning cart, and the air was full of the sound of the blazing stones of the great arch crashing down behind them.

The cold night, with its scents and its normality, folded itself magically about her. Many hands reached out to support her as she slithered down from the horse, but she struggled free from them. 'Which way did Rannick go?' she heard Levrik asking.

A hand touched her shoulder. As she turned, an arm encircled her neck and she felt her hot cheek pressed against an even hotter one. It was Aaren, leaning down precariously from her horse. 'Bravely done. Bravely done,' she said simply, her voice hoarse with smoke and her eyes shining wet in the light of the burning castle. 'We're in your debt.'

Before Marna could reply, however, she had pulled away, and the four were galloping off into the darkness.

Chapter 26

Derwyn peered into the darkness at the men around him. The sound of the horns had succeeded in extricating most of them from the carnage of the camp but, dimly lit by the distant glow of the campfires shining through the trees, they were milling about him in considerable disorder. Their behaviour vividly reflected the emotions that were tumbling through him: a numbing mixture of shock, fear, and choking guilt; and an urge to flee from this now terrible fringe of the Forest, back to the safety of his lodge and the ways he knew and had always known. Yet, it was combined with an equally powerful urge to charge back amongst the men who had done such harm, to work some dreadful vengeance on them.

But, despite this turmoil, the qualities that had made him the quiet leader of his people were subtly asserting themselves, calming the ancient racial frenzy in which he and his men had tried to hide from the alien strangeness of the quest that Farnor had brought on them. In its wake came a clearer, if no less troubling, knowledge. Warrior he was not, nor any of his men. But they *were* hunters, and their ancient ancestors had been warriors. It was surely not beyond their resources to find some way of dealing with these intruders?

It occurred to Derwyn briefly that, Farnor's assessment of these men having been so fearfully accurate, his assessment of the creature was probably no less so, and that they might indeed find themselves contending with it as well as Nilsson's men. And, of course, there was the man, Rannick, with his mysterious powers.

With an effort, he set the thoughts aside. One thing at a time. He had first to bring his men back into some semblance of order. Standing high in his stirrups he bellowed out, 'Be quiet, all of you!' His powerful voice rose above much of the noise, but he had to call out twice more before it was quiet enough for him to speak and be heard.

He wanted to ask who had been injured, who killed, who had gathered around the frantic horn calling, who scattered into the trees, but a panic-stricken voice nearby focused his thinking sharply. 'This is dreadful. Let's get away from here while we can.' It was a young voice, but echoes of it sprang up in the darkness.

His eyes reflecting the distant lights of the camp, Derwyn turned grimly towards the speaker. He could not allow time for the leisurely niceties that normally decorated their decision making.

'No,' he shouted. 'Maybe it was a madness that drew us into that reckless charge, but it would be a greater madness if we forgot our duties as Valderen. If we fly now, how can we ever look to the protection of the Forest again? And how could any of us sit at peace by our hearths knowing that we betrayed both our ancient obligations and those who've just fallen to these outsiders?' He waited for no reply. 'Like it or not, we're warriors now, and we stay here until this evil's been driven from the Forest.'

'It was that black-haired devil of an outsider who brought this on us,' someone shouted.

Derwyn pushed his horse forward in the direction of the voice. 'That black-haired devil was chosen to visit the most ancient, I'd remind you,' he replied furiously. 'It was he who *warned* us about these people, if we'd had the wit to listen. And without him, who can say how much harm they'd have done before we knew of them?'

There was no answer. Derwyn seized back his people. 'Melarn,' he shouted. 'Take a dozen men and move back towards that camp, carefully. We need to know what they're doing.'

Nilsson leaned forward earnestly, hoping to catch some indication of what the distant shouting meant, but it was too far away and there was too much noise about him. The blasting horn calls that had drawn the riders back into the trees had startled him. Were there reinforcements out there? Was there indeed some infantry force making its way towards them right now? And, again, who *were* these people?

He dashed aside the persistent question. It didn't matter who they were. His first impression remained; whatever else they were, they weren't fighters, and that was what mattered. But they'd still have to be dealt with, and dealt with tonight; there was little point in forming a defensive enclave and holding, as *he* definitely had no reinforcements to draw upon. And any delay might prove disastrous if indeed some other force were heading towards him. He must move out and attack before matters deteriorated.

Few changes were needed to the positions that his men had already taken up, and he noted with some satisfaction that many of them, anticipating a return by the riders, were hacking down long branches to use in lieu of pikes.

Within minutes of his decision, his men were moving into the darkness in the direction that the riders had taken. They retained their small, tight groupings, and many were carrying burning brands.

The news reached Derwyn almost immediately, and he suddenly found himself the centre of a fear-laden silence. He knew that all eyes were turned towards him in the darkness. He watched the lights of the enemy moving towards him; a flickering, firefly tide, spreading out from the fires of the distant camp. Fighting men, Farnor had called them, and for the first time in his life Derwyn felt the peculiar terror of knowing that someone was intent upon seeking his life; *his* life.

Yet he must lead his men against them, or they would be scattered about the fringe of the Forest here and perhaps lost for ever, and who knew what consequences would flow from that? Images of Angwen and Edrien and the other women they had left at their camp came to him, chilling him.

But what did he know about fighting? Nothing.

But . . .

'Do as they did,' he shouted urgently. 'Do as they did. Stay in small groups. Six, eight. Keep moving. And keep together, whatever happens. Protect one another. Drop your lances if you're pressed and use your machetes.'

'And if you're downed, then climb. They won't be able to do that like we can.' It was Marken who finished Derwyn's hasty battle order. Derwyn felt his men's spirits lift as some strained laughter greeted this.

Thus it was that the Valderen began to avenge their first fallen. Guided by the brands that Nilsson's men were carrying, they burst out of the darkness, sharp-pointed lances and keen-edged machetes taking their toll, then they vanished as suddenly as they had appeared.

Almost all of the groups took some losses, but while one or two broke and scattered, to be cut down or trampled underfoot, the majority closed about their injured companions and held.

Nilsson swore silently to himself, but no sign of his feelings showed on his face except his characteristic snarl. Had these people launched their initial sacrificial charge just to lure him into an ambush? Surely not. It made no sense. But the alternative held little comfort for him; they had learned from their first mistake. 'Retreat to the camp,' he ordered, his voice icy. 'We'll see how well they fight when we can see them coming.'

As the groups withdrew, the Valderen pressed on with their swift assaults, though these became increasingly less effective and more dangerous as they drew nearer to the bright glow of the fires illuminating the camp. Then there was silence, save for the sound of the fires and the awful cries of the wounded and dying.

Nilsson's men retrenched, more of them hacking down branches either for use as pikes or to be driven into the ground to form defensive hedges. The Valderen walked like sinister shadows around the dark edges of the firelit circle, lance points glinting in the firelight.

The two leaders pondered fretfully, Nilsson on the identity of these mysterious attackers and the possibility of a further force arriving before dawn; Derwyn on the impossibility of attacking this increasingly entrenched group and the difficulty of maintaining the spirit of his men now that the fury of the action had ceased. And too, *he* was beginning to consider the possibility that there might be other groups of these outsiders nearby, ready to come to the aid of their companions. And what of the creature? And Rannick?

Neither man dared wait. Neither dared move.

Both were spared.

From the south came a sound. Everyone seemed to hear it at the same time, though none could have said how long it had been there. At first it was like the irritating buzz of some tiny trapped insect. Then it grew louder and louder, its tone tearing into its hearers like that of fingernails drawn down glass, but worse by far.

None, either in or around the camp, could do other than

concentrate on it in deepening fear, and each forgot their sudden foe totally.

Even Nilsson found his mind drawn from his dilemma. Then he heard a quality in the sound that he recognized. 'It's Lord Rannick,' he shouted, though as much in fear as in anticipation at what must be their relief. It was of no consequence however, for no one heard him. He pushed his way through the front ranks of his men. Vaguely he was aware of the circling Valderen, struggling to control their mounts as the sound grew. 'Their horses are panicking,' he roared. 'Get ready to attack.' But though he was bellowing directly into the faces of his men he could still scarcely be heard. And too, they seemed paralysed by the sound.

Then Rannick was on them, crashing into the beleaguered camp at a speed that no normal mount could attain, and with a sound like thunder and a howling wind tumbling in the wake of his dreadful scream. The wind snatched at the watching men and made the fires roar and blaze triumphantly.

Nilsson, like his men, was now transfixed, for though the figure on the horse was indisputably Rannick, he was not the man he had chosen to follow, even thought to manipulate to his own ends. He was something that radiated a malevolence that was beyond anything Nilsson had ever known. About him ran streams of a strange fire that crackled and flared, consuming everything it touched, save Rannick. And his mount. For the thing that had been a horse was as evilly transformed as its master. Its head strained against Rannick's fire-laced restraint, its eyes gleamed, and a steaming foam poured from its mouth and nostrils. Both rider and mount seemed unaware of the scene they had entered. They were swaying from side to side, as if scenting for something.

The sight banished all coherent thought from Nilsson, save one: the appalling wrongness of Rannick. The power that his erstwhile master had used had been greater by far than Rannick's, but its use had been rare and sparing. The thing he saw before him now was without any semblance of restraint, and beyond all controlling. What had been Rannick was, perhaps, quite destroyed, and what was left was not merely death, it was the antithesis of life.

A sensation passed through Nilsson that he had not known in many, many years. A sensation whose birth pangs had perhaps begun with the violent jolt he had experienced when he had thought the approaching Valderen were his long pursuing countrymen come to call him to account.

Guilt.

This abomination was his fault.

It menaced everything! – *everything!* It could not be allowed to live.

A life in which immediate and cruel action had been the inevitable solution to most problems, took inexorable command of him. Aware of nothing now, save the flickering figure swaying before him, Nilsson stepped forward. The word 'Lord' formed in his mind as he drew his sword. Rannick's swaying stopped abruptly as if he had heard the call, and he turned to look at Nilsson.

'No!' Nilsson bellowed into the thunder of Rannick's presence, and taking his sword in both hands, he swung it up in a whistling curve for a blow that would have cut Rannick and his awful steed in half.

Had it landed.

But with the air of a great lord casually dismissing a tiresome servant, Rannick delicately raised his hand. A terrible, unseen blow struck Nilsson, lifting him clear of the ground and sending him crashing down on to the Forest floor, a dozen paces away. His sword arced up, glittering through the firelight, twisting and turning, until it fell somewhere in the darkness beyond the camp.

For an instant, silence hung over the scene, and Rannick's brow furrowed a little, as if a troublesome memory had just occurred to him. Then the moment was gone and, his fearful scream returning, he was riding from the camp as precipitously as he had arrived.

The camp fires swirled up as if in homage to his passing, throwing flames high into the night sky.

Some of Nilsson's men started forward as the flickering light gave a semblance of movement to their downed leader.

But Nilsson's many subtle and devious concerns had ended the instant that Rannick's will had touched him.

He was dead.

Farnor moved slowly up the rocky slope, carefully testing the ground ahead with Marrin's staff. He needed no guide for the direction now, for the creature's presence had become as sharp and as clear to him as if it had been the Dalmas sunstone. Yet it had stopped its headlong rush. It had even stopped its desperate struggle to open again that which Farnor had made whole. It was

330

waiting. For the nonce it was deprived of its terrible powers from the worlds beyond, but it had still the power of this world and its cunning and strength, and Farnor was but just another inconsequential prey animal while he chose to hold the way closed and thus deny himself those same powers.

And Rannick was coming, Farnor knew. He had heard the creature's command reaching across the valley in that last awful roar. And command it had been. Who then was master, and who servant? he wondered.

Somewhere in the distance he heard the sound of thunder. He glanced up. To the south, the sky was glowing red. He frowned uncertainly. What was happening at the village? What was happening to the Valderen? With an effort, he set both thoughts aside and turned his attention back into the darkness. Whatever was happening, he could do nothing about it except what he was doing now.

Despite his clear intent however, fears tore at him. Even without its enhanced powers, this thing was a vicious night-time predator, quite devoid of fear. How big was it? How strong? He remembered the great pieces torn from the slaughtered sheep. Could it see in the dark? How silently could it move?

The thoughts circled and circled, until he found himself trembling again. For a moment he tried to resist it, then again, he paused and gave it free rein.

And he was quiet again.

He swung the stick forward.

It struck something soft. Then it was torn violently from his hand. He heard hard claws scrabbling on the rocks, and an awful rumbling snarl. And, as if a numbing fog had just lifted from him, he felt the creature all about him.

Without thinking, he dropped to the ground and brought his hands over his head for protection. Something caught him a glancing blow and he heard the breathy thud of the creature landing heavily behind him. His nostrils filled with the acrid smell of dank fur. Strangely, the sounds and the smell reassured him a little. Anchored him in this world. Here he might live or die now, but there was no strangeness, only savagery.

A thought exploded in his mind. If you were made thus by humans, creature, and you must have been, then all your attributes will be less than human, for no man would create his superior, even if he could.

On that black, rocky mountainside, then, for all his weakness, he, the man, was the greater savage, the more terrible opponent. Farnor heard himself snarling, as if in confirmation of this revelation. His hand swept over the rocky ground and almost immediately lit upon Marrin's staff. He seized it, rolled over and swung it in the place where he had heard the creature land. It struck nothing, but Farnor could hear the creature pacing slowly around him, suddenly hesitant. Feel it, do you? he thought. Feel the presence of one of those who made you. Be afraid, creature. Be afraid.

A menacing rumble came through the darkness in reply. It turned abruptly into a snarl and Farnor sensed rather than heard feet gripping the ground and muscles tensing.

He jumped to one side and swung the staff. His arms caught the side of the creature and in an instant he felt its great weight and muscular power. The impact knocked him over and he fell heavily, something driving into his ribs and sending pain to every part of his body. He cried out, his voice strange in his own ears, but somehow he kept hold of the staff and, fear overriding his pain, he rolled over, away from the sound of the creature, scrabbling once more over the damp rocks to recover its balance. If only he could see! If only there was a vestige of light to guide him!

Then there was a pause. Farnor swung the staff tentatively in a low arc about him. It struck nothing again, and though he could hear the creature breathing, the sound was coming from all around him. Then he felt it trying once again to draw on the power beyond, trying to rend open that which he had sealed. That part of him that healed such wounds cried out, No, here we decide this, you hellhound. But there was no response except a vaguely familiar sound in front of him. His mind searched to identify it.

It had dropped down on the ground. The damned thing was lying down! Waiting!

The sound of thunder reached him again.

It was going to wait for Rannick!

Man and beast must overwhelm him for sure.

He glanced quickly at the glowing sky to the south.

What was happening to the village? And to Derwyn? he thought again. And with the thought of Derwyn came the memory of Angwen. One hand still waving the staff in front of him, he fumbled through his pockets.

It was still there. Angwen's lantern. As he scrambled to his feet, he heard the creature doing the same. Then he threw open the shutter on the lantern.

The light burst into his face, blinding him. Frantically he turned the lantern round. There was an angry snarl and, through the myriad coloured patterns dancing in his vision, he caught a glimpse of a huge black shape, turning away and disappearing into the darkness.

With desperate slowness his vision cleared, and though the small lantern did not throw a great deal of light, it did show him that he was standing by the entrance to a cave.

His eyes widened in shock. Accidentally he had almost walked directly into the creature's den!

Now, however, he must do it deliberately. He must face this creature before Rannick arrived. Face it in its own lair. Gripping the staff, he stepped inside. A musty foulness greeted him.

The light gave him some comfort. At least he would be able to see the creature this time. At least he would be able to aim some kind of purposeful blow. And – he checked – he still had his mother's knife in his belt. With the light, he had a chance.

The smell grew worse, making him want to retch, and a chilling dampness started to strike through him. He was sodden with rain and sweat. He walked on, carefully shining the lantern into the many shadows that the uneven walls and floor formed. The light reflected back off glistening dampness, until the cave suddenly opened out and the lantern's beam faded into darkness, revealing nothing but the floor. There was blackness to either side of him.

Which way should he go? Suddenly very afraid, he stopped and listened. Nothing was to be heard except a faint dripping in the distance. He swung the lantern slowly from side to side, leaning forward to search into the shadows. Then bright, malignant eyes flared out, pinioning him, and the pool of darkness from which they had emerged surged towards him.

His fear saved him, for only at the very last moment did some reflex manage to twist him to one side. The movement however, did not prevent the creature crashing into him heavily and knocking him down. The lantern spun from his hand and, tumbling across the rocky floor, sent wild shadows dancing into the darkness. Marrin's staff snapped as he fell on it. He barely had time to cry out before the creature was upon him, its saliva dropping on to his face and its powerful forelegs rigid on his chest. The light from the rolling lantern fell momentarily on its face, lighting its eyes a savage red and revealing its gaping maw and terrible teeth. Its head jerked back a little as the light struck it. Farnor's hands came up frantically and seized its throat. The muscles and sinews that he grasped told him immediately that he could not hope to strangle it, nor best it in any kind of physical contest. He let out a great cry of fear and rage and, pushing upward with his left hand, brought his clenched right fist up and struck the creature on the side of the head. It produced no noticeable effect except to make it hesitate again slightly.

I won't die here, Farnor roared inwardly. I won't die here. Countless images burst simultaneously into his mind: sunset watches, solstice festivals, his journey through the Great Forest, Bildar, Edrien, Gryss, Marna, his mother, his father, Uldaneth . . .

Uldaneth!

'Why do you carry a kitchen knife with you, Farnor?'

The images vanished, and his right hand began to grope towards his belt.

The creature's forelegs pounded painfully into his chest and he felt its back legs scrabbling for purchase on the rocky floor. He also felt his left arm, screaming with effort, beginning to buckle under the increasing pressure. The creature's foul breath gusted over his face and saliva sprayed hotly into it as the savage jaws snapped shut the merest fraction in front of him.

'How did you do that?' he heard himself asking Uldaneth.

'I didn't, you did,' came the reply.

With a final effort he reached the knife and drew it, then jerking his head desperately to one side to avoid the descending jaws, he closed his eyes.

'I didn't, you did.'

He let his left arm collapse.

The creature crashed on to the upturned blade.

It let out a strange cry and stiffened. Despite the crushing impact of the fall, Farnor felt his own blood fury grow as the creature's faded, and with the last residue of his strength he thrust the creature to one side and dragged the knife up the length of its chest. He felt blood spilling hot over his arms.

Then he was rolling free, gasping with terror. To his horror however, he saw the shadow that was the creature struggling to regain its feet. He could not move. His mind told him to stab the creature again, quickly. Stab it over and over until it was still. But his trembling hands would not obey. And still it struggled, a great pool of blood spreading, black in the dim, reflected lantern light.

Then it turned to look at him, and, inclining its head on one side, it whimpered. The sound, unexpectedly poignant, seemed to fill Farnor's head, until he realized that the sound he was hearing was no longer that of the creature. It was something else. And a flickering uneasy light was pervading the cave. The sound formed itself into words. Words as full of horror as they were of menace.

'What have you done?'

And Rannick was kneeling by the creature, cradling its head tenderly. Farnor, barely conscious, shook his head. It seemed to him that flames were dancing about Rannick, and that part of him was elsewhere.

Slowly Rannick turned. His hand came out and took the knife from him. Farnor could not resist. Then Rannick raised the bloodstained blade to his mouth and licked it.

Good . . .

Farnor felt the exhilaration and desire run through him. They turned into Rannick's laughter. 'Yes, cousin,' he was saying. 'You feel it, don't you? All this time you've been the same as me and we never knew.' Farnor tried to shake his head in denial but he could not.

Rannick spoke again. 'I liked you, Farnor. Such things we could have achieved; you, me and . . .' He looked down at the creature. His mouth curled viciously. 'But *we* will yet, cousin. She and I. You may have a gift of sorts, but it is perverse and twisted, and hers is beyond yours by far. And perhaps you would only have become a rival to me in time.' He let the knife fall and held out a bloodstained hand. 'Look at what you've done,' he said, his voice suddenly rasping and full of hatred. Yet though his eyes were blazing, it seemed as if he were going to weep as he cradled the creature's head. He turned sharply away from Farnor and bent low over the creature, speaking to it softly, comfortingly.

'I can mend this hurt you've done to her,' he said, looking up again. 'And all the other hurts that have been wrought tonight. But you'll see none of it. You, I'll destroy as I destroyed your insolent father. Only more slowly. Far more slowly. I'll squeeze all her pain and an eternity more into each wretched heartbeat that you have left. As you've sown, so must you reap. And I've skills now that I'd scarcely dreamed of when your father was sacrificed to my greater learning.'

'No,' Farnor whispered, struggling to lever himself up on to his elbows.

'Oh yes, Farnor. Oh yes. Have no doubts about it. All is mine now.'

'No,' Farnor whispered again. 'I shall destroy you. You abomination.'

Rannick sneered. 'You weary me, Farnor. Weary me beyond measure,' he said. Then, in a voice that seemed to penetrate every part of Farnor's body, he cried, 'Know my power, Farnor Yarrance. Know the power to which I have access. Look on it and weep, before I begin to kill you. For it could have been yours too.'

Farnor stared, wild eyed, as he became aware of a strange sound, so deep that it could scarcely be heard, permeating the cave. Permeating him. Permeating all things.

And then it was done, and he was looking into one of the worlds beyond. But it was no world of nightmare and terror. It was sunlit and wooded, and in the distance, over rolling countryside, snow-covered mountains rose sharp and clear.

It was beautiful.

And he saw yet more worlds. Worlds beyond number. And the shifting, flickering spaces between them. The spaces that should not be entered other than by those who had the true knowledge, and where Rannick and the creature moved so freely, malevolent trespassers.

His every fibre protested at what he saw and felt as he looked at Rannick and his grotesque mentor. It seemed to him that they were both far and near, the focus of the fearful gash that had been wrought in this reality. For it was not the worlds beyond that wrought the harm. It was their nature to be where they were, just as it was the nature of this world to be where it was. It was only in the wild conjoining of the two that the imbalance, the chaos, could be made manifest.

Agonizingly, Farnor forced himself up into a sitting position. As he did so, his hand fell on the jagged end of Marrin's broken staff. Faintly, in the long dead wood, he felt again the presence of the most ancient. And with it came the memory of the Forest, awash with the dawn sun and the ringing sounds of the horns of the Valderen. And too the remembrance that whatever else, he must hold to his resolve to honour the lives and the love of his parents by being as they had been, and as they would have wished him to be: true to himself.

Human he was, and thus savage and cruel he could be, as need arose. But always he had choice. Always everyone had choice. His savagery and cruelty had saved him from the creature, but perhaps the creature itself had had no choice in its nature. Rannick however, did. And he could do no other than help him.

He held out a hand towards him. 'Rannick, no,' he shouted into the eerie stillness. 'Come back. Nothing there belongs here. There's only loneliness, pain and madness for you if you go on. Come back.'

He hesitated for a moment, then he cried out, '*I forgive you the death of my parents.*'

Rannick started violently and his hand clutched at the creature feverishly. 'No!' he cried, his face alive with horror. He began to sway unsteadily. The vision of the worlds beyond shifted and changed, and Farnor felt Rannick reaching out, moving further and further into those places beyond, gathering as never before that which might give him the power to protect himself from the fearful revelation he heard in Farnor's words.

Farnor reached after him. Rannick's doubts and pain filled him, as did his desires. 'No, Rannick. I forgive you, truly. Come back.' But even as he spoke, he knew that in reaching for him he was reaching out once more to make whole the rent that Rannick had torn in the fabric of this reality. For therein lay Rannick's pain. And he knew too that Rannick had bound himself dreadfully to those places beyond.

Yet there was hope.

'No, Rannick!' he cried out again, in desperation. 'Come back! Let go! Let go! LET GO!'

Then there was silence . . .

Save for the lingering echo of Farnor's final, plaintive cry . . .

And the howl of the creature.

And when that was no more, Farnor, pain-racked, was alone in a damp, empty cave, dimly lit by Angwen's lantern. Both Rannick and the creature were gone, and no sense of either lingered anywhere. 'No,' Farnor whispered faintly, over and over. 'Let go. Let go.'

Then he wept.

Chapter 27

Farnor was found the following day by a search party of villagers and Valderen. He was leaning against a rock at the entrance to the cave, exhausted and covered in blood. Apart from some bad bruising, however, he was unhurt.

There was all manner of speculation about what had happened to Rannick and the creature, but despite every entreaty Farnor would say nothing except, 'They're gone.'

Besides Farnor's mysterious reappearance and the apparent destruction at his hand of Rannick and the creature, many other tales from that night went down into village and Valderen legend. Marna's desperate leap through the burning gate to rescue the four strangers. Rannick's screaming flight into the night. The death of Nilsson. And the strange and terrible fire that had consumed even the stonework of the castle until it had suddenly flickered out, as if it had never truly been there.

And too there was the appearance out of the woods of the Valderen and the four strangers escorting the remainder of Nilsson's men to join those held by the villagers at the castle. Following the death of their leader at the hands of their new lord, most of Nilsson's men had thrown down their weapons, though a few had fled into the Forest. It proved to be a costly mistake for them however, as Angwen, quiet and graceful, had listened to Farnor and trusted him, and she and the other women were waiting, bows and vicious hunting arrows ready, for the sudden arrival of armed strangers. They killed all of them without mercy, as is the way with women when they choose to kill.

And they killed Rannick's awful steed also, as, both masterless and riderless it careened, howling, through the Forest.

In due course, the survivors were given to the charge of a contingent of the king's army which had eventually been drawn to the area by news of Rannick's depredations in the surrounding countryside.

'Others will be sent to take them, in time,' Engir told the king's commander. 'We must return home as soon as possible.'

'What did they do that you travelled so far and for so long to find them?' Marna asked Aaren.

Aaren looked down at her hands. 'Wearing a false livery, they rode into a quiet village one misty autumn morning and killed everyone they could find,' she said without emotion. 'Men – women – children. None were spared. Then they burned the houses.'

The starkness of the telling shook Marna more than any amount of passion could have. 'Why?' she asked, rather hoarsely, after a moment.

'To start a war,' Aaren replied, as flatly as before. 'A civil war.'

'Which you won, I presume,' Marna retorted savagely, suddenly desperately angry at this coldness.

Aaren looked up sharply, but though she saw the torment in Marna's face, she did not spare her. 'You stood with us all amid the Valderen's grief when the butchered remains of their dead were buried. You saw the terrible wounds that came out of the Forest. And you heard the screams of people maimed for ever. And there're injuries you can't see.' She fidgeted with her damaged finger, then tapped her head. 'In here. Like the memory of the one you killed. He'll never leave you, Marna.' She seemed to relent a little. 'And that was barely a skirmish.' She paused. 'No one wins a war, Marna. Least of all a civil war. The more fortunate survive and grow a little wiser. But no one ever forgets. Not a day passes for as long as they live but some memory doesn't come back to them.'

'Why do you stay a soldier, then?' Marna asked. She had not intended it, but again there was a hint of anger and reproach in her voice.

There was an equal note of annoyance in Aaren's reply. 'Because circumstances made me such. And just as it was right for me then, so it's still right for me now.' Marna could not tear her eyes away from Aaren's bleak gaze. 'There are evils in this world, Marna, and there are always people who choose to forget that, and then they need people like me and the others – with our particular skills – because of the inevitable consequences of that forgetting.'

Marna suddenly felt very ashamed. 'I'm sorry,' she said. 'I won't forget.'

Unexpectedly Aaren embraced her. 'I know,' she said. 'I know. Circumstances have made you one of us, haven't they?'

They talked a lot after that. And Marna thought a lot.

The Valderen and the villagers became cautious friends. As did the villagers and those people from other villages who had been brought there as captives. Indeed, after the kind tending of these unfortunates, the villagers did much to help the communities over the hill that had suffered from Rannick's ambitions. It became much less . . . eccentric . . . for villagers to travel abroad.

While they remained in the village, Engir and his companions found themselves engaged in long discussions with Gryss and elders from the other villages, all anxious to make preparations to ensure that no such tragedy could befall them again. Derwyn, too, listened thoughtfully and sorrowfully, and made his own resolutions for the future.

Farnor, with the help of his neighbours, began to rebuild his farmhouse, and very soon part of it was fit to live in. Gryss and his other friends watched approvingly, but grieved a little at the sadness that now seemed to lie just below the surface of the young man.

One evening Aaren, Yehna, Levrik and Engir rode into the Yarrance farmyard, together with Marna. Farnor welcomed them warmly, and in his still rough-and-ready home, he entertained them as well as he could, recounting yet again his journey through the Great Forest and his encounter with the most ancient of the trees. The four exchanged significant glances when he talked of Uldaneth, but said nothing. Then they, in their turn, talked of their own land and their long journeyings.

A silence fell over the group. Farnor grinned sheepishly and was about to remark on it when Engir spoke. 'We're leaving tomorrow,' he said. 'The Valderen are going to allow us through the Forest. It'll save us a great deal of time, and there's much we both need to learn from one another.' Then, 'Marna's coming with us.'

Farnor started and looked at Marna. He said the first thing that came into his head. 'Does your father know?'

Marna gave a sad smile and a nod. 'Yes, of course he does, you

341

donkey.' She gestured at the others. 'We've all of us spent days talking about it.'

Farnor took her hands and looked at her earnestly.

'He's glad that I'm alive, and doing what I want to do,' Marna added.

'Well, so am I then, I suppose,' Farnor said hesitantly. 'Though I'll miss you. I'll miss you a lot.'

'I'll be back,' she replied, smiling. 'This is a good place.'

Farnor lowered his head. There was another awkward silence.

'Farnor, do you want to tell us what happened to Rannick and the creature?' Engir asked.

Farnor shook his head and repeated his litany. 'They're gone.'

Engir became more urgent. 'There's much we haven't told you about our lands, Farnor. But you know we've suffered at the hands of – people – who used the power as Rannick used it, don't you?'

Farnor nodded and Engir continued. 'It worries us greatly that this power returned again when we'd all thought its very source destroyed. It worries us that that very destruction may have wakened the creature and drawn it from the depths, and we fear what else might have been stirred. Please tell us what happened. It may be more important than you realize. And I think it may help you too. Lift some of the shadows from you.' He paused, then added finally, 'Uldaneth will want to know.'

Farnor stood up as if he wanted to leave the room suddenly. Then he sat down again and, without further bidding, told them what he could of his final encounter with Rannick and the creature.

They asked few questions, but listened with great intensity. Engir's response when Farnor had finished was unexpected. 'Will you come with us too?' he asked. 'There are people there who will understand your strange powers and what should be done with them. And people who can help to ease your deeper pain.'

Farnor looked at him thoughtfully and then at Marna. Then he said quietly but unequivocally, 'No. What I had to do, I did. I need to stay here now. To take back the threads of my life – my family's life. That too, is important.'

'You may be needed,' Engir said finally, with a hint of anxiety.

Farnor thought for a moment. 'Send for me then, and I'll come,' he replied, simply.

Aaren chuckled a little. 'I told you,' she said to Engir, who sat back with a rueful smile. 'He's one of us, like Marna.' But she did not amplify the remark.

When they parted a little later, it was with promises that they would call on him the following day before they left. Rather self-consciously, Farnor leaned forward to kiss Marna on the cheek, but she took his face in her hands and kissed him on the mouth. There was a little ironic applause from the four watchers, and Marna blushed as she waved a fist at them.

Farnor went for a walk after they had left. He took the dogs with him. It was a bright moonlit night, but warm and full of summer calm. He reached out to the trees, and they welcomed him, as they would always. Coming to the top of a rise, he stood for a long time staring at the remains of the castle, bleached by the moonlight. What had been merely part of the landscape, a relic of the need to stand against evil times now long since forgotten, had become a jagged reminder of the inevitable consequences of such forgetfulness.

Then he turned away. Many things had changed as well as the castle but, he judged, on balance they had changed for the better, despite the pain that had come with the changing. A few mysteries had been lost, but there were as many as ever in the world, bad and good, and now the villagers had far more friends to face them with, and greater knowledge.

As he walked through the warm night, it came to him that, despite all he had lost from his life, he was, nonetheless, happy. He could, and he would honour his parents and the life they had given him by living it well.

And with this simple realization, his mind, like his boisterous dogs chasing their cavorting black shadows in the moonlight, ran ahead of him. Once home, he would close his new door behind him, and – a new habit – he would touch the Threshold Sword that hung there, as it did in most of the cottages now. Then he would go up to his old bedroom, lie on his soft new bed and look up at the new beamed ceiling and wait patiently, and happily, until sleep carried him off into its welcoming darkness.

ROGER TAYLOR

THE CALL OF THE SWORD

The Chronicles of Hawklan

Behind its Great Gate the castle of Anderras Darion has stood abandoned and majestic for as long as anyone can remember. Then from out of the mountains comes the healer, Hawklan – a man with no memory of anything that has gone before – to take possession of the keep with his sole companion, the raven Gavor.

Across the country, the great fortress of Narsindalvak, commanding the inky wastes of Lake Kedrieth, is a constant reminder of the peace won by the hero Ethriss and the Guardians in alliance with the three realms of Orthlund, Riddin and Fyorlund against the Dark Lord, Sumeral. But Rgoric, the ailing king of Fyorlund and protector of the peace, has fallen under the malign influence of the Lord Dan-Tor and from the bleakness of Narsindal come ugly rumours. It is whispered that Mandrocs are abroad again, that the terrible mines of the northern mountains have been re-opened, and that the Dark Lord himself is stirring.

And in the remote fastness of Anderras Darion, Hawklan feels deep within himself the echoes of an ancient power and the unknown, yet strangely familiar, call to arms . . .

FICTION/FANTASY   0 7472 3117 6

A selection of bestsellers from Headline

THE PARASITE	Ramsey Campbell	£4.99 ☐
GAMEWORLD	J V Gallagher	£4.99 ☐
SCHEHERAZADE'S NIGHT OUT	Craig Shaw Gardner	£4.99 ☐
THE GIANT OF INISHKERRY	Sheila Gilluly	£4.99 ☐
THE HOODOO MAN	Steve Harris	£5.99 ☐
LIES AND FLAMES	Jenny Jones	£5.99 ☐
THE DOOR TO DECEMBER	Dean Koontz	£5.99 ☐
HIDEAWAY	Dean Koontz	£5.99 ☐
MIDNIGHT'S LAIR	Richard Laymon	£4.99 ☐
HEART-BEAST	Tanith Lee	£4.99 ☐
CHILDREN OF THE NIGHT	Dan Simmons	£4.99 ☐
FARNOR	Roger Taylor	£5.99 ☐

All Headline books are available at your local bookshop or newsagent, or can be ordered direct from the publisher. Just tick the titles you want and fill in the form below. Prices and availability subject to change without notice.

Headline Book Publishing PLC, Cash Sales Department, Bookpoint, 39 Milton Park, Abingdon, OXON, OX14 4TD, UK. If you have a credit card you may order by telephone — 0235 831700.

Please enclose a cheque or postal order made payable to Bookpoint Ltd to the value of the cover price and allow the following for postage and packing:
UK & BFPO: £1.00 for the first book, 50p for the second book and 30p for each additional book ordered up to a maximum charge of £3.00.
OVERSEAS & EIRE: £2.00 for the first book, £1.00 for the second book and 50p for each additional book.

Name ....

Address ....

....

....

If you would prefer to pay by credit card, please complete:
Please debit my Visa/Access/Diner's Card/American Express (delete as applicable) card no:

Signature ....Expiry Date ....